# explorer's revenge

NEW YORK TIMES BESTSELLING AUTHOR

## K.A. KNIGHT

Explorer's Revenge

Copyright © 2025 by K.A. Knight

Written by K.A. Knight.

Edited By Jess from Elemental Editing and Proofreading.

Proofreading by Norma's Nook.

Internal Formatting by The Nutty Formatter.

Art by Dily Iola Designs

Cover by LLewellen Designs

# READER CONSIDERATION:

This is a very dark book not meant for anybody under the age of 18. Content includes: explicit sex, explicit violence, gore, loss of limbs, depression, extreme weather, PTSD, loss of a family member, child abuse and much more.

# PROLOGUE

*Five years earlier . . .*

I stare down at the street hundreds of feet below, my heart racing with both adrenaline and fear. My toes hang off the edge of the roof seventy stories above the city. The sounds are almost muted up here, the city noise unable to pierce the sky surrounding me. Closing my eyes, I spread my arms to feel the wind like a bird. My hair blows back in the breeze, and I smile as I see myself going over the edge and free-falling to the streets below.

Opening my eyes, I look up at the sky and grin. "Not lost," I whisper to my dad, wishing he could see me now. The thought of him and the news we got last week has my heart plummeting. For a second, I debate if this is the best thing to do, but I need this feeling. I need to be free of the pain licking at my insides like flames.

I glance down at the city and take a deep breath.

It's now or never.

Time to take the leap.

Just as I'm about to step off, I hear the door to the roof opening, the telltale creak making me glance over my shoulder to see a confused security guard in his three-piece suit, his walkie-talkie on his hip. His pudgy

1

face pales when he sees me on the edge of the rooftop. His hand comes up in a halt motion, as if that will physically stop me from tumbling over the precipice. His brown eyes widen in fear, his eyebrows rising into his receding hairline.

"Ma'am, what are you doing?" he asks. "Get down now!"

Looking back at the city, I grin before turning to face him, my heels hanging over the edge, my back to the wind that tries to give me a helpful push.

"Ma'am, please!" he yells, blocking his face from the gust to see me. "You need to get down from there."

"Get down?" I call, reaching up to hold the ties of my pack. "Are you sure?"

"Yes!" he shouts. "Get down now!"

"Okay, if you insist." I salute him and then tip backwards. I see his screaming face appear at the lip of the roof before I flip in the air and spread my arms and legs. I hoot in ecstasy as adrenaline races through my body and lights up all my nerves, bringing me to life. The weightless feeling makes me laugh hysterically as I plummet closer to the ground.

My stomach flips as it does when you're falling, and I kick without meaning to, a knee-jerk reaction I ignore. My brain quiets like it always does when I do something crazy. I feel peaceful, just experiencing my body and the excitement.

I see people looking up and pointing, but I still wait.

Holding off . . .

*Holding . . .*

Now!

I pull the chute with a laugh, and it explodes out of me, hoisting me back into the air. Gripping the handles, I soar above the people and traffic, directing myself to the landing area I located earlier, and when my feet touch down, I run to a stop. I look around to see everyone turned to me, but then I spot the camera.

They move closer, so I grab the random spectator's hand with the camera and put my face near it. "Did you see that? Want more? Then make sure to watch out for me!" I call as I step back, stripping off my pack as I hear police sirens approaching.

"What's your name?" the man with the camera asks as I shove everything inside the pack. Looking up, I wink as I toss it over my shoulder.

"Maeve. Maeve motherfucking Carter!" I shout as I hop onto my bike and race away from there before I get arrested again.

If only I knew just how much today would change my life . . . .

# ONE
## WILDER

*Five years later . . .*

"Did you see that stunt Carter pulled?" Rick, my young brother, says as we ascend in the elevator. His phone is held in one hand, his silver rings glistening in the fluorescent lights. He turns to show me, and I crane my neck down, scoffing at the image of her free-climbing a mountain. Her smile is wide, and her eyes are bright. Despite the fact that she works for the same people we do, she is nothing like us.

We are explorers, while she is nothing but a crazy adrenaline junkie looking for her next fix.

"Carter is a fucking idiot." I mutter.

There's a snicker behind me, and I turn to meet my cousin's eyes. Logan is almost the same height as me, and for a moment, I see the young boy turning up at our doorstep, all his worldly possessions in two bags at his feet, his shoulders rounded in pain. Now he stands tall, his gray eyes alight with mischief as he grins at me, flashing his pearly whites. "Yeah, but she's hot."

"All the crazy ones are," Way mutters at his side, his eyes closed as he leans back against the wall, the lights flashing across the new ink on his head. When he feels my gaze, he opens his eyes to wink at me. Despite the fact that he's not blood related to Rick, Logan, or me, he's just as much family. I glance at Aiyaret next to him, who's purposely looking at the doors, ready to get this over with. He feels uncomfortable in this high-rise building, just like the rest of us. We prefer to be in wide open spaces, not this mechanical prison with too many people and too much noise—not to mention the monkey suits we were forced to don to visit the bosses.

They pay our bills, though, and give us the freedom to explore like our hearts call us to, so we play nice, even if we hate it. "Put your phone away," I mutter to Rick as the doors open. "And remember to keep that smart mouth shut. We don't need another probation because you called one of the board members an old, fat bastard who couldn't get an erection if a whore was riding him like a bronco."

Rick laughs, as do Logan and Way, but I just roll my eyes, fighting a smile even as I glare at him, showing him I'm serious. He mimes zipping his lips as we step off onto the top level of Venture Enterprises, the company we all work for as a team. They have their fingers in a lot of shit, from racing to drinks and equipment. We are their Adreno Squad, as they call us, due to the nature of our jobs.

I ignore the looks we get and the photos being taken as we traverse the corridor. We are used to it by now, even though I remember the first time we nervously walked these halls as cocky teenagers and no one knew who we were. Now, the whole world does, and we are the best at our jobs.

We are a wandering family living wild. We explore every inch of the world together. Men love us and want to be us, while women want us, and Venture? They made us.

Without bothering to knock, I open the glass door to the conference room filled with board members. They are sitting around the large table in their stuffy suits with their bottles of water and laptops, looking like zombies—apart from the man who hired us and the reason I took this job.

Ajax is the son of the man who founded this company and the one who made it about excitement and adventure. He understands my need for exploring, and he wants to be out there himself, but instead, Ajax is stuck in boardrooms. Behind him are framed photos of him climbing Mount Everest and diving in the deepest, darkest holes in the world. He is a businessman, but his heart is wild like ours.

"Wilder!" he calls with a genuine grin, clapping my back. I return the greeting, a smile on my lips.

"Hey, Ajax, how are you?" Despite the fact that he's my boss, I genuinely like the guy, and I knew the first moment he asked us to join them that I would. He had the same fire and excitement we feel. He's older now, but he's still the same young man who wanted to take Venture into the twenty-first century and do things no other company dared, and he has. Hence why he's the richest man alive.

"Better now that you're here, friend. Take a seat." He gestures at the free chairs on the other side of the table. I sit, with Rick lounging in the chair next to me. Logan takes a seat, but Way and Aiy lean near the door, wanting to escape. The men in the room shift uncomfortably at our rugged appearances—tattoos, piercings, tan skin, and worn hands—compared to their silken, unblemished richness. I smirk, knowing they wish they looked like us, all hard edges and muscles, but only because it suits our needs.

The strength we need is hard earned and keeps my family safe when we explore. The tan protects my skin and is a perk. The hard calluses are finally strong enough not to hurt when I climb.

Every inch of us is carefully crafted, not for aesthetics or pleasure, but for work. The plus side of it is it creates envy in men and lust in women.

"We are so excited you agreed to come in. We know you were relaxing after your successful win of the Adventure Race." Ajax grins. "Which, by the way, congratulations on again. You guys were amazing."

I just nod, and he carries on, knowing I only speak when I feel like it.

"However, we have something for you, something that's time sensitive. No other person in the world knows about this, and no others could ever hope to find the lost city of Apear." He lets that sink in as I frown. It sounds familiar, but I can't figure out why. Luckily, he doesn't make me guess—another reason I like him.

"It is also known as the city of gold. It was thought to be lost hundreds of years ago and hasn't been mapped or found ever since, but recently, a survivor of a boat wreck stumbled upon an island they swear has gold ruins that have never been explored before. We paid him off, but who knows how long he will hold his silence, which is where you come in. If you and your team want to, we would like to send you there to find this city for us and document it. Of course, whatever is found will be given to museums, but the press it will bring the company is invaluable, and you have free rein and an endless budget." He leans forward, pressing his hands to the table. "I mean it, Wilder, whatever you want, name it. Your team has all our resources and no rules. Find us this city, and for the rest of your life, you can do whatever you want."

The press is important to them, but for us, an unexplored lost city on an island in the middle of nowhere? I can't deny the excitement that builds within me as I think about the things that could be there and what would be needed. I glance at the others and see the same emotion reflected in their eyes.

This is a big deal. We will be the first ones there in hundreds of years, and we can finally show Carter who the real explorers are.

"We're in."

# TWO

# MAEVE

I stride into Venture Enterprises, the company who scouted me five years ago after I freebased from a skyscraper and gained internet fame, grinning and waving at Bob, the security guy behind the desk. I scared the shit out of him five years ago. I did go back and apologize after, but he laughed it off, telling me he'd framed the news article, and then he asked me to sign it. When Venture came knocking, offering everything on a silver platter, I brought him with me. He loves his new job, even if he sometimes finds me doing crazy stuff.

I was overjoyed and slightly starstruck when they approached me. Once a boring business, Venture gained notoriety for its new CEO, Ajax Howard. He's a sexy as hell adventurer who stepped up when his father died. He brought the company into the modern century, and I had been dreaming of working for them for years, but I still brought my dad with me to read the contracts, needing his approval and knowledge. I don't do anything like that without his approval, and despite his condition, he said yes and was overjoyed, and my dad made fast friends with Ajax, even if he did threaten him and tell him to look after his baby girl.

It's been five amazing years, and I get the best of both worlds. My bills are paid, and I have the freedom to follow the wildness my father said we were both born with. I do the events they ask, like cliff diving,

9

climbing, racing, and so on, and then in my free time, they pay me to explore. Their dick squad hates that. Wilder, Merrick, Way, Logan, and Aiyaret are five sexy explorers who were already signed with Venture. I think Ajax hoped I would join them, but they made it very clear they are a family and no one else will ever be allowed to work with them.

I hate them. The cocky assholes look down on me. They clearly think I am nothing more than a woman trying too hard to be like them. They have made it known that they find me lacking, so yes, the dick squad might be sexy as hell, but I'd rather punch their smug faces than sit on them.

One day, I'll show them and get my name out there before theirs as the best explorer of all time, and then I'll shove it in their pretty boy faces as I drive off in my Ferrari toward my mansion.

My dad always says it's good to have dreams, but I don't think that's quite what he meant. Oh well.

Pushing all thoughts of those assholes away, I take the stairs to the top floor, racing my last time as I leap and drag myself up until I break out onto the floor. I grin at a startled businesswoman as I straighten my blouse and pants. That's about as good as they will get. I still have my sneakers on, and they will never get me in heels no matter how much they ask. They are death traps meant to slow women so men can catch them.

I hurry to the boardroom we always meet in.

They are all waiting inside as I enter like a ball of chaos. Ajax grins at me as he hugs me. "Fashionably late, as usual, Maeve."

"Sorry, I was exploring an abandoned hotel." I shrug as I sit, flinging my shoes onto the table, ignoring the disgruntled looks from some of the board dudes. They don't have to like me. Ajax holds all the votes and he does. He sits down and watches me, uncaring about my lack of manners or business sense.

"Of course you were. I hope you recorded it." He raises his eyebrow, and I nod.

"You know it." I grab some water and down it as I peer at him. "So, what's with the formal meeting? I didn't start any international fights or sink a boat again."

"No, no, nothing like that. You aren't in trouble for once. We actually have another job for you." He waves, and I groan.

"Not another picture-perfect event," I grumble, hating them as much as they love them, but it's part of the job to be the face for the adventure units like the dick squad. They said they wanted to get more women into the sport, but to me, it's just torture.

"Not this time." He grins, making me eye him worriedly. "This time you'll be doing what you do best, exploring the unknown."

I sit up, excitement beginning to course through me. "Don't tease me."

"I'm not. This is an all-expenses paid trip—no limits or rules. You can take a team if you want or go alone . . ." He waits, knowing I'll bite.

"What's the job?" I ask.

"To find and document the infamous lost city of Apear."

"Oh shit," I mutter. Not many people know, but my love of exploring came from tales about that city. "They found it?"

"Maybe. A man was shipwrecked, and he swears he stumbled into the ruins. No one else knows yet, and he didn't claim the discovery. You are going to, aren't you?" he asks, smiling at me.

"You bet your sexy ass I am. Where do I sign up?" He laughs with me and starts clapping his hands. "Let's get you started. The quicker you leave, the better, right?"

"You know it." I leap to my feet, grinning.

This is it, my chance to prove I am better than all others.

The world will always remember Maeve Carter, the first solo woman to find the lost ruins of Apear.

Eat a bag of dicks, Adreno Squad, because I'm about to be your daddy.

"Dad!" I yell as I slam his front door, kicking off my shoes.

"Kitchen!" he calls back, laughter in his shaky voice.

Grinning, I head past the living room and find him sitting in the kitchen with a cup of tea and a book. For a moment, I just stare at the man who raised me to love the world. I grew up in different countries, seeing everything the world has to offer. Some found it weird and said I had a bad childhood, but I wouldn't change it for anything. Other girls got to go to prom, but I got to swim with sharks, explore ruins, cross the world on sailing boats, climb mountains, and dive into the deepest parts of the ocean.

We did everything together until he got sick. Now, it's just me representing everything we love. I wanted to quit, unable to do it without him, but he wouldn't let me, saying it's in my blood and now I need to do it for both of us. It still hurts seeing him like this when he should be doing it with me, knowing it causes him pain as well as joy when I do things he can now only dream of.

"Hey, baby girl," he says as I sit and take his mug, sipping it and gagging. He laughs. "Green tea. Apparently, it's good for me," he jokes as I wipe my mouth.

"Or Sandy is trying to kill you," I tease as he laughs. "Speaking of, where's the monster in law?" When he married, I joked she would be a monster, but I was so wrong. She's an incredible woman who loves both my father and me. She shouldered the burden of having a kid who wasn't hers and a husband who preferred to spend his weekends doing dangerous shit that gave her sleepless nights, yet she never once complained. She came with us to every ceremony and was there for me in a way my own mother never was since she'd abandoned me as a kid. When Dad got his diagnosis, she quit her job and became his full-time caregiver despite the fact that he isn't as bad now as he will be. She learned everything she could about MS.

Dad was diagnosed a few years ago after many bouts of lost balance, blurry vision, and his body just generally not doing what he wanted. Seeing such an incredibly strong man who'd spent his days climbing mountains reduced to this breaks my heart, especially knowing he's still an adventurer at heart. We got unlucky—or lucky, depending on how you look at it—because he has primary progressive MS, which means it will only get worse, and the years since he was diagnosed have only proven that. He now walks with a cane and sometimes struggles with balance and seeing, and his coordination is disappearing while his brain becomes foggy. He hates it, but just like anyone with a lifelong condition, he has his good and bad days.

It ended his explorer career though.

That's something we both resent, even if we have learned to live with it. He changed, but he found happiness in the mundane, creating a life with the woman he loves. When he reaches for the mug, I see his arm shaking, and I swallow as I hand it over, knowing better than to point it out. It will only upset us. Plus, he's happy, and I don't want to ruin that.

"So what has you bouncing around like a bunny, kid?" he asks.

"How was treatment yesterday?" I ask instead, tempering my excitement.

"The same as always. Spill it, kid. Nothing exciting happens in my life—"

"Not true, you found a dog and rescued it last week. Sandy said so!" I tell him, and his eyebrows rise in his iconic expression I always get, which is why I could never keep secrets from him. He's always been my best friend, and his only rule was that we do it together.

Now we can't, though, and it hurts because we should be, but I'll do it for both of us. I'll get our name out there, so they remember him for his achievements, not just his illness.

Dexter Carter will go down in history as the best explorer ever. I will ensure it.

"Ajax gave me the opportunity of a lifetime." I quickly dive into where I'm going and why, holding nothing back despite the secrecy of this job. My dad will always know everything and help me plan. He's my best friend and my teammate, even if he's stuck here now.

He nods, asking questions and giving me ideas for equipment I might need. I see the excitement in his eyes before it dampens with a little pain —because he won't be there with me. His longing is clear on his face, even as he tries to hide it so he doesn't hurt me.

I guess you never think about getting old or sick when you're young and in your prime. He never thought he'd be anything but an explorer. That's where his heart lies and it always will, but I know he's proud of me and wouldn't want me to keep it from him.

K.A. KNIGHT

"So when do you leave?" he asks, holding my hand tightly, but I can feel the weakness in his grip.

"Tomorrow. I came to say goodbye." I cup his hand. "I'm doing this for us, Dad. You should be there, but I will find it, and when I do, I'll make sure everyone knows you helped me."

"No, kid, *you* are doing this. You were always destined for great things, so don't diminish that."

I kiss his hand. "But without you, there is no me." I blink and look down. "I wish you could be there."

"I will be, kid. Remember my lessons, and I'll be right there with you, cheering you on, and when you come back, I'll be waiting." He grabs me and pulls me in. "I'm so proud of you, Maeve. Show the world what a woman is capable of . . . what *you* are capable of. Give them hell."

"Always, Dad."

## THREE
## MERRICK

**S**hoving another pair of shorts into my duffel bag, I straighten and inspect the chaos on my bed. I threw everything on it I thought I might need. We know it's going to be a jungle with a hot climate, so that helps. It's horrible when you don't know what the weather will be like so you can't pack for it. After the number of times I've nearly frozen my balls off because of lack of packing, I've learned to adapt quickly. I like my balls where they are, thank you very much.

I check my mental list as I go, making sure I have everything I need.

I forgot my stuff once, and Wilder, my older brother, has never let me live it down, so now I double-check. He calls my bag organized chaos, but it works for me. The others are all doing the same, knowing the faster we fly out of here, the faster we can find the ruins and stake our claim. It's a race against time and others going for it.

We need to be first.

Once I'm sure I have everything, I zip up my bag and then throw myself down next to it on my bed, bouncing as I unplug my phone from the charger and scroll through my notifications. Opening Instagram, I reply to a few comments and DMs on our team's page before looking through others' stories. I sit up when I land on Maeve Carter's. Despite Wilder's hatred for her, she's one hell of a woman and sexy with that

15

dimpled smile that makes my knees weak. Even if she is our competition and enemy as Wilder believes, I can't help but root for her. She's brave, crazier than us, and has an amazing record, drawing more notice to our team and Venture.

She's walking through an abandoned hotel before she starts to climb the elevator shaft, making me shake my head as I laugh. If these two didn't hate each other so much, they would be perfect for each other. There is a reason we call him Wild, and it isn't just because of his name.

Once the story is done, I shut and lock the phone then close my eyes for a moment, breathing in the peace of my room. Despite the fact that we spend most of our time across the world, we do have a shared house to come home to. I don't know when we will be back here, so I make the most of my privacy since I won't get any when we're exploring.

Speaking of . . .

My eyes open, and I check that my door is shut before I grab my phone again and open her Instagram page, scrolling through the bikini shots of her explorations. She looks fucking sexy as hell with a body I've spent more time jerking off to than I should for our competitor.

Pushing my hands into my sweatpants, I grip my hardening cock and stroke myself, imagining her pushing that tiny white bikini to the side before impaling herself on my cock. She would be wet, wild, and crazy like she is in real life, riding me like a fucking pro.

I pump harder, visualizing her licking down my abs to my dick, her eyes filled with mocking laughter as she swallows me into her hot mouth. I shut my eyes, my phone still gripped in one hand as I fuck my fist faster and faster. I force my eyes open so I can see her picture, needing to see her when I come. My grip tightens on the phone as I imagine Carter sucking me down, her pouty lips wrapped around my cock, and without warning, my orgasm slams through me, and ropes of hot cum splash over my bare chest and fist.

Collapsing back, I lock my phone and close my eyes. I must drift off because when I wake up, I hear the others yelling at each other, which makes me laugh because yelling is their way of showing love. We are a dysfunctional family but a family, nonetheless. Wilder and I grew up together, and although he's older than me by five years, we have always been inseparable. Logan came to live with us when he was fourteen. We had been close before, but after that, we were inseparable. We protected him as he healed from losing his parents in a car accident, and our parents treated him like one of their kids. The others came along later on. Despite it all, we are family.

They say I'm the joker who helps them calm Wilder down, so I guess that works.

I get up, washing off the remains of my release, and head down to interrupt the yelling and get them to laugh it out together—as usual.

What is family without a few fights?

## FOUR
## LOGAN

**W**e fly private. It isn't the first time, but I'll never get used to it. It shows exactly just how much Venture is invested in this exploration. It also means I get to stretch out my legs without my six-six frame being cramped on those tiny plane seats while trying not to touch the person next to me. I sleep most of the way there, much to Wild's chagrin because he wants to plan.

It doesn't matter that we've gone over everything a hundred times already; he has to check continually to make sure there is nothing that can go wrong and anything that could go wrong already has a counter-plan in place. I help with logistics, but now he's just being paranoid. There is only so much we can do before we have to just dive in and trust yourself and your team. There is no map or trail where we're going. Getting to the island itself will be a task, and anything could happen, so planning isn't as important as sleeping.

When I see the worry in Wilder's eyes, I sit up and run over his notes and maps, double-checking them for him, knowing he does everything possible to keep his family safe.

I am his family, more brother than cousin. He's made that clear since the day I was dropped at their house with my bags after losing my parents. We had always been close, living down the street from one another, and our fathers were brothers as well as best friends. We grew up together. Wilder, Ricky, and I were always together.

They loved my parents like their own, but when they died, my uncle and auntie didn't hesitate to take me in. They stayed with me through it all. Rick and Wilder held my hands through the entire funeral, even though they got mocked for it. Ever since, they've always been protective. When I got bullied at school and people would tease me for my dead parents, Wilder and Rick would work together to silence them. When I cried myself to sleep for a year or on my birthdays or Christmas when I missed them something fierce, they were there then too.

Now, over twenty years later, I barely remember my parents.

I don't remember the color of my mom's eyes or the sound of my dad's voice, but I still miss them, and at times like this, I wish they were here to see me. Wilder's mom and dad always support us and love me, but it's not the same.

The crinkled picture of them I always keep feels heavy in my pocket as I drift into my memories, only blinking when Wilder covers my hand on the map. "You with us, brother?" he murmurs.

I nod, meeting his eyes. I don't have to say what I'm thinking—he already knows.

"They would be so proud of you," he murmurs softly.

"I know." I do, but it doesn't stop it from hurting. They say grief lessens with time, but they are fucking liars—you just get better at dealing with it.

Aiyaret claps me on the shoulder, resting his head there after. I close my eyes, soaking in their warmth and friendship, which has saved us all throughout everything we have endured, especially Aiy . . . .

Shaking it off, I concentrate on the map. "So what's the plan, boss man?" I joke, and Wilder grins and lets me change the subject, thank God.

Rick and Way crowd closer as Wild launches into detailing where we will land before we have to get a seaplane. We will have a hotel for the night as Wilder meets with someone he chartered a boat from, and then the next morning, we'll set off towards the island at dawn, which we have rough coordinates for and no more information.

It's the best time of exploration—the unknown kind.

Excitement pours through me, chasing away my demons, and I see it doing the same for the others as I grin at them. "Let's find that lost city and make it our bitch!"

FIVE
# MAEVE

I double-check my list and then glance back at my bags on the bed. Most are filled with equipment I might need. I can order more when I get there, but some of my favorites come with me. I trust it more than a random new set I haven't had the chance to test. I only have a small backpack with clothes and supplies, but I end up hauling several duffels and bags of equipment down to the car Venture sent. I wave off the driver's help and load it myself, and then we're off to a private airstrip.

I've flown private a few times when they needed to pick me up from the middle of nowhere at random hours or when they bribed me to attend an event like kayak racing, but I never get used to it. I always feel out of place, my worn shoes treading on the perfectly posh carpet. My jacket has a patched hole, my face is clean of makeup, and my clothes are comfy. I stand out, but I force myself to sit and smile when I'm served before we take off.

I'll sleep most of the way, having gone over the maps and plans with my father before I left, and then I can hit the ground running when I land. I can't fly directly to the island on this plane, though, so I'm stopping at a nearby island and taking a boat there. From there, I've chartered a small plane I can jump from with my equipment. There are easier ways, but hell, what's life without a bit of excitement? And when will I have the chance to jump from a plane into the middle of the ocean in search of a mysterious island and lost city?

Never.

So you bet your ass I am.

Reclining in my seat, I close my eyes and nod off. I only wake for food and to check the time to our destination, then I fall asleep again, only to be woken when we land. I thank the crew, grab my bag, and head down where my stuff is already being loaded into the back of a truck on the private airfield.

The sun is blazing down on me, and the ocean stretches before us. Something in my shoulders eases, and I relax with the scent of the salty ocean and the freshness of the warm air. Pulling on my sunglasses, I strip off my jacket and greet the driver before climbing in.

He takes off at a breakneck speed down old dirt tracks, and I whoop as we fly over mounds and hills. Once back on normal roads, I grab my satellite phone and do my last check-in with Dad.

"Remember our rules. Stay sharp and safe, and baby girl, don't take too many risks, okay?"

I laugh. "Okay, Dad, love you."

"Love you. Find it for me."

I hang up, having nothing else left to say. Throwing my legs out of the open window, I watch the jungle as we speed across the island to the dock. I have to grab a boat from here, the mainland, to the next island over where the plane port is, and then I'll be on my way. When I find the lost city, I'll rub it in the Adreno assholes' faces.

I can picture their anger now as I smugly show them pictures. That ridiculously hot prick, Wilder, will hate me even more, and it will be so worth it to see his envy.

Pulling out my camera, I snap a few pictures and videos, and when we stop at the port, I climb into the back of the truck and ask the driver to take a few more. After he does, I take some short recordings on the camera they gave me—I have to document the exploration. They automatically upload to the office when there is a signal, so I switch it off after it's done its thing and strip at the port, putting on some shorts and a tank top over my bikini. I change my sneakers for boots and thick socks before braiding my hair and winding it on my head to keep my neck bare.

I hoist my backpack up, testing the weight, then grab my equipment in both hands and head to the boat. I'm betting not many people come through here, since it isn't exactly a tourist attraction. The other side of the island is filled with luxury resorts and floating villas, but this side is for the locals and fishermen.

"Hey, I'm Carter." I shake the captain's hand. Wearing nothing but some low-slung shorts and sunglasses, he's my type of guy. He's relaxed and knowledgeable, which is evident in his boat and how swiftly he escorts me on and gets settled.

"Welcome to paradise, Carter," he calls as we maneuver into the open ocean.

"It sure feels like it," I shout over the wind as I watch the choppy blue waters on either side of us. "I don't suppose this thing goes any faster, does it?" I grin.

He turns and meets my eyes with his own grin. "Hold on, city girl."

He guns it. Laughing, I tip my head back and close my eyes, letting the wind flow through my hair and the sun heat my face while we speed through the ocean. Each moment brings me closer to what I know is going to be an incredible adventure.

I can feel it in the anticipation and rightness of being here in the air, like when you're on the verge of jumping off a cliff. I can't wait to get there, but my dad used to remind me to enjoy the journey there because that is half the experience.

I focus on the present, keeping myself grounded as I look out. He was right—it's paradise. The blue ocean beckons me to dive in to learn its secrets. The green, jungle-covered oasis of islands are close enough to see but not get to by swimming. The sky is a bright blue, shining with the type of sun that overheats your skin if you aren't careful.

The crossing takes just over an hour, and I spend some of the time stretching my body and double-checking my bags for the supplies I will need, and then I take pictures and videos for Venture and my dad. The captain is nice enough to stop for one in the middle of the ocean with the island behind me, my bikini on display as I grin. I know Dad will frame it alongside the others I've sent him from all over the world.

Once we arrive at the other island holding only jungles and locals, I unload and hand cash to the captain. "Good luck," he tells me, and I grin as I drop my bags on the dock.

I have to wait two hours for the plane to be ready, and I plan to spend that time finding the man who discovered the island. Venture made sure he was here. I like to get my information from the source, and like it or not, he's the closest thing I'll get. Leaving my bags with the person who will load them onto the plane, I hoist my backpack onto my shoulders and set off on foot into the jungle, taking the shortcut into town.

An hour later, I'm sweaty but grinning after exploring the jungle and coming upon the town. It's filled with cute shanty shops and shacks, some built into the lake water, and I can't help but take more pictures. I love the bright colors and friendly, curious faces. I greet as many people as I can before asking for directions. They point me across some dock planks fastened together to create a walk over the lake to a floating bar.

After thanking them for the directions, I set off across the boards. They shift slightly with the water but seem stable, so I wander across them, looking out at the tiny town. It's the opposite of a tourist attraction, which I love. I can feel the culture. I stand out for sure, and I don't plan to cause any trouble or even showcase this place, since they deserve their privacy. That's the one rule I follow—respect their world since you are just a tourist in it.

The dock splits off almost like a junction, but I take the wooden steps up into the bar, which is a mix of driftwood and old boats without doors or windows, just an open front. Tables are spread out across a floating wooden balcony. Some of them are made from crates, boxes, and even a surfboard. Grinning, I look inside to see more tables and an old bar with a door leading to a kitchen. It's warm as hell but so amazing. There's a fridge buzzing with cold drinks, and a surprised woman greets me in her native tongue.

"Sorry, I don't speak your language." I wince, and she laughs. I start to pull out my translator, since I'm the tourist here, when she speaks again in a thick, accented voice.

"English?"

I look up in surprise, and she grins.

"You want a drink?"

"I'll take a cold beer if you have one, and a water please," I reply.

"Sure. Take a seat wherever. We are never busy at this time of day. You want some food too?" she asks, wiping her hands on her shorts.

"Anything you have will be great." I hand over a wad of cash, and she blinks in shock, but I gesture for her to keep it. "I'm looking for someone named Conrad."

She huffs, her black hair moving as she turns and points to a table outside in the corner where a man is hunched over, snoring, with a half drank beer in his grip. "You've found him. Don't expect to get any sense out of him though." She hurries to the back.

Shrugging, I drop my bag at the table closest to him then stand above him.

He doesn't stop snoring. "Conrad?" I ask loudly.

Nothing.

"Hey, I have money," I say, but he still doesn't respond. Rolling my eyes, I kick his chair. It screeches back, and he windmills his arms as he glares up at me.

"The fuck?" he slurs with a heavy accent as I sit and slide money over.

"I need to know everything about what you found down to the tiniest detail, so sober up and answer my questions and I'll pay your tab for the night before I leave."

His eyes narrow before he drains his beer. "Deal."

"Good." Sitting back, I grin at him as the woman drops off a plate of fish and my drinks. I tuck into it, groaning at the flavor as Conrad watches. Once I'm done, I sip the beer.

"Get on with it then," he snaps, and I hide my smile as I lean back in my chair.

"How did you get there?"

"I've already been through that," he retorts.

"Fine, so you crashed there. Where exactly, a beach? Any other entry points you found that might be better? What about shade?

Anything I need to be aware of in terms of risk? And this city, how far in was it?"

"Fuck, I need a beer," he mutters. "There was a beach, but it was a huge trek through the jungle. I was hoping to find someone or get to the other side in hopes there was a better beach."

"Why? What was wrong with that beach?" I ask.

"It had huge cliffs next to it, and I thought it would be impossible to get a boat to it. Anyway, the cliffs lead straight to a path deeper into the jungle and the city. Wish I had taken that way."

"Okay, so cliffs," I murmur. "And through the jungle?"

"You're smart," he mutters sarcastically as I narrow my eyes. "Don't remember much after that. I was too fucking terrified and running just to get away from that shit show."

"But you remember seeing ruins, and that's why I am here," I hedge.

"Vaguely." He shoots me a look that holds more intelligence than I thought he was capable of.

"So why not go back and sell all this for yourself?" I ask, voicing something I've been wondering.

"I'm not ever going back there." He shivers in fear. "Not ever."

"Why is that?" I press, sensing it's deeper than him simply not liking the rough terrain or ruins. There is something that puts an uneasy look in his eye. I need to know what it is, because whatever scares him sends a shiver of excitement through me.

"Shit that I saw there," he mutters, eyeing me warily.

"But I thought you only vaguely remember?" I counter, getting sick of his runaround.

"I vaguely remember enough to know to stay the fuck away from that place. No money or shit is worth the evil I felt there. The skeletons . . . You're a fool, but go right ahead and get yourself killed searching for gold."

I want to tell him it isn't about the gold, but he's not worth it. Skeletons? It could be from plane crashes, shipwrecks, or, hell, ancient tribes, so that doesn't scare me, but something clearly traumatized him. You don't travel the world and experience the shit I have without believing a little about the supernatural, so I'll respect what he thinks he saw and use extra caution.

"Believe me or not, but I saw what I saw," he snaps.

"I do believe you." I stand, tossing money on the table. "Which is why I'm here."

I grab my backpack and wave goodbye to the waitress, but he calls out, stopping me. Turning back, I meet his eyes.

"Be careful, okay? Something there is . . . hungry."

"Always am."

I pay for my stuff and walk to the plane, his words echoing in my head.

*Evil* . . .

What makes a forgotten island evil?

I guess I'm about to find out.

SIX
# WAY

When we land on the main island, we head straight for the port and load our equipment onto the seaplane. We warned them there would be a lot of stuff, and we booked the whole thing out, but it's still a tight squeeze, especially when you are a big guy. We make it work, though, and we've been in tighter and weirder places when diving or climbing. Our bodies are used to us putting them to the test, and that's what makes us feel alive.

The seaplane doesn't take long to get to the other island, and once there, we check into a hotel for the night. Leaving first thing tomorrow is better, since we will have the full day to explore. Honestly, exploring at night is fun, but Wilder wants to make sure this is done by the book. We have to get good footage but also stay safe. Aiyaret makes most of the recordings while we explore the little town, not wanting to stay in the hotel—all of us need to stretch our legs.

The town is set in the cliffs with steep steps and ramps leading to higher sections of roads. It's filled with incredibly beautiful white houses with the area near the harbor full of shops, restaurants, and a bar or two, but it's more for locals than tourists. It truly is a beautiful place, and we climb to the old castle at the top where we take pictures and study the history before heading down to eat something.

Despite the fact that we each have a hotel room, we crash in the same one, spread across the floor, sofa, and bed. Before Venture, this was how we lived, crammed into tiny, cheap hotels, and now it's just a comforting habit—a reminder we aren't alone, especially for Aiy and me who struggle to sleep by ourselves. Aiy doesn't like the dark, but for me, it's the reminder of everything I lost when I dream. Logan, Rick, and Wild are used to sharing a room, having done so when they were kids, so there wasn't much adjusting there, even if Wilder complains.

"You are both too big to be in this bed with me," he mutters, his hands fisted on his hips as he glares at them, stretched out on the queen-sized bed. "One on the floor."

"Nope," Logan replies.

"If you want one of us on the floor, then you sleep on the floor, brother. We were here first." Rick grins at him.

"I mean it, don't make me drag you. I'm the oldest and in charge—"

"I'm the oldest and in charge," Rick mocks, making him and Logan laugh. I duck my head when Wilder starts to glare. When I first joined the team, hearing their familiar, brotherly banter used to hurt.

It hurt a lot, but now it keeps me centered. It's a reminder of what I lost and what I gained—a family.

"Mer, he's going to kick your ass," Aiy deadpans, chewing on the fruit he bought, his legs kicked over the sofa he claimed.

"Nah, he can try, but he's getting slow in his old age," Merrick jokes.

"Old age? Old age? I'm thirty-six!" Wilder scoffs.

"Exactly. Soon, you'll be in a retirement home." Rick pats Wilder's leg. "Don't worry, brother. You'll still have pussy and adventures in your memories."

"That's it!" Wilder snaps, reaching for Merrick, who rolls and ducks out of the way. They chase each other around the small space while we just watch, used to it. Aiyaret continues eating, and I move closer, stealing some fruit.

"Ten on Merrick winning," I mutter.

"Don't want your money anymore, Way, but I'll take the bet for your limited edition, signed Everest poster."

"Shit, okay, deal," I reply as we wait to see who will win. Merrick is faster, but Wilder? Well, he's Wilder.

By the time Wilder has Merrick pinned, I owe Aiy my poster, just like I knew I would. "Okay, now go to sleep," Wilder orders after kicking Merrick to the floor. "Early morning tomorrow, and I need you to be rested."

"Night," I call as I roll to my back on my sleeping bag.

"Night," Logan and Merrick say in unison, making them laugh as the lights go out. Without a word, Wilder heads to the bathroom and opens the door a crack, enough for Aiy to see, and the tight grip he had on the sofa edge eases.

"Thanks, brother, night," Aiyaret whispers. Wilder just nods as he climbs back into bed.

Lying in the dark, I find my hand reaching out before I realize what I'm doing and pull it back. All these years later, I still reach for him like I did when we were kids. Sometimes in those moments between wakefulness and sleep, I actually think he's still alive, and then I remember he's gone and the pain and guilt crash down again. The other half of my soul is gone, like a puzzle missing one piece. That's how I've always felt, and it's obvious to everyone else I'm not a whole person.

Not without him.

Then again, I don't think any of us are, which is why we travel the world, hoping the more we see and find, the less broken we will be. It never works because what we are searching for can't be found anywhere but inside.

I always find it hard to fall asleep, as if my mind is trying to stop me from drifting off to that oblivion, but just like every night, I lose the battle and tumble into an exhausted, fitful dream.

*"Come on, don't be such a girl!" I call with a laugh as I reach up, having to stand on my tiptoes to grasp the bar above me. Without waiting for a response, I haul myself up onto the next ledge before I look down at him below me. "Come on, chicken!" I make chicken noises, and his expression transforms, just like I knew it would. He hesitantly takes a step forward then hoists himself up the metal bars, climbing up after me, his movements more careful and unsure.*

*He just needs to be pushed to do anything—to make friends, go out, speak, and even eat. He's always been this way, and I've always helped him by being outgoing and dragging him with me.*

*"Mom wouldn't like this," he mutters, staring at me with wide eyes. "Why don't we just go back and play a game?"*

*"No, that's boring," I scoff. "I want to get to the top and pretend I'm a superhero." I glance up at the huge tower we are climbing. We found it a few days ago in the woods, and ever since, I knew I needed to climb it and feel that rush I always get when I do something stupid—something that usually ends up with me getting grounded.*

*Like last week when I took Dad's car for a joyride around the block.*

*"I don't like heights," he mumbles.*

*"You don't like anything," I retort, still climbing with him slowly following behind.*

*When I get higher, I look down to see him hesitating about halfway up.*

*"Come on!" I yell, and as he goes to reach for the next bar, he slips.*

*"No!"*

"No!" The horror-filled scream rips me from my dreams, and for a moment, I blink, wondering if it was from him in my dreams, but then it comes again. I'm the closest, so I get to my knees and crawl over to Aiyaret, gripping his hand.

"You're okay, brother. You aren't there. You're here. Come back to us. It's just a bad fucking memory. You're safe. You're okay." His eyes slowly blink open, his body covered in sweat. "Shh . . ." I sense the others drawing closer, offering their support.

"Say it with me: You're safe. You are with your family. She can't hurt you anymore. Say it," I demand, holding his face to force him to look at me.

"I'm safe with my family. She can't hurt me," he whispers shakily before he says it again, repeating the words until his voice is stronger. Once I'm sure the lingering fear is gone, I pull him in for a hug.

"I'm sorry," he mutters, voice cracking.

"Never apologize to us. I just wish I could take the fucking nightmare away from you," Wilder replies, gripping his shoulder.

"Me too, brother," Merrick says, sounding serious for once.

"We would all bear them for you if we could," Logan adds as we circle around Aiy, protecting him from the invisible force reaching for him beyond the grave.

"I know," he whispers, letting us hold him together.

"Do you want to talk about it?" I ask. He always says no, but I keep asking anyway. When I was younger, my therapist explained how important it was for me to talk about what happened. She said it would help me, but it never did. Maybe I'm just too broken, or I didn't trust her since I'm pretty sure my parents only took me to her to find something wrong so they could get rid of me.

It might work for Aiy though.

I wait for the usually clipped refusal, but he hesitates before shaking his head. I'm wearing him down. I don't need to know the details of what happened, since we'd worked it out before he calmly explained some of it. I won't pry, but I don't want him bottling it all up and exploding. He needs to heal. If anyone deserves to, it's Aiyaret.

"Okay, will you be able to sleep?" I ask softly.

He swallows and looks away. "Not yet. I'm going to shower, then I'll try."

It's a lie, but we don't call him on it. He's going in there to cry, and there's nothing we can do but keep proving we are here for him, so we let him slip away. All of us watch him enter the bathroom before climbing into our beds, but I know we will lie awake, staring at the ceiling as we listen to his muffled sobs.

Our hearts crack with each one, his pain becoming ours until we are one.

Maybe that's why we all get along so well, because we are all broken beyond repair and instead of doing ourselves in, we throw ourselves into situations where all we have to feel is adrenaline.

That's the thing about adrenaline, though, and going full speed for so long—eventually the high wears off and you are left in the aftermath.

Then you have to worry because you can't outrun your demons forever.

# SEVEN
## AIYARET

**M**y bloodshot eyes burn, and no matter how many times I splash them with cold water, they don't reduce in puffiness. My hair is wild, sticking up at all angles, as I grip the sink and glare at myself, seeing nothing but a stranger.

I am a broken, pathetic man.

I turn away, her voice floating through my head.

*Men don't cry. Stop crying. You're so fucking pathetic. Look at you, just pathetic.*

Gripping the shower faucet, I turn it on and step inside, pressing my hands to the tile. The warm water flows over me, trying to wash her away. Today is an important day. I should be excited, but instead I'm hiding in the bathroom after keeping my friends up, screaming like a wimp from nightmares.

*Pathetic. What do pathetic men get?*

Grabbing the handle, I make the water hotter until it scalds me. The burn grounds me, keeping me in the present rather than the past, and her laughter floats away. My head feels clearer and my thoughts are my own once more, which is important. I can't be exhausted on this kind of mission. It could get me hurt, or, worse, one of my brothers could be killed. They are depending on me, and I won't let them down. They've been so good to me, taking me in and giving me a job, a family, and purpose.

They are a true family, something that took me a really long time to understand. For the first few years, I was always suspicious, wondering why they wanted to help me. Everything felt like a trap, a trick, but it wasn't. I still struggle with that now, but I know they only want what's best for me.

The door opens without the person knocking, and I grab the shampoo, pretending I was just washing my hair. "Fuck, dude, you take so long in the shower," Merrick teases as he flips the toilet seat up and pisses. I roll my eyes and scrub my hair. He flushes the toilet, and I glare at him, making him laugh.

"Oops, sorry." The bastard comes closer, and before I can warn him or turn it down, he sticks his hands under the shower spray to wash his hands.

"Fuck!" he yells, pulling his hands out and looking at the reddening skin on his palms. "What the fuck, Aiy?" he shouts, grabbing the handle with a hiss and turning the heat down. "Are you trying to burn your skin off, dude?" He becomes quiet, watching me with knowing eyes. They see too much, so I look away, scrubbing my scalp viciously.

"Brother," he murmurs, "we can go home—"

"No," I snap.

"Okay then, but you need to take better care of yourself. I know you are working through . . . what happened in your own way, but hurting yourself isn't the way to do it. We're worried about you."

"Worried?" I bark, my protective instinct rearing its ugly head, and I lash out like a cornered snake. "You cover your pain with jokes and sarcasm. Wilder is a fucking control freak who pushes everyone away. Logan is still fucked up from his parents, and Way has worse dreams than I do, and you want to talk about my issues?"

His expression becomes sad, but he doesn't let me push him away. "We are all messed up in our own ways. It doesn't mean we let our issues blind us to everyone else's suffering too. You aren't alone anymore, and we aren't going anywhere. When you realize that, we'll be waiting." He walks out, shutting the door softly behind him, which is worse than him slamming it.

Fuck! I smash my fist into the wall, feeling the skin break on my knuckles as blood pools in the shower drain. I shouldn't have hurt Rick. He means well, and he's sensitive under all that bravado. He'll take it to heart. I need to apologize, but I finish my shower first and wrap a towel around my waist, only hesitating for a moment. They've all seen the wicked scars on my back.

Opening the door, I ignore the looks and head straight for Merrick, who's sitting with his back to me as he shoves things into his bag. Wilder shoots me a concerned look and then glances at his brother. I nod, and he sighs before clapping me on the shoulder and using the bathroom next.

"Merrick," I murmur as I stop in front of him. He freezes but doesn't look up. "That was cruel of me. I know you are only trying to help. I'm not used to that. I lash out to protect myself, and that was mean. I'm sorry, brother."

He lifts his head, searching my gaze, and then a wide smile curls his lips. "I knew you liked me."

I chuckle with my own smile, something that's impossible to fight around him. Standing, he pats my shoulders, ignoring my flinch. They are getting me used to physical touch one step at a time. "Don't worry about it. Brothers fight. Now, get dressed. I don't want to start feeling inadequate with that dick near my face."

Smirking, I fake thrust at him, and he shoves me as I turn away. Way winks at me, and Logan grins, all unbothered by my moods, and I'm grateful. By the time I'm dressed and packed, the others have showered. We make quick work of packing up what little belongings we brought, grab our bags and equipment, and then head down to the boat. After we load it all up, we eat a quick breakfast at a local restaurant, leaving a generous tip, and then we stand in front of the boat and take our first picture.

We all wear wide smiles, but it's a lie. No one really knows us or the shit we have seen or done. They only get to see the good parts, and that's what Venture wants.

We are their pretty Adreno guys.

The waves are soothing, rocking the private dive boat as we make our way across the water. We paid all the staff off, so we only have the captain and an engineer—the less people who know, the better. They are going to drop us off at the beach in a tender, and they won't stay near the island, but they are coming back for us in seven days. They said there is a superstition about it.

We'll have a radio, but there's no telling if it will work. It will just be us on an abandoned island, searching for a lost city.

The excitement I once felt for this mission comes back, and I grin, watching Merrick as he and Way twerk and smack each other's asses to the song playing on the radio. Wilder is bent over his maps, but he keeps stopping to watch with a wide grin. Even he can't fight the pull of excitement when we are this close to this kind of exploration.

Logan sits near me, checking our gear and singing along.

Everyone's mood gets higher the closer we get to our destination. Heading inside, I wave at the captain, who nods before turning to his engineer. I grab a water and drain it, about to walk back outside, when they begin to talk.

"Did you hear about those divers who got stuck? Yeah, it isn't too far from here. Let's hope they manage to get them out."

I wince, wanting to ask about it, but it's none of my business. Diving is a dangerous gig. We do some, but not as experts, and especially not cave diving. It's one of the most dangerous things you can do. I hope whoever is stuck down there is okay.

My thoughts soon divert from them as I return outside because the island we are looking for is appearing on the horizon—one thought to be lost.

Rising from the water like an avenging god of old, the green jungle glimmers in the sun.

"There she is," I call, and the music cuts out as we crowd around the bow of the boat.

"This is our big break, boys." Wilder grips my shoulder, standing next to me. "Let's find ourselves a lost city."

# EIGHT
## MAEVE

The plane is small, but big enough for what I need. After communicating the drop zone with the pilots, I prepare my gear. I will have to throw it from the plane, so I attached floatation devices, which I will tie on the cliff to be picked up at a later date. It will be easier to haul the stuff up that way. I don't bring too much, knowing the more I bring, the more I have to haul, but I have my food, clothes, water, map, compass, cameras, ropes and pulleys, snorkel and dive mask, flashlight, pick, and a few other tools I might need. I condensed a lot, not wanting to die while traveling through the jungle. That's the only issue with exploring alone. Before, Dad would have taken half the gear, and we could have brought more with us, but not now.

It doesn't matter because no matter what I'll face there, I can do it. Climb it, swim it, dig it, explore it—I can do anything. That confidence is what pisses a lot of men off in my field. They don't like a woman saying that she can do it the same if not better than they can. Mansplaining is the worst, as if I'm not a fucking expert. Idiots. I think that's why the Adreno Squad hates me so much, because I can do exactly what they can, just better.

That or they are just miserable fucks who hate sharing the spotlight.

Yeah, that's more likely since they are plastered all over social media. Their fan clubs are notorious. Their profiles all have pretty ab snapshots and perfectly timed pictures to make them look their best.

Me? I show the real side of exploring, even the hard stuff, so no one goes into this with a lie. My behind-the-scenes vlogs are famous, from showing the weather conditions in Malaysia to the bad stomach bug I got in Bali—my own fault. I show the good stuff too, of course, like ruins and heights normal people might never get to see otherwise. I show them the beauty of the world and how they can safely explore it themselves.

I encourage men, women, and kids, showing them that they can do anything if they put their minds to it. In the end, the fear they create by setting restrictions is their only limitation.

I feel that same fear before I do something like this. It never goes away, not really. You just get better at dealing with it. Like now, as I move to the open door as we draw closer to the island. A moment of loneliness hits me. I wish I could turn and see my dad with his grin. Instead, I close my eyes and reach for him, and when I'm ready, I open them again, vibrating with excitement.

"You should see the island any minute now," the pilot calls, and I nod, leaning out of the door to look. A few moments later, I see it.

The luscious, bright green jungle obscures the terrain beneath. It would take at least four days to walk from one side to the other, and that's without getting lost. We circle it, passing the beach until we find the cliffs, and then we go in for the run. I drop the gear first before saluting the pilot, then I grin as they call out and throw myself backwards.

I whoop as I flip midair, my arms and legs spread as I free fall. Adrenaline makes my heart pound. The drop will come quickly, so I flip again, cross my arms, and lock my ankles before I hit the water.

I enter hard, slipping under, then wait a beat before kicking to the surface with a laugh. Swimming hard, I reach my gear and grab the rope I tied to it. I shield my eyes as I look up, waving to the plane as it leaves.

When the sounds of the engines fade, I'm left with the lapping waves and the crash as they hit the cliffs and nothing else, just nature.

Tying the rope to my waist, I start to swim, having to paddle harder against the current to pull the equipment, but I manage it, and when I get to the base of the cliffs, there's a ledge. I haul myself up and sit with my legs dangling, then I pull the equipment up. I lay it out to dry as I stand and look out at the water. The cameras on my chest are recording, so I start to talk.

"See that? That is an empty ocean, no man-made structures anywhere in sight, just nature. This island was forgotten many years ago until a recent storm washed a man ashore. It's said many will never venture to this part of the world. How about we see why?"

I glance up at the cliff and dry my hands. "Now, to get my stuff up there, I'm going to free climb the cliff, placing lines as I go. Once I reach the top, I'll repel back down, clip the equipment, climb, and haul it up after me. I won't leave the lines in place, since I won't leave the island from here, and you never know what you will need. Plus, you need to respect your environment when adventuring. You know the saying, 'Leave it as you find it.' This island has stood for many years and will stand after we're gone, so we'll respect it."

Finished with my little pep talk, I get my equipment ready and check all the safety features before chalking my hands. I walk the base of the cliff, looking for the best route up, and when I have it, I grip the crumbling rock and begin to climb. It's slow going, as I check every hand and foothold, knowing I could drop at any minute. I lay line as I go, double-checking it is locked and safe with carabiners before moving onto the next section. I reach the top in under thirty minutes.

I drop my backpack there and tie myself up, step back over the edge, and throw myself down. My feet hit the base, and I secure the other equipment bag and start to pull myself up. My arms shake with the effort as the bag dangles midair.

When I get to the top, I haul the equipment over the ledge, slowly unlatch all my lines, and wind them up. Leaving the anchors there in case I need them for the way back. Stretching out my arms and legs, I slip off my waterproof jacket and roll it up into my bag, leaving me in shorts, socks, boots, and a white tank. I'm not wearing a bra because who's going to see my nipples out here? I put as much in my bag as I can, testing the weight before I bury it at the base of a tree and mark it. It's my emergency kit, stuff I don't think I'll need, but you never know. I have everything else with me, including flares and a flare gun.

Lifting my bag up, I pull on my sunglasses, apply more sunscreen, tug my hat down, and turn to the jungle. The sound of wildlife is loud now, the insects buzzing and birds calling to each other.

It's incredible.

"Time to explore." I grin and let out a hoot. Birds take flight, and predators sink deeper, and I laugh, unable to help it.

I set off into the jungle, making sure to keep my eyes peeled. There could be snakes or venomous spiders anywhere. They won't attack unless threatened, but I could wander too close or scare them, and I don't want that. I'd be dead before anyone even realized something was wrong. Plus, I never know what I'll find, but I've always felt more at home in the jungle than in a city.

I take some photos as I stroll through the flora, using my compass to keep me on the right path. A worn route through the trees becomes apparent the farther I go, which is helpful but also has me wondering who or what made it. Maybe someone has been here before, but surely it would have been recorded. I don't know, but I know I'll find the ruins if they are here, and that's all there is to it.

Whistling to myself, I stop a few hours in to drink some water and have a quick snack before setting out again. The air is hot, sweat dripping down my body, and my muscles start to ache, but I push through it. I want to get close to the middle of the island before I make camp for the night, which will mainly entail a hammock. That way I'll stay off the ground where most of the smaller predators hunt.

An hour or so later, I hear a waterfall. I follow the sound, and when I come upon the sight, I gape in amazement.

Crystal-blue water flows heavily over a small fall, lined with rocks on either side to climb, before flowing into a pool. I move closer and test the water with a rock before filtering it, filling my canteens, and taking a big drink. Then, I strip to my bikini bottom and test it with a rock again. When nothing moves, I step back and take a running leap.

I splash down and stay under the surface as I swim to the falls, coming up under them in a small alcove. Climbing the ledge, I explore and find nothing before diving back under and coming up in the pool. I swim and float for a while. The water is warmish, but definitely cooler than the air. Closing my eyes, I float across the surface, letting the sun hit my skin. It's so peaceful and perfect. There is only nature, no city noise or pollution, just animals and their surroundings. This whole island is beautiful, from the brilliance of the jungle to the hidden gem of this waterfall.

I'm excited to see what else I can find while I'm here. After all, I almost have two weeks completely alone out here.

It's time to make history.

# NINE
## MAEVE

After playing in the waterfall a little longer, I eat some lunch and set off into the jungle. It would be easy to get lost here. The trees all look the same, and there are no landmarks or high points, just foliage as far as the eye can see. I make sure to keep a careful route, leaving some indicators in the unlikely event I get turned around. It's never happened before, but you can't be too careful. It does slow me down, though, as does having to hack through the underbrush. Whatever was left of a trail has long since disappeared, and I am completely engulfed by nature. I try to do as little harm as possible, but I have to get through somehow.

The sun will set soon, and it would be stupid to continue forward, since you should always set up camp during daylight, so I find the biggest clearing I can and get to work. The hammock is easy enough. I string it up between the biggest trees, their leaves offering shelter and warmth since the temperature will drop quickly after nightfall. I test it a few times before plugging the cameras and sat phone into the portable battery to charge for an hour. Next, I make a fire. I'll leave it burning all night if I can to ward off predators and offer some protection, but I also need it to cook. I burned a lot of calories today, and it's important not only to stay hydrated, but also to eat properly so I have enough energy to go on. Some adventurers try to ration their food, but I packed enough to last me at least three weeks, so I'm not too worried as I build the base of the fire and press my lighter into the kindling. It catches alight, and I blow into it until flames engulf the pit. Sitting back, I pull out my pans and add pasta I sectioned off, warming it over the flame. I tug the pot off and begin to eat as I glance around. The sun is lowering rapidly, turning the sky orange, pink, and then black.

Once I'm done, I clean up my mess and tie my food bag to a tree away from my camp just in case, and then with my shovel in hand, I head away from my camp, using my fire as a directional marker. I dig a shallow hole and do my business before covering it up and returning. After wiping my face and hands with my wet wipes, I wrap myself up in my fleece and stare into the jungle. My mind is at peace.

The silence is comforting, not restricting or scary like most believe.

I feel alive here. I feel free.

When a yawn splits my lips, I climb up into my hammock, taking my flashlight with me just in case, and I settle in for the night, swinging ever so gently in the slight breeze, my eyes on the stars and moon I can see through small breaks in the canopy above me.

My mind, as always, returns to my father. Is he okay? Is he looking at the stars right now, wondering where I am? I reach for my camera and sit up in the hammock, then I hit record.

"Hi, Dad." I swing it around. "I'm at camp for the night. You should see this place. It makes the jungles in Peru look like child's play. I found an incredible waterfall today. I'll show you all of it when I get back." Hopefully, this reaches him before then. The uplink is a little spotty, but it should reconnect when the satellite is close enough. Some days, it won't, but others, it should. "I miss you right now because if you were here, you would maintain the fire," I joke.

Lapsing into silence for a moment, I take a deep breath. "I hope you know, Dad, that you're here with me, and everything I'm doing is for you—for us. I know you're probably sitting at home, telling everyone you're fine and you aren't worried, but we know each other too well for that. I'm sorry, Dad, that you can't be here when you want to be. I'm sorry your body is betraying you, but you are still the strongest person I know, and when I find the lost city, it won't be because of me, but because of you. You taught me everything I know, you inspire me, and you guide me, and even when you're under a different sky, know I am with you." Taking a deep breath, I blow it out. "Got deep, huh? You'd probably hit me if you were here. Alright, I'm going to get some sleep. Big day tomorrow. Speak then." Hitting end, I hold the camera to my chest and let the tears I will never let him see fall.

I grieve for him and everything he will never do.

I know he tells everyone he's lived a full life with no regrets, but when he sees me walking out the door, going off on adventures, he wishes it were him, and so do I. I'd gladly take away the disease if I could, but I can't, so instead I have to live for him.

Wiping my eyes, I remind myself that although I do this for us, this life is mine and I have to live it. He would be angry if I did everything just for him, and I don't. I love exploring. I just wish he were with me sometimes.

Hunkering down for the night, I let my gaze drift across the sky as rain starts to fall on me, so I wrap myself up tighter. A little rain never hurt anyone, after all.

I must drift off fairly easily, but a loud snap from above wakes me. I'm a light sleeper, but in a place like this, I have to be. After all, this is their world, not mine. I'm the invader. I slowly move my head to scan my surroundings. It could be nothing, but sharp, jerky, fear-filled movements would draw a predator's attention when I'm trying to figure out if I'm tonight's midnight snack or not.

In Australia, I once woke up to an eastern brown snake just slithering across my bag, and the only thing that kept me alive was remaining calm until it passed.

My eyes scan the ground, but I don't see anything, so I look up. My heart pounds in my chest, and my hands clench the bag in case I need to rip it off and run, though it wouldn't do much good because peering down at me are two bright glowing orbs.

Its eyes are a little set apart, and as my own adjust, I make out the shadow of the animal.

The jaguar is perched right above me on a branch, leaning down to stare. It doesn't attack or hiss, just stares, and I relax a little, staring back.

There's something . . . old about those eyes, ancient even, as if it's seen the world grow and change and is just curious. It isn't afraid of me, but why would it be? It's never had to be here.

It doesn't know the depths of cruelty humans are capable of. It is simply curious.

"I won't hurt you," I murmur softly as it blinks. "I mean no harm at all."

I speak gently, infusing my words with the truth, hoping it senses I am not a threat. If it attacks, it would be my own fault. I came into its home, but if anything, it seems more inquisitive as I speak.

For a moment, we just stare at each other, worlds apart yet both filled with curiosity, until a noise deeper in the jungle makes us both whirl around. We share a look, and then with a swish of its tail, the jaguar is gone, loping back into the trees and leaving me alone once more.

I look at the camera attached to my bunk and grin for the viewers. "Well, wasn't that a sight? It's never had to fear humans, never been hunted or trapped or killed. It just proves nature is beautiful, and if humans were less cruel, animals would trust us more. I'm going back to sleep now. Let me know if I have any more midnight visitors. Hopefully, they are just as nice."

I am used to talking to myself. I used to feel like I was crazy, especially in public, but on long trips and treks like this, it almost becomes a comfort. My viewers, although not here, bring me peace because I know I'm not alone. Even in the wildest most remote sections of our world, they are with me.

I wake as the sun starts to rise, and when I stretch in my hammock, I groan at the sight that greets me. A mixture of snakes and insects is spread across the ground, more than I've ever seen.

Eyes wide, I search for gaps, and luckily, there are some. I have no idea if these are venomous, but I'm going on the assumption that they are.

Grabbing my camera, I pan it around the resting snakes. "I have never seen so many gathered like this before. It's as if they fled from something."

I slowly slip from my sleeping bag and—thank fuck I kept my boots on—I put my feet in a space on the ground, moving gradually as I slide across to unhook my hammock. The takedown process is slow so I can avoid hurting the snakes or disturbing them, but once my bag is over my shoulder, I pan the camera around again.

"Bye-bye to our newest friends, sleep well." Hopping through the small gaps and into the jungle, I leave the snakes and their strangeness behind.

Everything on this island seems backwards, but the oddness of it appeals to me.

If this is really where the lost city is located, then I hope finding it won't change it too much.

There's a wild beauty here that deserves to be undisturbed.

## TEN
## WILDER

**O**ur boat anchors off the south side of the island where a low beach heads into the jungle, which is the best place for insertion that I could see. Plans adapt and change, but I like to have the basics in my head, unlike the others.

Sometimes, plans might just save your life.

From here, the island looks dormant and forgotten. Overgrown jungle spreads up to the beach, and crashing waves hit the cliffs to our right, the water as blue as a gem. It's a stunning sight, especially with the sun hitting it, and I know all too well that beauty hides secrets.

I can't wait to devour the ones we find.

"We will go no farther, and we won't wait here," the captain calls. When I turn, he is eyeing the land with something close to fear.

"Why?" Rick asks curiously as he ties off his bag and stands, the boat rocking slightly in the waves.

"It's cursed," the captain replies. "That is why nobody goes here. The locals forgot about it, protecting it to stop the curse. You shouldn't disturb it."

"How would you know it's cursed if no one ever comes here?" Aiyaret asks conversationally, his eyebrows raised.

The captain's eyes narrow on him in irritation. "Some things, you don't need to see to believe. The curse is real. Ignore me if you want to, but don't come crying to us when it swallows you up." He storms away, and I sigh.

Aiy smirks. "What? How could we cry to him if it swallowed us up like he said?"

"One of these days, your mouth will get us into trouble," I mutter as I sling my bag over my shoulder.

"I wish mine would." Logan sighs wistfully. "It's been too long since I was in trouble. Do you think it would swallow us for fun or food?"

Way smacks him for me as he walks past, and we head to the edge of the boat as the captain reappears and throws something at me.

"Just because you don't believe in the curse, doesn't mean it doesn't believe in you. Wear that, it will keep you safe. Don't ever go into the darkness alone, and you might just make it out alive." Lifting the necklace, I eye the green and black stone carving at the end. It's a face with teeth, and it's a little terrifying. Superstitions are often based on truth, so I drop it over my head and nod my thanks.

"Uh . . ." Rick lifts his hand. "Don't I get one too? I'm all for swallowing in the right circumstances, but not this one."

The captain smirks. "I only have one."

"Well, shit," Logan grumbles. "Guess we share the creepy necklace to keep us safe."

"Alright, enough," I warn them. "Game faces, boys. It's go time. I want to be on that beach in five minutes. No diving or playing around. The sun is high, and we need to cover a lot of ground fast. Is that understood?"

"Sir, yes, sir!" Logan mocks with a salute.

"I'm surrounded by idiots," I mutter as I turn to the water.

"Speak for yourself," Way scoffs as he slings his legs over the edge of the boat. "Now, let's go before the captain murders Logan or Rick and offers them to the gods or something."

"I heard that!" the captain calls.

"Yup, time to go." Waving at the captain, I throw myself backwards into the water, letting the waves consume me as I push away from the boat and resurface farther out. With a whoop, Logan flings himself after me, and Rick flips in. Way rolls his eyes and steps in, followed by Aiyaret, and before we are very far away, the boat speeds off into the distance.

"Guess he really believes in being swallowed." Logan chuckles as he catches up to me and then turns to Rick. "Race you to the shore. Whoever loses will be sacrificed to the curse."

"Shit, you're cheating!" Rick shouts as Logan dives under and sets off before they even agree.

I watch them race away, but I hang back, waiting for everyone else to pass me before I start to swim. I'm the team leader, so it's my job to keep them safe, which means being first in the water and the last one out. As soon as my feet hit the sand, I open my bag and slip on a shirt and hat as the others do the same and prepare. I tie my boots on and sling my bag over my shoulder, peering up at the thick jungle.

The darkness within makes me think of the captain's words, but I nod at my team and walk closer anyway.

I'm not afraid of a curse—it should be afraid of me.

I am going to find the lost city, and when I do, I'll make the world forget all about Maeve Carter and those other phonies.

"I think we should enter the jungle up there," I tell them as I scan the beach. "It seems less dense. We'll waste energy hacking through it here."

"Then let's go up there." Way shrugs. "Logan, tie your shorts. We don't want your dick slipping out."

"Boring," Logan mutters, but he does as he's told, and as a unit, we set off down the beach, our cameras capturing everything.

Logan and Rick film some short videos as well, playing in the sea and chasing each other. They also interview us as we walk. We let them, since our fans love it, and they keep us at the top of our game so we get to do what we love.

It's why we give them almost complete access to our lives, even the personal side.

"Wilder, say hello to your loyal fans." Rick shoves the camera in my face, pressing his cheek to mine so we're more stumbling than walking.

"Hello," I say, my eyes scanning the horizon.

"Our fearless leader is in work mode, but how cute is his new haircut?" Rolling my eyes, I let him film until I see something in the distance.

"What is that?"

They all turn to look, our eyes straining as we tread closer until we can finally make it out.

"Holy shit," we say in unison.

## ELEVEN
# MERRICK

"Rick, wait!" my brother yells, but I scramble over the sand and gape at the giant shipwreck emerging from the water. I don't know how we didn't see it farther down the beach, but up close, it's huge. The old, scarred, knotted wood is covered in sea life, and there are some holes in the sides. It's unlike anything from this century.

"Shit, that's ancient," Aiyaret confirms. "Probably a cargo ship that ran aground and washed up here."

"Um, guys," Logan calls, and we hurry around the front to see him pointing behind it. "There are at least four wreckages here."

We sputter because he's right. Hidden behind the mostly intact ship are four smaller wrecks. Some are mainly just pieces, but one is a tiny fishing boat, probably from a few years ago. The others span in size and time, but they are all here.

As Logan strides over, he picks up a piece of wood and shows it to us. There are teeth marks on the side. "Probably a shark," I remark, but I can't help scanning the rest, looking for more. There aren't any.

What made them wreck here?

Storms?

Mechanical failure?

"I guess other people have been here before," Way murmurs, sharing a look with Wilder, but we are all thinking the same thing—if they have been here before, then why haven't they reported their findings?

Unless they didn't make it out alive or they didn't tell for a reason.

Neither option bodes well, but we can't let the mood sour, so I turn the camera and pose in front of the ship, grinning. "I am the captain now," I mock.

It does the trick, breaking the tension, and Wilder rolls his eyes. "Whatever the reason, we'll leave them here. This doesn't affect us. Shoot some footage if you want, but be respectful. We might need to show it when we get back so they can help identify the boats if anyone is still missing."

I read between the lines—if there are any bodies, we need to be careful.

We shoot from all angles before turning our attention to the jungle. We can't afford to be distracted, not in there, and it's already late morning, which means we need to get moving if we want to cover ground. We plan to be in the city within the next two days, which means setting a grueling pace of trekking from sunup to sundown.

It's nothing we haven't done before, but in this heat and with the unknown factors, it spells trouble, so I promise myself I'll keep them laughing. Otherwise, there's no point. Wilder's moods have the tendency to sour, especially on long excursions or if things go wrong.

It's my job to keep him smiling and enjoying the adventure. He's my big brother, and the only reason he is here is because of me.

They call him Wild, but if it wasn't for me, he'd probably have a normal, mundane life. I was the one who needed adrenaline, adventure, and an outlet to keep me out of jail. He simply gave me one, and he fell in love with it along the way, but I know deep down Wilder is the same as I am—a lost spirit in search of a purpose.

"Rick, keep up." Wilder grabs my shoulder and shoves me in front of him. Way is in the lead, Wilder is at the back, and the rest of us are in the middle. It's how we always do things. Way and Wilder keep us safe.

An hour in, Wilder hands me my bottle, silently demanding I drink. I roll my eyes but do as I'm told, knowing better than to defy him.

"Thanks, Dad," I tease, and he rolls his eyes, but his smile grows.

He is like my dad. Our parents are amazing people, and we love them, but they could never handle me. They didn't know what to do with me, so I always got into trouble. Only Wilder could calm me down and keep me sane. He's the reason I made it through school and out into the world. Without him, my life would be very different.

He's the brains, I'm the brawn, and that's the way I like it.

He does all my thinking for me. "Look at that." Aiy points, and we all follow his gesture through the densely packed trees.

"Is that—" I squint. "A building?"

"Looks to be," Wilder murmurs.

"Let's check it out." Logan marches in that direction, and we have no choice but to follow, even as Wilder's sigh fills the air.

Oh well, he should be used to it by now.

**M**ost of the jungle looks the same. It would be easy to get lost if I didn't keep checking my compass. I don't want to leave many markings behind if I can help it, wanting to preserve as much of the island as possible.

Unfortunately, I don't find a waterfall today, so I'm dripping with sweat. The heat is almost unbearable, and it also means I have to make more stops than I would like to hydrate and rest, but I don't want to make myself sick or get heat stroke simply to get there a day quicker.

I'm sitting on a log when a little lizard scrambles across my leg and freezes. I know from its coloring its venomous, but I gently lift it into the air. He doesn't bite, just stares at me. "You're beautiful," I tell him honestly as I look around. "You might get squished here though." Standing, I head over to a boulder a little bit away and lay him on it. "There you go. You should be safe up there." I watch him scurry away with a smile before packing up and carrying on.

I'm deep in the jungle at this point. I can't hear the ocean anymore, and I'm at what we call the danger point. If anything were to happen, I'm too far to make it back and not deep enough to make it through to the other side, so I'm being extra careful.

I might be an adrenaline junkie, but I'm not dumb, not like those Adreno fuckers.

Just after dinner, I find an entrance to a cave in the middle of the jungle floor. It's overgrown around the edges, but when I peer inside, I notice it stretches deep into the earth. It's a pit stop I don't need, but who is to say there isn't an entrance or clues down there?

Besides, exploring a cave no one else has sounds like a good time.

I make a quick plan, crack some lights, then toss them inside so I can take a look around. It's about seventy feet deep and looks pretty big from what I can see. Pulling out my gear, I secure my rope to two trees, testing it first, then I pull on my helmet, grab my flashlight, and sling my bag over my shoulder just in case. With a grin at the camera, I take a running jump and leap into the hole, spinning as I go. The momentum takes me about halfway, so I use the ropes and my legs to swing myself down the rest of the distance. When my boots hit the slightly wet rock below, I untie myself from the rope and swing my flashlight around.

It's not a huge cavern despite what I initially thought, maybe around a hundred feet wide. It's jagged and uneven, the rock is slick down here, and foliage grows from cracks in the walls and floor.

I can't see any other holes or entrances and exits, which means there isn't much in terms of the lost city down here, but it doesn't mean it isn't cool to explore.

I investigate the area under the entrance first, finding some cool, old markings along the floor, and then I head farther into the shadows, spinning my light over the walls. The lights I threw down glow red, and maybe it's that, but something here makes me shiver.

I'm scanning the back wall when something makes me still.

Narrowing my eyes, I shine my flashlight on what caught my attention, and I silently tread across the slick cavern, walking past my rope and into the shadows.

On the black rock are gray furrows. Five of them drag down, the jagged marks deep enough to scar the surface. Tilting my head, I eye them. Is it an animal mark? Did it fall and get trapped?

Something protrudes from one of the furrows, and I pluck it free, my blood running cold when I realize it's a broken, bloody fingernail.

Holding out my hand, I press it to the marks and slide it down, realization settling in.

These are from a human hand.

Spinning, I scan the cavern with new eyes.

Did someone fall down here? Did they get trapped and try to claw their way out? Staying quiet, I walk the perimeter, knowing what I will find.

At the very back, huddled, as if trying to hide or avoid death, is a body.

The skeleton is positioned with one hand out, its head turned away. I don't know how long ago they fell down here, but it's clear nature has eaten away at the flesh. Crouching, I eye it sadly.

How horrible it must have been to starve, alone and terrified, while trapped down here when the exit is just above.

I could try to haul the body out and bury it, but that seems more disrespectful than just leaving it. I don't want to disturb their resting place. Instead, I bow my head and close my eyes, offering my condolences and hopes for a peaceful afterlife for them, and I make a note to delete any camera footage from down here.

Heading back to my rope, I tie myself in it, and with one last glance around, I push off and start to climb up, ignoring all the other scratches and marks of desperation. Once I'm in the sunshine, I lie back, my heart aching for that person. My legs dangle into the hole when I swear something passes under them.

Yanking them up, I peer inside, but there's nothing there, so I let out a bitter laugh.

"Imagination, my girl," I mutter as I untie my rope, wind it up, and tug my pack on. Shaking off the clinging feeling of dread, I grab a piece of wood and use my blade to carve it into a cross, then I place it before the hole for when I come back. Hopefully once I find the city, someone can collect the body.

Just in case, I send my wishes down again and head off into the jungle.

My heart is heavy, my excitement gone at the reminder of the brutality of nature and how easy it would be to perish in my line of work with no one the wiser.

Would I just be forgotten, left to rot and die alone?

Would anyone care?

## THIRTEEN
### WAY

**A**s we come upon the building, I realize two things very quickly.

First, there is more than one.

Second, they are very old.

These are made from wood, clearly well-constructed, and small but homey. They are in an encampment of sorts, the jungle reclaiming a few of them and growing over. It's obviously been years since they were inhabited, but it means more than one person lived here at some point.

Is this where the curse rumor started?

Who knows, but it's exciting to think people have been here before, maybe even found the city and left it—or protected it.

"Be careful." I jerk Logan back as he steps onto the entrance of a structure. "The wood might be rotten. We don't need you falling through and breaking an ankle or something."

"Yes, Daddy," he teases, but he heads inside one of the homes anyway. Rolling my eyes, I scan the area. There's a clear space where they cooked and had fires, the homes circling it. There are even some posts where a fence may have been, and I swear I even see planks up in the trees.

"It's a village," Aiy says, appearing from behind a hut.

I nod in amazement. "It is."

"Not just a village. You guys need to check this out," Rick calls from somewhere beyond the last home. We follow his voice and come upon a bigger, wider building with a huge awning covering the entrance.

Inside is a wooden table with figurines on it, and as I spin, I take in all the drawings on the wall. "Is this a temple?"

"It looks to be," Wilder murmurs. "Or at least a place of importance for them."

"Hey, check out these drawings," Logan murmurs. We follow him over to the wall. Some of them make no sense, but I get what he means.

They are . . . *odd.*

There is a depiction of a hole in the ground and somebody being thrown inside, and next to it are large shapes coming from the hole, chasing people. There are more images of the village and shadows surrounding it.

"It almost looks like there's an animal that haunts them or this place," he murmurs.

"The curse?" I shrug. "Could be a myth or simply a tale. The shapes are black, so maybe a jaguar?"

"Maybe," Wilder says as he looks around. "Whatever it is, they believed in it enough to build a temple to ward it off."

Nodding, I wander around and look at the drawings. There are more of humans running and more shapes than I can count, but never a clear image of what.

"We shouldn't touch anything," I warn with a glance around. "I feel their ghosts haunting this place. We don't want to disrespect or disturb them."

"I agree," Rick replies with a shiver. "I can feel them watching us. We shouldn't be here."

"Then let's keep moving," Wilder orders, and we file out of the temple and back into the jungle, leaving the village to be claimed by nature.

Whatever they feared, it has to be long gone.

Right?

# FOURTEEN
## LOGAN

W e made good progress today. We didn't cover as much ground as we would have liked, but we got some amazing footage that Ajax will be happy with, and we are deep in the jungle now. If the lost city is anywhere on this island, it has to be in the middle.

At least, that's what Wilder thinks, and we agree with him as we swiftly and efficiently set up camp, falling into our usual routine without needing to be ordered or asked. It's one thing that works well for us. We have been together so long, we know and can anticipate each other's needs.

I help Aiyaret string up our hammocks in a circle around the fire, where Wilder is preparing food while Way and Rick clear the edges of the camp and filter our water. When we are all sitting, tucking into our metal tins, we fall into a companionable silence.

The jungle is alive around us, the fire crackling between us.

It's how we like it out here in the middle of nowhere, be it sand, snow, or jungle. It's just us and nature and nothing else. We are free of expectations, pressure, and the horrors that press down on us from our memories.

"You think it's actually here?" Rick asks as he leans back, resting his head on Wilder's shoulder. "The city, I mean?"

"We'll find out," Wilder mutters, always the practical one.

Leaning forward, I grin mischievously at Rick. "I think so. I think it will be dripping with gold, and we are going to be the first to find it. Can you imagine what it will be like when we go back? We'll be famous, maybe given some sort of award—hell, the best part will be shoving it in Carter's face."

"I'd like to shove something else in her face." Rick wiggles his eyebrows as Wilder shoves him off, making him fall back with a laugh. Rick loves to wind his brother up about Maeve Carter, especially since the two hate each other after he rejected her as one of us.

We all know why he did it. If it had been anybody else . . . if it had been a man, he would have given them a chance. My eyes drift to Aiy, who looks away at the mention of her name. Nobody said it or brought it up, and we didn't even tell Ajax the full reason, but Aiyaret is why Maeve Carter wasn't allowed on the team.

This is his family, his safe space from the world, and she would threaten that by simply being a woman.

We couldn't let it happen. We couldn't let the slow healing we have seen with our brother disappear with one look at her. He will never discuss it, but I know he was relieved. He didn't refuse to let her join, but he didn't have to. We would never put his mental well-being in jeopardy like that. Being around a woman twenty-four seven in close proximity is different than being around women in general.

I think Ajax and Carter believe we did it to spite her and that Wilder didn't like her. Nothing could be further from the truth, but the indifference on Wilder's part soon turned to annoyance as they went from would-be coworkers to enemies, always trying to one up each other and show off. Honestly, the two should just fuck and get it over with. We all know they want to. Beneath all that anger and hostility is a level of sexual attraction that even makes me want to look away.

When they are going toe-to-toe, it's almost a private interaction that you feel weird intruding on.

It's why Ajax keeps them separate, I think, worried about losing one or both of them.

"Enough," Wilder snaps, his eyes flashing with fire like they always do when he hears her name. I truly can't figure out if he hates her or hates how much he wants her. It's fun to watch.

"I heard her dad is really sick," Way says, and we all look at him. He shrugs, shoving another forkful of food into his mouth and chewing. "She doesn't talk about it, but I overheard Ajax. He has MS. Apparently, they were a team, but when he got sick, she ended up with Venture to keep his legacy going. She's raised millions for charities related to it, I think, in hopes of helping him."

"How the hell do you know that?" I ask.

"I listen." He shrugs. "She isn't a bad person."

"Nobody said she was," Wilder mutters. "She's just—"

"Annoying?" I add.

"A know-it-all?" Rick grins, leaning forward.

"Too crazy for her own good?" I say.

"Wild?" Rick chimes in.

Wilder has called her all these things before.

Wilder barks, "Enough about Carter. She isn't here, and we are. Leave her to base jump or throw herself from hot air balloons again. We are real explorers. There is a difference."

"Yeah, baby, exploring the bush." I wiggle my eyebrows, and Rick laughs as the others sigh.

We lapse into comfortable silence.

"She's not . . . bad." We startle when Aiyaret speaks, our mouths dropping open. He feels our stares and shrugs, looking away. "I understand wanting to help the one you love. Besides, we spoke once or twice at Venture. I think she realized I was uncomfortable and was kind about it."

I share a look with Wilder. That's news to us. I didn't even think Aiyaret had met Maeve Carter, let alone could think any woman was kind.

"Well, that's good," Wilder comments slowly, and then he stands. "Okay, time for bed."

"Aww, let's tell some spooky stories, Dad," I joke.

"No, last time Rick climbed into my sleeping bag with me after you freaked him out. No ghost stories here," Wilder admonishes.

"I just wanted a cuddle." Rick sighs, pouting dramatically.

"Cuddle Logan. He'll probably like it," Wilder retorts as he adds logs to the fire and checks the camp once more before climbing into his hammock. "I don't want stories. Go to bed. We have a long day ahead of us tomorrow. You need your sleep."

"Yes, Dad," we say and burst into laughter. He ignores us, but I see the smile curling his lips as we climb into our sleeping bags and hunker down for the night.

The sounds of the jungle fill our ears with relaxing white noise.

# FIFTEEN
## AIYARET

I should be asleep. My body is tired after a long day of trekking through the jungle, but my mind is wide awake. A change in the atmosphere or location and I struggle to sleep, worried old trauma will rise. After years in this job, you would think it would get better, but no. It's just something I have grown accustomed to. I love this occupation and my brothers enough to endure it. Besides, I feel safer out here with them than I ever did in a bedroom in the city, with too many doors and locks to keep me in.

I still wear the scars from my childhood like brands, but it's the mental ones I can never escape.

I haven't spoken to the others about what happened, but they've put enough pieces together. I also know they try their best to protect me, so it doesn't surprise me that when I get up to sit by the fire, wrapping my bag around me, Way finds his way to me, ducking under the material to share the heat.

"Can't sleep?" he asks after a moment, his voice low so he doesn't wake the others.

I shake my head, unable to look at him, ashamed of how fragile my mind is. I feel like I'm their weakness. It must be exhausting always having to protect and monitor me, but they have never complained. They just call themselves my brothers and hold me until I'm better.

I'm not the only one with issues. Normal people don't choose to do what we do. We are all trying to escape something, be it our pasts, our minds, or how we feel.

We look for answers in the unknown, and we find the beauty in what others deem terrifying.

I suppose most people look for guidance and answers in the mundane, but not us. We search mountains, explore caves, swim in oceans, and scale glaciers in search of them. They call us adrenaline junkies, but they don't see the peace we find together in nature.

"Memories?" he asks after a moment.

"My mind is just too loud to relax," I murmur softly. "It's always like this. I'll be okay, go back to bed."

"Not a chance, we're brothers." He moves closer. "You're up, so I'm up."

I know Way misses his brother, and he envies the bond Rick and Wilder have. Every time he calls us "brother," it's tinged with both sadness and happiness.

Yes, we all have our own demons.

We sit in silence for a bit, and I feel him looking at me, his eyes running over my face. He's started to do that more, and I don't know why, but it makes me nervous. When I glance over, he meets my eyes as his hand slides over the jungle floor and grips mine. I turn mine over and twine our fingers. Something about it makes my cheeks heat, and the small smile he aims my way dazzles me for a moment.

Way is handsome, and he knows it. When we are like this, it's my favorite time of the day.

He always seeks me out in the dark, sleeping by my side, waking with every nightmare, and sitting with me on sleepless nights.

I don't know why. Is it because he wants to protect me like he couldn't protect his brother?

His smile slowly drops, and I swear his gaze slips down my face, though I'm not sure why. When his eyes meet mine again, they are filled with something that scares me as much as it has me holding his hand tighter.

A snore breaks the moment, filling the air and making us jolt apart, and it's only then I realize we were leaning into each other. Another snore makes us look back, and Logan turns in his hammock, his arms windmilling for a second as he almost falls before he rights himself and goes straight back to snoring.

Shaking my head, I look at the fire as Way chuckles. "Some things never change."

"Some things do," I reply, and I feel him staring at me again. It's different this time, questioning, but I'm not sure why.

"Did you really speak to Carter? Like, actually manage to speak to her?" Way murmurs, and I hear the shock in his words. I don't blame him. I've never been able to before.

Pursing my lips, I nod. "For a little bit. Nothing important, she was just making jokes and trying to get to know me."

It was a passing moment for her, but it was a big, momentous occasion for me.

We brushed past each other on the way to the offices.

Her body touched mine, and I usually would have gone into a meltdown, but she looked at me and smiled, and something about it seemed to calm my racing heart. I barely remember what she said, but I couldn't seem to stop myself from staring at her. I should have walked away, but I lingered.

When she went to slap my side after a joke, however, I stepped back. Her expression hadn't changed, no offense was taken, but something in her eyes seemed knowing, and I hated that.

"And?" Way prompts when I say no more.

"I didn't have a panic attack," I tell him.

"Aiy, that's huge," he whispers. "Why didn't you tell us?"

"I figured it was just a freak moment and it wasn't important," I mutter.

"Of course it's important. You're doing so great with healing and moving on. I'm proud of you for not running from her." There is pure pride in his voice, and when I glance at him, he's grinning widely.

"Why?" I ask, my voice thick. "Why are you proud of me for doing what others can do without thinking?"

"Fuck others. I don't care about them. I care about you. This was a big deal, so of course I'm proud of you. I want you to be happy, Aiyaret." The way he says my name, rolling his tongue over it, sends a shiver through me that I can't explain. "I want you to be able to live the life you want."

"It was just a conversation," I remind him.

"Yes, but tomorrow, it could be a meeting, and the next, it could be a hangout. The time after, who knows?" He nudges my shoulder. "I want you to be happy, brother."

I stare at him again, wondering what he means.

He wants me to be happy . . . like, with someone?

With a woman?

As I stare at him, I start to wonder. If he or I were a girl, would this be different? I don't know, but I look away at the strange thought.

"I want you to be happy too," I murmur. Way has . . . flings, not relationships. He never lets anyone get too close. He gives them part of his life, not all, but not us—we get everything.

I get it all, but I'm his brother, so that's normal.

"One day, this will all change." I don't realize I'm speaking out loud until his voice comes.

"What do you mean?"

"One day, Wilder will settle down, or Rick will, hell, even you or Logan. We'll slowly splinter apart. We'll go from living with each other and seeing each other every day to once a week, then a month . . . then on holidays. We'll get normal jobs and have families." Well, they will, not me. "We'll forget all about these adventures and the way it felt when we were on them. That's what happens, right? People calm down and move on, but I'll still be here, waiting for all of you. Our brotherhood will change."

"Change is the only constant in the world, Aiy, but we will never leave or forget you," he promises, and when I glance at him, he grabs my hand tighter. "I promise. There is no breaking us apart. I will go wherever you go. If the others . . . If they do eventually settle down and start a family or whatever, you'll still have me. I'm not going anywhere, but neither are they. Not everyone wants that type of life, Aiyaret. It might be normal for some, but not for us. We've never done anything the traditional way. We'll be out in jungles and mountains until they have to force us into graves."

"Really?"

"Really. We'll be in hospital beds side by side, and when the time comes, we'll go together. Nothing in this world can separate us, Aiyaret, be it time or age. We are in this for the long run," he vows, and I know he means it. "Do you believe me?"

I nod silently, and he smiles brightly. "Brothers," I whisper.

"Brothers," he agrees, but why does the word feel like we are saying something else?

Dragging my eyes away, I focus on the low flames of the fire as our friends and brothers sleep around us.

His arm slides around my shoulders, and I rest my head against him. He holds me as time passes, letting me soak in his warmth.

After a while, something makes me lift my head and peer into the jungle. There's no change in the noise or any movement, but something made me look, and an unknown fear courses through me for a moment.

"What is it?" Way murmurs.

"Something is watching us," I whisper. The hair on the back of my neck rises, and an old instinct kicks in—the one that kept me alive.

"What do you mean?" he asks.

"I don't know, but . . . I think something is watching us," I reply quietly.

Way gazes into the jungle, picking up a flashlight and shining it in the trees before glancing at me when neither of us sees anything. "There's nothing there. It's just that captain getting in your head with tales of boogeymen and curses. Don't let him spook you . . . like that time in Berlin with the ghost, or in New Zealand with the made-up creature stalking the night. There's nothing here but ruins and history," he assures me. "You have enough horrors in your life, Aiy, so don't make any more up."

I look back at the trees, the fear not going away.

History has a way of clawing at you, even from the past. I know that all too well.

## SIXTEEN
## MAEVE

I wake before the sun. The birds and insects chirp happily, and after a quick breakfast, I break my camp down and repack my bags. I take a little bath to treat myself, since my skin is already sticky with sweat from the heat. It mainly consists of using the wipes from my bag and changing into clean shorts, but it's surprising how that can make me feel like a new woman.

Tying a scarf on my head to keep my hair back, I set off into the jungle. It seems like the deeper I go, the thicker the foliage gets. It's obvious no one has been here in a very long time, maybe never, so I take time shooting more footage. I carefully climb a tree to film from high above before continuing on my path.

By midmorning, the heat is almost unbearable, and I've worked through my first water canister faster than I would have liked. I need to ration my second and last, since I haven't seen a water source since the waterfall.

I hide my second bottle to stop myself, and instead, I eat some of the nuts I brought to keep my hands busy. I have to reapply sunscreen and insect spray a few times, and my feet grow tired as I become bored. I search for something other than greenery, like any hint of this lost city so I know I didn't waste a week just walking across a random island.

It has to be here. He wasn't lying, right? No, he saw it, and he was terrified.

Recalling his reaction makes me impatient, which is a flaw of mine. I crave adrenaline and exploration. I love days like this and have spent many just walking trails and sightseeing, but it's lonely without someone beside me.

I'm just starting to feel a little tired and dejected when I hear something.

Tilting my head, I close my eyes and concentrate to make sure I'm not hearing things, which is very common with explorers on isolated areas.

No, it's definitely the sound of water. I head in the direction I think it's coming from. The ground turns muddy and tilts down, then the trees break open, and I smile. It's a river!

"Yes!" I shout as I slide down the embankment to the water. It's dirty for sure, almost greenish in color, but water is water, and in this kind of environment, beggars can't be choosers. Pulling out my canisters, I down the last of my supply and fill them up, adding tablets and letting them clear it. I could boil it, but this is easier and safer. The last thing I need is to get sick on a remote island where I'm alone. I could easily die from something as simple as vomiting out here.

Eyeing the river and the shoreline, I look for any wild animals that might attack me, then I pick up some rocks and toss a few into the water. When nothing emerges or snaps, I shrug. There are no bubbles or signs of anything hiding. They could be under the surface somewhere, but everything out here involves risk. I have waded through enough swamps with crocs and alligators not to be too worried anyway. They aren't the monsters people make them out to be.

They are beautiful creatures, just misunderstood.

I could continue trekking through the jungle, but this river is flowing in the same direction I am traveling in. I can cool down as I go, and hopefully it will lead to something. I place my phone and cameras in my waterproof bag and bury it deep in my pack before doing the same to my food, then I strip my outer layer off and add that as well. Holding my backpack against my chest, I slip and slide down the rest of the embankment, and I splash into the water. It's shallow at first, and then it drops off.

Moving my bag in front of me, I use it as a floatation device to save my arms and just kick my legs until it grows shallower, then I basically walk and wade. It changes a few times, and I end up swimming most of the way as I scan the jungle on either side, looking for any hints or signs.

The water is nice and cold compared to the heat of the jungle, and I know I'll be shivering when I get out. Luckily, I have other things to change into. I wish I could film some of this, but it's also nice just to experience it. Some things should be kept for myself, and although I try to replicate the feeling of exploring like this, it's impossible unless I'm doing it myself.

I can show them, but I can't make them feel the way the sun warms my skin or smell the wild wind. They can't feel the unknown, excitement, and pure joy like I do now.

I swim for another hour or so. The river winds and becomes narrow at some point before suddenly widening, and I can stand. I sling my pack on and look around a full marshland. Checking my compass, I see it's heading the way I need to go, so I set off across it, taking my camera out and shooting some footage.

"Okay, so I just traversed a wild river that led to this marshland. We are still heading north across the island, so hopefully we'll come across something soon, but look at this—water and trees as far as the eye can see." I pan the camera around. "No other person in sight."

A snake swims past me, and I film it. "Plenty of wild animals though." I spend the next thirty minutes shooting some footage of snakes, spiders, and even a monkey or two before putting my camera away and focusing on my destination.

The water is hip deep now, clearly a flooded area from the looks of it, with trees growing up and out of it as the ground squishes under my feet.

My legs are aching and tired, but I push forward. I've had a lot worse, and this is precisely why I work out, so I can push my body to its limits. I knew this wouldn't be easy, but when it gets hard, I just tell myself it's mental, and there are so many people in the world who wish they could do what I do. Those who might have limitations or struggles, just like my father, would do anything to be here, complaining their legs ache. My dad would suffer any exhaustion, pain, or wet socks to see what I am seeing.

Also, when I'm old, if I manage to get to that age, I won't care about how tired I was. I'll only care about what I saw and experienced. Life is too damn short to hold myself back or talk myself out of it. I'm lucky I don't have a voice that tells me to. I know so many others do, and I think they are stronger than I am because they fight and overcome it to get to the same places I do.

Whether the battles are mental or physical, I am in awe of everyone who wakes up each day, no matter what they are going through, and survives it.

After taking more pictures, I eat some snacks and keep wading forward. My arms have goose bumps, but it's better than sweating my tits off. There is nothing worse than underboob sweat.

A noise makes me frown, so I scan the area and see bubbles floating past me.

I turn slowly, trying not to make any sudden movements. The sound comes again, and I see bubbles about two feet away. It could be a trick of my imagination or random fish, but I wait just in case.

Most wild animals will attack if they are hungry, their nests are disturbed, or something scares them. Otherwise, they tend to leave you alone—it's humans who are usually the assholes—so I wait, hoping whatever it is goes on its merry way.

As time crawls by, though, I swear I feel something watching me.

I'm going mad—that's what it is. The environment and my mind are playing tricks on me. When nothing pops up or attacks, I slowly continue on, and I see the water flowing to the left, so I head that way and get my boots out on solid land. I could take a break and dry my gear, but I head straight into the jungle until I'm a little ways away, and then I change my socks. The rest can wait, but keeping my feet dry is important.

I'm just slinging my bag on when I feel something behind me.

Slowly, so I don't startle whatever it is, I turn, only to freeze as a jaguar appears. It slinks between the trees, stopping right in front of me. It can't be the same one. That would mean it's either tracking me or I'm crossing its path, which doesn't feel right. It feels like the same one, though, and it's watching me the same way.

I wait to see what it will do, but it just observes.

I turn and slowly start to walk sideways, keeping it in my vision, but it tracks me, and when I try to head north, it jumps in my path and hisses. I fall back, holding my hands up.

"Okay, okay." I tilt my head, copying it. "Are you warning me about going that way?"

It stops hissing, stops baring its teeth, so I back up, and it keeps its eyes on me, but when I try to pass it to head north, it hisses once more, swiping out a paw in warning.

What the actual fuck?

This isn't normal.

Suddenly, it flattens its ears and turns its head, looking at something in the distance. A scared hiss leaves it before it spares me one last glance and lopes off in the opposite direction, as if something is chasing it.

Eyes wide, I watch it go then look back the way it was staring.

That was the direction I was aiming for, but something in me says, "Nope." If that wild animal is running, then I shouldn't ignore it. I turn east instead and travel that way.

There is no way I am ignoring that jaguar.

Crazy or not.

I have a general idea of where I am on the island, and although I'm heading deeper, eventually I'll need to trek north. I just want to give whatever upset the jaguar a wide berth. Anything that can scare a wild cat like that . . . Yeah, I don't want to meet it.

The afternoon sun is moving quickly across the sky as the jungle opens into a large clearing. Blinking in surprise, I push my sunglasses up and gape in shock at the giant circle stretching as far as the eye can see.

How and why aren't there any trees here? I step hesitantly onto the high, thick grass and walk forward, only to stop when I get to the middle.

Something under my feet doesn't feel right. Crouching down, I rip away some of the grass with my machete, then I freeze.

It's soil with something hard under it. Brushing it away, I swiftly stand up and step back when I see bones.

*Human bones.*

Turning, I realize the grass is hiding a mass grave.

Bodies are buried just below the surface.

I carefully pick my way toward the edges, not wanting to disturb the dead. Nothing good can come from it, and they deserve peace. They were buried to rest, not for me to dig them up or take pictures of them. Toward the edge of the field, though, where the soil is dug up and bones protrude from the ground, I swear I see gnaw marks on them. They look like animal teeth marks, round and sharp, but something has definitely been chewing on the bones.

Why?

A bad feeling causes a shiver to travel down my spine, so I head toward the trees to leave this place, but at the tree line, I see a body, not a skeleton.

Half of his face is missing, exposed down to the bone, his chest is ripped open, and one of his legs is gone. His hands are up as if to protect himself or ward off whatever did this.

Fuck, I turn way, gagging at the stench and sight.

It's fresh, maybe a week or two? More? I'm not sure, but it hasn't been years like the others behind me. Who exactly is this? Did he wash up here? Was he another explorer? I'm not sure, but I can't leave without checking. Someone could be searching for him. If something happened to me, I would want someone to take the time to tell my father.

Pulling my scarf down, I tie it around my face to mask the smell, and before I lose my courage, I head over. I don't look too closely at his face, but I search his ripped pants. I have to slide my hand into the pocket, and I gag, turning my head away when it seems to plunge deeper into his skin. Something hard is in there, and I hook my fingers in it then yank it out. When I fall back on my ass, I see the blood-covered wallet and scramble away to the closest tree. I pull my scarf down and retch, throwing up the contents of my stomach.

It keeps coming as flies buzz around me, but eventually I'm just dry heaving. Spitting to clear my mouth, I lean back against a tree, breathing deeply before grabbing my bag.

I wash my mouth out with water and breathe through the queasiness. When it abates, I wipe my face and tie my scarf around my hair, then I look at the wallet on the grass where I dropped it.

Wincing, I pick it up, sparing some of my water to wash it off as much as I can so it's not as . . . sticky, then I pull my camera out and take some footage of the inside.

He was a Californian named Thomas Wardle, and he was twenty-nine. There's a polaroid of him and another man embracing. I spare him a look, saddened by how he died, before I close the wallet and carefully put it in my bag. Hopefully my camera will link up, and they'll see the footage and let his partner and parents know.

I debate whether or not I should bury him, but I honestly don't know if I could manage it. It would also make it harder to retrieve his body if they tried, not to mention what has been . . . snacking on him will probably come back and dig him up anyway, so although it feels wrong, I head back into the jungle and leave him there.

My heart is heavy, and my good mood is nowhere in sight.

It's a reminder of just how brutal nature can be if I'm not careful.

## SEVENTEEN
## MERRICK

I wake with the sun hitting my face and roll over, only to fall from my hammock. I hit the ground with a thump and hiss as I rub at my eyes, then I glance over at the others to see them waking as well.

My eyes land on Way's bunk and widen. His arms are wrapped around Aiyaret, both of them huddled together. Aiy lifts his head groggily and looks around. When he meets my gaze, I look away with a knowing smile. I'm glad my brother is finally moving forward.

I say nothing as the others stir, not wanting to draw attention to it. I know Way and Aiy have been getting closer. Way is the only one who is able to comfort and calm him down, but it isn't any of our business unless they say it is.

"Going to be a hot one," I grouse to Aiy as I sit at his side by the campfire. I feel his eyes on me. He's worried about what I'll ask when I meet his gaze. "Let's start breakfast while they wake up."

He nods, and we work together out of habit. Aiy relaxes over time when I don't say anything, and when breakfast is served and everyone else is walking over, I slap his shoulder gently. "Don't overthink too much, brother. It isn't good for the soul," I whisper to him before handing a metal tray to Wilder.

Aiy hands one to Way, who slumps next to him after going to the bathroom, and for a moment, their eyes meet and something passes between them. I have the insane urge to squeal, but I feel like I'm intruding, so I turn to Logan and steal a forkful of his oatmeal.

"Hey," he grumbles around a mouthful.

"Yours looks nicer." I shrug, and his eyes narrow. Before I know it, I'm tackled to the ground. Our oatmeal is forgotten as we roll across the leaves, slapping and kicking each other. Wilder simply steps over us and heads to the fire, and we finally roll to a stop.

"Truce?" I suggest.

"Fine," Logan mutters, and then he offers me a hand up and we walk over to the fire, grabbing our breakfast and eating.

"So what's the plan, boss man?" I ask Wilder, eyeing Aiy and Way, who are in their own little world, their heads bent together as they eat. A small smile curves my brother's lips before he clears his throat.

"I want to cover at least four miles. It's a hard hike today. No stops if we can help it."

We groan, but Wilder just grins like a psychopath. "If we can, then we will be at the center of the island by tomorrow, and the real fun will begin."

"Wilder," Logan whines, and we press our faces together, wearing pouts we've practiced a million times.

"Wilder," I echo. "Can't we have some fun?"

His eyes narrow as he glances between us, knowing he's fighting a losing battle. "Like what?" he mutters.

"Merrick and I saw a waterfall not far from here last night. Can we play there for a bit, maybe do some rock climbing and diving?" Logan asks, and I nod.

"It will be good for footage. Ajax will like it," I add.

"They are right," Way says, and Wilder sighs, a sound that lets me know we won.

"Fine, but only if you're ready to go in ten minutes."

Our whoops of joy fill the air as we scramble to pack.

You bet your ass we were ready in nine minutes, and Wilder reluctantly let Logan and I lead the way to the waterfall we found. It doesn't take long, and we dump our packs along the boulders at the edge. It's not overly large, not like the one we found in New Zealand, but it's pretty with sparkling, clear water crashing over rocks.

Wilder checks the perimeter and water before nodding at us. "Fine, have at it." He knows better than to fight us.

Logan and I share a look and rip off our shirts, laughing as we race toward the water's edge and dive in. I hit first, and when I surface, I push my hair back and grin at Logan. "First up the wall wins first pick of the annual vacation spot," I call.

"Deal. Cheater!" he shouts as I dive under and swim hard toward the back. When I break through, I waste no time grabbing the rock there and hauling myself up. It's slippery, and when I start to climb, I hear a splash. Glancing back, I chuckle as I realize Logan plummeted back into the water. Focusing on the wall, I move swiftly, climbing as high as I can, but I soon hear Logan behind me, and when I crest the edge, he is just seconds away.

When we reach the top, we are both panting and grinning. I wave at Wilder, who's at the bottom, shirtless and filming us. Way and Aiy watch us with twin looks of amusement and incredulity.

"Together?" I look at Logan and hold out my hand.

"Always." He slaps his palm in mine, and we take a running leap, jumping off.

I feel weightless as we plummet, our laughter echoing around the jungle until it is swallowed by crystal-clear water. When we kick to the surface, I can't help but smile. "Come on, it's fun!" I call to the others. "Wilder, Wilder, Wilder," I chant.

His eyes narrow as Logan joins in, then Way and Aiy. "Fuck it, fine." He kicks off his pants and boots, placing the camera on the portable tripod before he heads toward the wall. We turn to watch him as he quickly and effortlessly scales it, moving so fast he's a blur. It's his specialty, and it's always impressive. No matter how much we try, we can never beat him.

At the top, he gives us a wave and then turns around, the real Wilder coming out to play when he flips backwards. We shout in encouragement, and when he hits the water, he splashes all of us.

His head appears, and he's grinning. "Don't you dare!" I yell before I'm yanked under.

Everyone's laughter filters to me while Wilder fights me underwater. Despite it, I can't stop smiling. It's rare for my brother to let go, but I love seeing this side of him.

We play for hours, competing in diving and swimming, picking crazier paths up and down until we collapse onto the boulders at the side to dry off before we head into the jungle.

"Hey, did you see this?" Aiyaret calls, and we stride over, Wilder tugging his shirt on as he goes.

"What?" he asks as Aiy points at the ground where he's crouched. "Am I crazy or are those . . . footsteps? Human ones?"

We turn to where he's pointing. He's right.

The tracks are maybe a few days old, but distinct.

Those are human footsteps on a deserted island where we are supposed to be the only people here.

"Well, shit just got interesting," I mutter.

Wilder does not look happy, his eyes scanning the jungle. "He's right. Those are human. We need to be extra careful. If someone is here, then they might not be happy we are as well."

"Oh, come on," Logan mutters. "It could be an animal."

"It's a boot," I scoff.

"Wilder is right. We need to be careful," Way murmurs, and they share a look. I know fun time is over. They'll be anxious about this all day now—hell, all trip.

It does make me curious. If someone else is on this island, then why?

Do they live here?

Are they after the same thing?

If they are, what happens if we get in their way?

It's clear Wilder is having the same thoughts because he stalks back to his bag, dresses, then turns to us.

"Alright, playtime is over," Wilder states, studiously ignoring the tracks, none of us wanting to read too much into what it means. "Time to hike."

Our groans fill the air, even as he smiles sadistically at us.

# EIGHTEEN
## WILDER

Istay at the back as we trek, holding a protective position just in case. Way leads the crew after my careful order. He knew what I meant with one look, so we move slower than normal but also more carefully.

We are less likely to leave tracks.

It's likely someone is inhabiting this island, which means they are probably here for the same thing we are, and not all who seek places like this are explorers.

Most are treasure hunters, and they can be more dangerous than anything else in the jungle ever could be.

They are more likely to kill first and ask questions later, prepared to succeed and claim their gold. Money is everything to them. It isn't about history or heritage or even knowledge. It's about profit. We've run into a few in the past, and I have a scar on my shoulder to prove it. We had a narrow escape when we were exploring caves in southern Africa, which apparently used to be for smugglers, something we didn't know until later.

It didn't end well, and we were lucky to escape with our lives.

We don't cover as much ground as we would like, and the

atmosphere is definitely more tense despite Logan's and Rick's best efforts.

An hour before the sun is due to set, I call it a day, and we erect the camp. This time, we make sure to find a position that's hidden between the trees, and I'm tempted to keep watch tonight just in case.

I have a bad feeling in my gut—one that is usually right. I hate feeling it and not knowing what's going to happen. All we can do is wait.

When the sun does go down, our fire lights up the trees, and it throws the once beautiful jungle into a shadowy trap. That alarm in my gut only grows until I'm pacing. The others watch me, sensing something is wrong but unable to help.

"Maybe we should keep moving," Rick suggests.

"No, not in the dark. We could get hurt. No, it's better to stay here until we have light again," I mutter, scanning the trees, and I freeze when I see something ruffling the foliage.

"Okay, what if we—" Logan begins.

"Shh," I hiss. "Something is watching us."

"You're imagining things," Rick mutters, but he sounds concerned.

"Everyone, stay calm and do not move." When I glance back at them, they are on their feet around the fire, their eyes narrowed as they search the jungle for what I saw. Leaves don't move like that unless they are disturbed, and from that height, it has to be something big.

I'm trapped between the darkness of the jungle and the fire at my back when a shape slowly slinks from the trees, stopping about ten feet away.

"Fuck," I mutter.

"Is that a jaguar?" Aiy hisses.

I nod, keeping my hand up and very still. "Do not move. It seems curious."

It isn't attacking, which is a good sign, and its ears are up. We could simply be in the way or in its territory. My mind spins with a million possibilities and plans on how to get out of this unhurt.

It isn't the first time we've faced a dangerous, wild animal. There was a black bear in Canada, sharks in Australia, and snakes on an abandoned string of islands. It's about remaining calm and in control. We are in their world, not the other way around.

"I think we'll leave the stuff and come back in the morning," I murmur. Its ears twitch as it paces closer.

"Wilder," Rick whispers, and I hear him move ever so slightly. The jaguar hisses, flattening its ears.

"Don't move." I want to yell, but I keep my voice soft and quiet as the jaguar paces before me, hissing every so often.

Our voices seem to have agitated the animal, and it keeps glancing at us and then back to the jungle, as if debating leaving, but the swish of its tail is fast and jerky, and the alarm within me only grows. I slowly inch to the right to block the others in case it attacks, and the movement doesn't go unnoticed.

The big cat's paw lifts and swipes through the air. I want to leap back, but I remain rooted in place, trying to stay as calm as possible, even as I hear the others audibly panicking for me.

"Wilder," my brother whispers as it swipes again, closer this time.

I need a plan. How do we get out of here?

My eyes narrow on the animal for a moment. It's pacing and swiping randomly as if it's trying to warn us away rather than hurt us. Rick, however, doesn't notice and instead strides forward to circle the animal, but it notices and seems enraged. The jaguar's eyes lock on Rick.

"Rick!" I shout and tackle my brother to the ground just as the jaguar swipes and pounces with a hiss.

Bowing over his body to protect him, I grunt in agony as I feel claws swipe my side, but then a loud whistle cuts through the air. My head jerks up as the jaguar spins and steps away from us.

Something crashes through the jungle, heading our way, beams of light parting the foliage as the person continues to whistle loudly to draw the animal's attention. I keep bowing over my brother, refusing to let him be hurt.

The whistle grows louder, and the jaguar snarls, its head down as it waits for whatever is moving through the forest. It's a person; it has to be. Is it the same one who made the footprints? My eyes narrow on the approaching shape.

I realize it's a woman as she bursts into our camp and waves the flaming flare in front of her, backing the animal toward the jungle.

My blood seeps into the dirt below us, but I ignore it.

My eyes stay on the woman racing through the forest who's holding a fiery stick in her hand and calling loudly to the animal. It looks back at us and then at her again before leaping into the trees. She skids to a stop in front of us, waving the flare to keep anything else away.

She glances over her shoulder and meets my gaze.

"Carter?" I blurt in shock.

# NINETEEN
## MAEVE

"The one and only." I grin as I look around their scattered camp, my flare still in hand. I didn't want to hurt the animal, especially since I think it's the one that kept me company and meant no harm, but I wanted to scare it off. Luckily, it worked, thank fuck. "Looks like you got lucky."

Wilder groans, pushing off Rick, and sits back. His hand goes to his side, pressing against jagged claw marks that cut through his shirt to his skin below.

"Lucky? We almost died," he grumbles.

"Almost being the word there." I wink. "If it wanted to gut you, it would have. It didn't want you dead." I shrug as I drop the flare and prop my hands on my hips as they gape at me. "What? No thank you? Here I thought I'd get a hero's welcome."

Muttering, I head over to their fire and drop my bag there, then I pull out my rations and start to eat as the silence stretches on.

"Maeve Carter?" Wilder says again.

Lifting my head, I meet his incredulous gaze. "I know you've probably dreamed about me enough that it's hard to imagine I'm real, but I am," I quip.

His cheeks flame red, but his eyes narrow in irritation. It's always like this between us, and it's fun to tease him. "What the fuck are you doing here?" Rick and Logan are at his side now, trying to check his wound.

Way stands in front of Aiyaret, his arm out as if to protect him from me, and that saddens me a little.

"Oh, you know, felt like taking a walk." I nod at his side. "Better dress that before the smell attracts any other predators. Oh, I don't suppose you have any ketchup? I ran out two days ago and it's killing me."

They share a silent look, which I ignore as I take another bite.

"Maeve fucking Carter," Logan scoffs as he grins at me. "Our hero."

I wink. "Don't forget it, pretty boy."

"Let me," I say, pushing Rick aside. Wilder is lying back on the ground, his bare chest showing three wicked claw marks on his side. They aren't deep, but they are bleeding. Rick was dabbing at the wound, but I swiftly open the medical kit and, despite Wilder's glare, I clean the wound and bandage it.

"You'll need a shot when you get back. Keep it dry and clean." I shut the kit and take my seat at the fire.

I make sure to keep distance between Aiyaret and me and to not speak to him directly. Instead, I stay near Wilder and Rick, who is unnaturally quiet for a loudmouth. Logan hands me warm water, and I nod my thanks.

"Seriously, Carter, what the fuck are you doing here?" Wilder snaps as he tugs his shirt on with a wince, uncaring that I just saved his life. That's Wilder for you, a total asshole even in this situation.

"Taking a vacation?" I joke as I sip, and when his eyes narrow, I roll mine.

"You didn't think Ajax only sent you, did you? The more people, the more likely we are to find the lost city."

"You're here for that too?" Way murmurs.

"Well, I'm not here for the scenery," I say with a wink. "Ajax asked me to come, so I came."

"Fucking brilliant, and he didn't think to tell us that bit?" Wilder grumbles.

"Oh, stop complaining. If I weren't here, you would be dead," I snap.

"She's right," Rick murmurs, his voice unceremoniously choked. "It was my fault. I'm sorry, brother. I didn't think—"

"Shh, we all act on instinct in such situations." Wilder ruffles his brother's hair and throws me a glare. "She's right though."

I smirk. "I think you meant to say, 'thank you.'"

"Not a chance. Now get out of our camp," he demands.

"Seriously? I saved your ass and you're kicking me out? Rude. I was setting up mine when I heard the commotion, and now you want me to find somewhere else in the dark?" I mutter.

"She's right," Aiyaret interrupts, surprising us all. "It's too dangerous, and she did save us. Thank you, Carter." He nods at me before looking away, his hands clenched on his thighs, and I watch as Way covers one and gives me a narrow-eyed look.

"You're welcome," I reply truthfully for once, my voice soft. "Though, if I had known it was Wilder getting eaten, I would have waited a few seconds. Might have knocked him down a peg."

Logan chuckles at my side. "Doubtful. Well, you're here now—"

"She's not staying," Wilder snarls, getting to his feet.

I leap to mine and get in his face. "What is your fucking problem, Adreno junkie?"

"You are, money grabber."

"Limp-dick prick."

"Cheating twat."

"Okay, okay," Logan cuts in, sliding an arm between us to separate us. "Like it or not, Wilder, she saved us. We would be dead without her. We can't help that she's here, since Ajax chooses whom to send. She can't go out there tonight, so she'll stay. We'll set her up between you and me, and Aiy and Way can go way over there. It will be fine for one night, right?" He glances back, and Aiyaret nods jerkily.

"One night," Wilder snaps, pointing in my face. "I want you gone by dawn."

"Might as well work together now that we are here," I suggest. It's something I would hate to do, but the truth is, I could use more eyes, and if things are getting dangerous around here, then they might not be bad to have around in a bind. I like it as much as they do, which isn't at all. I want to find this city for my father, and knowing they are here makes it that much harder, but at least if we stick together, I can keep tabs on them at all times.

"Not a chance. Ajax might have sent you, but it doesn't mean we are on the same team. It means this is a race." Wilder steps closer again, until I can feel his body heat.

"Fine." I smirk. "A race it is. Want to take a bet on who will win?"

"Wilder," Rick warns.

"Fine. What do we get when we do?" He grins maliciously.

"What do you want?" I ask, and I swear for a moment his eyes drop to my lips before he looks away.

"If we win, you quit Venture," he says. I jolt at his words, and I see amusement enter his expression. He expects me to back down.

He doesn't know me very well.

"Fine. If I win, you have to record a video saying that I am the best and post it everywhere." I grin as I stick out my hand. "Deal?"

"Deal." He slaps my hand before stepping back. "Now stay out of our way. If you cause trouble or even so much as talk too loudly, you're gone, jaguar or no jaguar."

"Asshole," I mutter as he turns away.

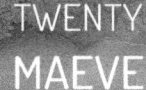

# TWENTY
## MAEVE

"Honestly, would you two just fuck already?" Logan mutters to Wilder as they pass, and I pretend I don't hear it. Wilder and I butt heads, but it's because we hate each other—that's it. He prevented me from potentially joining their team and tried to get Ajax to fire me. I wasn't good enough for his boys' club, and he lets me know that every time we meet.

I hate that cocky fucker, and I definitely don't want to bang him.

My eyes stay on the flames as I ignore them. It's obvious they don't want me here, which is fine by me. I don't want to be here either, but we all know it's dumb for me to go off alone right now. The jaguar seemed harmless when it approached me, but it is a wild animal, and I can't deny that something about this island gives me the creeps, even though it's stunningly beautiful.

It's better this way, safety in numbers, but I don't have to like it.

If that little limp-dick prick doesn't want me with them, then fine, I won't be. He called it a race, and I plan to find the city first to prove them all wrong.

"He just doesn't know how to say thank you." The unsure voice makes me lift my head, and my eyes widen when I find Aiy lingering next to me.

"If you say so," I reply softly.

Aiyaret continues to dawdle when he would usually run as fast and as far away from me as he could. A protective instinct I didn't realize I had rises to the surface.

He looks at the log and then me. "Sit if you want to," I whisper, not daring to speak too loudly in case I spook him. He hesitates before sitting on the other log a little ways away from me. It doesn't sting. When I accidently touched him at the office, the look in his eyes was enough to let me know he has his reasons.

He was terrified.

I'm very careful now. I don't want my presence here to hurt him and whatever peace he feels. His eyes stay on the fire, and I look back at it too, unsure what to say or do. I don't want to scare him or cross any boundaries, but it's hard when I don't know what they are.

Touching is a big no, and being close probably is too.

He doesn't seem to want to talk to me either, so I keep quiet, knowing it must have cost him a lot to approach me. I don't know his story or his past, and I don't need to. Whatever happened is his story, not anyone else's, but I won't make it worse with my own naivety and blindness.

"Thank you. You risked your life by coming to help us. Wilder might not say it, but he's grateful," he says, and I make sure to keep my eyes on the fire.

I shrug. "He doesn't like me much, a sentiment I return, but I wouldn't let him get hurt out of spite. We have to look after each other."

"Do you hate us for rejecting you?" My eyes jerk up, and I scan the camp to see the others quickly settling in. No one is really paying attention, but I know better—they are probably all listening intently.

"No." I smile. "Okay, maybe I did at first, but it was more the way I was rejected."

"They did it for me," he tells me, glancing away. "They didn't tell me, but I know."

Ah, well, fuck, that makes a whole lot more sense. My irritation with Wilder disperses a little, but he could have been nicer about it.

"They are loyal to you, and that's good. I know the kind of bond you create when you explore together. I miss that. It was the only reason I even let Ajax think about putting me on a team. In all honesty, the idea of being on another one hurts."

"Your father?" he asks, and I eye him. "I overheard."

"My father. He'd been my partner for longer than I can remember, and then it was just me. It almost felt like I was betraying him by going to Venture, and the thought of joining a team? I felt bad," I admit, sharing something I haven't even told Ajax or my father.

"If he loves you, then he would want you to be safe and happy," he responds after a while. "I don't think he would mind."

"You're probably right. He's a good man. He would have loved it here." I smile fondly as I look around the jungle. "He was always most at home in places like this. He loved nature more than life. It's where my love for it came from. I was in jungles and forests before I could even speak. I wish he could see this place."

"You can show him when you get back," Aiy offers.

"It isn't the same, but yeah, I will. It's why I keep going, why I'm determined to find it. More recognition means more money, and more money means supporting research to help others like him," I explain, though I'm not sure why.

"Not him?" he asks, his eyes searching my face curiously.

"It's too late for him." The words are choked, and I look back into the flames. "We both know it. We just don't like to admit it."

"I'm sorry, Maeve. That must be very hard," he replies.

I nod, and we lapse into comfortable silence.

I stare into the fire, my shoulders relaxing as I watch the dancing flames until a noise makes my head jerk up, and I see a figure next to us.

"Aiy, you okay?" Way asks cautiously as he looks between us.

"I'm okay."

"Time to sleep." Way offers him his hand and helps him up, but Aiy hesitates, glancing back at me.

"Goodnight, Maeve." He swiftly looks away and lets Way lead him as far from me as he can.

"Goodnight, Aiyaret," I respond softly.

I don't really sleep. I stare up at the stars through the break in the canopy before my bladder makes itself known. I left all my gear and stuff back at my camp, so I am sleeping on a borrowed blanket they loaned me. Before morning, I'll need to head back to where I dropped it.

If Wilder wants a race, then he'll get one.

I head through the trees—not far since I'm not stupid—and when I'm far enough away that I can't see them clearly, I crouch and do my business. I'm just standing and buttoning my pants when there's a crack behind me.

I spin, raising my machete as a deterrent, when a flashlight runs over me.

"Put it down," I snap.

It lowers to the forest floor, and I get a look at a smirking Wilder. "Caught with your pants down, Carter?"

"At least my fly is down on purpose," I retort, and he swears as he looks down and zips his. "What are you doing out here?"

"Checking the perimeter to keep us safe," he replies before he seems to remember whom he's talking to. "Enough questions, get back to camp. I told you to be quiet, remember?"

"Stop being an asshole for one fucking second, Jesus," I mutter as I drop my hands to my hips.

He steps back, leaning into a tree, running his eyes over me. "We only let you stay because you'd be dead out there alone. That doesn't mean we like you, Carter."

He recoils as my machete embeds in the tree at his side. His eyes widen as I walk over and pluck it free, our faces almost touching. "I can take care of myself. Never forget that or that I was the one who saved you."

I trek back in the darkness and lie down, ignoring him as he marches into camp and gets into his bunk. Within minutes, snores fill the jungle, loud enough for one of them to scare any predator.

I doze on and off, jerking awake at every little noise until I finally give up.

I move around silently so as not to wake them, cleaning up the area I rested in and leaving it like I was never there.

Before dawn even arrives, I am on my feet, and with one last glance at their sleeping camp, I smirk.

Game on, Adreno junkies.

# TWENTY-ONE
## WAY

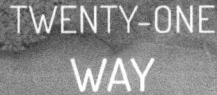

**S**taring down at the space where Maeve Carter was sleeping, I rub my aching head, already knowing how well this will go down—like a shot of bourbon before seven in the morning.

"What do you mean, she's gone?" Wilder roars.

Yup, called it.

Aiy went to wake him, and when I turn, Logan is in the middle of falling from his hammock, half asleep. Merrick is sitting up, looking confused as his head swings between us.

"She was there, and now she's not. Therefore, she is gone," Aiy scoffs as he gestures at the spot. "You did tell her to be gone by dawn, and it's past dawn."

I bite back my smile at his sass as Wilder's eyes narrow in anger. "How the fuck did she get past us? Fuck, she's trying to beat us to the city." He leaps from his hammock and starts packing up. "No breakfast. We need to move now. We have to catch up to her."

"Wilder," Logan whines. "I need breakfast. I'm a growing boy."

"Then you should have gotten up when your girlfriend left," Wilder snaps as he shoves things into his bag.

"Wait, girlfriend . . . Do you think she would?" Logan asks hopefully, and he doesn't have time to duck before the bag smacks him back into the ground.

"Get ready now!" Wilder shouts.

That gets us moving, and I spare the forest another look, wondering just how far of a head start Maeve Carter got.

Wilder won't even let us take a break. He's pissed as hell that she managed to sneak past us without us knowing—something none of us can do. Wilder is like an eagle. Aiyaret and I once tried to sneak out in Thailand to go for food at three in the morning, and the man was waiting at the door like he knew. Nothing gets past him . . . apart from Maeve Carter, apparently.

"You know, I still think this anger you have toward her is undercut with sexual tension," I comment idly as I walk at his side. He hacks at the bushes, his expression tight, but that's never stopped me before. I usually leave it to Rick or Logan to tease him, but it's just too much fun today.

"The only tension between Carter and me is how long I can hold out before I kill the stubborn woman," Wilder mutters.

"Or fuck her," Rick adds helpfully.

"I'm betting fuck," Logan says.

I turn to them. "Want to bet?"

"Whatchya offering?" they ask in unison.

"My limited edition, signed *Alice in Borderland*." That gets their attention, and they nod rapidly as I look at Wilder. "Don't let those idiots win. I love that comic."

"I'll get in on that." We turn at Aiy's voice, and he blinks. "It's obvious Wilder wants to sleep with her. He keeps denying it and pretending he hates her because it's easier."

"I do not," Wilder sputters as he gapes at us. "I just think she's annoying, stubborn, and a know-it-all who thinks she's better than everyone—"

"With the most perfect body," Logan adds.

"And sass that makes me hard," Rick joins in.

"I hate you all," Wilder mutters as he focuses on cutting the trees away. Five minutes later, he looks back at us. "I don't want to fuck her."

"Sure you don't," I agree as I hang back to walk at Aiyaret's side. He looks tired, maybe from more nightmares, so I keep pace with him, adjusting my strides so he doesn't try to go too fast to keep up.

"I like Maeve," he remarks randomly. "If she finds it before us, I wouldn't be mad."

"No?" I ask curiously. "Even after all our hard work?"

"She's worked just as hard, maybe harder. We have a team, and she's by herself. I think she deserves to find it." He must feel my gaze because he lifts his head and smiles at me. "I'm not saying we invite her to join the team or anything, but people who work hard deserve their wins. We should celebrate that with her, not act against her. There is enough of the world for all of us to explore. Why does it have to be a competition?"

"Because that's who we are," Logan scoffs. "Besides, try telling Maeve Carter you don't want to compete with her. The woman thrives on a challenge. She doesn't want to be treated lesser because she's a woman. She wants to win fair and square, which means pushing as hard as we can to beat her."

"Fuck, when did you get so smart?" I ask as I tug Aiyaret out of the path of a fallen log he didn't see. He nods in thanks, and we keep walking until Wilder finally lets us have a break.

Sitting in the dirt, I rip open one of the pouches and hand it to Aiy, and then I give him his bottle. The smile he gives me is blinding, and I'm happy just watching him eat. I was so proud of him last night for talking to Maeve, but I know it cost him.

When he's done, he hands over the pouch, and I finish it off with his water. "Don't you need more?" he asks.

"I'm fine. You needed it more." I shrug as I pack my bag and lean back. I rest my head on my arms as I close my eyes for a moment. The heat is oppressive, making me a sweaty mess, but none of us care, and Aiy definitely doesn't seem to mind as he leans into my side, resting his head on my shoulder.

"She can't be that much farther ahead," Wilder grouses, and I open one eye to see him looking at us. He must notice our fatigue because despite the impending loss, he leans back against a tree. "Get some rest. I'll stay awake."

Logan and Rick waste no time bracketing Wilder and using him as a pillow before closing their eyes. He nods at me, and I close mine again too, wrapping one arm around Aiy so he can be comfortable.

I don't sleep, but I let my brain wander and my body recover.

Besides, Aiy might have another nightmare, and he doesn't need to go through that alone. As if my thoughts conjure it, his whimper cuts through the air. Opening my eyes, I turn my head to see his brow furrowed as he jerks in his sleep. Lifting my other arm, I softly rub away the lines between his eyebrows. "You're safe. You're here with us. You're safe . . . ." I repeat it until he settles down, but I don't pull my hand away like I should.

Instead, I watch him, stroking his soft, beautiful face. I wish more than anything I could take his pain away from him.

Leaning down, I press my lips to his forehead as softly as I can so I don't disturb him. "Don't worry anymore, okay? I'll always protect you. I'll always keep you safe. Nobody will ever hurt you again."

Pulling back, I turn my head and meet Wilder's knowing eyes. I wait for his words, but he simply smiles and closes his eyes, his brothers leaning into his sides like twins.

Twenty minutes later, he sits up and softly shakes Logan and Rick, so I lift Aiy. "Time to keep going," I murmur as he groans and opens his eyes, wincing at the sun.

"Ten more minutes," he whispers.

"Nope. Come on, hot stuff, let's move." Rubbing his back, I wait for him to fully wake up before I help him to his feet and sling both our bags on since he's tired, and then we are off again.

The sun moves through the sky, and it's late in the afternoon. Either we will need to call it soon and find somewhere to stay or risk it by pushing on. One look at Wilder, though, and I can tell he has no intention of stopping.

He's determined to catch up to her, so we say nothing and follow him.

"I'll take point," Logan calls. "You can watch our backs." He must have noticed that Wilder is favoring one side—his uninjured one. It's a nice way of ensuring he doesn't do too much, so we switch, and Logan whistles as Rick walks past him, taking point and hacking at the foliage that only seems to get thicker.

He finally stops, panting and sweating as he shakes his head.

"We should stop for the night," I suggest. "We aren't getting far."

"It has to be around here somewhere, right? Maybe if we keep going —motherfucking tits!" Rick shouts, reaching back as his body moves forward, and my eyes widen when I see the tree he just pushed aside is atop a steep hill. We leap toward him, but it's too late, and he tumbles over the edge.

Stopping at the precipice, I stare down as he rolls and hits everything on his way down, his voice reaching us.

"Ass!"

"Dick!"

"Too young to die!"

"Send help!"

"My balls!"

He's finally quiet as he disappears into the thick foliage below.

For a moment, we are silent, and then Wilder leaps over the edge and slides down after him.

Sighing, I glance at Aiy. "Come on, let's rescue the idiots."

E verything hurts, and not in a good, I spent the night drinking and fucking type of way, but in a more I tried to fight Godzilla and lost sort of way.

I hear the others yelling my name, but my head is spinning and my ears are ringing, so I let that dissipate before I try to answer.

"Rick!" My brother's desperate voice is what gets me moving, and I lift my arm.

"I'm alive," I call before I cough and spit out some dirt. Lifting my head, I take inventory of my body. My pants and shirt are ripped, and I have some cuts and bruises, but nothing seems broken, which is a fucking miracle.

I've always been lucky.

I should probably be mortified, but I wasn't embarrassed when I waxed my balls in high school on a dare to ask out Missy Collins, so I certainly won't start now.

"Rick!" The yells draw nearer, and I don't want them to find me on my back. Wilder will freak and try to pull us out of here. He was attacked by a jaguar, fine, but I fall down a hill and that's a no go.

With a groan, I rub my sore ass and sit up, looking around as the others make their way through the thick foliage to find me. Trees

111

surround me on most sides, so I peer through the closest one to find them, only to freeze at the sight before me.

Holy shit!

The jungle opens up into a clearing below, and even from here, I can tell what it is—an abandoned city.

Lost . . .

"We found it!" I shout as I climb to my knees, ignoring their concern and especially Wilder, who is scanning me as he kneels by my side. "Wilder!" I grab his chin and tilt him around until he sees it too. "Look, this has to be it."

"I fucking found it!" I whoop. "It's all skill, baby!"

"More like all klutz, baby," Logan scoffs. "Glad you didn't die though."

"You think that's really it?" Way whispers as we huddle around the opening I created and stare down.

It's deep inside a crater, but there are crudely carved steps leading down toward it on each side. Buildings are carved into the stone walls in a random pattern. It's ancient and rough, but it's a city. There even appear to be paths or roads of some kind, but it's a strange layout, like circles leading inwards, growing tighter and tighter.

"It has to be," Wilder confirms, but then he looks me over. "Are you hurt?"

"I'm fine. Focus on that, brother. We did it." I grin, and he finally relaxes enough to aim one back at me.

"We did."

"And we beat Carter," Logan says. "Win-win."

"What was that, morons?" We all whirl around to see a figure waving at us on the steps leading down. "It took you long enough. Are you going to lie there all day, or are you going to come see what I found while you were sleeping?"

"Motherfucker," Wilder shouts, and her laughter fills the air.

I guess Aiy was right—she deserves it.

Maeve Carter found the lost city of Apear.

It's all hers.

## TWENTY-THREE

# WILDER

After making sure Rick really is okay, we push through the foliage, walk across the rocky terrain, and descend the steps Maeve Carter is trekking back down—no doubt after hearing Rick yell.

They are steep as hell and uneven, so I go first, taking a couple at a time before turning around to check on my team. Holding out my hand, I help them down and then continue, moving slowly so we don't fall. Bits crumble away as we walk and tumble into the crater below.

The jungle must have hidden this from aerial view. No wonder it was lost. If we hadn't stumbled into it, we probably never would have found it.

By the time we are halfway down, the buildings start to appear. They are crude but beautifully built with open windows and doors, which allow us to peek inside.

The houses are empty, but they look as if people were just here one day and gone the next. The steps get steeper the farther we go, but I finally reach the last one and step out onto dusty gray rock. Maeve is peeling an apple with a sharp blade, leaning against one of the houses in the shade as she waits for us.

"About time," she mumbles around a bite before wiping her knife off and putting it away. "I thought I was going to have to go back and leave a map for you," she scoffs. "How did you find it?"

"I sort of . . . stumbled into it," Rick replies, blushing.

Logan chuckles. "More like fell."

"Ah, that explains the yelling. Did you tell a tree to eat your ass?" She laughs.

"Shit, actually," Rick replies as he looks around. "How long have you been here?"

"About an hour. I was just about to start exploring." She eyes me. "If you can agree that I found this first—well, since I have footage as proof and all—we can share. I'll even let you film."

"Let us? Like you could stop us," I snarl.

She pushes off the structure and doesn't stop until I have to crane my head down to meet her gaze, shielding my eyes from the sun to see her. "Yes, let you. You were too slow, Wilder. Just accept it. Now, what was it I won again?" She taps her chin in thought as I grind my teeth. "Don't worry, big boy, I'll collect later. For now, I'm going to document my amazing discovery. I have to get all the good angles."

She walks past me, making sure to knock into my shoulder as she does.

Rick hurries after her, and I gape. He meets my eyes. "What? I want to see it all too." Logan strides after him, and then Way and Aiyaret follow as well.

"Traitors," I hiss.

"Just give in, Wilder. It would be easier." Way laughs and smacks my shoulder before they follow her down the dirt path, leaving me staring after them, grinding my teeth.

I can't leave them with her, though, so I trail after them, angry that I let her get the jump on us. She found it, which means the discovery and the money is hers—something I loathe to admit.

It should have been us, but hopefully we can get some good footage so this trip isn't a total waste. Besides, we are only second to her in a place where people haven't been in a very long time.

That means something.

We break off into the circular pathways, wandering around the houses while we shoot. It's eerily quiet, and we remain silent, as if sensing something happened here.

I see belongings within the houses that were left behind. It's creepy, and I've been to some creepy places.

"Anyone else getting the heebie-jeebies?" Logan whispers.

"Me." Rick takes Logan's arm, and they look around.

Maeve stops as we branch off into what must be the main walkway, and we look at what is left. Items are discarded across the stone, baking in the sun, and wagons and bricks are dotted around as if forgotten.

"I didn't expect it to look like this," she murmurs, and we share a worried glance as she turns and heads down the next street. More wagons are abandoned, and one is even right side up with bricks inside. "It's like they just left one day."

"Or died," I murmur, but how did an entire city just up and go missing?

"What were you expecting? Gold?" I ask her when she frowns and comes to a standstill.

"Honestly? Kind of." She shoots me a smile that, for once, isn't filled with hostility or anger. "I guess this is beautiful as well though, but you're right. It has a . . . haunted feeling to it."

I nod in understanding. I feel it too, not that I would tell her, but my gut tells me something transpired here.

"I don't think we should be here at nightfall. We can set up camp up there." I nod toward the tip of the crater.

"You want me to stay with you again?" she teases, nudging me.

"Just for now," I reply.

That makes her frown as she watches me. "Must be bad for you to let me into your little nest again, but I agree."

"Don't think I'm being nice. It's purely about survival," I protest.

"Got it." She winks as Logan calls her name, hurrying past me.

It's obvious they all want to see the middle of the village, so we rush there instead of wasting time since we are losing daylight. The city was either built around it or it ripped through the center, but there is a gaping black hole in the middle.

Peering over the rough edge, I strain to see any color or earth inside, but the hole seems to go on forever. There is only inky blackness, which makes it impossible to see, so I lean back, but my boots slip in the loose rocks at the rim.

Rocks shift under my feet, crashing into the cavern, and I start to tumble forward, when Maeve catches my arm, pulling me back. "Careful, idiot." She chuckles before following the others, circling as they film. I watch her for a moment, trying to calm my erratic heartbeat. I tell myself it's from the near miss and not the warmth of her touch.

Dragging my gaze away from her and my team, I scan the edge of the hole, wondering if it was a natural disaster or if it has always been here. Something farther down catches my eye. Moving in the opposite direction of my team, I carefully pick my way across the uneven rock until I can crouch closer to it.

For a moment, I can't seem to comprehend what I'm seeing, or maybe it's my brain, but when it does, I go cold all over. That same feeling from the other night when I knew something was wrong courses through me.

In the dirt and rocks, there are claw marks leading from the edge of the hole, as if whatever creature made it had climbed in or out.

Putting my hand up against the grooves, I frown at the size. What wild animal did this, and was it before or after the people who lived here left?

"Yo, Wild, come get in the picture!" Rick calls, and I lift my head to see them gathered before the chasm, crouched together with a camera set up a few feet from them. Even Maeve is involved, positioned between Way and Rick. Rolling my eyes, I spare the claw marks one last look before I stand and dust off my hands. I tell myself it could have been here for years, maybe as long as the village. It's nothing to worry about.

Nothing at all.

I squeeze in on the end, and Logan wraps his arm around me, dragging me closer until we squish together. "Okay, everyone, shout, 'Maeve won!'" she yells, and the camera captures our exact reaction to that comment. I can't help but laugh at the angry look I must be aiming her way, and the camera snaps again.

"Alright, fuckers. Get out of the frame. I'm going to record some footage since I'm the one who found it." She winks at me, purposely trying to piss me off, and I wonder if Way is right. Do we like fighting with each other? Turning away before she can read my thoughts on my face, I move over and take a seat on one of the rocks. She fiddles with her camera and begins recording, then she starts to speak as she moves around, showing everyone what she found.

She's a natural—I'll give her that. Her excitement is palpable and real, and she breaks it down easily enough for people to understand. If I overlook her daredevil, no fucks attitude, she's a good explorer. It doesn't surprise me that Ajax recruited her, though I'll never tell her or him that.

"Starting to hate her less, are we?" a mocking voice remarks as Logan sits on my right, grinning at me.

"The way he's staring at her ass makes me wonder if it's something else," Rick teases as he perches on my left. They cage me in, and I roll my eyes, purposely looking at Way and Aiy instead of her, but as she speaks, I keep stealing glances. She's dangerously close to the edge, and I worry she will fall.

That's all.

"Hey, moron, don't get too close to the edge. If you fall, we aren't helping you!" I shout.

She turns and flips me off, but she's smiling. "The only one who almost fell was you, dickhead!"

I know her camera is still rolling, and I can't help but smile. Despite her retort, she steps farther away from the pit and gestures to it and then me as if to say, "Happy now?"

"She's good, you know. I've seen her records, and she holds some killer titles and wins. She's an all-rounder like you, Wilder, wanting to be the best at everything. It wouldn't be the worst thing for us to work together while she's here," Rick says.

"Aiy," I start.

"Doesn't seem to mind," Logan interrupts, pointing at Aiy, who is watching her with a ghost of a smile on his lips. I don't know what they spoke about, but he seems more comfortable with her. However, I won't risk the hard-won safety and comfort he has found with us for anything.

Carter can't stay, no matter who wishes she could.

"So what now?" Rick asks when I don't respond.

I shrug. "We document and send the footage back, then I guess call for pickup and head back to the beach. She won this one, but there will be others."

"Are you conceding defeat?" Logan gasps and pretends to swoon. "The horror! The shock! It must be love."

I shove him off the rock and focus on Carter. He's right, I hate admitting defeat, but I'll give credit where it's due. She found it, so it's hers. I'll let her take all the accolades with Ajax and the world—she deserves it.

"Okay, I'm done," she calls. "I'm thinking we should explore the cavern. It can't be that deep. We can send a camera down first then repel down."

I head over, and the others follow. "We don't need to."

"No, we don't, but why wouldn't we while we're here? Come on, Wilder. I can see your curiosity too. Deny it all you want, but you're a daredevil like I am. You want to go in the hole and see what's down there," she taunts.

Fuck her, but she's right, and she knows it.

She peers down at the chasm and then turns to us, her eyebrows arched as she waits for us to disagree, but none of us do. She knows she has us.

Propping her hands on her hips, her back to the gaping hole, she grins at us. "Who's going first? Rock, paper, scissors?" When we groan, she laughs. "What? Oldest first—" Her words are cut off as something appears from the darkness within the hole. The shape moves too fast to see, and it snatches Maeve then drags her down with it.

Her scream echoes around us.

One second, she was there, and the next, she was gone.

All that is left are claw marks in the dirt where she stood.

# TWENTY-FOUR
## MAEVE

The first thing that pierces the floating comfort I'm in is pain. It stabs through me—mainly my head, back, ass, and legs. My eyes are closed, but I keep them that way for a moment as I scan my body. My head hurts, but it isn't to a point where I'm worried I cracked my skull—did that once, thanks, so I know what that feels like. My back feels like I hit something hard, but I can twitch my toes, which means nothing is broken, but moving them brings a whole lot of agony to my left leg—the type that means a big injury.

I just breathe through the pain, trying to remember what happened. Did I slip? It doesn't seem like a mistake I would make, but I must have. The guys' shocked faces are the last thing I remember seeing before oblivion swallowed me.

The pure horror in their gazes haunts me.

I don't remember hitting the bottom of wherever I am. All I remember is intense pain, the feeling of free-falling, and then nothing.

*Okay, enough, Carter. Time to get moving.*

It's my dad's voice, like that time I slipped into a glacier and he called instructions from the top. Accidents happen, but I can't let fear overwhelm me. I have to deal with it as it comes and adapt. I am clearly in that hole.

First things first . . .

Blinking my eyes open, I realize I can't see anything. Wherever I am is pitch black. Panic starts to consume me, so I slam my eyelids shut and force myself to relax.

I strain my ears for any familiar sounds, like the guys or anything, and wait. All I can hear is a soft lap of water and dripping somewhere farther away. Nothing else. No yells. No screams.

I don't hear my name being called either, which isn't a good sign.

Once I have myself somewhat in control, I make a list.

First, I need to find out what's broken or hurt in my body.

Second, I have to figure out where I am and find a way up for help.

I can't expect anyone to save me; I need to save myself. It's what I was taught—it's the way of the world. I can't lie around feeling sorry for myself.

Opening my eyes again, I try to get my vision to adjust, which it does, albeit slowly. Shapes and shades of gray come into view. I can't see far, but I can see my hands when I lift them, which is something. Sliding one into my right pocket, I search for my keychain that's attached to the inner pocket. I unhook it from the carabiner, tug it out, and turn on the small light attached to it. It blinds me for a moment before I shine it around. This isn't good.

There's water to my left, and it seems to go for a while, beyond the light's capabilities. There are rocky outcroppings surrounding me, almost like a barrier in the front and right. There are a few to the left as well, but I can still see the water, and if I reached out, I could probably touch it. The light doesn't pierce the ceiling, but I'm lying on rock and wet sand.

I'm not dead, so at least there's that.

Okay, now my injuries. I've been putting it off, knowing there's something wrong with my left leg, but I can't anymore.

Licking my dry lips, I place the light on a rock to my left, angling it up. It only reaches the immediate area, but it's better than nothing.

Taking a deep breath, I look down at my legs. My first thought is I'm fucking lucky. They are straight before me and not broken, which is a fucking miracle. I don't know how I didn't break any bones. Running my gaze down my right one, I only see surface wounds, scrapes, cuts, and torn pants. Nothing major.

Now to my left.

At first, I can't make out much. My pants are completely torn into shreds from mid-thigh down. I carefully try to pull a hole farther apart so I can see the skin below, and I hiss through my teeth, but I can finally spot the injury. It covers most of my thigh and past my knee. My skin is a strange color, and blood pumps steadily from the raw wound, which looks like a chewed-up mess. No bones are poking through, though, which I guess is a mercy.

My boot is missing, and I don't know why that pisses me off, but it does.

My thigh is bad, though, really bad. I'm losing a lot of blood. It's sliding through wet sand and down a small slope into a pool of water, tinting it red.

I need to stop the blood loss, which means I need a tourniquet tight enough to restrict the vessels, but I'll need to remember to release it every now and again so I don't lose circulation. The torn muscles and skin are an issue, as is the risk of infection, but I can worry about that later.

Sliding my belt off, I use the sharp tip to pierce another hole in the leather with much difficulty after measuring. I lift my leg as much as I can, and a sharp scream leaves my lips before I cut it off, then I wrap the belt around my upper thigh and tighten it. The agony is indescribable, and once it's done, I fall back, panting and sweating.

It hurts, but it's better than bleeding out.

I need to clean the wound, but there is only that water, which probably has more bacteria in it than anything else, so I decide not to. The edges of my skin are torn as hell, like I slammed into a rock and ripped it open. It's a jagged mess. If I don't get out of here soon, I could lose my leg or worse. Infection will set in, and I'll become septic and die a horrible death. It's an idle thought, but it makes me want to laugh hysterically. I know if I start, I won't stop, so I swallow it down.

*Think, Carter. Focus.*

Okay, my leg is hurt, which means I probably can't climb, and that means I need to look for another way out. There has to be another way, right? I need to move and bind my leg. The longer I wait, the more blood I will lose, and the pain will get worse, making it hard.

At least it's not cold. It's almost too hot, oppressively so. I don't know if that's good or bad. I'll lose more precious water from my body, but at least I won't freeze since shock is already setting in.

Glancing down at my wound, I debate the best course of action. Should I try to close it? But I don't have anything with me, only what I have on my body.

Grabbing my light, I spin it around again, but nothing has changed. There's just rock, sand, and water. My back aches then, reminding me of my other pains and that sitting up hunched like this isn't helping. My leg is useless right now, though, so I hold my light between my teeth and dig into the wet sand until it's under my nails.

Using my hands, I scoot backward, resting my back against the rock as my eyes close and my head lolls.

*Come on, Carter, think.*

*Think!*

An idea comes to mind—a terrible, crazy one, but I don't have much choice.

At least it will be a story to tell and I'll add an epic scar to my collection.

"Okay, Maeve, fucking do it," I mutter, placing my light down. I wince as I tug off my boot. It's useless anyway. I lost the other one, so I'd just be unbalanced. Unthreading my laces, which are luckily thin since I hate the thick ones, I lay it out on my thigh before reaching into my shirt. I manage to get my bra out. The one I'm wearing today has a wire in it. I don't usually wear one like that, but it was all I had left— lucky me.

Ripping the material, I yank the wire out and try to manipulate it. It's stiff, but I manage to snap off a piece and then, using a rock, I bend it into a curve. The end is sharp from being broken but too ragged, so I sharpen it on the rock. I keep pulling it back and testing it until it finally draws a pinprick of blood from my finger. Wrapping the lace around it, I lean down to my leg.

I hesitate, knowing it's going to hurt, but then I hook the makeshift needle into my skin. The pain makes me grimace as I pull it through, threading the lace. The skin ripples, and the pain is so intense, I nearly pass out, but I keep going, gritting my teeth. I'll need to remove the lace at some point, but it might help stop the bleeding and save my leg.

The pain grows so intense as I continue that I almost throw up, and I'm on the verge of passing out. If I do, I'll die, so I focus on good things, trying to go to my happy place.

"Iced tea with Dad on a summer day." I push it through my skin again, fighting unconsciousness. "Hitting the peak on a mountain." I thread it again, wanting to cry and scream. "The feeling of flying through the air."

I sew it back and forth, tightening the wound and closing it. It's inexpressible how much it hurts, but I keep going despite the dots dancing in my vision and the blood thundering in my ears. My body feels hot all over as the world seems to slant.

"The look on Wilder's face when I beat him." I chuckle as I tug the next stitch. "Aiy when he was able to speak to me." Groaning, I thread again. "Rick's and Logan's laughs." There's one more to go. I thread it through. "Way's protectiveness."

There.

It's done.

Bending over, I bite off the rest of the lace and tie it. It won't last forever, but hopefully it will do the trick until I get out of here. I feel dizzy as hell, though, so I close my eyes and lean back, allowing myself a moment to rest. I could use some sugar, but I don't have anything, so I just have to make do and hope I'm strong enough to overcome it.

I must lean to the side because something sharp pokes me, making me jerk upright. The sudden movement causes me to groan out loud in pain, and I blindly reach for whatever it was, only to yank it from the sand and pull it in front of me. My eyes widen in horror when I realize what I'm holding—a bone.

It's human from the looks of it.

It's a fucking human bone.

Grabbing my light, I sweep the beam around the sand, terror washing through me as I see more protruding.

I'm sitting in a fucking graveyard.

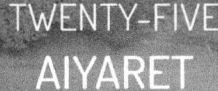

## TWENTY-FIVE
## AIYARET

I t's silent for a moment before we scramble to the hole, but she's
gone.

"Carter!"

"Maeve!"

We all yell into the chasm, but there's no answer. Wilder looks at
something over the edge and pales, grabbing and pulling us.

"Get away from there." Wilder yanks us back so we are farther away.

"What the hell was that?" Rick yells, sounding panicked.

Way is wide-eyed and shocked, and Logan is searching around as if
Carter will appear.

"Wilder!" Rick yells.

"I don't know!" Wilder roars. "She's gone."

That's when the shocked bubble seems to burst.

"We have to go down there."

"We don't know how far it is or what happened."

"So, what? We leave her to die?"

"We need to call for help."

"No, they will take too long to get here. She'll be dead."

"If she isn't already."

"What if she fell?"

"You saw what we did. She didn't fall."

The voices all blend together as I stare at the hole. She was there one second and gone the next. I don't know what I saw. I don't feel like I can trust my eyes. All I know is that she's in there, hurt, alone, and probably terrified.

She was nice to me. Nobody deserves this, but especially not her. We have to help her. That's what it boils down to.

"Her camera is still recording," Way says calmly, but I sense the shock in his tone.

"Then let's look." They rush over to her camera, but I leave them to it. It won't change the truth. She's down there, and she needs help. However she got down there doesn't matter. Not right now. They are right—assistance will take too long. It would take at least seven days to even get to us. She'd be dead.

I have to believe she's alive. If anyone could survive a fall into that abyss, it would be Carter, but we can't leave her there.

We have to help her. She would help us.

Scooting to the edge, I peer in once more.

"Aiy, get away from there!" Way snaps, and I glance back to see him glaring at me, so I step away. He nods before focusing on the camera again.

I know I need to do something. Wilder will argue until he's blue in the face, wasting time. We can't do that. Slipping on my bag, I uncoil the ropes we prepared to venture in, slam the hook into a rock, and secure myself into the harness, then I take a running jump into the hole, turning as I do so I repel backwards.

Their yells chase me into the blackness when they realize what I've done.

Way's terrified voice reaches me, making me hesitate before I keep going.

They would do the same if it were me.

My flashlight on my chest turns on as I repel lower, slowing down since I can't see much. Reaching into my bag, I pull out glow sticks and crack them, dropping them below me.

They spin, throwing a red glow across the rock. The cavern is wide, and I'm just dangling in the blackness. They keep going until they finally hit bottom. The red glow is tiny from here, but it isn't endless.

I repel down, speeding toward the red light, and it grows brighter as the rock opens up into a huge cavern. I run my eyes over it, searching for her, but I don't see any signs of her—no body or lumps. That doesn't mean she isn't here though. When my feet touch the rocky ground, I unhook my rope, pull my flashlight from my shoulder, and shine it around.

"Maeve?" I call, but there's no response. Heading away from my rope, I kick the glow sticks, spreading them out until I can see more. The cavern is massive, and there are different layers of rock, so I circle slowly, searching until I find what I'm looking for.

Drag marks cut along the floor, wide enough for a person.

Did she drag herself away?

That's good. It means she's awake.

It means she's alive.

There's a metallic twang and a snap, and I spin, my flashlight shining across the cavern in time to see my rope crash down, hitting the rock I was standing on. Hurrying over, I coil it up and search for any problem, when I reach the end to find it jagged and torn—like it has been ripped in two.

Glancing up into the dark hole, I see the sunlight above and something moving in the shadows.

Something that bit through my rope, trapping me down here and standing between my team and me.

Our eyes weren't wrong.

She didn't fall.

She was yanked.

"Don't come down here!" I yell, cupping my mouth to warn them, but I know they won't listen. "Don't come down here—" My words cut off when there's a feminine scream. I spin rapidly, trying to pinpoint its location.

"Maeve? Carter? Maeve? Can you hear me?"

It comes again, and then nothing.

"Maeve?" I call, my yell tapering off as the hair on the back of my neck stands on end. "Maeve?" I whisper as I slowly turn, my eyes widening as something huge emerges from the shadows and charges me.

I turn to run at the last second, but I know it's too late.

## WAY

"Aiyaret!" I shout as I rush to the edge.

My heart stopped the moment he went over.

I can see his rope, but I can't see him. "Aiyaret!" I bellow as Wilder grabs me, stopping me from falling. He yanks me back and turns me to him. "Wilder, Aiy!" I yell, struggling in his arms.

"I know, I know, brother." Wilder grips my face. "We'll get him back."

I panic as I stare at him. "I can't—I can't lose him."

"You won't. Come on, get our gear ready now!" Wilder roars.

"You saw what we did, Wild. Something took her," Logan whispers.

"So we leave him?" I shout as I grab the bag he's holding and rush to the edge. "Fine. You stay; I'll go."

"I'm not saying that," Logan replies. "I'm just saying we need to be prepared. Something is down there, and it's dangerous. We can't go in blind."

He isn't wrong. What I saw on that footage before I realized Aiy was going over still haunts me, and knowing he's going down there with that . . . thing?

Terror claws at my chest until I can barely breathe. He's all I have. He might be their family, but he's always been more to me. He's my everything. I didn't understand it until this moment, but I can't live without Aiyaret.

"We are wasting time," Wilder snaps. "Each second that passes is another that both Aiy and Carter are in trouble. Anchor our ropes here, send out the SOS, and let's get down there. Logan, Rick, you stay here."

"Not a chance in hell," they snap in unison.

"If help comes, we need you up here," Wilder protests.

"No, you're trying to protect us. That's our family down there too. We are going. We'll send the SOS and leave proof here, but we'll go down. They won't be here for days, and you need our help. Maeve will be hurt. You can't get her up by yourself. Let's go," Logan says, sounding more serious than I've ever heard him.

I'm in love with Aiyaret, and if something happens to him . . . *No.* That realization haunts me, distracting me from their arguments as I look at the hole.

Grabbing my bag, I hook in and plummet over the side after him. My heart rips apart with every second I'm separated from him. Their yells follow me down, but I won't waste another second.

*I'm coming, Aiy, just hold on. I'm coming.*

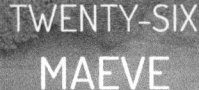

## TWENTY-SIX
## MAEVE

A noise wakes me up. I must have fallen asleep. I didn't mean to, but luckily, I must not have been asleep long. I don't feel like I'm going to pass out at any given moment, which is good.

I try to hear what woke me when there's a different type of noise. It's like something sliding across rock, something heavy. Everything in me goes cold, and I don't know why, but I grab my light and lift it. My mind screams at me, telling me not to even as I sweep it around the area.

The noise gets louder and louder. It's hard to pinpoint, so I focus hard, until I realize it's coming from my right. I turn my head slowly, knowing I don't want to see whatever it is, and shine the light there.

It's a shape that's moving oddly and heading my way. For a moment, my brain seems to come to a halt as I notice black and green scales covering the entire form. I trace them with my gaze, trying to make sense of what it is, surprised when I find a large tail at the end of the body. With terror gripping my heart, I shine the light back across the shape, my brain not working properly.

My light catches two large eyes shining brightly in the dark, and I quickly slam my light off and carefully set it down. My hand scrambles through the sand as I search for what I need while I try to slow my heartbeat.

When I find what I was looking for, I grip the sharp bone.

Terror and instincts urge me to remain as still as possible as the noise only grows closer. My eyelids flutter halfway shut, as if that will stop whatever is coming.

I grip the bone, ready in case that thing lunges at me. I don't think it will do much, but I'm not going down without a fight.

Just because I taste nice doesn't mean I'm going to become monster chow, because that thing is fucking ginormous.

My brain seems to pop then, allowing me to remember the pain of teeth in my thigh. I didn't fall or slip—I was pulled into this place by that thing. I have no idea how or why, but that . . . that crocodile thing tried to kill me.

It probably thought it did. It's bigger than any crocodile I have ever seen, the snout and body shape distinctive. It suddenly releases a hissing noise that makes my hair stand on end as it keeps crawling closer.

I strain my eyes as it approaches, coming close enough to touch. I smell stale water and rotten meat, making me want to gag. Its tail flicks in the sand, hitting my bad leg, and I bite back my scream. refusing to move or react. If I do, it will turn that monstrous jaw and snap me in two.

Something drops from its jaw and lands in the sand with a thud, and I realize it's a body—a person.

One of the guys? I don't look as it lifts its head, making that noise again—a bellow? It's horrific and beautiful at the same time, but it flashes huge, sharp teeth that have been inside my leg, and I don't want to feel that again.

I hear another sound, this one farther away than the creature before me.

Voices! It dawns on me at the same time that thing notices.

It spins faster than I thought possible, knocking me over with its tail. The impact causes agony to splinter through me, but I don't make a sound as I watch it slide into the water and return to wherever it came from. There are no bubbles or movement. I lie still, knowing it could be waiting. When it doesn't spring up, I slowly slide across the sand. I dare not turn the light on, so my hands search in the dark until I hit a body.

Ignoring the pain racing through me, I skim my hands up a chest to a face, feeling it as my vision adjusts again.

Aiyaret.

It's Aiyaret.

Blood drips down his forehead, so I lift him slowly and feel his head. His hair is a bloody, matted mess, but he releases a groan that lets me know he's alive. Loathing the fact that I have to touch him since I know he hates it, I glide my hands down and check for injuries. He has a few cuts on his legs where he was obviously carried, but nothing major except for his head.

He is very lucky.

I know the moment he wakes up—his heart starts to pound under my hand and he jerks. Covering his mouth, I lean closer so he can see me.

"Quiet," I hiss as he struggles against me.

"Maeve," he murmurs, and I press my hand tighter against his mouth, cutting off his words.

"Shh." I glance at the water, but nothing moves, so I relax a little, and he nods with a wince.

He reaches for his head and seems to remember, then he sits up, his eyes wide and panicked. Aiyaret tries to stand, so I hold him down with as much strength as I can muster, but he's still panicking. His breathing picks up, and it's too loud. It echoes around the chamber, and my terror increases at the idea of the creature hearing and coming back to finish off what it started.

"Breathe," I command, holding his hand to my chest so he can copy my breaths, forgetting his aversion to touch, but if he keeps panicking, then we are both dead.

His wide eyes lock on me, and he nods, wincing as he slows his breathing. I let go of his hand, and his touch lingers for a moment before he snatches it back. I move a little farther away now that he's more awake so he doesn't get upset because I'm touching him.

"What happened?" I whisper.

"I came down looking for you. The others are going to follow, I think. I was in a cavern below the opening when something . . ." He frowns, his eyes far away. "Something hit me. That's all I remember."

"You have a wound on your head where you met the ground," I murmur.

"Why are we whispering?" he asks.

"That thing that hit you? It's down here with us," I tell him. "I don't know if it's gone or waiting, but we can't risk it. We are both injured, and we wouldn't stand a chance."

"What was it?" he asks. "I only saw a shape. How can something even live down here?"

"I don't know, but I'm guessing this is where all the villagers went." It's a thought I keep having, but I don't know for sure. "As for what it was . . ." I glance at the water again. "It looked like a crocodile, but it was bigger than any I have ever seen. It was massive."

"Fuck." He rubs his head with a wince, and I tear off a strip of my shirt and dress his wound, trying to staunch the bleeding. "Thanks."

"It's about as good as we are going to get down here. Hey, your bag! You still have it." His eyes widen, and he swings it around from his back and digs inside. When he hands over a water bottle, I take a sip, even though I want to guzzle it down. We need to reserve it. He pulls out some bars, and we each take one. Neither of us really want to eat, but we force the food down, knowing we need the energy and sugar.

"I don't have a first-aid kit," he says as he rifles around in his bag.

"It's okay. We just need to get away from here," I murmur softly as I wipe my mouth. I keep stealing glances at the water, knowing before long, that thing will return, and we shouldn't be here when it does.

"The others will look for us. We need to stop them," he hisses as if remembering again, and I worry how badly his head is injured, but there is nothing I can do for him right now.

"I know." I glance at my leg, and he follows my gaze.

"Shit, Carter." He reaches for me before stopping himself. "Are you okay?"

"Just peachy. I never liked that leg anyway," I tease before turning serious at his worried look. "I'll live, but I'll need medical help as soon as possible."

"Why are we alive?" he whispers as he glances around.

"From what I remember, crocodiles like to keep their prey for weeks, usually dead. It must have thought I was. I think this is its nest and feeding area. It was interrupted with you by voices. We are lucky, but it won't last long. We need to get out of here and to the others and back up for help." Sliding back, I glance around once more. "It pulled you in here from there, so there has to be a way through. We'll go that way."

"Your leg," he reminds me.

"I'll be fine. I'm Maeve Carter, remember?" I joke, but it falls flat. We are both too scared to appreciate humor right now. "Hey, it will be fine," I promise as I reach for his hand before remembering. "They will be okay."

I help him up, ignoring the agony it sends through my injured body, then take a look at the water. I use the rock behind me to climb unsteadily to my feet, then I take one step forward, then another. Each time I put my foot down, fire flares up my injured leg, but at least I can walk, so that's something. Aiyaret keeps a close eye on me, though, and I move closer, turning my flashlight on. We need the light or we could fall and injure ourselves more. "It came from that direction. That has to be a way out."

Nodding, he lets me take the lead, his eyes on the water as we slowly make our way through the rocky room. I trip once, almost going down, and he catches me. As soon as I'm up, I move away, knowing his aversion to touch.

Across the room, hidden in the darkness, is a tunnel. It's big enough for us to walk through, and from the slide marks in the mud, it's clear this is the entrance to its feeding ground. It isn't a good place to get caught, but it's now or never, so I step inside. My flashlight barely illuminates the twisting corridor before me. Keeping one hand on the damp, rough rock, I lean into it as I shuffle forward. The more I move, the more the pain grows, but my body is loosening up, making it easier even if it hurts more. There isn't much I can do about the pain, so I just ignore it as best as I can, peeking around a corner before shuffling around.

"What happened?" Aiy asks barely above a whisper. Neither of us want to draw that thing's attention.

"I don't really remember. One second, I was standing up there with you, and the next, I woke up back there," I answer, having to grit my teeth through the pain. Each step is heavy and sends sparks shooting up my leg. It's a good thing I can feel it though, right?

"It's probably better that you can't remember," Aiyaret murmurs. "Your leg isn't broken?"

I shake my head, feeling woozy, so I stop for a moment and lean into the wall on my left. We can't afford to waste time, but the hot flash indicates I'm on the verge of passing out.

"Maeve," he says, "answer me."

I know he's keeping me talking to distract me from the pain, and in this moment, I love him for that.

Forcing a smile, I push off and carry on. "Not broken. Some muscle is torn, and the skin is punctured for sure. I don't know how deep. It didn't hit an artery or I would be dead, but it hurts like a son of a bitch."

"I bet." He laughs softly, keeping pace behind me. "Most people would have given up. Not you."

"I sewed it shut with my lace," I admit. "Thank God for Girl Scouts and their training."

He chuckles, and we continue walking, following the slide marks. It must be where it came from, which has to be where the others are. I can't hear them now, but that doesn't mean anything.

"How did it get you?" I ask. He mentioned something before, but it's a blur, the pain making my mind foggy. Besides, I need his voice, since it gives me something to focus on.

He's quiet, and I glance back before focusing on walking. "I came down after you."

I turn, flashing my light over his face, making him wince. "Alone?" I hiss.

"You were in trouble. We couldn't wait. They were planning, but it was taking too long, so I made the first move. I knew they would follow." He smiles. "Especially Way. He'll follow wherever I go."

"And here I thought you were oblivious, poor guy," I scoff.

"What do you mean?" He frowns. "He's my best friend. Of course he would."

"Sure, friends." I chuckle as I turn forward. "The others followed?"

"I think so, but before I could shout a warning, it was on me, and then I woke up next to you. Guess I found you, huh?" he quips.

I can't believe Aiyaret risked it all and came down here for me. I thought he didn't like me, but he jeopardized his life to find me, and that warms my heart toward the big guy.

"What did you mean when you said, 'sure, friends?'" he asks.

My breathing is labored, and I hate it. I focus on trying to control it as much as I can, not wanting that thing's attention. Who knows how well it can hear out of water.

"Aiyaret, it's very clear that Way is in love with you. Even the damn birds up there could see it. You act like a married couple. Haven't you ever thought about it?" I respond, focusing on our talk to keep going.

He's quiet, and I worry I overstepped until his hushed voice comes. "We're friends, always have been. I didn't think anyone would ever want me like that, especially someone who knows my past."

"But you've thought about it?" I deduce.

He's quiet, and I take that for a yes.

"Then what's stopping you? As you can see, life is too short," I scoff.

"I don't want to lose him," he whispers.

I can understand that, so I simply nod and shuffle another step forward. He could leave me and go faster, warn Way and the others, but he never once complains, sticking with me.

A sharp noise has us whirling around, my light splashing across his shoulders until he turns his head to see me. "You hear that?" I nod, and he looks around before grabbing me and shoving us both in a tiny alcove between the rocks. It's barely big enough to fit us, so we are pushed together, scarcely able to breathe. Reaching down, he shuts my light off and covers my mouth.

My chest rises rapidly—not in fear but exhaustion. I close my eyes, focusing on the softness of his skin and his warmth, letting it calm me until I can breathe normally. When my eyes flutter open, Aiy's face is so close to mine, I back up so we don't touch. His hand slides behind my head, protecting it from hitting the rocks. "Are you okay?"

I nod, and he lapses into silence for a moment, but his eyes never leave mine, and I realize we are touching. "I'm so sorry. I swear there isn't more room. If I could—"

"It's okay," he whispers. "Surprisingly, it doesn't bother me."

I don't know what to say to that, so I glance into the tunnel. When there is no more noise, I slip out, but he reaches to pull me back in. "It's okay. I think whatever made the noise is gone. Come on, we need to warn the others."

We don't get far, however, before my leg gives out. I crash into the rocks, sliding down to my ass. Gritting my teeth against a cry of pain, I glance at my watch and release my tourniquet. The blood flow is instantaneous, and it hurts so badly tears squeeze from my eyes. I count as I wiggle my toes before tying it off again. When I lean back, I find Aiyaret waiting for me.

"Are you okay?" he asks.

"Fine, just hurting," I admit, something I hate. "My leg is slowing us down. You need to go warn the others. I'll catch up."

Crouching down, he covers my good leg with his hand, eyeing me. "I'm not leaving you, so tell me how I can help."

"You can't," I reply, and he frowns. I stumble to my feet, but he catches me again when I struggle. I try to pull away, but he keeps hold of me, the tunnel allowing us to lean into each other.

"Come on, I'll help you walk," he offers.

"You hate touch," I remind him, though I don't know why.

"Like I said, I don't hate yours, not as much as I expected. Maybe it makes me feel less alone and scared right now, or it's because we need it, but I'm fine." He seems surprised by his own words.

"You're scared?" I whisper as we move faster. I don't have to use my bad leg as much with Aiyaret helping.

"Everyone would be in this situation. I'm not foolish enough to pretend like I'm not. I'm scared of whatever that thing is, that it hurt my family, and that I won't be able to get you out. Doesn't mean I'm not going to try, though, but yeah, Maeve. I'm scared." He looks down at me, and I meet his gaze once more before focusing on the path in front of us.

138

"I'm scared too," I tell him, "but I promise, Aiyaret, that I'll get us all out of here. I won't let anything happen to you."

"You know, Maeve Carter, you were born to be one of us. Shame it might never happen."

"Yeah, shame," I say, and we share a small smile.

# TWENTY-SEVEN

# LOGAN

We follow Aiyaret down as quickly as we can, but it takes us a couple of minutes to anchor in enough rope and get our packs together. Wilder sends an SOS on the satellite phone before we leave, just in case we get lucky, and then we are over the edge. Way's in the lead, his face pale and anxious as he repels faster than he should.

His boots aren't even on the ground before he unhooks, dropping the rest of the distance. "Aiy!" he screams, swinging his flashlight around as my feet touch the rock next to him.

I unhook and grab my own flashlight as I slap his shoulder. "We'll find him, okay?"

He nods, and Wilder looks around when he joins us.

"Split up and search for exits. I want constant communication," he orders.

We are all subdued and quiet for once as we spread out, our head-lamps turning on as we walk to the edges of the cavern.

There's a whistle, and I glance back. Rick looks worried as he holds up Aiy's rope, showing the torn end. I hurry over and finger the frayed edges. "Did it snap?"

"Impossible," Wilder murmurs as he takes it from me and plays with the end. "It looks like it was cut by something."

"A rock maybe?" I suggest as I glance up.

"Maybe," Wilder responds, but when I look back at him, he doesn't seem convinced. "Let's keep looking."

"Blood," Rick whispers, and we look at him. "That's blood." We follow his pointing finger, our flashlights shining on what he sees. A couple of feet away, glistening on a rock, is red liquid. We all rush over, Wilder crouching as he dips his fingers in it and lifts it in front of his flashlight. "He's right."

Way joins us at that moment, and he turns even paler. "Aiyaret! Aiyaret!" His panicked shouts echo around us, and Wilder grabs his shoulders, shaking him.

"Keep it together," he hisses. "It could be either of theirs. We don't know, okay? I need you to calm down. I can't be looking after you while we search for them."

Way nods, but it's too fast, and he looks absolutely petrified.

"Okay, we need to play this smart," Wilder begins, taking charge despite the fact that he's worried. "I want us in pairs, searching for which way they went, okay? No one goes anywhere alone. We will figure out what happened, but we'll be smart about it. No more injuries."

Nodding, I head off with Rick, leaving Way to Wilder. We start in front of the ropes, scanning the wall with our flashlights for any caves or tunnels, anything to give us a clue as to where they could have gone. Something catches my eye, and I stop, inspecting the marks. "Rick, do those look like claw marks to you?"

He turns, shining his light on the wall I'm standing near, and his face pales as he nods. "Come on." His voice is softer now. "Let's keep moving. We have to find them. I don't like whatever is down here."

"Me either," I admit quietly as I move closer, fear filling me. "Do you think this is the place from those paintings in that temple, where they were throwing people down here? Human sacrifices?"

"Probably," he replies, "which means there's something down here, and I don't want to be here when it hunts for its next victim, so let's get our team together and get the hell out."

We spend the next twenty minutes or so searching for an exit. There are a few tunnels, but they look far too small for them to have gone through without crawling, and they must be injured, so we discount them for now. If we don't find any others, then we will have to make our choice and pick one at random, but none of us seem particularly excited about that as we meet up in the middle.

"He didn't just disappear," Way snaps.

"Both of them will be okay," Wild promises. "There's something we missed. That's all."

"We are going to have to pick one of those smaller tunnels and just go for it," Rick says, sounding surprisingly logical for once.

"He's right." Wilder sighs. "Okay, I found five. We'll go two by two and set our watches. We'll be in and out in ten minutes and meet back here to check in, no matter what we find, okay?" Wilder tells us, and I nod, glancing at the wall and trying to pick one.

"Wait, do you hear that?" We turn around at Rick's urging, and it takes a second or two, but then I hear it as well.

Groaning.

Human groaning is coming from a tunnel we must have missed in the corner, and out steps Aiyaret and Maeve fucking Carter.

She looks up at us, her eyes widening before her cocky, if slightly breathless, voice comes. "Did you miss me?"

# TWENTY-EIGHT
## AIYARET

**M**y head jerks up at Maeve's words, and I see my entire team turned toward us. My heart slams in relief. I didn't want to admit it to her, but I was terrified we were alone down here or, worse, something happened to them. They rush toward me, and I pull her back, warding them off.

"Careful, Maeve is hurt pretty badly." That slows them down before they gather around us. Wilder gives me a look, and I nod before he glances at Maeve, his eyes widening when he sees the damage.

"Fuck," he hisses.

"Shit, I must look terrible if your expression is anything to go by, or are you that kind to all the girls?" she replies.

Way grips my arm, checking me over frantically.

"I'm okay, just a bump to the head. Maeve saved me," I say.

"What happened?" Wilder asks, his eyes on Maeve's leg.

"Oh, you know, I just look so fucking tasty that some ancient fucking monster of a croc decided to eat me," she replies, and all gazes swing to her. "Not joking."

"She isn't," I murmur. "It attacked me too, knocked me out and dragged me to its feeding ground where Maeve was. I don't remember much, but it was fucking massive."

"And angry," she adds. "We're lucky to be alive, but I'd like to keep it that way." She glances over her shoulder into the tunnel, and I get her meaning. We need to get out of here as soon as possible.

"Let's get away from the tunnel," I comment, and she nods, taking another step, but Wilder suddenly scoops her up and carries her away, ignoring her protests. He places her gently on a rock near the ropes.

I follow them over, but Way pulls me to a stop, running his eyes over me with so much worry, I soften and let him.

Way cradles my head, turning it left and right, running his hands over every inch of me. "Are you sure you're okay?" he asks. "Aiyaret, is anything hurt?" He finds every scrape and cut, and I can't help but smile as I watch him. He looks so worried and uncharacteristically serious that my heart skips a beat.

Is Maeve right?

This isn't the time to think about it, that's for sure, but then his hands grip my cheeks and he leans in, resting his forehead into mine. "I was so fucking scared," he whispers. "Don't ever do that again, you hear me?"

"I'm sorry," I respond, but I refuse to make that promise, and he notices. Reaching up, I grip the nape of his neck and hold him for a moment. "Thanks for coming for me."

"Always," he murmurs, holding my gaze. "What are friends for?" The way he stumbles over the word "friends" has me recalling Maeve's observation. Is she right? Have I been ignoring this all along?

The searching look he gives me makes me release him and step back, and I head over to Maeve to see how she is. Way's hand slides down my back to my waist as if he thinks I'll disappear again. It's comforting, so I don't say anything. Instead, I lean into his touch, needing his support after everything that happened.

Wilder is crouched next to Maeve, his bag beside him as he eyes her wounds before reaching for her leg and turning it back and forth, making her hiss.

"Wilder!" she snaps, smacking his hands away as he sits back. "Ignore it. I've survived so far. We need to get out of here before it comes back, okay? We can worry about me losing my leg once we are out of this hole."

"You could bleed out before we get up there," he retorts, refusing to back down, "so shut the fuck up for once, Carter, and let me deal with your injury." His touch is soft as he pulls her tourniquet away. "Shit, this must be so painful." He eyes her anxiously. "Did you sew this?"

"With my shoelace. It was better than bleeding out." She leans back, clearly feeling weak, and Rick drops to his knees, letting her lean back into him as Logan crouches on the other side.

"That's hardcore," Rick teases.

Wilder smirks slightly as he opens his bag. "You saved your own life, so I guess you aren't a total idiot."

"Really? I nearly got eaten, and you're still an ass?" she complains as he douses the wound with cleaning fluid, making her jerk and scream.

He grabs her neck, eyeing her hard until she stops. "So fucking weak, Carter. I thought you were hardcore."

"I fucking am," she growls, and I know he's starting a fight to distract her from what he needs to do.

Turning to his bag, he pops something and hands it to her. "These are strong, and they might make you feel sick, but it should block the pain for a while." Without asking any more questions, she throws them back as Wilder lays out what he needs, and then he looks at her.

"Fucking do it," she grumbles.

"I'm going to need to clean it again. I'll keep your stitches in. There's no point in agitating the wound and reopening it, but we need to bandage it. I have some antibiotics as well as adrenaline. It will help with shock and fatigue, but it's going to make you crash later and feel like shit."

"Wilder, just fucking do it," she orders, and he nods.

He's the best person to deal with this. He even started med school before dropping out, but her wound is extensive. He's clearly concerned, but he doesn't say it as he starts to clean and dress it.

Her scream echoes around the cavern once more before she cuts it off, turning her head and burying it in Rick's chest to muffle it so the creature doesn't hear. When Wilder sits back, she slumps and pants as she turns her head to see her leg. It's wrapped as best as he could manage. That's about all we can do down here.

"Don't worry, you're still as hot as ever," Logan teases, making her grin despite the pain.

Wilder loads up a shot and then looks at her. "You're a pain in the ass, Carter, you know that?"

"You bastard." She groans as he stabs her with the adrenaline, making her narrow her eyes on him. "Prick," she finishes.

"There, that's all we can do here. We need to get you to a hospital as soon as possible. Can you climb up the rope on that leg, or should we create a pulley system?"

"I'll be fine," she snaps as she sits up. "Don't worry, I won't slow you down. Let's get the fuck out of here." Despite her words, when she stands, she slips, and Rick catches her.

"I'll tie her to me," Way offers. "I'm the strongest. I can get her up there."

"I'll be fine," she promises.

"No, you won't," Way says, his voice soft. "It's okay to need our help." He looks at me and then at her. "Let me do this."

I can tell she hates it, but she nods, her shoulders slumping in defeat. "I'm sorry," she murmurs.

Wilder claps her shoulder, being surprisingly gentle for once, as he slings his bag over his shoulder. "You can pay us back later, Carter. Stop being so stubborn." He heads over to the ropes. Rick and Logan follow to help him set them up, and I walk to her side, offering her my arm. She leans into it with a grateful smile as Way comes to her other side, offering his.

"Lean on me." The rest of his words are unsaid—instead of me.

She begins to let go, and I cover her hand. "It's okay," I assure them. "Are you okay?"

"Peachy," she teases. "I know I'm damn tasty, but this motherfucker couldn't have gone for one of you? More meat. Idiot."

I laugh, and when I look up, Way is frowning and glancing between us, but when he sees me watching, he clears his expression. "You're lucky to be alive," he says.

"Don't I know it," she replies tightly. "I wouldn't have made it without Aiy."

"You would have," I reply. "You're Maeve fucking Carter, remember?"

"Too right. Alright, let's do this. Get me the fuck out of this hole."

Way and I help her to the ropes. She seems to walk better as time passes, so I guess the drugs are kicking in. Once there, we hook Way up first and then start on Maeve, ready to tie them together, but a hair-raising growl fills the air, making us freeze.

We turn just in time to see a huge shape lunging from the shadows.

I push Way and Maeve away just as it snaps its maw between us, where they were just standing.

I hit the ground hard, its massive body before me. Its green scales are bigger than the palm of my hand.

Its tail slides across the rock as it curls before the creature looks at them.

"Run!" someone yells.

# TWENTY-NINE
## MAEVE

**W**ay is still hooked to the rope, so he's a sitting duck. The creature focuses on him as he struggles with the line, eyeing it as Wilder, Rick, and Logan gawk in shock. Way glances from it to the rope as Aiy's voice comes from its other side.

"Run!"

It snaps us all into motion, and the croc slides closer to Way. He freezes, knowing he's going to be too late.

With my good foot, I kick the side of its snout. It snaps and turns its head, focusing on me. I start to back up, but it whirls around and concentrates on the others. They must have gotten its attention somehow.

It's the chance we need.

Turning to Way, I see him gaping at the croc, his hands frozen.

I grab his knife from his side, cut his rope, and kick him out of the way. "Run, idiot!" Keeping the knife, I turn just as the croc's tail swings for me. It hits me in the stomach, sending me flying. I smack back into the rocks with a groan, the force making my head spin for a moment.

Sitting up, I see Aiy backing away from the thing as it prowls toward him. Way is trying to get its attention, but it isn't working. Climbing unsteadily to my feet, I look around for a big rock, then I palm one, but when I look up, the creature is focused on Wilder, who has pushed Rick and Logan toward Aiyaret and is yelling, smacking his palms into the wall he's in front of.

It lunges at him, and he rolls out of the way at the last second. When he stands, it whips its head around and looks at him. "Go, get out!" he orders. "I'll keep its attention."

When it snaps again, Wilder lunges at the last second and gets tossed to the ground. The croc is going to attack again, and he's a wide-open target.

I throw the rock with all my might, and it smacks into the side of the croc. It spins, lashing out with his tail as he hisses, and I cup my mouth. "That's it, you ugly fuck, over here!" I back up as I yell, smacking my hands against anything I can.

"Fucking damsels in distress!" I shout, but we are spread around the room, and the croc is in the way of the ropes. It's like it knows that's our exit and is blocking it on purpose.

It keeps lumbering my way, obviously annoyed by us and deciding I'm the easiest target. "That's it, you ugly fucking prehistoric dinosaur wannabe!" I bellow as I step backwards.

My back hits the wall, and I know I'm fucked, until I feel air blowing across my legs. I don't dare look in case it lunges, but I glance over the creature to the others who are in a line, trying to get its attention.

"Go, get the fuck out of here!" I scream.

"Carter!" Wilder roars, walking toward me, but I shake my head.

"Go!" I yell just as the croc opens its maw and lunges at me. I take the chance, turning and throwing myself into the space where I felt the wind. I find a tiny tunnel and crawl as fast as I can. The smash of the animal against the wall is loud, sending rocks flying across me, but I keep crawling, feeling its hot breath panting in the air. Stopping, I turn on my back to see its huge fangs snapping at the entrance, the monster still not wanting to give up its prey.

I can't hear the others anymore, and all I can do is hope they listened to me. I turn and crawl as fast as I can, hoping it comes out somewhere that isn't in the jaws of that beast. The drugs they gave me have kicked in, but it won't be long until I feel pain again. It means I have a couple of hours to get out of this place without their help and hope I can find them and get the hell out of here. I check my watch and set a timer as I go. Pain pulses every now and again, but I ignore it. My life depends on it.

The sound of the croc slowly disappears, and that makes my heartbeat slow slightly, the adrenaline Wilder gave me causing it to beat faster. It's probably the only thing keeping me from crashing, so I make the most of it. I cut my hands on the rock, having to duck my head so I don't smack it on the roof of the tunnel. I lost my light a while back, and it gets darker as I go, leaving me blind, but I still crawl. Even as something scuttles over my hand, I keep going, but I only realize the tunnel is tilting down too late.

I start to slip as I try to crawl backwards, but it's slick, so I slide down and out, plunging into something wet and solid—water.

I float under it for a moment before I swim to the surface, taking a deep breath as I look around. I know where I am.

I'm back where I started—its feeding ground.

A growl makes my head snap around, and I see the outline of the croc in the tunnel. I won't make it out of here in time, so with no other option, I silently swim back under the water, holding my breath. My eyes remain locked on the surface before I realize the stupidity of that. Water is where they see and hear best.

Fuck.

Swimming backwards as gently as I can, I feel the rock around the edge, and I debate trying to get out when the water ripples around me like something big slid into it.

Yeah, fuck this.

I am not being ripped apart today. Gripping the edge of the rock, I push myself up and out as silently as I can. My leg cramps up, and I try to breathe as noiselessly as possible as I scoot backwards across the rock. I stare into the water, holding my breath, when the monster suddenly bursts from it and lunges at me.

With a yell, I throw myself to the side, narrowly missing being eaten, and then I'm up and running. I can hear it following me as it crashes from the water. It snaps again, and I throw my arm up as stones tumble over me, and then I race into the tunnel. I slip into the darkness, but I push myself to move faster, knowing it will chase me. When I glance back, I see it trapped under some rock, giving me a chance to get away. I run as fast as I can, which is slower than normal due to my fucked-up leg, but it's all I have. This time, I pass through the tunnel much faster, wishing Aiy were here to help. When I burst out into the cavern, I don't see anyone there, nor bodies, which gives me a moment of relief, but a bellow behind me has me ignoring my worry for anyone else and diving from the edge of the tunnel.

Racing across the rocky surface of the cavern, I see a dangling rope and know it's for me. With a yell as I feel the creature behind me, I push off the ground and leap. When I hit the rope, I wrap myself around it, dangling in the air just as jaws close below me, missing me by inches.

Glancing down, I see the rope in its mouth, and I hope like hell the line can hold up. The croc falls back on its tail, the edge of the rope in its jaws. I look up and start to climb, using my upper body instead of my legs. Luckily, I have my strength there, and I move quickly as I hear the croc below me. I have no idea how it usually gets up here, nor do I want to find out.

The darkness recedes the higher I get, and when I look up, I see five faces peering over the edge before they start calling out.

I climb faster.

The rope begins to move, and I look up to see the guys there, hauling me up and over. We fall back together, safe on solid ground.

"Well, that was fun," I tease just as something tugs me—the rope.

It yanks me back toward the edge.

*Oh fuck.*

# THIRTY

# WILDER

**S**crambling around, I manage to grab Maeve's dropped knife as she screams, being dragged to the edge. I slam the blade down on the rope, snapping it, and with a twang, it falls back into the hole as Logan hauls her away from the rim.

She's panting, soaked, and wide-eyed, but she's alive.

Gripping her face, I run my eyes over her. "How the fuck did you get out?"

"Just lucky, I guess," she rasps, "but we won't be if we stay here. We need to move."

She's right, but I steal one last look at the hole before helping her to her feet. I didn't want to leave her, but I had to get my team to safety. I threw the rope in to head back down myself in search of her, but she beat me to it again. I guess I just keep losing to her.

Our bags are packed, so we toss them on, then I grab Maeve's. "Way, give me your bag." I grab the one he throws, and he understands instinctively, hauling her up on his back despite her grumbling. The heavens open, and rain lashes down. When I look up at the darkening sky, I realize it isn't just a little rain.

"Shit, I knew the weather was getting bad. It's a fucking storm. Our boat won't come back in this. I hope it lets up," I lament.

Logan pulls something out and looks at me with an anxious expression. "Not just a storm, it's a fucking hurricane, and we are in its path. They aren't getting to us anytime soon."

"We have bigger issues," I comment as I glance around at the city.

"Like what?" Rick asks worriedly before looking at the hole.

"We are in a valley. If this is a hurricane, then it's likely this whole place will flood and be under water." I meet their eyes. "That would turn it into a perfect hunting ground for that thing. We need to get to high ground now."

That gets everyone moving.

The dirt roads turn into a maze of slippery slopes, but we climb up as fast as we can. Maeve clings to Way, and I know she hates it, but it's faster for us, and when we reach the steps, I let them go first. I keep my eyes on them as Way climbs, holding her under her thighs to secure her.

"Go," I order Aiy. He nods and keeps his hand on her back as he ascends behind them.

"Brother," Rick begins.

"Go," I demand, pushing him and Logan up the steps. I stay in the back, my machete out just in case—not that it would do much against that . . . thing.

The ground shakes, and a bellow reaches us. That monster is mad.

I glance up to find Maeve and my team near the top, so I spare the chasm one last look before I turn and sprint up the stairs faster than I have ever moved in the past.

I find them waiting at the top, all looking into the city. No wonder no one has found it. They probably have but didn't survive to tell the tale.

I glance back to see the hole filling with water. The rain is going to flood the valley. The creature is next to it, looking massive even from this far away, and as it lifts its head, bellowing a strangely beautiful sound into the storm, I realize just how truly fucked we are.

"Wilder," Rick murmurs.

"I know. High ground, now. We'll take shelter only when we get there. It will eventually grow bored," I say.

"Are you sure?" Logan asks as he stares at it. "It looks mad as hell."

"I'm sure. We didn't see it outside of the island, so it has to stick close to here. Animals are territorial. We probably stumbled into its home and made it angry. Out of sight, out of mind." I push my wet hair out of my face. "Let's move."

## THIRTY-ONE
## MAEVE

**L**eaning into Way's back, I shiver. I'm not moving, and I'm soaked from the torrential downpour, meaning I'm cold. I know it's probably due to blood loss as well, but still. "I can walk now," I tell him, but he just keeps going. "Way, put me down so I can walk."

"No." He glances at me before focusing on following Aiy's path, Wilder and the others behind us. "You're hurt. You'll slow us down."

I flinch, but he's right.

He softens as he glances at me. "I didn't mean it like that. We need to get to safety, and you're injured. The longer we take, the worse it will be for you. I'm fine. I could carry you the entire trip over and over if needed."

Nodding, I shiver again and tighten my hands on his neck to help support my weight, not wanting to be a burden.

"Here," a soft voice whispers, and I glance up to see Rick there. He drapes his coat over my back and ties it as he covers my head with it. "Just hold on, okay? We'll get somewhere safe soon."

I nod and snuggle deeper into it, trusting them. The croc doesn't seem to be following us, but the storm is picking up in ferocity, and we need to get out of it before it worsens.

I must pass out for a while because I wake up to being jostled, and I lift my head to see we are climbing. "Sorry," Way says. "Didn't mean to wake you, just needed to shift your weight."

"It's okay. I can climb—"

He laughs, cutting me off, and I know I'm not getting down. Luckily, the hill we are climbing isn't overly steep, so he just takes extra care with his steps, and I notice he shields my bad leg from any rocks. When we reach the top, he isn't even winded, which makes my estimation of him rise. We look around at the flattened hills. "Wilder spotted them on our way in," Way explains. "We'll find something up here to take shelter in for a while to wait out the storm."

I relax back into his hold as they scout the area and talk between themselves.

Way carefully lays me down under the shelter of a copse of trees a little while later, helping me arrange my legs in front of me. "Are you okay?"

I nod, and Rick appears, handing me some water. I drink it as the others prepare around us, working in synchronization to set up a camp.

"Are we safe here?" I ask.

"For now," Way replies. "Rest, we will be right here." He ducks out of the trees to help the others, and Rick smiles and follows him.

Leaning back against a tree, I watch them. I should help, but I'm exhausted, and the pain is starting to return. They set up camp with an ease that shows they have done this together a hundred times, and for a moment, my heart clenches and I miss my dad.

My bag is at my side, so I rip it open, grabbing my camera. I don't know if it will update to the server with the storm overhead, but I need to do this just in case.

Fiddling with it, I debate what I want to say before turning it on and aiming it at myself, forcing a smile. "Hey, Dad, sorry I didn't update you before. It's been a little . . . well, crazy." I laugh bitterly. "You'll never guess what we ran in to here. Well, you wouldn't believe me even if I tried to tell you. I'm hurt, but I'll be okay. I'm with Ajax's other team." I pan the camera around so he can see, careful not to show him my leg or anything else. "Hopefully this storm will pass soon and we'll find our way home, okay? So don't worry. I know by now you probably are." Taking a deep breath, I surge ahead. They can hear me, but it's important.

"If this gets to you and I don't get home, please don't be sad, okay? Don't blame yourself. I know you will, but don't. It was my choice to come here. I fell in love with exploring just like you. Like father, like daughter, eh? There is nothing you could have done. You being here wouldn't have changed anything. I need you to know that I love you so much, Daddy, for everything you did for me. You gave me the best life I could have ever wished for, and you didn't try to make me like everyone else. Thank you for exploring the world with me, even when your heart was broken, and I'm so happy you have step-monster. Let her look after you, alright? I'm sorry I can't be there, but don't be sad for long. Remember what you always told me? Death isn't the end; it's just a new beginning—another adventure. It will hurt for a while, but there is nowhere else in this world I would rather be right now. There isn't much else I can say, but I just needed you to know that I love you, and I'm so grateful you are my father." Biting my lip, I force back my tears, not wanting to upset him. "Goodbye, Daddy." Looking away, I take a deep breath and glance into the camera.

"Ajax, if I don't make it back, make sure this gets to my dad along with the insurance money. If I do, delete this so he never sees it," I instruct. "Take care of him like you promised me." I shut it off, letting it drop into my lap. I never thought I'd have to say goodbye to him. No parent should outlive their child, but I'm so fucking grateful he isn't here right now. As much as I ache for his strength, his absence means he's safe.

"What are you doing?" Aiy asks, and I notice the others are looking too.

"Saying goodbye, just in case," I admit. "I don't want him to always wonder what happened to me." I hold out the camera. "Do you have anyone you want to say goodbye to? Just in case?"

"No. My family is all here," he replies softly.

"We don't need to say goodbye because we are getting out of here," Wilder promises as he comes to my side and hands me some rations which are protein bars. "Eat this while we cook. You need all the strength you can get. Those shots will make you feel sick."

"But what if—"

He shoves some into my mouth and forces my jaw to chew as he speaks.

"No what-ifs. We are getting out of here. You'll be fine, so no good-byes, okay?" he tells me. His face is hard, but his eyes are soft. "Trust me, Carter, I'll get us out of here."

Faith, I realize, is what I feel as I nod.

They set out a tarp in front of the trees to create a tent and then arrange the bedding. Logan helps me to my feet and gets me comfortable there as they build a fire and start heating their rations. We can hear the wind and rain, but we are shielded from it, and we all start to dry off, our socks and boots to the side since none of us want gangrene.

I barely manage to scarf down the food they cook before my eyes begin to close, a mix of pain, exhaustion, and drugs hitting me like a truck. Before I know it, I'm out cold.

When my eyelids flutter open, I see flames dancing in the dark night. Snores fill the air, and bodies lie around the fire. The pain in my leg is back to a dull ache, but my head is cushioned by something soft, and there's a blanket wrapped tightly around me.

Frowning, I shift my head higher, and I freeze when I hear a grunt, realizing it's a person.

I look up to see Wilder, the firelight reflected in his eyes as he peers at me. "Sorry," I mutter as I go to move away, knowing he won't like me being this close.

"You're fine." Grabbing my neck gently, he guides me until I lay my head on his shoulder. "Rest, you need it."

I should argue, but it's better than the cold, hard ground, so I close my eyes once more, knowing my cheeks are hot, and go back to sleep.

Pain wakes me. The sun isn't up yet, and I try to bite back my whine, but I must wake Wilder, who is at my side. He has one hand on my back, and the other is in my hair. I see Way move and realize he was on watch at the entrance. He scoots over, crouching before me.

"Maeve?" he whispers softly. "Are you okay?"

"Sorry." I wince, trying to move my leg to alleviate the throbbing, but nothing helps. It's burning and aching, and I know that isn't a good sign. "Just the pain."

"You're due for more pain pills," Wilder murmurs groggily. "I'll get them."

"I've got it, Wild." Way hurries away, and when he comes back, he offers me the pills and some water. They help me lift my head, and I take the painkillers before they lay me back down.

I can't do anything but wait for the medicine to kick in. Way sits cross-legged before me, and I look up at him. "Want me to distract you with some stories?"

"Please," I whisper.

"How about the time Wilder tried to fight a moose?" I grin, and he smiles. "Or when Rick and Logan had to climb a mountain in Peru totally naked?" I laugh, and his smile grows. "Or my personal favorite? Okay, so we were in this tiny little village . . ."

I listen as he talks about everything and anything, embarrassing every single one of his teammates. The distraction helps me manage the pain, and when he's done, he brushes some hair from my face.

"Sleep, okay? You need the rest. We'll be right here." Despite it all, I snuggle closer to Wilder and shut my eyes again, letting the pop and crack of the fire soothe me to sleep.

I snooze on and off all day. When I wake, someone is always there to feed me or offer me water. I know I should get moving, since we should do *something*, but I can't. I keep slipping into an exhausted slumber, and besides, the storm isn't letting up.

The howl of the hurricane follows me into my dreams.

## THIRTY-TWO
## RICK

**M**aeve is pale, but at least she's awake. She slept all day and night, which makes sense considering what she went through. Aiy's head wound is bad but okay, and Wilder is fussing over them both. With nothing else to do but take shelter, we pass the time slowly. The storm doesn't lessen, though, and I know it's worrying Wilder, although he won't admit it.

"We need to check her wound," Wilder murmurs, and I help him. Maeve sighs, turning her head away, and we slowly peel off the blood-saturated dressing. It doesn't look good at all. There's no pus or odor, but the skin is a strange color. She whimpers but doesn't wake as we touch near the wound.

Wilder and I share a look, knowing there's a problem. She could have an infection or worse. She needs a hospital, and it's clear this storm isn't passing anytime soon. We could be stranded here forever, and we can't let that happen. We need to move and find help.

Covering her up, we gather the others at the edge of the tent, so we aren't in the rain. Wilder's voice is low as he speaks so he doesn't wake her. "She needs help and soon or she'll lose the leg . . . or worse. We can't stay here."

Aiyaret frowns. "But the storm—"

"We have to risk it," Wilder says. "They won't be able to get to us here anyway. We need to be near the water so they can drop in quickly. We'll pack up and move this afternoon. If we can get down the mountain and a little ways away, that's good with me, okay?"

There is a noise, and we turn to see Maeve sitting up.

"We're leaving?" she murmurs, having overheard us.

Wilder nods. "It's our best bet. If we stay here, then we can't guarantee they will come for us or that our call will even get out. We need to find a way off this island or something that can help us. Your leg is only going to get worse. It's now or never." He looks concerned.

"I can do it." She clambers to her feet using the tree, waving off our hands. "I got it. I'm stronger than I look."

"We know," I tease. "You survived a fucking crocodile attack and still got us the hell out of there. You're one badass bitch, Maeve Carter."

"Don't forget it when we get back," she teases, some color returning to her cheeks. "You're right. The storm isn't passing. We need to push on."

"Then it's decided." Wilder nods. "Pack up. We'll move as soon as we can."

We're quiet as we work, and I shoulder Maeve's bag as Wilder puts her on his back despite his wound. We're all rundown and wet, but we are determined as we head down the hill. The storm is wild again, lashing us. I walk to Logan's side, link our arms, and start to sing loudly and off-key.

He soon joins in, and then Maeve, Way, and Aiy begin singing as well. Wilder doesn't, and she smacks his shoulder. "Don't be boring." She starts singing again, while the rest of us wait for Wild.

With a sigh, he finally joins in, and we can't help but laugh as we sing loudly to old-school party tunes the entire hike down. The rain finally stops for a bit, and we make the most of the break to clear our path. The forest is waterlogged, our boots sinking deep into the mud, and it slows us down, but Wilder is unwavering, setting a hard pace toward the outer shore of the island.

We don't stop at all, eating and drinking as we walk, and as the sun starts to descend and the rain begins again, we know we need to find shelter. We spread out in a line, close enough to see but able to cover more ground to find somewhere for us to spend the night. None of us want to sleep in the dirt again and on the ground where that thing could get us, but we might not have any choice.

"I see something!" I call, breaking the line as I slog through the mud and trees to the glint that caught my eye. I stop when I realize what it is. My eyes bulge, and I hear the others join me.

"Holy shit, is that a truck?" Logan whispers. "How?"

"Someone before us must have dropped it here when they came to explore. Idiots, it clearly wasn't going to get far," I mutter as I turn to Wilder. "It will do the trick though, right?"

"It should." He frowns, eyeing it. It's only one or two years old, black, and meant for off-roading with an extended back.

"I'll check it over," I say, and Way follows me. I yank on the door, finding it unlocked, and peek in the front seat. It's empty. There's a chain with a cross dangling from the mirror and some wrappers shoved in the middle compartment, but not much else. Looking between the seats, I find Way in the back. "Nothing but some insects that we'll clear out."

"All clean!" I call to Wilder, and he heads over. He lets Maeve down at the door, and we help her onto the back bench seat. We push it back as far as it can go so she can stretch her leg, and I climb in opposite her, sitting with my back to the passenger seat and propping her ankle on my knee. Way and Aiy climb into the front, shutting doors against the storm, as Wilder and Logan climb into the back and close the door. The engine is long since dead, so we hand out some lanterns that we spread out.

"At least we aren't wet anymore," I tease, shaking my head like a dog to wring out my hair. Maeve laughs and squeezes hers out as she looks around.

"This can't have been here long. It isn't even overtaken by nature yet. It seems we aren't the first people here. You think that thing got them too?"

The question sobers us, and I look at my brother.

"Probably, or simple exposure." Wilder shrugs. "It doesn't matter. We'll take shelter for the night."

Logan climbs over Wilder, who grunts, and once in the back, we hear him rummaging around.

"What are you doing?" Wilder asks.

"There are some kits here. They must have left them because they were too much to carry," he calls, and I climb over Wilder to help him. There are several black boxes, and we search through them. Many items are way too big to carry, the idiots, but others are helpful. I put together a pile of flares, hoping they still work. There's a small camping stove and some rations that might not be expired. Logan finds some medical supplies and hands them over to Wilder as we keep searching. At the bottom of a box, my hand connects with a metal item, and I freeze.

Pulling it free, I hold it up, and Logan's eyes widen. "Is that a gun?"

"A pistol," I clarify, and Wilder and Maeve turn to see us.

"Put it back," Wilder demands. "You idiots can't be trusted with a gun. Besides, it's probably empty."

Maeve reaches over and grabs it. "Hey!" I protest, but we watch as she deftly checks it with sure fingers. "It's loaded. Are there any more clips back there?"

"Uh . . ." I rifle through the box and retrieve two more, handing them over. "Just these."

"It's better than nothing." She shrugs. "My dad taught me to shoot when I was younger. It might not kill that motherfucker, but it might help if it comes at us again."

"We lost it," Wilder says, "but keep it if it makes you feel better. Now, this is going to suck, but we need to redress your wound and stitch it properly."

Her eyes widen, and she looks at us for help.

I wince for her. "Sorry, cupcake. Hope you like pain."

"Not like that," she says, but she nods. "You're right. Let's do it."

Climbing over, I glance at Wilder, who appears anxious. "Maeve, just look at me, okay?" I tell her. "I'm much more beautiful."

She smiles, and I give her one of my own as I take her hand and squeeze it, hoping like hell we get out of here soon so we can get her help.

This world would be a boring place without Maeve Carter, and the idea that she could die here terrifies me more than that creature we faced.

# THIRTY-THREE
## MAEVE

Wilder turns me and stretches my leg out on the seat. My sock is already off—one I stole from the others, as well as their spare boots—leaving my foot bare as I lean back against the truck door. I reach up and grip the oh shit handle as Wilder looks at me.

"Ready?" he asks.

"Do it," I order, and he peels off the bandages. I grunt but bite down on the pain. It's bad but not unbearable. As he exposes the wound, though, I know this is going to be terrible. He has a sterilized setup before him, and he grabs scissors and tweezers.

"I need to get rid of your stitches. If we were being rescued tomorrow, I wouldn't, but I'm worried about the damage. There is a staple gun here, which will be better," he explains as he leans over my leg. "This will hurt."

"No shit—fuck me!" I scream as he cuts through the shoelace and starts to pick it out with the tweezers. Each tug of my torn flesh creates pure agony. I'm sweating profusely and trying not to punch him. My tongue bleeds from how hard I bite it to stifle my bloodcurdling screams, not wanting to draw anything's attention.

"Just pass out," Rick tells me, gripping my hand. "It's okay."

I can't, I don't, and the pain only worsens as he slides the lace through my flesh. My leg jerks, and he looks at Logan. "Hold her down." Climbing over me, he pins my legs as I cry and whimper.

"Fuck you, Wilder! You piece of shit. You're enjoying this!" I rant, even if it doesn't help. "You've always hated me, and now you're enjoying this way too fucking much, you beautiful fucking bastard—ah!" I cry out as he continues unthreading the stitches.

"Maeve," Rick says, and I turn my head, panting. "I'll distract you, okay? Just don't punch me."

"What—" Before I can question him, his lips press against mine and his hand slides into my hair to hold me to him, even as I struggle.

My eyes are wide open, but when his brother hits something in my leg, I jerk and gasp, and his tongue slides into my mouth, allowing him to deepen the kiss. Without meaning to, I shut my eyes and give myself over to him, needing an escape from the agony.

"Keep her distracted," Wilder tells his brother. "I'm going to clean the wound."

His head moves higher as his kiss becomes hard, and he swallows my whimper of pain, tilting my head back for better access. Our heaving breaths fog the windows as he groans and breaks us apart.

His lips brush over my ear, his voice a shocked whisper as he says, "Do you know how many times I've imagined kissing you, Maeve Carter?" I shiver, and he holds my head firmly as I feel burning liquid pour over my wound. "How many times I've jerked off while thinking of you? You'll kill me later for saying that, but it's true. I'm your fucking stalker." He guides my lips back to his, swallowing my screams as Wilder begins to staple my leg.

Wilder is quick and efficient as his brother eats at my mouth so hard our teeth clash together, but it does the trick, diverting my attention. It's the most feral kiss I've ever had in my entire life, as if he needs me more than air.

The pain suddenly stops, and I feel my leg being covered, but Rick keeps going. He groans, kissing me deeper, and then someone coughs.

"I'm done," Wilder says, and I jerk back, breaking apart from his brother.

My cheeks are hot with embarrassment and pain, but I don't avoid their gazes. What's the point? They all saw it. Aiy's eyebrows are raised, and he's gripping Way's hand, which is trying to cover his eyes. Logan strokes my other leg as Wilder cleans up, blood on his hands and arms.

Rick pants as he grins at me, and I look at Wilder.

"All done." He nods as he leans back.

"Good." I slam my fist into Rick's stomach. He doubles over, coughing. "That's for taking advantage of me." Gripping his head, I jerk him up and kiss him. "And that's for helping." I slump back, feeling exhausted.

He stares at me in bewilderment, but he's smiling. "Worth it," he mutters.

Settling in my seat, I let them pass me some water and rations. We can't cook tonight, so we make do as they stretch out. Wilder slips onto the floor with his brother, and Logan squeezes in on the seat, lifting my legs onto his lap. I should move, but I don't as I press my face against the cool window.

"We'll get up early tomorrow. I want to cover as much ground as possible. We'll reach the beach and retry the emergency signal. If not, it should only be a few days before our boat arrives. We can make do until then," Wilder says, "so sleep and conserve your energy. It's going to be a grueling few days."

He doesn't turn out the lights, though, and no one seems eager to sleep.

"Despite it all"—I indicate my leg—"I'm glad I came, and I'm glad I met you guys here."

"Don't go acting nice, Carter." Wilder smirks. "We are still enemies."

I grin, and Aiy pops his head through again, smiling softly at me. "Where's your favorite place to travel?"

"Hm, I really liked Peru and Norway," I reply. "I love exploring and traveling. Doing crazy stuff is a bonus, but seeing the land and things others might never get to is my favorite part. That's why I do it."

"Your dad took you to those places?" he asks.

"Hmm." I nod. "Peru was the last place we visited together before he got his diagnosis. I didn't explore for a while after that, staying close, but he demanded I stop fussing and get my ass back out there. Ajax took me in and gave me a chance."

"He saw what we do—you're made to be an adventurer," Way says as he leans against Aiy. "You're one hell of an explorer, Carter."

Not a woman.

Not anything else.

Explorer.

That makes me grin. "Yeah, well, you guys aren't so bad yourselves, but if you tell anyone I said that, I'll kick your asses."

They laugh, and we lapse into silence.

"I liked Antarctica. There aren't many people, and it was desolate but beautiful," Wilder murmurs.

"Tibet," Logan says.

"Greenland," Way adds.

"Brazil," Aiy shares.

"Canada," Rick says, and we turn to him as he grins. "What? I like the food, and it was fun."

We laugh again.

"What's the scariest thing you've done?" Logan asks a while later.

"Besides getting a killer crocodile to chase me?" I tease as I look at him. "Leaving my dad behind. I don't know if he'll be there when I get back, and it terrifies me."

I feel their gazes on me after that admission, making me feel vulnerable.

"We should get some sleep," Wilder says, saving me. "We move again at daylight."

"Will you guys be comfortable enough to sleep?" I ask curiously, since we are on top of each other and scrunched up.

"Eh, we've slept in worse places," Logan replies softly. "Try to get some rest, okay?"

Nodding, I close my eyes and scoot down, trying to get comfortable, but it's useless. My body is one big, giant ache. The inside of the truck lapses into silence, and before long, snores fill the air. Annoyance bubbles up at how easily they passed out, but I try to temper it since they've been taking care of me and helping me as much as they can.

"I'll make sure you get back to your father." Wilder's soft whisper makes my eyes snap open, and I swear I see him leaning into me. "I promise, Carter, you're going to make it back to him."

Self-consciousness raises its ugly head for a moment as I stare at him. I'm always so strong and sure of myself. I've been in situations others would only have nightmares of and come out alive, but as I look at his face, I allow some of my vulnerability to come through. "If I don't, please tell him I love him."

He covers my hand with his, offering comfort. Despite our differences and the bad blood between us, he doesn't hesitate to give me that. "You can tell him yourself. Now get some sleep, okay?"

"Thank you, Wilder, for helping me and coming in after me. You didn't have to," I tell him as I hold his hand, needing that connection.

"Eh, I just didn't want Ajax to blame me," he teases, and I chuckle, closing my eyes as I relax as much as I can. "We're in this together, Carter. You don't need to thank us. You saved us down there in that cave, so let us return the favor."

Nodding, I clutch his hand like a lifeline. "Can you keep talking until I fall asleep? Part of me is terrified I'm going to wake up in that cave."

It isn't something I want to admit, but the terror is there. The moment I woke up alone and in pain will be ingrained in me for life.

"Did you ever hear about the time I got drunk when we were in a cabin in Alaska and had to fight off a bear?" I smile as he launches into this elaborate, soft whisper of a story, and my brain finally shuts down enough to allow me to rest.

I have a fitful sleep. Every time my body unconsciously turns, pain flares up my leg. It isn't as bad as before, but it's unexpected and wakes me for a bit.

Sometime later, when something rocks the truck, I groan, my eyelids feeling heavy as I force them open and look around. Everyone else is snoring, but I definitely felt something. Grabbing the light that's near me on low, I crank it up and press it against the foggy window, trying to peer outside.

Was it a jaguar or a falling branch?

The light reflects back, however, and I struggle to see past the glass. Did I imagine it?

Frowning, I put the light down and glance around at the others. They are still sleeping, no one else seems to have felt it, so it has to be me. My other hand is still clutched in Wilder's, and I focus on that as I try to get comfortable again, when something smashes into the truck. The force spins it, and I bolt upright.

The others do the same. "What is that?"

"What's happening?"

Their voices blend together as I stare out of the window, searching for the source. "Shh," I order, and they fall silent. "That wasn't an accident or a falling branch." I turn to Wilder. "I think it followed us."

"How would it even do that?" he mutters, but he looks worried as well.

"I don't know, but something with the strength to spin a truck?" I mutter as I turn my head to look out of the window, only to freeze. The rain has eased slightly, just a small sheet, but under the shelter of the trees I see glowing eyes staring back at me.

Way, who's in the front, must see it at the same time I do. "Holy fuck!" he yells. "Yeah, it definitely found us."

I pull the gun out as it stares at us. "What do we do?"

"Stay in the truck," Wilder commands. "It's hitting it for a reason. It knows we are here, but it can't get to us."

At that moment, it rams us again, as if sensing what we are talking about. The truck spins from the force, and when it finally stops, Logan is gagging, and Rick is on his knees. "I'm a tasty snack, but stop, okay? The only one who gets to eat me is Carter."

I blink incredulously at him despite the situation.

"Are you sure the engine won't start?" Wilder asks, never taking his eyes off the creature, which is now circling us, no doubt looking for a way in.

"Nah, it's fucked," Aiy replies. "We are sitting ducks."

"If we go out there, we will be worse off," Logan says. "We just need to stay where we are and pretend that thing isn't acting like we are

Happy Meals trapped behind bars. This is some *Jurassic Park* shit right here, and I always made fun of them in that scene."

"Me too, but I like to think I'd be more of a Big Mac," I remark, and he reaches over and high-fives me before we fall silent. The darkness outside makes it hard to see the croc, and we are all turning and craning our necks to keep it in view.

"Does anyone see it?" Way murmurs.

"Not back here," I respond, eyes straining as I press closer to the window just as it smacks into it. Yelping, I tumble back into Wilder's side as the glass splinters like a spiderweb, but luckily it doesn't shatter.

"I think it wants in," I mutter. "Why do I suddenly feel like a tin of sardines ready to be popped open and eaten?"

"I'll eat you," Rick retorts, but I ignore him as the creature hits the other door, right at Wilder's side. We all whirl around as it rams the truck again and then again, when suddenly, huge teeth spear through the metal door. Rick yells and scrambles back into Logan, his arm and leg bleeding from where he was grazed.

The teeth yank out of the metal, and we stare in wide-eyed horror as it chomps through again, yanking until the door is torn off. The cold, rainy air hits us as the creature appears in the gap, its eyes locked on us, and then it lunges inside.

Wilder shouts, dragging Rick back and slamming his booted feet into the creature's snout. He must hit something because it hisses and slides away.

"We need to get away from this thing. It will come back," I warn.

As if summoned by my words, it appears in the gap again, so I reach back, open my door, and tumble out. The others follow as I stumble to my feet, pain flaring through my body as Wilder slams the door in its face as it dives across the back seat.

"Run into the trees!" Wilder roars. "We'll try to lose it!"

Just as he says that, it bursts from the truck and lands in front of us. We clamber backward as it hisses and tries to keep us in view. I don't look where I'm going, not wanting to take my eyes off that thing. I simply back up, but my foot catches on a rock, and I almost fall, letting out a pained yell, and its head snaps to me.

My eyes widen, and I throw myself to the side just as it lunges. I narrowly avoid being eaten as the guys shout my name. I crawl backward before getting to my feet as it turns to them, hissing and snapping as they move back, the distance between us growing.

"Carter!" Wilder snaps, and I look at him over the creature. "Run now!"

Déjà vu fills me for a moment.

"Get out of there!" I tell him as it snaps at them again, moving closer as I pick up a bag that fell from the truck and sling it on. A flare falls and hits the ground, and I groan as I bend to pick it up, only to freeze when I hear them yell.

My head jerks up, and I meet the creature's eyes as it turns.

"Not again, motherfucker," I mutter. Grabbing the flare, I light it up, drawing it to me once more. "Run, we'll meet in the trees or at the beach!" I turn and sprint as fast as I can into the jungle.

I hear it behind me. It smacks into trees, the only thing slowing it down as it races after me. I stumble over roots but keep running, only glancing back to see it catching up. It's fast, moving quickly on all fours, wrapping its teeth around anything that gets in its way.

The guys' yells are far off as I almost fall, focusing on running. I feel blood trickling down my leg, but I ignore it, lurching forward as it suddenly latches onto my bag and drags me back. My scream fills the air as I'm tossed like a rag doll. I'm airborne for a moment before I come down hard, rolling to a stop against a tree. The flare burns brightly between us as I blink and lift my head to see the croc coming toward me.

Pulling the gun out, I climb to my knee, my bad leg extended so I don't put weight on it as I take a deep breath. I blow it out as I turn off the safety with my thumb, then I squeeze the trigger, remembering my dad's training. The sound it makes as it hits the croc's flesh is audible, but it doesn't even make it pause as it moves closer.

I fire again . . . and then again.

Shells fly back and hit my cheek as my arms shake. The bullets are hitting it, but it doesn't stop.

I keep firing, needing to kill this bastard.

My eyes widen as I hit one of its eyes, but all that does is enrage it, and I have to roll out of the way at the last moment when it lunges for me again, snapping in the space I just was.

I aim once more, but the chamber is empty, and when its head turns, I know I'm toast. I can't outrun or kill it.

I'm dead fucking meat, but that doesn't mean I'm going down without a fight. As it jumps at me, I roll forward, grabbing the flare, then I slam it into its other eye before rolling away, keeping hold of the light as it roars.

"Why won't you fuck off?" I snap at it. "Just fuck off and go back to eating . . ." My words trail off as I recall the body I found.

All the skeletons.

Did this thing eat them?

What the fuck?

"I'm not fucking dying here, you hear me?" I scream at it. "Fuck you and fuck this island!"

A blur shoots past me, and I fall back on my ass as there's a roar and a hiss. Clambering to my feet, I see a black blur ripping at the creature's neck as the croc tosses its head, trying to dislodge it.

The jaguar.

It's attacking the creature, and I swear for a moment those glowing eyes meet mine and tell me to run. I turn and take off, leaving them behind, the stick and gun still in my hands. The rain seems to increase, blinding me as I pant and try to move faster despite the pain in my leg, and I don't see the slope of the hill until I tumble over the edge of it.

A scream erupts from my mouth as my back hits the ground. The rainfall has turned it into a mudslide, so I flip and roll all the way down, scrambling to grab anything. I try my best to keep hold of the gun and light, but when I hit something hard at the bottom, my hands spasm and my vision goes dark.

The very last thing I see is the flare dying out and plunging me into darkness once more.

# THIRTY-FOUR
## WAY

**W**e need to find Maeve. We ran off into the jungle when she did, but that thing followed her. We trace our steps back to the truck. It's still wrecked, but we manage to grab some stuff as Wilder shines his flashlight around, picking up their tracks.

"They went that way. Spread out and remain in shouting distance at all times, okay?" he orders. We could leave her, but not a single one of us would ever do that. She needs us, and we need to find her.

Spreading out in a line, we head into the forest, careful to keep our noise to a minimum in case the creature is lurking somewhere nearby. I swear I hear a scream in the distance, but the rain soon swallows it. Wilder and I share a look as Aiy moves closer to me. All of us are worried and terrified. We walk for a while, following the broken branches and marks in the muddy ground until it starts to disappear and we have nothing to go on.

Whatever trail she left is long gone, thanks to the rain, but we try our best.

"Maeve!" Aiyaret yells, and I pull him closer, covering his mouth as his eyes widen.

"Shh, that thing is still around," I murmur.

He nods, and I release him, but his head is still turned to me, his hair soaked and eyes worried as he leans into my side. "We have to find her. She's hurt."

"I know, and we will," I promise, but he looks so concerned. I lift my hand and cup his face. "I promise we'll find her, alright? Maeve is smart. She'll be okay."

"What if she's injured?"

"More than before?" I scoff as I pull him closer by the neck. "She's capable. Trust in that, okay?"

He closes his eyes. "I'm scared, Way," he admits. "I have this horrible feeling none of us are going to make it off this island alive. We never should have come here."

"There's no point regretting our actions, babe. It's done, and we are here. We can't let the past control us." His eyelids flutter open, and he meets my gaze. "I'll always protect you. You believe that, right? I will always keep you safe."

"I know," he croaks, "but what if something happens to you—" He hiccups over the word, a tear sliding down his cheek. "I don't think I could survive without you."

"Of course you can." I smile, but it fades. "Aiy, you can do anything. You are so much stronger than you know. You don't need me."

"I do." He fists my jacket as he looks up at me. "I need you, Way. I can't do this without you, so don't be a hero and get hurt, okay?"

"Okay," I murmur softly as I press my forehead to his. "I'm scared too," I admit. "But we are going to get out of here, and when we're old, it will just be a story we tell."

"To your kids," he murmurs.

"No, to our kids," I correct, my heart hammering despite where we are and what's happening. "You're my future, Aiy. Okay? I'm never leaving you, not here and not then. It's us. Do you believe me?"

His eyes meet mine for a moment, and I swear they glance down to my lips. Something moves through me—something I've never told him about and never will. I will never be someone who hurts or uses Aiy like everyone else has. He needs a best friend, and that's what I am and will always be.

"I do," he murmurs. "We'll make it out together?" he asks, his chest rising rapidly, and I frown.

"Of course, together," I promise. "It will be okay—" I freeze as he presses his lips to my cheek in a soft, chaste kiss.

"Okay, then let's get moving. I want to go home." He pulls away, and it's like the kiss never happened, but my cheek burns from his touch. It was such an innocent gesture, but it rocked me to my core. He moves back into line, and I keep glancing at him before I focus on where I'm walking.

I remind myself we are looking for Maeve.

A roar rocks the earth, and we freeze, sharing a look.

It was the creature, and it sounded close.

Too close.

"Maeve," I murmur at the same time as Wilder. Forgetting all about our hesitation, we run into the jungle, following that roar.

The earth seems to shake from it, and I keep Aiyaret behind me as we burst into a clearing, my heart pounding in terror at what we might find. As I search the dark, though, all I see is turned-up mud and slide marks.

It was here, but now it isn't, and the world around us seems to fall deathly silent. Wilder slips from the jungle like a ghost, his finger to his lips, then he points in a direction farther away from us. I scan the area, straining my eyes, and see the slide marks leading away.

Did it leave?

Why?

I get his message though. Logan and Rick emerge, and we silently move closer, freezing when we see the gun lying carelessly in the mud. Maeve had it, and there was no way she would let it go. Rick scoops it up, his eyes wide and worried as he looks at Wilder like a child demanding comfort.

Wilder's expression is grim, however, and even my stomach rolls at the implication. There's an abrupt tug on my arm, and I spin to see Logan pointing over the brim of a small hill to the left. I tread over and carefully walk along the edge, unsure what he's trying to show me, but then I notice it.

Hand and feet marks, followed by what looks like slide indentations are etched down the slope. Wilder's flashlight joins mine, and we search the bottom until our light catches on something big and unmoving—a body.

She's covered in mud and being rained on, but it's Maeve.

Rick goes to throw himself down the hill, but Wilder stops him, eyeing me. The message is clear—keep him here in case she's dead. Nodding, I point at Aiy, who has tears dripping from his eyes, and then to Rick and Logan. It's clear they understand, even if they hate it. Wilder and I carefully lower onto our sides and slide down the hill. My feet and hands slip in the deep mud, causing me to descend faster than I would like. I land on my ass at the bottom, but I ignore it and hurry to Maeve, dropping to my knees at her side. She's facing away from us, her bad leg bent, and for a moment, she's too still.

Wilder is beside me, and we share another look before he props up his flashlight and carefully turns her over. A whine leaves her throat, and relief almost makes me collapse before I get a look at her face. It's pale, and blood slides down her cheeks like raindrops.

Lifting my flashlight to give Wilder a better view, I watch as he examines her and finds an epic cut on her head. It's bleeding, and there isn't much we can do about it, but he checks her pulse and breathing then nods.

She's alive, but for how long?

Who knows what damage has been done? We need to get somewhere safe and dry to assess the extent of her injuries.

Handing Wilder my flashlight, I slide my arms under her, the mud making it easier, and carefully lift her as I stand. I eye the hill, the others watching from above, and realize I won't make it back up with her.

"There." Wilder's voice is quiet, and I see him pointing to the left, where the hill tapers off into the jungle. "We will meet them there."

I hesitate. The idea of leaving not only Aiy up there, but the others as well with that thing about, terrifies me.

We don't have much choice, though, so I incline my head and carefully pick my way through the mud as he conveys the message. My boots slip, and I try not to jostle her as much as I can. With each bumpy step, she lets out a tiny groan that stabs daggers into my fragile heart.

She looks so small and weak right now.

How much can one person endure?

Every time there's danger, she throws herself into it to protect us and comes out just a little worse for wear. If we don't get her help soon, she'll die on this island.

Nervously waiting at the bottom of the ridge, I turn my back to shelter her from the rain even though she's already drenched. It's pointless, but it's all I can do.

I see blood dripping down her face, carving a path over her beautiful features.

"Is she okay?" Logan's hurried question reaches me as he slides to my side. His hands flutter over her uselessly as he looks at Wilder for answers.

"She's unconscious. She hit her head. We need to get somewhere dry and safe to check her wounds," he murmurs as Rick appears.

"Is she alive?" he asks frantically.

Sighing, I hold her closer when a jacket is suddenly draped over her and tucked up under her chin, protecting her from the rain. My head jerks up, and I meet Aiy's worried gaze. "We should move now, get some distance between us and it, then find somewhere to let her rest."

"You'll be cold," I scold, but he shakes his head.

"I'll be fine. She needs it more. Come on." I've never heard him bark orders before, but we listen, even Wilder, silently following him through the almost pitch-black jungle. It's not advisable to move at night, but we don't have much choice.

We walk until the rain stops, something we are all grateful for, but Maeve shivers in my arms, and she's way too pale. I worry about what that means, so when the sun rises, and Wilder deems it safe to make camp for a few hours on a small section of land protected on one side by big trees, I let the others work around us while I continue to hold her.

I lower my voice and lean closer to her, my words just for her. "Stay with us, okay? You're going to be okay. We've got you. Just keep fighting. It's what you do Maeve—fight."

"She'll be okay," Rick says as he comes to my side, his eyes on her. "She's Maeve fucking Carter, after all."

I nod, but deep inside, I'm worried. Our bodies can only handle so much.

# THIRTY-FIVE

# LOGAN

**W**e managed to set up windbreakers to protect us from the harsh gusts. The rain has stopped, but who knows for how long. We started a fire and got our bed rolls out, wrapping them around her after Wilder treated her head wound. He said the cut is deep, and she might even have a concussion. He looks concerned, especially when she doesn't wake up when he prods the wound. He also inspects her leg and gives her a shot of something, but from the tightening around his eyes, it's clear he's very worried.

Wrapping my hands around the steel mug, I blow on the water, watching her through the steam.

"When was the first time you met Maeve?" I ask curiously. "Mine was at the Red Bull awards. You guys didn't want to go to the after-party, but I went anyway, and she was there, surrounded by people. Her laugh was so loud, it caught my attention, and she looked happy. I had no idea who she was at the time. The next day, I noticed she'd signed with Ajax, and, well, the rest is history."

"Mine was online. Does that count?" Rick asks. "I was scrolling on our night flight back from Peru and found her channel. I watched her for hours. The first video was her jumping from a hot-air balloon and doing backflips. She looked like she had no cares in the world."

"Or was batshit insane," Wilder scoffs.

"The first time I met her was at Venture with Wilder, when Ajax tried to convince us to let her join our team. She'd just met with him, and she stomped out. She was glaring at Wilder, and they argued. She didn't even notice me"—Way smiles—"but she made an impression, considering the way she went toe-to-toe with Wilder."

"Mine was at Venture too." Aiyaret moves closer to Way as he looks at her. "The one I told you about. I heard about her from you guys and saw her online, but it was my first time meeting her. She wasn't loud or angry. She was . . . kind."

"It's like she knows what each of us needs," I say then look at Wild. "When did you meet her?"

For a moment, I don't think he'll answer, but then he speaks. "The one she will remember is at Venture when we argued."

"What do you remember? Why would it be different from what Maeve recollects?" I frown, unsure what he means.

"I met her years before that." My eyes widen. He never mentioned knowing her before Venture. "I didn't know her name back then. We were strangers. It was only years later, when I met her at Venture, that I learned it."

"What? When? How did you meet?" Rick asks as he shuffles closer, propping his chin on his hands.

Wilder sighs, looking at Maeve. "It was brief. Do you remember when we went skiing and there was that avalanche, and I was trapped in a cabin for a few days with all those strangers who had been in the restaurant?"

I nod, and he looks from her to the fire.

"She was there. She'd just come in from the slopes. Her face was red, and she was covered in snow. When it happened, she stayed calm and helped people who were scared. She made them laugh and lightened everyone's mood. I kept to myself after helping out, so I thought she didn't notice me, but that night, she came over, sat by my side, and told me it would be okay. I got so mad and told her I wasn't scared and to leave me alone. She said, 'Hey, it's okay to be scared. I am, but you have to have hope too.' I was scared because you guys were out on the slopes, and I didn't know what had happened to you, but I wouldn't admit it. I was prickly and rude, yet she stayed at my side all night. We didn't really talk, just sat side by side. It was the longest night of my life. I was terrified for you, but somehow, she lessened my fear, and when we were rescued the next day, she just left, and you guys were safe and sound."

"You never talked about what happened there," I murmur softly. I remember that night. We were so fucking terrified he'd been lost in the snow. It was chaos, and when he walked out of the snowed in main building the next day, I'd never felt so much relief.

"I forgot for a while. She was just a passing stranger, one who'd loaned me a shoulder without complaint. When I met her again, I recalled who she was, but she didn't recognize me, so I guess it pissed me off," he admits.

Wilder's eyes soften as they land on Maeve, and I see something in those depths that surprises me. I think he's finally stopped fighting his attraction, and his anger has faded, leaving only the truth behind.

He cares for her.

I've lived with Rick and Wilder nearly all my life, and I have never seen that tenderness in his eyes. He never lets anyone close enough for him to care about them, always worried about protecting us. Wilder has his reasons, though, just like we all do.

"Do you still hate her?" I ask.

"I don't think I ever really did," he divulges, which is something. "She just—"

"Called you on your shit?" Way laughs, making Wilder crack a smile.

"Yeah, and pushed my buttons. She made me feel things I had no right feeling. I need to be strong and calm to keep our family together. I felt unbalanced when I was with her, and I blamed her for that."

"It isn't all on you, brother," Rick tells him. "It isn't your job to take responsibility for us. You take too much on yourself . . . always have. You are allowed to feel things, date, and be happy. You are allowed to live for yourself, not just for us."

His gaze sweeps over us and then moves back to her before he rubs his head. "We'll see once we're out of this. Right now, you need me to get you off this island."

There's no point in arguing when Wilder has made up his mind, so we slip into silence. I don't know what the others are thinking about, but I'm thinking about her. I wonder if I'll ever hear her laugh again. Suddenly, Aiy's voice jerks me from my thoughts, and I turn to stare at him. It's unlike him to talk a lot, but he seems oddly fond of her.

"She doesn't even hesitate," he murmurs. "When there's danger, she throws herself at it, despite whatever it means for her well-being, to keep us safe. Her first instinct is to run at it and save us. We were wrong about her. I was wrong about her. She was always one of us, and I worry she'll never wake up for us to tell her that."

"She will," Way promises as he takes Aiy's hand and kisses his head. "We have to believe that."

"Maeve Carter would never let something like a head injury win," Wilder states calmly. "She will wake up, and when she does, we can tell her ourselves."

He sounds so confident, but I see the truth in his eyes. I don't say anything, though, knowing Aiy needs comfort.

Wilder moves away, keeping watch, while the others go to settle down for the night, and I set my lukewarm mug to the side and scoot closer to her.

While the others are distracted, I take her cold hand, warming it between mine as I lean in, my words just for her. "I lost my parents when I was young," I tell her. "I can barely remember them now, to be honest. I used to struggle to remember the color of their eyes, their scents, the way they would laugh . . . . It disappears after a while, but I remember loving them, and when they died, they left a hole in my heart that never healed. I distract myself and pretend I'm fine, but deep inside, I'm still that kid in the oversized big black suit, watching his parents' coffins being lowered into the ground. So, Maeve, don't you do that to me again, okay? I can't lose anyone else. I can't attend any more funerals." I kiss the back of her hand. "We need you. We need your insanity, and we need you to call Wilder on his shit, sooth Aiy, and play with us, so wake your ass up, Carter. If you do, I promise I won't let you explore alone anymore. We'll be your family who explores with you while your dad can't."

Blowing out a breath, I sit back and make myself comfortable at her side, her hand in mine. I feel eyes on me, but I avoid them, hiding the wetness in my own. I don't want to upset them anymore or stress them out.

We all have our pain, from Way's brother to Aiyaret's past, Wilder's guilt, and Maeve's dad. We are all damaged toys.

# THIRTY-SIX

# WILDER

**M**aeve woke up this morning. She was groggy and confused, but she came around enough to have something to drink and eat before going back to sleep. She couldn't seem to fight it, and that's probably not a good sign, but there isn't much more I can do for her here. I don't say that of course, nor do I share how I'm worried that she's pale and burning up. All I can do is keep going, keep giving them hope. It's my duty as a leader.

"I'm worried. Shouldn't she be awake by now?" Aiy asks as he looks at her sleeping form while we pack up. The storm isn't giving in. If anything, it's getting worse, but we need to push forward.

"She probably needs the rest. Her body has been through a lot. She's waking every now and again, which is good and all we can hope for. We need to focus on getting to the beach and safety so she can be treated before infection sets in," I explain. "We'll take turns carrying her until we get to the shore. Once we get there, everything will be okay." It's a lie, but one they need to hear. All but Way cling to it as I turn away. He looks from her to me, a knowing gleam in his eyes.

I busy myself, and he crouches before me as I shove things into my bag, his voice lowered. "How bad is it?"

"I don't know what you mean," I force out.

"Wilder, I'm your best friend. You can't lie to me. Aiy cares for her, so tell me . . . how bad is it?" he inquires tightly, his hands clenching my bag to stop my movements.

Biting my lip, I debate whether or not I should tell him the truth, but honestly, I'm tired and scared. "I think she has an infection, maybe even sepsis. The wound on her head isn't serious, but coupled with her other injuries, it could be life-threatening. We need to get her to a hospital now. She's strong, but the drugs I have won't help her for long."

He stares at me before blowing out a breath. "Okay then." Standing, he claps his hands. "Let's get going, losers. First one to the beach wins an all-expense paid weekend trip from Wilder."

That gets them moving, and I thank him with a nod as I head back over to Maeve. She groans as I lean down and touch her cheek. "Time to move," I murmur softly.

Her eyes open slowly. "Wilder?"

"Shh, it's me. Just rest, your body needs it. Let me do this for once, Carter," I offer as I scoop her up into my arms. She groans when it hurts her bad leg, and I try to cradle her head as much as I can.

"I can walk," she complains lazily.

"I know you can. Just let me feel like a hero and carry you though, okay?" I implore.

"Fine, but only because I know you like to win," she grumbles, pressing her face against my chest. "Your heart is beating fast." Her head tilts back as I look down at her, a smile curving her lips. "Is it because I'm so close?"

"You wish, Carter," I scoff, even as I hold her closer. Under the blood and sweat, I still smell her scent, making me think thoughts I shouldn't, and damn, it makes my heart beat faster. When she reaches up and lays her hand on my chest, my heart kicks at her touch, and I freeze, my eyes widening.

"I kind of do," she admits, and I have to remind myself it's the drugs talking. "You know, if we didn't hate each other so much, Wilder, I think being loved by you would be something amazing. In another life, maybe I'd really like exploring with you."

Her words crack something open within me, and I press my forehead to hers, lending her my strength. "Why not this life, Carter? Don't tell me you're giving up already. Are you really going to let me win?"

Chuckling, she drops her hand. "Never," she replies.

"Good, rest." Before I can stop myself, I press my lips to her forehead, soaking in her warmth to give me the strength to keep moving. I've thrived on our fighting, our competitiveness pushing me to be better, faster, and stronger, and now I need it more than ever.

Lifting my head, I notice the others are giving us privacy, and I clear my throat, my voice sounding odd when I speak. "Let's keep moving. We need to get to the beach."

They nod, and then we are off, our boots sinking into the waterlogged earth. The heat hasn't let up, even if the rain has paused for a while, but the drops fall from the canopy, soaking us as we force our way through the jungle.

All of us know what price we will pay if we fall behind.

We hike for days, only stopping to eat and get an hour or two of sleep. Maeve doesn't get stronger as the days pass, but she doesn't get weaker either, which is something. She sleeps a lot, only walking for an hour or so every day before growing exhausted, but we are all too happy to carry her, even if she hates it. Honestly, though, it's quicker, but I worry about how rapidly she will decline. The storm seems to have passed, or so we hope, but it's hard to tell if or when another will hit. We haven't seen our crocodile friend in days, which is good news, but I'm on edge. Things are going too well. After everything we have endured, can our luck truly be looking up?

I don't believe in good fortune, so I keep walking until we finally break out of the foliage and onto the shoreline.

"We did it," Rick whispers, and then he whoops, "We did it!"

I nod, not counting my chickens yet. "Let's set up shelter. Way and Aiyaret, get on that. Rick and Logan, I want you in the ocean, but not too deep, to see if you can catch something to eat. I'll work on getting fresh water and setting a signal for the team." When everyone groans, I arch an eyebrow, and they hurry off to do as they are told. Carrying Maeve over to the closest tree, I prop her head up with a backpack.

"Just shout if something happens, okay? We'll be here," I promise as I crouch in front of her.

She nods, moving slightly, and I reach out. "What is it?"

"I'm going to perv on them." She nods, moving so she can see around me, and I glance back to see Rick and Logan with their shirts off as they wade into the blue ocean. Scoffing, I look at her and shake my head, but I smile. If she can joke, then she's okay.

"Have fun with that," I tell her as I stand.

"Feel free to take off your shirt if you're feeling left out," she teases, "but I have to tell you, your brother is built." She reaches out, making grabby motions with her hands. "I want to bury my face between his pecs."

"Dear God." Turning away, I get started on a signal, all while keeping my shirt on, thank you very much.

Within an hour, we have shelter, water, and are grilling fish, as well as have signals set up on the beach. We sit under ferns on the edge of the jungle, enjoying the shade. Being in the sun would exhaust and dehydrate us, and we already risk being snuck up on by that thing, so while the fish cooks, Way and I lay some traps and warning systems. By the time we are done, we're hungry and sweating, and I collapse next to Aiy with a sigh as he meticulously picks the bones out of a fish. I hold my hand out, expecting him to pass it to me, but he turns and stands, feeding it to Maeve. I gawk, and she winks at me as I shake my head. For someone who's so stubborn and independent, she sure does like being waited on.

"I could really get used to this service," she teases around bites. "Maybe I should get chomped on more often."

"Or get a butler," I scoff.

"In the buff? Good idea." She nods as she takes a bite from Aiy.

"I volunteer!" Logan yells, making her grin. She shakes her head as Aiy offers her another bite.

"Eat," I order in a tone that brooks no argument. Her eyes narrow, and I wait, but then she grumbles something about asshats under her breath before she eats. I nod in approval, and then she glares at me like a kitten, only this kitten knows how to kill me. She's still adorable though.

By the time everyone has finished, Maeve is asleep again, and Aiy and Way lay her down in the shelter and cover her while I check the satellite phone. The distress signal went out, so now it's just a waiting game, and hopefully they will find us in time. With nothing else to do, I watch her sleep, check her pulse as often as I can, and try to make her comfortable.

By nightfall, she still hasn't woken up, and everyone is worried. Logan tries to start a game, but no one wants to play, so they eventually sleep as well while I keep watch. The fire we built burns brightly enough to scare off any other predators, apart from the creature who attacked us in the first place.

There's a beep, and I search around until I realize it's coming from Maeve's bag. I hesitate, but I don't want to wake her, so I open it and find her camera beeping as it uploads. She must finally have a signal. I should put it away, but it's frozen on a recording. Sparing her a look, I give them my back and load it, keeping it quiet.

It's a message to her dad, and it breaks my heart. I scroll through her footage, seeing snippets and clips of her adventure here. She's smiling in the ones before, the sunlight bathing her, and I click them at random, watching the journey she took.

She truly is a force of nature—fearless and skilled.

I scroll further back and pull a video up at random. She's sticking her tongue out, and when she turns the camera, I see Ajax talking and walking in front of her. Grinning, I watch her mock him behind his back, and when he turns, his eyes narrowed, he yells her name. She laughs and races away with the camera.

Chuckling, I spare her a glance as I keep scrolling, picking another one at random.

She's somewhere icy and wearing a hat, goggles, and a big jacket. Her nose and cheeks are red, but she's grinning widely as she looks into the camera.

"Hey, Dad, how did the doctor's appointment go? I'm sorry I couldn't be there, but you know how it is. We both know you would rather be here with me." She pans the camera around to show a mountain completely covered in snow, and there isn't another soul in sight. "Apparently it's the gnarliest slide ever, but we shall see." She grins at the camera.

"I miss you so much, Dad. I wish you could be here with me. I always do, but I'm doing this for you. I'll leave your name everywhere, so you'll see it with me." Her smile fades a little. "I'm sorry, Dad. I didn't know what to say when you told me. I'm sorry you're hurting and it stole your dream, but I love you. I will always love you, and whether I'm across the world, trekking through jungles, or in your living room, enjoying the crackling fire, we'll always be together. My adventures are yours, and I'll love them all for you. I love you, Dad, so much. We'll get through this together. See you when I'm home. It will be soon, I promise." She's gone, and I glance back, her camera falling into my lap.

I could hear her heartbreak and loneliness in every word despite her smile. I guess I never realized Maeve Carter was struggling before, so intent on hating her. She's looking for a place to belong, just like us.

She groans, and I hide her camera, turning to her just as her eyes open. "Hey, are you okay?" I ask.

"I need to pee so badly," she admits, making me grin.

"Come on." I help her up, and her hand shakes in mine, something I don't like. I guide her behind the nearest trees so she can have some privacy, and she looks at me.

"I can pull my own pants down," she mutters when I just stare.

"Carter, I think we are past boundaries now," I retort, but her eyebrow arches, so I turn my back. "I'm not going any farther. You're hurt."

"Perv," she grumbles. I hear her fumbling, and then she groans and hisses, no doubt struggling to crouch since her leg is bad.

"Lean on me," I murmur softly.

She hesitates but finally rests her head on my lower back, leaning against me as she does her business. When she stands, she rests against me for a moment more, her head on my shoulder as she pants. "I fucking hate being weak."

"You've never been weak a moment in your life, Carter, not even now," I tell her, and I turn, catching her as she stumbles at my sudden movement. She looks up from the safety of my arms, her nails digging into my skin. I let her leave her physical mark on me, since she's already left a mental one.

My entire life has revolved around Carter for years, whether I was hating her or competing with her. It's strange how easily my feelings went from hate to something . . . more.

"Liar," she whispers. "Look at me, I'm useless right now—"

"Never," I interject, cupping her chin and tilting her head back until she meets my eyes. "Even injured, tired, and smelly"—she huffs, and I grin—"you're the strongest person I know. Look at how far you've made it. No one else I know would have endured what you have. You brave, foolish, perfect woman."

We both freeze as the words slip out, the warm darkness of the jungle closing around us, and my eyes lower, tracing her lips.

"You hate me." I watch her mouth form the words, and I can't help but swallow, wanting to feel them against mine.

"You hate me too," I respond softly.

We don't pull away, instead leaning closer like magnets are drawing us together. Years of fighting, of butting heads, all just . . . leave in this moment as my eyes meet hers to see her uncertainty.

"Let's forget the world for a bit, forget our company and competition and all the reasons why we hate each other, and how about we just . . . do what we both want? How about we love each other for one stolen moment?" I murmur.

"One moment?" she asks.

"Maybe two," I admit as I tilt my head down. "Say yes."

From one heartbeat to the next, she tortures me, but then she speaks, her voice small and quiet. "Yes."

My lips are on hers before she can second-guess herself or either of us can question this. I swallow her little gasp as my tongue invades her mouth. It isn't a soft kiss—no, it's a battle, a fight for dominance as her fingertips dig into me, and I back her up against the tree.

My hand cradles her injured head before it can hit the tree trunk, and

I lift her with my free hand to relieve the pressure from her wounded leg so all she feels and tastes is me, not pain.

Deepening the kiss, I press her back into the bark, and she lets out a little moan that drives me crazy. I pull away, breaking the kiss. "Make that noise again," I demand roughly. "Fuck, I'd give anything for you to make that fucking noise again."

"Make me," she retorts breathlessly, sass in her tone.

Grunting, I slam my lips onto hers, kissing her like our lives depend on it, and she finally emits that noise. It vibrates through my body, making me tremble. My cock hardens despite how hurt she is, and my desire rivals the storm that hit us, but then I remember where we are and her injuries and I slow it down. She keeps up with me until we break apart, both of us panting.

"Two moments," she murmurs, licking her lips, and I nod, ordering my hands to let her go, but they won't listen.

"Maybe three." I press my lips to hers again, tasting her smile.

This time, she pulls away first, leaning trustingly into my hold. "They'll come looking for us."

"Let them. They would be doing the same thing," I admit, knowing I'm not wrong. I've seen the way they look at her. I can't blame them. One simple yes from her turned me into a demanding dog who's pawing at her.

"Who said I would let them?" she asks, arching a brow.

"Wouldn't you?" I ask curiously. Surprisingly, it doesn't bother me. I've always shared everything I have. It's my duty as a big brother, but I never realized that would extend to someone I wanted. With her, though, it seems . . . normal.

"I guess they'll have to find out." She gives me a quick peck that has my eyes widening as she slips from my embrace and limps back to our camp.

My hand drifts up and traces my lips. She claimed them for her own.

I can't even remember a kiss that wasn't hers. Maeve Carter has ruined me.

Maybe she did the very first moment I met her, I was just too hard-headed to understand.

# THIRTY-SEVEN
## MAEVE

The sun burns brightly, as if the storm that battered the island never was. It glints off the bright blue ocean, creating a perfect paradise—not to mention the shirtless men working on the beach, giving me an amazing view. All I need is a cocktail and I could almost imagine I was on vacation. *Almost.*

I glance down, no longer putting it off as I remove the bandage to look at my leg. I keep telling them I'm fine, but it's a lie. I'm hot, my stomach is aching, I feel sick, and my skin is sweaty, but not from the heat. It means something's wrong, and looking at my leg, I know why.

It's infected. I can smell and see it.

I should tell them, but there's nothing they can do. We're running low on medicine, and without a hospital, I'm fucked, but making them worry will accomplish nothing. Help is on the way. I just need to hold on. I don't want to stress or hinder them more than I already am.

I hear a noise and cover my leg, leaning back like I was resting as Rick appears. He sits at my side, sweaty and smiling. "How are you doing, cupcake?"

"Ah, you know, making the most of this five-star resort cabana," I joke, and he chuckles, leaning back on his elbows and looking out at his team before he nudges my good leg. I turn to see him wiggling his eyebrows.

"You know, I was taking a leak last night, and I saw something interesting." His tone is filled with amusement, and I freeze.

Shit.

His chuckle fills the air, and I feel my cheeks flush, but I refuse to be ashamed. Rick sobers, but he's still smiling. "I won't tell." He winks, and he's quiet for a moment. "Don't break his heart, Maeve Carter."

I gape at him, and his smile widens. "Wilder doesn't let anyone in, not all the way, not even us. He's always felt this . . . pressure to prove himself to everyone, protect us, and keep us happy. He never takes anything for himself, yet he took you. Read into that what you will."

I process his words, looking at Wilder, who is focused on the rocks as he realigns the signal. His expression is one of concentration, even as Logan chases Way around him. He's always so in control, the capable, dependable one. Is that because he feels like he has to be?

"We hate each other," I say.

My gaze moves to Rick. He's watching me with a knowing look in his eyes. "Hmm, isn't it strange how close hate can feel to love?"

My eyes flare, and I panic, knowing he sees right through me.

Patting my good leg, he stands and stretches. "I'll get you some water, just think on it." He's gone, and I'm left staring at Wilder, wondering if Rick is right.

Groaning, I close my eyes and must nod off because I wake to Way pressing a canteen against my lips. I drink, and he wipes my mouth before shifting back.

"How are you feeling?" he asks softly.

"Sick of people asking that," I admit, and despite the venom in my tone, he chuckles and sits down opposite me.

He's quiet, and I stare, wondering what he wants. When he glances at Aiyaret, I know. "You were down there with him. Was he . . . Is he okay?"

"What is this, circle time?" I tease, and he tilts his head in confusion. "Never mind. Everyone wants a heart-to-heart with me today, and I can't run away."

"That's probably why. They know you would otherwise," he teases.

"Fine, he's stronger than you think," I tell him, "but if you're worried about Aiyaret, you should ask him, not me."

He nods, hesitating.

"You love him," I state.

His head jerks up, his eyes wide with fear.

"Don't worry, I won't tell him, though it's the worst kept secret in the world. I know neither of you are ready. He's . . . fine, worried about all of you, but especially you. He's a good guy."

"He is." He looks at Aiy, who is glancing over at us, and Way quickly averts his gaze. "He likes you." I remain silent, and he stares at his feet in the sand. "He doesn't like any women, but he likes you. It's surprising."

"Yet you're worried," I surmise. "What, do you think because he tolerates me, he'll fall in love with me and leave you behind?" When he stares at me without answering, I know I'm right. "Idiots, all of you. Men. If you would just talk . . ." Leaning forward, I hide my wince. "Aiyaret isn't going anywhere. Want to know what he was like down there? He was worried about you all the time. Maybe you should ask him why or, better yet, figure out why the thought of him loving me terrifies you."

He looks at me, confusion etched on his features, when Aiyaret appears. "What's going on?"

We both startle, looking up to find him standing above us. I stretch out my good leg. "Oh ,you know, comparing notes on the weather. Aiy, can you do me a favor?"

"Sure, what's up?" he asks.

"Can you find me a nice shell from the beach? I always bring one back. Oh, but don't go alone. Take Way with you." I wink at Way, and he sighs at my clumsy attempt.

"Uh, sure." He glances at Way then me before walking off, and Way grumbles but goes after him.

"They really are pretty together." I sigh as I close my eyes again, hoping no one else wants free therapy. I'm not Dr. Phil.

I slept most of the afternoon, only waking long enough to eat and go to the bathroom, which is a hole in the ground. I'm bone-deep exhausted, so I fall back to sleep as the moon rises, but something wakes me soon after.

I'm groggy and confused. My skin feels hot to the touch, and I'm sweating despite the rough breeze blowing through our makeshift shelter. Frowning, I struggle to sit up. My head aches, but not as bad as my leg. I don't know what woke me. I scan the others, finding all but Rick sleeping. He's facing the jungle, scanning it, so I glance at it and then at the beach.

"Hey, why are you awake?" Rick asks softly, but I keep staring. Something is off out there. Is that what woke me up? "What is it?"

"I don't know," I admit, and I push to my feet. He's by my side in an instant, helping me, then he places his hand on my forehead and hisses.

"You're burning up. Shit, let me get Wilder."

I nod absentmindedly as he heads over to wake his brother.

Stumbling with my bad leg practically dragging behind me, I make it farther onto the shore when Wilder joins me. The others race after me, no doubt woken up by Rick.

"What's going on?" Wilder barks.

"Something is wrong."

He goes to touch me, but I shake my head.

"Not with me. I don't know. I just have this gut feeling, like an alarm bell going off." I don't know how to explain it. It's the same feeling I had when the avalanche happened, that shark snuck up on me, and I went to the doctor's office with my dad. It's there, and I struggle to breathe.

Wilder doesn't dismiss me, scanning the beach for clues. The others spread out next to us. "You think it's here?" Aiyaret asks.

"Maybe," Way grumbles.

I follow their gazes, but for some reason, my attention goes back to the ocean.

Straining my eyes, I finally realize why it looks weird. It's thrashing more than I've ever seen, with big waves crashing out in the darkness. It looks . . . angry.

Just then, lightning cracks across the sky, and we jump. The wind picks up, lashing us, and the water foams angrily over our feet.

The storm rages on around us as ferocity and beauty blend together, and we stand in the midst of it all. The water churns relentlessly, warning us to stay out of its deadly depths as our toes dig into the sand with no other option but to ride it out.

Either we need to make it through this or we'll die here like everyone who previously explored this island.

"What is that?" Rick asks, and we stare as the water pulls back, the tide or something else taking it away. Our feet are still damp from where it just crashed into us, but it doesn't come back. It exposes wet sand and rocks, pulling farther and farther back.

"Tsunami," I whisper, remembering a documentary I saw a few years ago about this very thing. My eyes widen, and I turn to them. "Run!"

It's too late.

I turn toward the ocean to see it barreling straight for us.

A wall of water so high it blocks out the moon races at us. There is no warning, no escape. Wilder grabs me as we rush into the jungle, but as we step into the leafy trees, the water reaches shore.

We can't outrun it.

Wilder throws me toward a tree, and I grip it with my fingers, but the water slams into me and sweeps me off my feet, carrying me away. I hear one of the guys scream before all sound is drowned out except for the roaring of the tsunami.

Saltwater flows over me, pulling me under. I flip and turn with the current, keeping my mouth shut as my training kicks in. Everything happens so quickly that I barely have time to breathe, never mind look for the others.

Something hits my side hard, and I want to scream, but I don't open my mouth because if I do, I'll drown. Paddling in the direction I think is up, I swim hard and break through the surface, gasping and drawing in a breath before I'm pushed under again. This time, a scream erupts as I'm slammed into a tree. It hits my arm, making it go numb, and then I'm above the water. If I'm forced under again, I'm dead.

I swing my head around wildly before I see what I'm looking for, and then I dive under and let the current carry me the way it's going. My arms are out, and when my body slams into the tree, I wrap myself around it with all my might and climb. I manage to get above the water, clinging to the trunk. Every part of me aches and hurts, and my fever still rages on. My bad leg slips, and I press my cheek against the wet trunk, watching the foaming water flow past me.

I see debris in it as well as trees and rocks. A snake lunges for me as it's dragged by, and I search for the others, but they could be anywhere. It separated us when it hit. Breathing slowly, I look up and force myself to climb as fast as I can to the next branch. I sit on it with my back to the trunk, my arms still wrapped around it just in case.

My heart hammers in my chest as I watch the water pass below, flooding the island.

I don't know how long I'm trapped here, but the whole time, all I can think about are the guys. Are they okay? Are they safe? Are they hurt? They are strong and smart, but nature doesn't care about that.

I lean my head back, and my eyelids must close because they open when I jerk to the side. Yelping, I scramble back, almost falling from my perch. The water has settled, moving slower and much lower, as if the waves have retreated. Everything is still waterlogged but nowhere near as deep.

The moon has moved farther across the sky. Fuck, was I out long?

What should I do?

I'm losing time. I need to find them.

Swallowing, I scoot down the branch and look out, straining to hear and see, then I finally catch a voice in the distance.

It has to be them.

Without a second thought, I climb down, but my bad leg slips, and I hit the water with a loud splash. Groaning, I stumble to my feet, grateful nothing was below me that could stab me, but I need to be more careful. I wade through the chest-high flood, limping and stumbling over the uneven ground and debris, all while blindly following that voice.

It grows louder and louder.

"Hello?" I yell before coughing.

It stops for a moment, and I freeze. "Maeve?" someone shouts, and my heart pounds.

Moving faster, I propel myself in the direction of the voice. My eyes strain in the dark, but then I finally see their outlines.

I move faster, dropping to my knee as I trip over something, but I get up and keep going until I can see them.

Logan holds onto a tree with one arm, holding Rick with the other. Rick's eyes are closed and blood drips down his face, his legs floating. "Maeve," he whispers. "Thank God. Thank God. Did you see any of the others?"

"No. Just you," I reply as I move closer, stroking Rick's face. He groans, and I nearly double over with relief.

"He's okay, but he hit his head hard. I can't let go. He won't wake up enough, so I'm trapped," Logan explains in a rush.

Moving past Rick, I grip Logan's head and press my cheek to his. "Shh, it's okay. You did really well. Let's get up into the tree, okay? Once we are safe, we can make a plan to find the others. If we swim or walk without a strategy, we could lose." He nods, and I look at Rick. "Okay, hand him to me while you climb up onto that low branch, and then I'll pass him to you."

We work quickly after that, wanting to get out of the water in case it gets worse again. You never know. He scales the tree swiftly and crouches on the thick branch just above the water, reaching as far down as he can while I hold Rick. His weight tugs me deeper into the water, but I dig my feet into the ground below.

"Okay, hand him over."

My hands slip on Rick's skin, but I keep hoisting, using all my strength. My bad leg screams at me, and my numb arm aches, but I ignore it all.

Grunting under his weight, I manage to get Rick high enough for Logan to grab him under his arms and lift him onto the branch. Breathing heavily, he settles Rick into the crook before leaning down and offering me his hand. "Okay, now you."

"Maeve . . . ," Rick groans, lifting his head and looking at me.

"Here, babe." I wink as I jump and try to reach Logan's hand. My wet palm slips through his grip, so I grit my teeth and try again. My fingers just hit his when something hard and large crashes into me under the water, dragging me down and away.

I hear their yells and a splash, but it's all secondary to a stabbing, burning pain in my arm.

My eyes widen as I stare into the empty orbs of the crocodile. My scream fills the water as it sinks its teeth into my arm and shoulder, rolling us deep into the murky abyss. Water fills my lungs, and I know I need to get free or I'll die. I frantically search the water until I see a sharp rock. I reach for it with my other arm, screaming as the monster yanks on the limb in its maw. I finally grasp it, and with a victorious yell, I swing my arm up, smashing the rock into its face. It gnaws on my arm, so I try again. This time, I hit its nose, and its jaws open as it recoils. I drive the rock deeper before pushing to the surface.

I choke as I splash and scream, blood filling the water around me.

"Carter!" The shout brings my attention upward, and I see Way, Wilder, and Aiy about twenty feet away. "Carter, we're here!"

I'm knocked to the side, the water moving in a wake as the croc cuts through it, swimming toward them. My throat burns, and I try to scream a warning, but I choke.

With no other choice, I grip the sharp rock and dive at the monster. I land on its back, and we sink under the surface. Pounding the rock against it, I try to hurt the creature, but its scales are too thick and its body is too big. It's like trying to hold onto a whale. Gripping its dorsal scales, I focus on my breathing and the creature below me as it dives deeper. Luckily, though, it's swimming away from the guys.

When it starts to roll, I know I don't stand a chance. My head smacks into the ground below, disorienting me, and my grip loosens. My eyes burn from the saltwater as I see it disappear into the darkness, then I push off the ground and break the surface once more.

My head is spinning, and every inch of my body both aches and feels numb. The muddy water around me is visibly red, even in the dark, with my blood, and I know it's only a matter of time before that monster returns to finish me off.

Arms unexpectedly wrap around me and lift.

I slam my head back out of instinct, and someone groans as I whirl. Way holds his busted nose, his eyes wide. "It's me! It's me!"

"Are you okay?" Wilder wades toward me, Aiy right behind him, then Logan and Rick appear, rushing through the water.

Nodding, I begin to speak when my legs suddenly give out. Way catches me, and I blink up at them all. "I think something is wrong," I slur.

"Shit, Wilder, look at her arm," Way snaps.

"We need to move her now!" he roars.

"This way," Logan yells, and I'm lifted. I must lose consciousness because the next time I'm aware of my surroundings, I'm lying on something in the water, the guys circling me. I glance down to see I'm on a small piece of wood, maybe from one of the ships, and they are pushing it through the water.

"What happened?" I rasp.

Aiy leans closer, his face pale. There's a cut across one eyebrow, and I try to lift my arm to wipe the blood away, but it's too heavy. "Shh, it's okay. Just rest. We are going back to the beach, I think. Rescue should be here soon. We just need to ride it out."

Turning my head, I see Logan smile at me, while Rick squeezes my other hand. Way kisses my forehead, surprising me. "Stay with us, Carter, okay? We need someone to keep us in line."

"Fucking hero shit," Wilder grumbles and then looks at me. "Don't try that shit again. We can save ourselves." His voice softens when he adds, "Just rest. I promise I'll get you out of here, Carter, and back to your dad."

They are talking like I'm dying. Maybe I am. Is that why everything is so . . . strange?

I probably lost a lot of blood between my leg, arm, and head, not to mention the infection, so maybe my body is finally giving in.

"If I die—"

"You aren't dying," Aiy snaps, sounding angrier than I've ever heard him.

"If I do . . ." I look at Wilder, hating that I'm adding this to his plate, but I know he can do it. "Tell my father I love him. Give him the videos."

"I will, but you aren't going anywhere," he murmurs. "Hold on, Carter." We travel faster, the soft lull of the water growing choppy.

"Something's wrong," Rick whispers, trying not to disturb me.

"Probably smaller waves coming—shit!" Way yells, and my eyes open just as another wave hits us. I'm thrown from the board, and I struggle under the churning water before I manage to resurface. Luckily the wood is near me, so I swim as hard as I can and throw myself at it. Clinging with the last ounce of strength I have, I look around for the guys, but I don't see them anywhere.

They are gone.

I try to scream, but my throat doesn't want to work. I float as time passes, until a bright light shines in my eyes, making them close. When I blink them open, I glance around in confusion. The water is moving weirdly and there's wind. The light grows stronger until it's right above me like a spotlight.

Tilting my head back, I glance up at it to make sense of what I'm seeing, my brain sluggish. The light is so bright it hurts, and that noise . . . it's like a whirring.

Helicopter.

It clicks. There is a helicopter above me.

I wave my good arm. "Help! Help!" My voice is more of a whisper, but it doesn't matter. A rope is dropped, then someone in a suit and helmet repels down. He stops next to me. "Miss, I'm here to help you. Are you able to grip the rope?"

I shake my head, almost slipping from the wood, and he speaks into his mic before smiling at me. "It's going to be okay now. We have you." Time moves strangely, but a rescue board arrives in moments, and he hauls me onto it, straps me in place, and waves his hand, and then we rise into the air and out of the water.

Turning my head, I see my good arm dangling down, but I can't seem to move it. I ignore it, searching the water for signs of them.

They were right there with me.

I want to scream, but my body's giving in, and they wouldn't hear me above the sounds of the blades. They have to see this. They have to be here.

I'll make sure the chopper doesn't leave without them.

Just then, something moves in the water, and hope blooms in my chest, even as we are steadily cranked up toward the hovering machine. When it breaches the surface, though, I realize it's not a person.

It's that thing.

My shout fills the air as I see the beast leap from the water, its jaws closing inches below the board before it plummets back into the sea.

"Holy shit!" the guy next to me yells. "Did you see that? Get us out of here!"

I'm slid onto the helicopter as two men start working on me, cutting away my clothes.

Everything feels . . . far away.

Everything but the thought of them down there.

"My team . . . My team is here," I tell them, or I think I do. My head is turned and my eyes are on the water and island below. "Save them, please. My team . . . We have to save them . . . ."

Everything goes black once more.

# THIRTY-EIGHT
## MAEVE

There's this annoying beeping noise piercing the fog in my brain. Every time I start to fade back into oblivion, the noise drags me out. For a moment, I float in the fog, the beep my only companion before it gets louder. I frown as I try to turn away from it, but something hinders me, further tugging me from that nothingness.

When my eyes finally open, I have to shut them again, the light blinding me and making them water. This time, I take it slowly, blinking them open and letting them adjust to the bright white ceiling above me and the sunlight.

Where am I?

What happened?

Lifting my head, I glance down and see I'm trapped under a thick blanket in what looks like a hospital bed, the sides up to protect me. I turn my head and find the source of the beeping—machines I'm hooked up to. The room is unlike any hospital I've ever seen, with wooden walls and large windows overlooking a strange city. It's beautiful and elegant and definitely private.

Why am I in a hospital?

Did I get hurt?

I try to recall, but everything is hazy.

"Kid, thank fuck you're awake!" a voice yells, and I turn my head, finding my dad in the doorway in a wheelchair. He rolls quickly toward me, tears in his eyes as he throws himself at me. I stare at him with a frown as he holds me tightly. "I was so worried. Don't you ever do that to me again."

"Dad?" My voice is rough, but he hears me, lifting his head. Tears stream down his face. "Hey, I'm okay."

Shaking his head, he wipes his cheeks and eyes before he helps me sit up and drink some water. "I've never felt such terror in my entire life, Maeve. When your videos stopped coming, I knew something was wrong. I went straight to Ajax. Luckily, he believed me and helped me get out here while they sent search and rescue. I knew something wasn't right. I could feel it. You would never forget to check in."

"Where am I?" I ask.

"You don't remember?" he inquires, appearing worried. "What is the last thing you do remember?"

"I don't know," I admit.

"It's okay. You hit your head pretty hard. You're going to be okay. We are on the outskirts—"

"My head!" I exclaim. "My leg, my arm—" I jerk upright despite his hands, and my wide eyes lock on him. "The guys . . . Where are they? Are they okay?"

Everything comes rushing back in stunning clarity, and my heart races, the beeping getting louder.

"Maeve, you need to calm down. You've been through a lot. Please lie down. You need to rest," he pleads.

"I can't. Where are they? Are they safe?" I swing my legs from the bed then stop. I don't feel any pain, probably due to whatever medicine they are pumping into me.

I'm in a hospital gown that must have rolled up when I moved, so it exposed my leg. I knew it would be bad, but fortunately, it's wrapped. I'm just glad I still have it. I test my foot, and when I find it still works, I breathe a sigh of relief.

"The doctor said you were very lucky. They wanted to amputate, but I begged them to try everything else first. I didn't want to take any

214

opportunities from you. The meds worked, so you were very fortunate." His voice is soft, almost scared. "You've been out for almost a week, Maeve. Your injuries were life-threatening. You might feel better now, but it's the meds. You need to rest." He sounds haunted.

The fact that he convinced them not to amputate is a relief, although I could have found a way to live if they had. It would have been difficult to adjust, and I wouldn't have let it change anything, but if they could save my leg, then I'm glad they did. "Dad, I'm sorry. I know you're scared and worried about me, but I need to know where the guys are. Are they safe?"

If I've been out cold for a week, then they have to be here, so why aren't they? It's not all in my imagination. We bonded on that island. They wouldn't let me wake up here alone.

He stares at me, and this pit opens in my stomach, but then the sliding of the door grabs our attention.

"I heard you're awake." I glance up as a heavily accented man in a suit walks in. My dad glares at him but says nothing. "We need to ask some questions—"

"Ajax said when she's ready, which isn't now," my dad snaps protectively, angling himself before me.

"Questions? I have my own. Where are they?" I ask.

He has to be a policeman or an investigator or something, considering the badge on his shoulder. He shares a look with my dad and sighs. "Miss Carter—"

"Cut the shit. Where are they?" I demand.

"We only found you." The words echo in my head. I see his lips moving as he continues to speak, but his answer is the only thing I hear.

*We only found you.*

It's impossible. They were right there.

I try to focus on his words, but I interrupt whatever spiel he is giving me. "How? They were right there with me."

"I'm very sorry. Our team searched for hours, and we didn't see anything. If they were there, they are most likely dead. The weather grew too bad for us to carry on, so we had no choice but to pull back."

"Is the storm still going?" I ask, my heart barely beating at the idea of them being there alone.

They aren't dead. I know it.

"It passed a few hours ago," he answers.

"Then why are you here? Get back out there!" I yell, falling from the bed. They both lunge toward me and help me back up. "They are alive, dammit!" I rip myself from their arms. "Get your ass back out there and find them."

"Maeve." The voice breaks through my panic, and I look up to see Ajax hurrying toward me. "I'm so glad you're okay. We were so worried—"

"Get your crew back out there and find them," I order him, and Ajax looks around before realizing what's happening.

"We will when the weather is better. Only a crazy person would head back out there in this storm, but Maeve, you need to prepare. They are now looking for bodies," Ajax cautions, wincing.

"They are alive," I hiss. "You know that better than I do. They wouldn't die so easily."

"Maeve," Ajax murmurs.

"Enough!" my father roars, and everyone falls silent. "I thought my daughter was dead for what felt like a lifetime, but now she's here, and she needs to rest. This can wait. Out. Now."

"Of course," Ajax replies. "Rest, Maeve. We will handle everything, so focus on getting better." He lays his hand on the other guy's arm, who nods, and both head out. I slump back before looking at my father, who's staring at me.

"Daddy," I begin, and he holds up his hand.

"I know what you're going to say, kid. I know you better than anyone. You're stubborn, relentless, and stupid, but not this time. Get back in bed," he orders.

"I have to get out of here. We have to go back," I beg.

"Maeve, Maeve, Maeve," he says.

"We have to get the search team—" I need him to understand.

"Maeve!" I freeze at his bellow. "I almost lost you. I thought my daughter was dead and I would never know what happened or find your body. I wasn't there, and I nearly lost you. I will not lose you again. Get back in bed."

My lip quivers as my eyes blur with tears. "Dad, I can't leave them."

"I nearly lost you. Do you understand that? Do you understand that I didn't know if you were alive or dead? That fear will never go away. I blamed myself for taking you on that first adventure. I ripped myself apart over and over, and when they found you, I still could have lost you. Maeve, please, don't ask this of me. I almost lost you once, and I can't risk losing you again."

The pain on his face tears me to shreds, and despite my injuries and the machines, I sink to my knees before him, covering his hands as my tears fall.

"Dad, I know you're scared," I whisper as I wipe away his tears, feeling his other hand shake in mine. "I am too, but I'm more scared of what type of person I would be if I got back in bed and didn't try. They saved my life. I wouldn't be here without them. I would be dead. They are my team, Dad. I can't leave them out there. I owe them, so I have to try. If anyone can survive, it's them. Please don't ask me to leave them when they wouldn't leave me."

He searches my eyes. "And if it gets you killed?" he snaps, his eyes glassy with tears.

"Then I'll die knowing I did everything I could, but I couldn't live with myself if I never tried. You don't know them like I do. If there's a chance, then they will be there. They will be alive. They are fighters just like us. I'm sorry to break your heart, Daddy, but I wouldn't be who you raised me to be if I got back in this bed. I can't lose them."

"You're asking me to let you go back to the place that almost took you from me," he croaks.

"I'm asking you to help me go back to that place and save the people who fought with me when I was injured, who carried me on their backs through storms and attacks to save my life. I'm asking you to let me save them the way they saved me. I'm asking you, Dad, to trust me to come back again."

His head bows, and I press mine against his as his shoulders shake. I try to bite back my tears, but I can't. Seeing my father so broken is not something I thought I would ever witness. He didn't even cry when he got his diagnosis, but as he lifts his head, I know this experience has changed him. It scarred him. I can't even imagine how he endured the worry and pain, and I wish I could stay here to ease that, but each moment I waste is another one they could be hurt or killed.

Wilder promised we would get off that island together. He broke it, so I'm going to find his ass and make him pay.

"They'll never let you out of the hospital," he murmurs, and my heart soars, knowing he's giving me his blessing. "It's on lockdown. Everyone wants your statement and picture. It's worldwide press."

"Then I guess I'll need help." I smile, and he purses his lips before blowing out a breath.

"I guess it's time for one last adventure," he mutters as his hands find mine. "Are you sure? You're still recovering—"

"They would come for me," I tell him as I kiss his knuckles. "If anyone can save them, it's me. You know that. Now, how the hell do we get me out of here? And clothes . . . I need underwear. There's no way I'm going on a rescue mission with my beaver in the breeze."

He laughs, and I smile with him.

We'll be okay. Now, I just need to find the guys.

I talk a big game, but fear lingers.

What if I'm too late?

# THIRTY-NINE

## WAY

The last few days have been hell. We are running out of water, and we are officially out of food, but it's more than that. It's the fact that we haven't seen any signs of rescuers for a while. It's like they left us here to die or gave up. I don't know how many days ago that was. They all blend together, especially since we are trapped.

When that second wave came, it dragged us away. We had nothing to cling to. I don't know if the storm or tsunami opened the entrance to this cave, but the water carried us right into it. We were lucky it was elevated so when the water went down, we didn't drown, but from that first moment we realized we were stuck here, we also realized that thing did too. It's been out there for days, waiting.

After we were swept in here, we tried to get out. Wilder nearly lost his arm. We've tried a few more times, especially when we heard helicopters. We needed to get their attention, but that beast is out there waiting for any splash or movement, and it lunges at us. Luckily, it's too big to get in here, but it knows it just needs to wait us out.

Fucking asshole.

Sighing, Rick rolls over and sprawls across my chest. I push him off, and he rolls the other way, curling up on Logan. Wilder sits near the entrance, perched on a rock. I don't know where we are, but it's nowhere near the beach. We need to get back there and figure a way out of the cave now that the water is receding. We've been waiting for it to lower as much as we can so we can see where that asshole is, but we are risking being too hungry and dehydrated to make it.

We need to make a decision soon.

"Nothing?" Aiyaret's voice is small. He lies next to me, his back to the rocky wall of the cave. It was where he felt safest, so we gave it to him since he struggles to sleep anyway. I make sure my body is between his and the entrance in case the worst happens.

"Go back to sleep," I murmur. He's only been resting an hour or so.

Sighing, he sits up and rests his head on the wall as he looks at me. His hair is slicked back, making him look younger, and he's still so handsome it hurts, so I glance at Wilder, but Aiyaret's voice brings my attention back to him.

"She's okay, right?" he asks softly, and I flinch. "If she was okay, she wouldn't stop until they found us. I'm scared something happened. I just hope she's okay. I hope she's resting and her dad is with her. It's what she would want."

"Maeve Carter is fine. There's nothing in this world that could kill her. She'll be in a nice hospital somewhere, giving them hell." He smiles, and I cover his hand with mine. "She'll be okay. We got her out of here. They'll take care of her, and I'm sure her dad is at her side, holding her hand. She won't be alone."

He nods, looking at our hands for a moment, and I debate drawing mine back, but honestly, I need his touch too. I'm scared, not that I'll tell him or the others. They need me to be strong. I can't implode.

"We are going to die here, aren't we?" he asks, and I startle as his lips curve in a sad smile. "It's okay. I know you all like to protect me, but I'm not scared of dying. Honestly, I'm surprised I made it this long. I spent my entire childhood thinking I was going to die each day, that one day she would take it too far. After a while, it just became something I knew would happen someday. Death doesn't scare me."

"Then what does?" I ask. "The thing out there?"

"No. Something much worse," he answers quietly.

"Then what?" I frown, not understanding. "Tell me, I'll make it better."

He watches me for a moment. "I'm scared I'll die without ever being brave enough to be honest with myself . . . and you. I'm scared I'll die never knowing."

"Knowing?" I hedge, something inside me waking up. Warmth flows through me, and my heart starts to hammer, but I don't know why.

His eyes search my face, and it's like he decides something when he nods. "If we are going to die here, then there's one thing I want to do before that."

I want to tell him we won't die, that I'll make sure I'll get him out, but all that comes out is a rough question. "What's that?"

"This." He grips the back of my neck firmly, and with more strength than I thought he had, he yanks me forward and presses his lips to mine. I freeze, staring into his eyes as he kisses me. I expect him to pull away, to apologize, but his eyes close, and he deepens the kiss. Before I know it, my eyes are shutting too and I'm kissing him back.

He gasps, and I pull away.

I stare at him before remembering the others. I glance at Wilder, but he's still keeping watch. He probably heard us, but he stays silent, giving us privacy.

"Aiyaret," I whisper, no other words filling my head.

"I've been scared my entire life, but I don't want to be anymore. If I'm going to die here, I'm going to do it knowing I gave it my all. I love you, and maybe I always have. You're my best friend, and I think that confused me for a while, thinking it was just friendship, but I don't feel the same way about the others as I feel for you. I can't live without you, Way. You're my light in the dark, my safe harbor. Maybe you don't feel the same way, but I don't care anymore. I have to tell you. For me, love was pain from a mother who hated me. I have nothing to offer other than this scared, flawed body and soul, but it's yours. It always has been."

Covering his mouth, I press my forehead to his. "You're confused—"

"Don't tell me how I feel," he snaps, tugging my hand away. " Stop being so calm and rational. For once, Way, tell me how you really feel instead of trying to protect me."

"Aiy, let's talk when we're out of here," I say, and he flinches and stands. I stare up at him, fear pounding in my chest as he locks me out.

"If you don't feel the same way, then just say it. Don't make excuses. That's worse. Stop being such a good guy and trying to protect me," he snaps, and then he goes to walk past me. I have this horrible, gut feeling that if he does, I'll lose him forever.

Grabbing his arm, I yank him down. His eyes widen as I pin him.

"I will always protect you. You're damn right about that, but it's not that . . . I'm terrified you're getting mixed up and saying it out of fear, offering me everything I want only to take it back later. I couldn't live with that. I can live with being your best friend as long as it keeps you in my life, but I can't go on if you give me a glimpse, a taste of what I want more than anything then take it away again." I'm breathing heavily, and so is he as he stares up at me, wide-eyed and shocked. "You're wrong, Aiyaret. It isn't you who can't live without me. It's me who can't live without you, and I'm terrified you'll realize that one day and leave me. Don't give me hope and take it away again. I know you have feelings for Maeve too—"

"So do you," he retorts, and I swallow.

"I do, but in a different way than you. You're both in my heart, but Aiyaret, I love you. I always have. If you aren't sure about this, then don't give me a chance. If you . . . If you feel the same way and you love me, then I'm yours."

We are both damp, and we smell like saltwater and sweat, but I don't care, not when he looks up at me with hope-filled eyes. "I love you. I don't want to be your best friend anymore."

"No? Then what do you want?" I ask as I lean closer, needing to know before I cross a line we can't come back from.

"I want to be yours," he whispers, and it's all I need. I slam my lips onto his. He arches below me, turning his hand in my grip and lacing our fingers as he groans, kissing me back. I force his mouth open, sweeping my tongue in and tangling it with his as we press together.

Despite how tired, dehydrated, and hungry I am, desire spirals through me, but I ignore it. This is about love, nothing else. I would never cross that line with him until he was ready. He might never be after his past, and that's okay as long as he doesn't leave me.

The little whimper he lets out has me hardening, so I pull away before I push him too hard. I rest my forehead against his and stare into his beautiful eyes.

"We'll get out of this, I promise, and when we do, I'll show you how serious I am."

His smile is slow but bright, and for once, it's unchecked, and it fixes something in my heart. "You better."

Grinning, I tug him into my arms. He snuggles into my chest like he has a million times, but it feels different now. I don't know if we'll make it out of here, but it doesn't matter, not now that I know he feels the same way.

After everything I've hidden, everything I've held back, he's in my arms. I don't know how long we'll get to be together, but it doesn't matter. We'll have a chance, and that's enough.

"It's about time," Logan mutters. "How much longer do we have to pretend to be asleep?"

"Logan . . ." Wilder sighs as I laugh, and Aiyaret hides his face against my chest, but he's smiling and holding me tightly.

"What?" Logan asks as he rolls to his back, his hand over his eyes. "I'm not looking, but if they start fucking, I'll be out there with the croc. There are some things I can't unsee."

I tug Aiyaret closer. "Idiots, all of you."

"I'm with him. We love both of you, but I don't need to see your balls," Rick teases.

"Jesus Christ," Wilder mutters. "Alright, since we're all awake, let's come up with a plan to get out of here." Rick and Logan groan, and Wilder laughs. "Come on, idiots, it's now or never."

"We're getting out?" I ask.

"Or we'll die trying," Wilder admits.

That sobers us all.

# FORTY
## MAEVE

"Y ou owe me, kid," my dad grumbles before he opens the door and rolls out. I wait behind it, dressed in clothes and gear he managed to get for me. I shouldn't be surprised, since my dad is resourceful and knows exactly what I need. I wear cargos, boots with two pairs of socks, a long Henley, and a waterproof jacket. He also managed to gather food, water, and ropes, amongst other supplies, everything I'll need to survive on the island. He doesn't like what I'm doing, but he's making sure I have the best chance at succeeding, and I love him for that.

I hear his wheels on the clean tile floor as he rounds a corner, putting our plan into action when I hear a crash then yelling. "Help me! Help me!" he shouts, and then there's running. Sliding the door open, I peek out to see him groaning as he lies on the floor, his wheelchair tipped. The police officer who was outside waiting to speak to me is at his side, along with nurses and doctors. Smirking, I wave at him and hurry down the corridor, breaking into a sort of run, the only limping type I can manage, when I hit the stairs and descend. He already gave me the hospital's layout. Luckily, the island we're on is the one I started on before all this, so I know my way around well enough to get out of here.

I escape the hospital with no trouble and tug on my hat. My leg still aches, as does my shoulder, but I got some pain meds and an antibiotic shot before I left—we assured it—which should keep me going for now. I could head to the marina, but I need to get there faster, and if the island is still flooded, then boats might not travel there.

That leaves air.

I manage to hitch a ride in a car with a local, and they drop me off outside the small airfield. I stride through the private bays and hangars, looking for what I need, and I find it on the back row.

The red helicopter looks like it's seen better days and clearly belongs to a tour guide. Rushing over to the guy in a big hat and floral shirt, I tap his shoulder. "Excuse me."

"Jesus." He spins, placing his hand on his heart. He's a bigger man and middle-aged, with wrinkled skin from sun and time, but he looks nice. "No tours today," he tells me in fragmented English.

"I don't need a tour." I pull out a wad of cash, and his eyes widen as he reaches for it. "I need a private trip to this island." I show him the GPS, and he holds up his hands as I pull out another wad of cash. "You get both if we leave now."

"Now?" Scratching his head, he looks around. "The storm only just settled. We aren't supposed to be flying—" I pull out more cash, and he grins. "But who am I to deny your rights? Let's go."

Ajax would help if I fought hard enough, but I don't have time for that. I need to get to them as quickly as possible, so this is the best way. He'll come after me, and when he does, I need to be with the guys.

The pilot takes my bag and helps me into the other seat, and I settle in, putting my headset on while he completes his checks. By the time we are in the air, it's already midmorning, so I won't have long to find them once we arrive. The island is dangerous during the day, but in the dark, it's a nightmare.

I need to find them before the sun sets, and then we'll get the hell out of there.

The flight seems longer than before, but I think that's just because I'm anxious to get there, worried they are in danger. I've already been gone too long. What if I'm too late?

I can't afford to consider that, though, so I focus on checking my equipment repeatedly until the island comes into view. Leaning against the window, I notice the water has retreated, which is good. That means they have land, but it also means it's going to be harder to find them. If the water washed them inland, they could be stuck.

"There's nowhere for me to land," he says into the mic.

"That's fine, I'll jump. Get lower." I unfasten my belt and climb to the door as he curses in his native tongue.

"You're crazy!" he yells, and I grin at him.

"I am, and when men in big trucks come looking for me, tell them where you dropped me as quickly as you can. When I get back, I'll give you more money than you could ever dream of." I slip my bag on my front and open the door. The wind instantly whips me, and I wrap my arms around my bag as I scoot to the edge. Ignoring my aches and pains, I nod at the pilot as he gets as low as he dares, and then I leap from the helicopter, keeping my legs straight.

The impact as I hit the water isn't too bad. I swim to the surface as quickly as I can and watch as he ascends again, observing me from his window. I salute him and swim toward shore.

When it's shallow enough for me to stand, I wade onto the beach, and my boots sink into the sand as I swing my bag around and strap it on, removing my hunting rifle just to be safe. By now, my dad will have told Ajax the truth and shared GPS coordinates, and he'll no doubt be scrambling to come after us. The clock is ticking, so with no time to spare, I head toward the jungle.

It looks completely different than it did before. Our shelter is gone, the trees are bent and stripped raw, and debris lines the beach, a reminder of the killer wave that swept in and stole us away. It means whatever markers we left are probably gone as well, so with nothing else to do, I simply head into the jungle with my compass and GPS and hope I can find them.

I won't stop until I do.

# FORTY-ONE
## AIYARET

"No," I snap, crossing my arms and glaring at them.

"I'm the fastest," Way responds softly, reaching out to placate me, but I jerk away.

"Okay, I'll go," Logan offers.

"No!" I snap again, and they share a look.

"Aiy, one of us has to do it," Wilder says. "You agreed to the plan too."

I did, but now that I'm faced with it, the idea of losing one of them—I can't stand it.

Terror makes it hard to swallow. "I can't lose you." It slips out, and they soften as they move closer.

"You won't," Rick promises, taking my hand. "We're fast and crazy. Nothing will get us. Just call us Maeve fucking Carter 2.0."

I smile despite myself.

"We have to do this. We are running low on supplies. If we stay here much longer, we'll die, so we either die here or we make a break for it and possibly die out there. I don't know about you, but I didn't spend my life exploring and taking risks to sit back and let death come for me," Wilder argues, never one to sugarcoat the facts. "We have to do this together or not at all."

"You're the only family I have," I murmur. "I couldn't live if something happened to any of you." Blowing out a breath, I stand taller. "I'll do it."

"No!" Way yells.

"Yes. I'm fast and smart. Way is too bulky, Logan is too cocky, and Wilder and Rick are needed for the other part of the plan. I'm not. I know you want to protect me—" I lift my hand to stop their protests. "You always have, but I can do this."

"He's right," Wilder admits, and I can tell he hates it, especially when Way gives him a glare that would frighten a lesser person.

Way guides me away until we are in the corner. "Aiy," he begins.

"I'm doing this. You would ask me to sit back and watch you, so why can't I do the same?"

"It's different," he argues.

"How?" I ask.

"Because if anything happened to you, I'd die as well," he retorts before softening. "If it's me, it's okay, you can live on, but I can't lose you."

"Have you considered that I feel the same way?" I reply softly as I cup his cheek. "You need to trust me. I know you always want to shield me from the world, but you can't this time. It's my choice, and I'm doing it. I'm the logical option, and you know it. If it had been anyone else, you would have already agreed."

"But you aren't anyone else," he says, the words tight. "You're my Aiy."

"Then make sure this works, okay?" I kiss him tenderly just in case it's the last time I'll ever get to do it. When I step away, he clings to me, but I face the others. "Let's do this. There's no time like the present."

Wilder nods, but I can tell he's worried, and Way is silent as he joins us.

"Do you remember the plan?" Logan asks.

"Of course. Distract the monster croc." I smirk. "What could possibly go wrong?"

"If we make it through this, I'll tell Maeve as well, that way both your boyfriend and girlfriend will reward your bravery," Rick teases before grunting as Wilder and Logan smack the back of his head.

I grin, though, just like he wanted, and remove the bag Way handed me and give it to them. I need to move fast, which means carrying as few belongings as possible. It outweighs the fact that I might need those supplies if we get separated.

Heading to the entrance, I leap onto the rock to the right of it and glance over, waiting for Wilder to take his spot on the opposite side of the cave entrance to give me a chance to get away. It's all about diversion.

Way takes Wilder's place, however, his dark eyes locked on me. "Don't you dare fucking die."

"Back at you," I call as he starts to smack the water, the ripples drawing its attention.

Way nods at me, and I turn toward the entrance, trusting in him to warn me as I grip the edge of the rock, ready to dive. I know it could be lurking right there, waiting with its mouth open, and adrenaline makes my heart pump faster until it's all I can hear. When Way yells, I don't look at him, blindly trusting him, before I dive into the water. As soon as I hit it, I swim as fast as I can toward the trees. I feel something big turn behind me as my team shouts to keep its attention, but I don't look back as I push myself harder.

I need to do this for them.

I have been a victim, a survivor, my entire life, enduring but never saving myself. Today, I will. I will save them and me.

Once I reach the trees, slogging from the remaining water, I start to run. I hear it splashing behind me and spare a glance back to see it sliding out of the water to give chase. That menacing maw is parted in a hiss, revealing huge, wicked teeth. I don't have long, but it's the break they need, and by now, they will be in the water too. We plan to meet up ahead, splitting its focus. It's the only chance we have.

There's a slight incline ahead, so I push myself faster, jumping toward it and digging my fingers into the mud as I drag myself up the hill. There's a roar behind me and a crack, and I glance down to see it lurking below, snapping at my legs. If I slip, I'm dead. Turning forward, I dig my fingers in until I feel my nails break and pull myself up and over, rolling across the rim, and then I'm on my feet again, running as fast as I can. I run so far, I don't even know how much time has passed until I slow and turn.

It's not there.

I must have lost it, or it went after the others. I send up a prayer, hoping they are okay, but like they trusted me, I have to trust them. Bending over, I suck in some slow breaths, trying to tame my hammering heart. My legs shake now that it's over, as do my arms, and I inspect my fingers to see blood and dirt covering them, but if it's the only injury I have, then I'm fine with that.

Standing straight, I let out the whistle we use when we're exploring and wait for the return signal. When it doesn't come, I start to worry. Maybe they are delayed. I pace for a minute, watching the jungle in case the monster is there, but there's only the usual din of other wildlife. No whistle. No croc.

That only makes my concern grow.

I whistle once more, and when there's no response this time, I decide I'm not waiting around to find out. As I dive into the trees, I make a whole lot of noise, knowing the risk it poses, but I need to get to them. I need to make sure they are okay. I have a general idea of which direction they went, so I travel that way, praying they are safe.

I've never felt anything like this terror before.

Not when my mom beat me or when her and her friends used to rape me.

I meant what I said—I can't live without them. Not just Way, but all of them. They are my family. If anything happens to them . . .

I sprint through the jungle, their names leaving my lips in desperate puffs of air that turn into screams until I smack into something hard.

Arms wrap around me, and then lips are on mine. I pull back to see Way. He's wet and sweaty but alive. I run my hands over him as he pulls me closer and kisses me again. When we break apart this time, I turn and find the others, panting and wet but okay.

"Please don't greet me like that," Rick teases. "I'm not secure enough to withstand that kind of kiss."

"You're okay." Tears fill my eyes. "I was so worried when I didn't hear your response."

"Sorry, we got caught up," Wilder whispers. "Fucker came out of nowhere. We had to sidetrack. We only just outran it."

"Uh, no, we haven't," Logan says helpfully, and we turn as the trees start to shake, the ground below us quivering. "We should get moving, like now. I don't want to be croc chow today. I refuse to die until I've tasted Maeve Carter."

"Fuck," Wilder grumbles, but he shoves Way and me past him, and then we run as the sounds catch up to us, and we know we are being hunted.

"What is it, the fucking Terminator?" Rick whispers. "It's always there, never giving up. Honestly, is it that hungry or just fucking pissed at us?"

"Probably both," Wilder replies. "We invaded its territory, but it's unnaturally vicious."

"It's also unnaturally large," Logan adds.

"Like my dick," Rick quips, but we ignore him.

"We are its prey, so let's not stick around until it catches us," Wilder orders.

The crashing sounds we make are loud as we race through the jungle, but not as noisy as that thing hunting us. Honestly, it's more relentless than Rick flirting with Maeve, and that's saying something. We either need to find high ground or get the fuck out of its way—something we are all acutely aware of—but having been washed away in the tsunami, we don't have a clue where we are on the island, so we just pick a direction and hope for the best. It's unrelenting, however, and only seems to pick up speed. I know we'll run out of energy and need to rest before long, and then we'll be screwed. All it has to do is wait us out, and it seems to know that.

"We need to find somewhere safe to rest and regroup," Wilder says. We are all exhausted, so as we run, we search for an opportunity, but the land is flat. Trees are down from the storm, bent or misshapen, and the ground is still soaked and covered with debris, slowing us down.

The croc lets out a roar so close, it hurts and shakes the earth, and I glance back to see it heading right for us.

"Move!" Wilder yells, and he drags Rick with him as we break through some dense brush at a sprint, only to come to an abrupt stop at the person standing there, waiting casually.

It can't be . . .

It's impossible.

My eyes widen as I meet the familiar, beautiful orbs of Maeve Carter, who's standing in front of me like the best figment of my imagination. I never thought I'd see her again, and for a moment, I drink in her beauty, wondering if she's real.

She wears a cocky, knowing smirk and raises a gun.

"Duck," she orders. I drop to the ground, and shots fire over my head. Turning, I see her hit the croc, and with a snap of its teeth, it starts to charge before she walks toward us, getting a few more shots off before the beast decides to spin and race away. It will be back, but for now, it's gone.

She saved our lives.

I climb to my knees and stare at her, silent, confused, and relieved. We got her off the island.

We assured her safety, so how is she here?

Why?

"Hey, boys, miss me?" she calls as she reloads and slings her gun across her chest.

# FORTY-TWO
## MAEVE

They converge on me as a group, huddling around me as they check me over.

I can't keep up with their rapid-fire questions, so I just chuckle and hold them. "I'm okay. I'm okay. I'm really here. Are you guys hurt?" I run my eyes over them again, barely believing they are safe.

When they quite literally ran into my path, I thought I was seeing things.

"What the fuck, Carter?" Wilder snaps. "How? Why?" It's clear he's confused as hell and worried.

"We can talk as we walk. We need to move," I reply. I want to examine them for injuries, but the longer we linger, the more likely it is that the croc will come back. We need to get going.

"You're right. Sorry, you were all clean." Wilder winces.

I laugh as I look down at the mud now covering me. "Meh, a little dirt never bothered me." I wink. "Come on, let's go."

He nods, and they fall into step at my side as I watch their backs with the gun. Their gazes keep slipping to me, though, and I can sense their desire for answers.

"Go ahead, ask." I keep scanning the area around us. I didn't find them again only to lose them the next second.

"What happened?" Way speaks first, which is surprising. "Last we saw, you were being airlifted out of here. We thought you were safe, then the water took us."

The fact that they saw my rescue and couldn't do anything to join me makes my heart ache. They must have been so afraid and utterly hopeless, especially when no one came back and found them. I wonder how they managed to survive, but he asked first, so I decide to answer their questions.

"I was knocked out for a while," I explain. "When I woke up in the hospital, they told me the search was called off because of the weather, so I bribed my dad to help me get out, and I paid off a pilot to get me here. By now, Ajax will know, and a search and rescue team will be on the way. My dad will make sure it happens. We just need to get back to the beach, okay? Just hold on a bit longer."

"We've survived this long," Way says. "What's a few more hours?"

"What happened?" I ask quietly.

"The water swept us away," Wilder replies. "When I woke up, we were in a cave. The last thing I remember was being washed away. The cave saved our lives, but it also trapped us. The flood water was so high, we would have had to swim out, but that thing found us and waited outside. We could hear helicopters every now and again, but we couldn't get out to signal them. They finally stopped coming, and I realized we needed to move or we were going to die there. We distracted it and managed to get out, and you saw the rest."

I chuckle. "Ballsy."

"Ajax? Your dad?" Aiyaret asks.

"Both are okay. It was my dad who realized something was wrong and set all of this in motion. Ajax flew him out here with a team to find me, trusting him. I don't remember much, since my body apparently shut down. I almost died, but I was very lucky. It took a week before I opened my eyes and saw my dad. When I learned they hadn't found you, I knew I had to come back. It was hard convincing my dad, but he caused a distraction so I could get out of the hospital."

"You broke out of the hospital to rescue us?" Rick gapes. "That's so fucking hot."

"Well, someone has to save your damsel asses," I tease. "I knew if I came, Ajax would have no choice but to get some teams out here. Besides, I couldn't waste any more time. What if something happened?" I cut off when we hear a roar.

We stay silent, our steps speeding up. We walk for hours before finding shelter on a small hill with trees for shade. Unloading my pack, I pass out rations and water, and they eagerly dive in. I wonder how long it's been since they have eaten and drunk anything. It makes me uneasy, but I only need to get them to the beach and then out of here.

It's then I notice Wilder holding his arm oddly, so I pull out my first-aid kit and crouch in front of him. "Let me see."

"I'm fine," he says around a mouthful, but I narrow my eyes.

"Now," I order sharply, and he grumbles but undoes his shirt and shows me his shoulder. There is some type of bandage wrapped around it, but it's soaked with blood. I carefully unpeel it. He doesn't make a noise, even though it has to hurt. I can feel his eyes on me, but I don't dare meet them, instead focusing on his wound.

When it's revealed, I gasp. There are teeth marks all around his shoulder, and it's a bleeding mess. "What happened?" I ask softly as I pull out what I need.

"I tried to get us out, but the croc wanted to play chew toy with my arm," he says as I clean the wound and redress it. "Thanks."

"You're lucky. You could have lost it," I murmur.

"I guess we have something in common now." His eyes drop to my leg, and I smile as I stand, shaking out the aches before sitting against a tree as they rest. I needed to put some space between us.

I was so fucking worried, and now that they are here, everything feels right again. I never thought I'd see them again, and I told myself if I did, I wouldn't hold anything back, but looking into Wilder's dark, hungry eyes is unnerving, so I keep mine on the jungle instead.

No one speaks for a little while, and I start to relax.

"Why did you come back?" Aiyaret asks softly, and my eyes move to him. He's sitting with Way leaning into him. I raise my eyebrows as I look at their joined hands, and he actually blushes. Chuckling to myself, I stretch out my legs as my bad one twinges.

"Why did you risk your life and come back here?" Wilder presses as he climbs to his feet. Whatever happiness he felt upon seeing me morphs to anger, and it makes my hackles rise. So much for gratitude. "You were saved. I kept my promise—"

"But broke the one about us getting out of here together," I snap before calming down. "I came back for you, you idiot, because I care about you all."

Logan sighs. "We could have been dead."

"I know that too, but I couldn't just lie there and wonder about you for the rest of my life. No matter what it cost, I had to find you," I argue, growing angry myself.

"Dammit, Carter, why?" Wilder yells.

"Because I care about you!" I shout back. "You think I could live with myself if I left you here? You never left me. You said we would do this together, didn't you? So yes, I came back, and I would do it again. I'm just sorry it took me this long to return. I'm so sorry I was late—"

My words end in a gasp as Wilder covers the distance between us and presses his lips to mine. I stare, wide-eyed, into his dark gaze. His eyes burn with desire and something infinitely more dangerous as he pulls back and lets me breathe.

"You stupid, beautiful woman," he whispers. "Don't you ever risk your life like that again, not for us."

When I don't respond, he wraps his hand around my throat and drags me forward until I fall into his chest, then his lips come down on mine again in a brutal, swift kiss. "Promise me. Promise me you won't risk your life for us again."

"I won't make that promise," I answer shortly. "You'd do the same for me."

"So sure, Carter?" he mutters, our old rivalry raising its head, but there's no heat, just teasing.

"Yes." I press against his chest, and he backs up until he hits the tree, his eyes widening. "I know you would, so don't give me that big bad

Wilder attitude when we both know you would risk your life over and over to save me. I came back, so you should be thanking me. Thank me."

His jaw clenches as he stares at me, and I raise my eyebrow. "Thank you, Carter," he grinds out.

"That didn't sound sincere. Thank me," I demand. The others are staring, but I ignore them. Wilder and I have always butted heads, and even our kisses taste like anger and a fight. I love it, but I refuse to back down now. If I do, Wilder will try to walk all over me. He's used to getting his way.

He needs someone to put him in his place.

"Carter," he warns.

"You know what? A real thank you should be done on your knees to show how truly grateful you are for me coming to rescue your stubborn asses."

"Don't push it," he growls, glancing from my lips to my eyes.

I wait, and he glares. Neither of us back off. I know one of the others will step in and cool us down, but he suddenly drops to his knees in the mud, and I freeze, gaping at him in shock.

Wilder kneels for no one.

"Thank you, Maeve, for coming back for us." His words sound so sincere, I just gawk. "Isn't that what you wanted? If I didn't know better, Carter, I'd say you like seeing me on my knees." His meaning is clear, and it breaks me from my stupidity.

I scoff as I step back. "Dream on, pretty boy." Turning away, I find the others gaping, completely shocked as Wilder chuckles behind me and climbs to his feet. His heat hits my back as his mouth brushes my ear.

"You think I'm pretty?"

I elbow him, making him grunt, and ignore the flush in my cheeks. I started it, but I should have known he doesn't play fair.

"Um, I missed you too, so do I get a kiss?" Logan jokes, and I know it's to defuse the tension, but I stride over, grip his chin as his eyes widen, and kiss him.

He stares up at me in shock. It's the first time I've ever seen him speechless.

"Well, fuck, that isn't fair." Rick stands up and purses his lips. "I missed you the most."

Laughing, I head over and kiss him softly, uncaring at this point. It's almost a game. Besides, it isn't something I haven't thought about before. I turn away and freeze. Aiyaret and Way are watching me, and I simply smile as I walk over and press my lips to Way's cheek. There is something between us, but I know he loves Aiyaret, and I'm happy for them since they seemed to have figured that out.

Turning to Aiyaret, I wait for permission, and when he offers me his cheek, I lean down to press my lips there, but he turns his head as if to check on me, and our lips meet. I pull away immediately, feeling guilty as he stares at me, but he isn't panicking.

"Sorry," he murmurs. "I didn't . . ." He stops as we stare at each other, and I glance at Way, but he doesn't seem bothered. He's simply observing us with a little smile on his lips.

"If we are done with the kissing booth, we should get moving," Wilder whispers, and I clear my throat and stand, going to my bag and slipping it on. I started it, but I'm the one left embarrassed and shy until I pull up my big-girl panties. I kissed them all. So what?

We've almost died a hundred times on this island, so what's a few friendly kisses?

Once we are off this island, this strange bond we built will be gone. They will go back to their team, and I'll return to being alone, so I'm going to make the most of having them on my side while I can.

Checking my GPS, I nod north. "That way. We should get there before nightfall if we move fast."

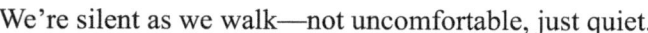

We're silent as we walk—not uncomfortable, just quiet.

Way falls into step at my side, and I glance at him, but he seems lost in his own thoughts, so I leave him to it until he's ready. "I told Aiy."

"I noticed." I nudge him with my arm. "It went well?"

He looks at me with an embarrassed, happy smile that warms my heart. "It did. He felt the same. You knew, didn't you?"

"Even the croc knew," I scoff. "I'm glad you two sorted it out. So you're dating?" I wiggle my eyebrows, and he looks away as I chuckle. "I'm happy for you both. You deserve to be happy. I hope you know that."

"Are you?" He takes a deep breath, meeting my eyes. "I know you like Aiy."

Well, shit, I guess we are going there.

"Maybe we should talk when we are off—"

"We have nothing better to do while we walk. You like him?" he presses, refusing to let me shrink away from the truth.

"I do," I admit as I glance at Aiy in front of us, but he's chatting with Logan about something.

"And Wilder?" Way continues, and I blink at him again. "I'm not shaming you. I'm just asking."

"Yes," I reply.

He nods, looking at them then me. "And Rick? Logan?"

"Yes to both," I respond, shocking myself. I haven't spent a lot of time with them, but what we have has been intense and hot, and I'll admit I like them a lot.

He nods like he already knew. I wait, but he doesn't ask about himself, so I do instead.

"You didn't ask about you," I say, biting my lip, and he stumbles, his head jerking around so he can gape at me, and I smile. "You didn't ask if I like you too."

"Do you?" he whispers.

"Yes," I answer, "but I also know you love Aiyaret, and I will never get between you two. I like you both, and I want you to be happy, which you are together."

"You like me?" He looks so incredulous, I can't help but laugh.

"You look surprised," I tell him.

"Well, I knew you liked Wilder, but me?" Shaking his head, he walks silently for a bit, then he comments, "This is so confusing."

"True, but when do we ever take the easy route?" I tease, and he shoots me a smile. "Besides, it doesn't matter. When we get off this island, we'll go back to our own lives, and you'll return to hating and avoiding me." I meant it as a joke, but it is a very real fear, and he must hear it.

"Do you really think that? Do you think we ever really hated you? Carter, we didn't, and being here with you changed everything." He reaches out and tucks me under his arm, offering me comfort. "We're not going anywhere, no matter what happens."

His words settle something inside me that I refuse to look too closely at right now.

"And I promise I won't say or do anything with Aiyaret. I really mean it. I want you both to be happy together."

He lets out a breath and is quiet for a minute. "He likes you too, you know? I know it. I'm jealous, but it's my own fault. I waited too long, and it gave him time to make room in his heart for you. I can't hate that. How could I when he's struggled so much and is finally learning to let people in? I thought I was hurt, but when I saw him kiss you earlier, I was happy to see him being so brave. I don't know what it means, but it's the truth."

I don't know what to say to that, so we just focus on our steps. Aiyaret glances back at us and smiles, seemingly unbothered by Way's arm around me, but I move out from under it anyway, and he looks at me, confused. When Aiy focuses on walking, I feel Way's eyes on me.

"I like you too, Carter." This time, I stumble, and he grabs me before I fall. "I didn't realize it at first, and then I tried to ignore it because I love Aiyaret and have for a long time. I couldn't believe that I started liking you, but I do. It's all messed up, and I'm confused as hell, but I need you to know, just in case, that I feel the same."

"Well, shit, we really don't do anything the easy way," I respond when I can speak again without sounding like an idiot.

He likes me. *They* like me.

I don't know what that means, so I focus on getting us out of here and nothing else. Once we are safe, maybe I can think about what to do, but for now, we need to get off this island alive.

# FORTY-THREE
## WILDER

We haven't heard or seen signs of the croc for miles, but that doesn't mean anything. It's probably waiting and watching. It won't let us go.

Maeve is hanging back. She said it's because she has a gun, but I'm worried it's due to her leg. One week of rest in a hospital doesn't miraculously cure someone with an injury as severe as hers, so I ask Way to take the lead for me and slip back, matching her pace.

Her eyes scan the jungle, her grip on the gun tight, but I know she senses me. "What is it, Wilder?" she whispers.

"How's your leg holding up?" I ask quietly so the others won't overhear. It's clear she doesn't want them to worry, but that shit doesn't work on me.

"Fine," she answers absentmindedly. She stops for a moment, her eyes on the bushes around us, before she continues walking. I know she's concerned—hell, I am too—but the croc isn't here right now, and she is, so I'm going to focus on her.

She came back for us.

I want to wring her fucking neck for putting herself at risk again, and then I want to kiss the shit out of her.

"Carter," I warn, and she flashes her eyes to mine and sees I'm serious. She never could lie to me. Even when all we did was fight, it was nothing but truthful, even in malice, and like my brothers so helpfully pointed out, it was mostly flirting rather than fighting now that I look back at it.

At least on my end.

I took out my need for Carter on her without even realizing what I was doing.

I don't know when my mindset began to change, but I can't deny that Carter is the one I want. If I were ever to take something for myself, it would be her. I might die today, tomorrow, or a year from now, but when I do, I'll regret the time I wasted not being hers.

She's crude, loud, excitable, and silly, but she's also highly intelligent, caring, loyal, and brave. She drives me crazy, but maybe I need that. Maybe I've even come to crave it.

I don't know what will happen when we make it from the island alive, but I do know that I'm tired of pretending I don't want Maeve Carter.

"It's fine," she grumbles, finally realizing I'm not backing down. "They gave me some good drugs. I should be resting, but I will when I get back, so until then, I just need to focus on moving and distracting myself from the ache."

So it's hurting her. We need to get off the island, but until we do, I can help a little, or maybe it's just my pervy thoughts that only seem to crop up around her.

"Fine, then let me distract you. Let's talk about our kiss."

Her head swings around, her eyes wide, and I chuckle.

"Really? You want to talk about that now?" she hisses, cutting the others a look.

"We don't have anything better to do. Are you embarrassed, Carter?" I tease.

Her eyes narrow in irritation, just like I expected, and damn if it doesn't make me hard when she rises to my bait. No one fights me like Carter. No one else dares to. "You call that a kiss? I barely remember it."

She's saying it out of embarrassment and trying to get me to argue with her. It's how we are, and she's trying to get us back to our norm, but I won't let her. I'm not going back now.

Not after I've had a taste of her.

I step into her path, and she bumps into my chest, her head coming up and eyes widening as I grip the nape of her neck and pull her closer. "Then let me remind you," I growl before I cover her lips with mine. Her gasp opens her mouth, and I slide my tongue inside, tangling it with hers as I deepen the kiss. She smacks my chest to push me away, but as we continue, she stops struggling and grips me tighter, hauling me closer. I smirk in victory as I pull away. Her eyes are closed, her lips are swollen and parted, and her cheeks are pink.

She's so fucking beautiful, I ache to kiss her again.

She would look so fucking good below me, all that fire and attitude. I'd fuck it right out of her. If there wasn't a croc on our tail, I would do just that right here and now, everyone else be damned.

Sweeping my thumb across her lips, I settle for just that kiss—for now. "You'll remember that one," I tease her.

She stares at me incredulously, and she's so fucking cute I can't help myself. Leaning down, I steal another peck, and she stumbles back, her hand covering her mouth as if to protect herself from me.

"I give it an eight out of ten." I glance back to see Rick grinning. "You needed more tongue, brother, but if you two are done dry humping and flirting, then we need to keep moving."

"We do not flirt!" Carter yells before glaring at me and giving me a wide berth, her eyes wide as she leads the way. Laughing, I lunge for her, and she yelps, moving until Logan is between us and glaring at me.

I can't help but smile, even as I hurry after them.

Maeve Carter is so fucking adorable, and when we are out of this jungle, I'm going to show her just what she does to me.

"It's too quiet," Logan murmurs, his eyes wide as he looks around. We are all worried about resting, but it's been hours. We need to sit down, drink, and eat, and there hasn't been any sign of it. Of course, that means nothing. Carter has her gun, and I'm on watch on the other side, not taking any risks with our team.

"It's probably resting or searching for us," Way says, but he doesn't seem sure. After all, this thing doesn't ever seem to give up. It finds us wherever we go. No wonder the island is deserted. I have no idea what happened here, and I don't think we ever will, but it's obvious it has something to do with that creature.

As if following my train of thought, Maeve looks around us. "I wonder if that monster is what happened here."

"There was a temple on our way in with drawings of people being tossed into a hole. We didn't make the connection before, but I'm betting they were human sacrifices," Aiy explains.

"Guess it didn't work," she whispers.

"Or they left." I shrug. "Either way, it doesn't matter. We need to make sure no one else comes here and gets hurt. Ten more minutes, then we are moving. We need to be at the beach when they arrive."

"I don't know about you," Rick says, "but I'm dying for a bath and pizza."

Way grins. "Burger."

"Small thinking, my friend. I want a five-course meal with all the alcohol I can drink and Maeve in a sexy, little dress," Logan teases.

"Wild?" Rick asks.

"I want our home. I want all of you bickering and chasing each other. I want our normal," I admit.

"I want my dad," Maeve murmurs, "sitting on his porch drinking tea. I want to sleep without worrying I will be eaten, but most of all, I want to shower."

We all laugh, since we feel the same way. We must stink, and after a long expedition, there is nothing better than that first shower. It's something only people like us understand.

"How mad do you think Ajax will be?" Aiy asks.

"At you guys? Not very. At me? Extremely, but then again, he's always mad at me," she says, and when Aiy looks scared, she adds, "Don't worry. I can handle Ajax. Besides, it doesn't matter as long as you guys are okay."

"I still can't believe you came back," Rick whispers. "You must really love me, Carter. I'm flattered. When should we set the wedding date?"

Her grin is infectious, and I turn away as they start flirting and arguing. Their laughter is a balm for my troubled heart, one that will only calm once we are away from this fucking island. Like Carter, I'll probably sleep for a week straight when I know we are all safe.

"What happens when we go home?" Aiyaret asks softly. I glance back to see Maeve looking at him tenderly.

"What do you mean?" Whenever she speaks to him, her tone always softens. With Rick and Logan, she's loud and boisterous, and with me, she's brave and strong, but with Aiyaret, she's soft and kind. She caters to us all, I realize, giving us what we need.

"With you." He looks around then back at her. "We just go our separate ways after this?"

"I—" She swallows. "I'm not part of your team, Aiy."

"Oh . . ." He looks so forlorn that Way pulls him into his side, and my heart aches for him. "I thought since we . . . Never mind."

It's uncharted territory for us, so we become quiet, none of us knowing what to say. I rejected Maeve as part of our team for Aiy, as well as some selfish reasons, but while we've been here, we have all grown close, and it's clear even Aiy doesn't want to let that go.

Worry tightens my chest at his question. Will she just leave us when we go back?

Moving closer to Aiy, she takes his hand and squeezes it softly until he looks at her. "Let's get off this island first, okay? When we are safe, we can talk about it, but I promise I'm not just going to disappear on you. We fought and survived a crocodile together, sweetie, and that bonds us," she teases. "No matter what, I'll be in your life if that's what you want."

"You promise?" he asks softly. She's the only woman he has ever trusted, ever let touch him, and as I watch them, something in me unwinds. She's healing him, or at least helping him, and despite the twinge of jealousy I feel, I couldn't be happier. Aiyaret has suffered for a long time, and the person who could fix him was right there.

I was just too blind to see it, thinking I knew best.

If we get out of here and she asks to be one of us, I'll let her in a heartbeat.

It's clear Maeve Carter belongs with us, but I will not tie her down if it isn't something she wants. I will never try to clip her wings. I love her wildness, and I will never take it from her.

"I promise." She presses her forehead to his. "Whatever happens, Aiyaret, you're not getting rid of me, okay?"

"Even if I'm dating Way?" he asks quietly, and I know that's one of his fears. He thought loving Way would mean losing her, but he doesn't know her very well.

"What does that have to do with anything?" she whispers. "I love that you both finally stopped being dumb and got together. Would you abandon me just because I like Wilder? Or Rick? Or Logan? Or even Way?"

"No," he answers without hesitation. "I'd be happy that someone I love likes the other person I love."

"Well then . . ." She grins. "That's your answer."

He stares at her for a moment. "I don't know if I could ever be with a woman after what my mother did." He doesn't speak about his past ever, so the fact that he's mentioning it to her tells me just how deeply Aiy trusts Maeve. "She hurt me, Maeve, a lot. She touched me . . . let others touch me. It ruined me, but I'd like to try letting you in. I know you'd never hurt me. I trust you. I love Way a lot, I can't live without him, but I'm starting to think I don't want to live without you either."

Holy shit.

Aiyaret has more bravery than all of us combined, and I'm so fucking happy he's being truthful with himself and giving himself a chance at being happy when he always thought he didn't deserve it.

"Then you don't have to," she replies. "I'm sorry for what you went through. You never have to speak of it, and you never have to touch me if you don't want to. How about you initiate anything, okay? If you want to touch me, then go for it, and I won't touch you at all."

"No," he protests. "I like it when you do, when you hold my hand or lean into me. It's . . . comforting. It makes me feel strong, like I'm someone who could protect you."

"Okay then, we'll figure it out," she vows. "Don't worry, alright? We have all the time in the world."

"Okay." He looks at Way. "You're not mad at me?"

"For what?" Way asks. "For being honest? For finally allowing yourself to be happy? I love you so much that all I want is for you to be happy. I don't care how you make that happen as long as I'm a part of it."

Way moves closer, and they hold Aiyaret between them. I glance away, giving them their privacy, until Maeve joins me at my side. Despite how soft she just was, her face is cold, furious, and when she speaks quietly, her tone is dangerous.

"Aiyaret's mother," she begins. "Is she still alive?"

I glance back to see Aiy talking to Way, not paying attention to us. "He doesn't speak about her, but we found out her name and looked ourselves. She died a few years ago from an illness."

"Too fucking quick," she snaps.

"What? Were you going to kill her?" I raise an eyebrow in amusement.

When she looks at me, her face is completely devoid of emotion, and it scares me. "I've been to the most remote places in the world and met some of the deadliest people. If you think I couldn't kill someone and get away with it, you're wrong." She turns and walks away, leaving me gawking after her.

I'm both turned on and afraid.

I remind myself never to piss her off again as I shake my head and turn to keep watch, giving Aiyaret and Way a few minutes to recover before I make us move.

It's quiet for a moment after that, and I focus on scanning the brush until there's a rustle. Frowning, I climb to my feet, trying to figure out where the sound is coming from.

There's a scream, and I whirl around just in time to see Rick being dragged back into the jungle, his arm and legs kicking before he disappears into the foliage, dragged away.

"Stay here!" I yell as I dive after him and come face-to-face with that creature.

It spins with a familiar hiss. Rick is lying on his side behind it where it dropped him. He isn't moving, and for a second, my heart stops as I stare at my silent, motionless brother.

I hear the others seconds behind me, and a gun fires close by, hitting the creature, who snarls, showing off rows of bloody teeth, and my heart stops.

"Get Rick!" Carter yells as she fires, hitting the creature's side and grabbing its attention. The croc lowers its head like it's going to charge, so she keeps moving back, pulling it away from Rick to give us the room we need.

I hesitate, hating that she's making herself a target again, but my brother isn't moving. I have to trust her to handle this. I run toward him, dropping to my knees when I get to his side. Blood coats his back, but I can't tell where it's coming from, and he's too still.

"Brother," I whisper, my heart beating so hard in my chest I can't breathe. I hesitate to touch him, my hands lingering above him before I turn him onto his back.

He groans, his eyes fluttering open. There's a cut across his head and blood covering his side, but his eyes open and his lips move. I lean in to hear what he says, and I almost cry.

"Women like scars, right?" he rasps.

I sag in relief and drag him into my arms, holding him tightly. "You're going to be okay. Let's get up." I help him to his feet as swiftly as I can, and he hangs onto my side. He's pale and bleeding, but he's alive, and that's all that matters for now. We need to get away before Carter runs out of ammo.

"Aiy, help me with Rick!" I yell when he just stands there, wide-eyed. Aiy rushes toward me, turning us so we can head into the jungle.

"Logan!" Maeve's terrified scream makes me whip around in time to see Logan dive at Carter, knocking her out of the way of that thing, but instead of getting her, it gets him.

Its mouth clamps down on his leg, dragging him off her as he screams, clawing at the dirt as he's hauled away. Maeve climbs to her feet and starts firing at its face as I race toward Logan, picking up a stick as I go.

Adrenaline pumps through me as his scream grows louder.

Leaping onto its back, I stab the stick into its head with all the strength I possess. It shakes from side to side, jarring Logan in its mouth as he howls, before I hit a sensitive spot that causes it to let him go. Maeve drags Logan away, and they fall into the dirt, him lying across her. His eyes are open, but he's bleeding from his leg, and he looks pale.

It jerks suddenly, and I'm thrown from its back. Rolling across the dirt, I smack into Way, who's coming over to help, knocking him back. That thing turns and focuses on Maeve and Logan again, and she pushes him aside, kneeling in front of him as she reloads. It gets closer and closer as I scramble to my feet. Finally, she lifts her arm and fires as it roars and spins, hitting her with its tail and knocking her into a tree. Her gun is gone.

Logan yells for her, and when it advances on her again, he's the closest.

"Logan, no!" I bellow, but it's too late. He throws himself into its path to protect Maeve, who's slowly sitting up, shaking her bleeding head. Wrapping himself around its mouth, he tries to hold it shut, yelling the entire time.

"The gun!" I yell at Way as I rush over. He hurries to find it as Aiyaret protects Rick. The croc jerks its head, and Logan flies off, rolling across the ground until he's by Maeve, but that thing keeps advancing, even when Way finds the rifle.

"Wilder!" he yells as he tosses it to me.

Catching it midair, I spin, ready to fire, but freeze.

Its jaw is open to swallow Maeve, but Logan presses his feet to the top and bottom of its mouth. When it snaps its maw shut, it catches his leg, and the agony-filled scream that leaves his mouth will haunt me for the rest of my life. He drops to the ground, screaming, and I fire.

I keep firing as it chomps, tossing something in his mouth, and I realize it's Logan's leg.

Horror makes my stomach roil as Maeve scrambles to staunch the bleeding, but I don't have time to check on them. I keep firing, and it snarls before diving into the jungle, racing away from us.

I keep the gun up, my arms shaking, but when it doesn't return, I glance back.

Logan is still screaming and writhing on the ground, and Way is with Maeve, both covering his right thigh, his leg missing just past the knee.

His leg is fucking gone.

Oh God.

# FORTY-FOUR
## MAEVE

Panic grips my chest and tears fill my eyes as I stare down at Logan. His face is pale and covered in sweat, and his eyes are too wide, showing too much white. He's still screaming, the horrible noise filled with terror and agony.

"My leg, my leg!" he finally shouts. "Is it gone? Is it gone? I can't—I can't feel it!"

"Carter, keep him calm!" Way orders. "The more he panics, the faster his heart pumps."

I feel tears drip down my cheeks as I pull my hands away from the stump where the bottom half of his leg used to be. I'm covered in blood, and Way swears as he tries to stop the bleeding, but Logan is moving so much, it's hard.

Gripping his face, I force him to look at me. "It's going to be okay. It's going to be okay," I insist, but tears won't stop falling from my eyes. "You're my hero, do you know that?"

"Maeve," he cries. "My leg . . . Is my leg gone?"

I glance at Way, who shakes his head, and I force a smile. "You're okay. You'll be okay," I repeat.

"I can't . . . I can't be an explorer without my leg. Is it gone? Please tell me!" he yells as Way does something and swears.

"Pin him down!" he shouts.

I force my full weight across him even as I cry, guilt and horror winding through me. I can still hear the bone crunching when the croc bit off his leg. My stomach churns as I shake my head, trying to focus on Logan and nothing else.

If it wasn't for him, that would have been me.

He saved me, but at what cost?

Logan eventually passes out, which is a relief. He won't be in pain this way, but it also gives us the chance we need to stop the bleeding.

"Here," Wilder says, but I'm so focused on Logan, I don't react. "Carter! I need you!"

I jerk my head up to see him holding the gun. "You're the best shot. I'm the best with medicine. Swap!"

Nodding, I grab the rifle with shaking, bloody hands and get to my feet, protecting them as I cry.

My grip slips on the barrel, and I glance from the jungle to Logan. Rick is on his knees, panting and pale, with Aiyaret helping him as Wilder and Way work on him, using my bag and supplies.

No matter what they do, he lost a limb—for me.

The atmosphere is tense and quiet as they work, and eventually, Logan wakes up, screaming once more, before he passes out again, and Wilder sits back. "That's all we can do for now. We need to get to the beach immediately!" He climbs to his feet. "Way, help me carry him. Carter, stay behind us with the gun. Aiyaret, help Rick. We need to run."

"I can keep up. Focus on Logan," Rick argues.

Wilder nods and turns to me.

"I'm sorry, I'm sorry," I chant. "It's my fault. He tried to protect me."

"Carter!" I startle as Wilder grips my cheeks. "I need you to focus. We have to get him out of here before we lose him. I can't do that without you, okay? We can cry later, but for now, we need you."

Nodding jerkily, I wipe my face, smearing Logan's blood across it. "I'm good. Let's move." I force myself to be okay. He needs me.

Logan saved my life, and now we need to save his.

We move fast. Logan wakes from the jostling, and his weak, pained moans are worse than anything. He lost a lot of blood, and his wound is life-threatening. I'm just praying Ajax will be there when we get to the beach.

*Please, please be on your way.*

Everything went from happy to shit in seconds, and I blame myself.

I can't lose him.

That thing doesn't come back, but we move fast. Sweat dries on me as I run, my stained hands flaking with Logan's blood. We don't stop to rest, and he tries to bite back his screams.

"Is Carter okay?" he rasps.

"I'm fine," I tell him, my voice tight. I'm scarcely able to believe he's worried about me right now.

"Rick?" he asks.

"He's fine, stop worrying," Way barks as he helps carry Logan. "Just focus on yourself, okay?"

"It was pretty badass, right?" he says through gritted teeth. "All heroic and shit. What do you think, Maeve?"

I force back the tears that want to fall. "So badass." My voice sounds weird, but I know he needs a distraction right now. "My hero. I'll have to find a way to thank you."

"I can think of a few ways," he jokes, but it falls flat when he screams in pain, and a shudder of horror passes through me.

We move faster after that, and we finally break out onto the beach, only to find it empty. Wilder looks at me, his eyes wide. "Where are they?"

"I don't know." I yank my bag open and grab the GPS and phone, searching for a signal. "They should be here."

They lay Rick and Logan down side by side, and I have to close my eyes for a second as they hold each other's hands. Rick turns to watch Logan as Wilder paces, and Way comforts Aiyaret, who is crying.

"Fuck!" Wilder roars at the ocean before he turns to me and drops to his knees. "Carter, please, where are they?"

Tears well in his eyes as he stares at me, looking so hopeless and lost. "Carter, please, I can't lose him."

My hands shake as I stare at him until the phone finally connects, and I hit speaker. "Maeve, is that you?" Ajax asks.

"It's me! It's me!" I rush out. "Where are you? We need you. Logan is hurt badly, really badly."

"We are on our way. Fifteen minutes out. The others?"

"Alive," I reply. "Rick is hurt, and so is Wilder, but Logan—please, Ajax, hurry."

"We'll be there. We have your position. I have two medics with me, just don't move, do you hear me? Do not move! Now, let me talk to Wilder." I hand the phone over. "Okay, Wilder, talk me through his condition. They are listening, and we might be able to help while you wait."

Wilder hurries to his brother's side, and I step back, watching them.

A hiss behind me has me turning, and I see the creature in the jungle, ready to attack again. They are all oblivious as they work on their brother, trying to keep him alive. Gripping the gun tighter, I spare them a look.

They won't be safe while that thing is here.

They saved my life, and now it's my turn to save theirs. I'll buy them the time until Ajax gets here. I allow myself one last look at them before I turn away, wishing I could tell them how much they mean to me, but they are focused on Logan, and if they realized what I planned to do, they would stop me.

No. I need to save them and give the rescue team time.

Silently, I head toward the jungle and dive into the brush. Grabbing a rock, I toss it at the creature. It hisses but moves farther away, so I grab another one and slice the palm of my hand so I'm bleeding, then I toss it again.

It turns as I keep throwing more, and I walk backwards into the jungle as it advances on me. I need to lead it away. I'm also running out of ammo, so I need my shots to be true.

"Come on, you ugly motherfucker!" I growl as it snaps and shuffles after me. "You can't have them, you understand me? They are mine!"

Smacking the gun into my side, I make as much noise as I can as I back up. "Come on, you prehistoric bitch. Are you hungry? I'm right here! Finish what you started!"

Glancing back, I see a huge rock on my right, and an idea comes to mind. It's a truly terrible one, but it's all I have. I back toward it as the croc snaps and hisses, lunging at me as I taunt it. I don't care how long this creature has been here or that we stumbled into its home and it's defending itself—I won't let it hurt any more of the guys.

I'll keep them safe no matter what.

"Come on!" I yell as I back up close to the rock, feeling it behind me just as it lunges.

My back hits the massive boulder hard, and I curl into it, screaming as the croc charges me, opening its mouth. It snaps into the rock, missing me, and moves back, shaking its head, and I see a tooth come loose.

It's working. The way the rock is slanted means it can't get to the curve in the middle. It's the only chance I have. I need to be close to kill this motherfucker. Raising the gun with steady hands, I feel everything in me go cold as I blow out a breath and extend my arms.

One of us will die here, and it won't be me.

I have too much to live for.

"Come on!" I shout. "I'm right here. You want to kill me? Go ahead. I'm taking you with me." It hisses again, and I snarl, "I'm right here! Come on!"

It finally lunges toward me.

I fire into its open mouth as its jaws close over me, hitting the rock above and the ground below. It struggles, trying to snap its mouth closed, but it's caught, and I keep firing, my arms and sides being torn by those vicious teeth as it tries its best to eat me.

I keep firing until the gun clicks empty, and it's only then I realize it isn't moving. Blood drips down my body, and I blink, breathing heavily as I look around. It's dead—it has to be. I slide up higher on the rock, freezing as a hiss escapes its mouth, and I swear its jaw clamps down before it suddenly snaps again. Screaming, I scramble for anything to help me as it shakes and struggles. My hand connects with something, so I lift it and stab. I keep stabbing as its mouth snaps again. Reaching through its sharp teeth, I swing over and over at its head with a bellow. I'm wild with my need to kill until my body gives into exhaustion. Heavy and done, I drop my arm and see the blood-covered tooth of the beast in my grip.

It's frozen, and I worry for a moment it's a trap until it collapses, seeming to deflate.

It's . . . It's dead.

Panting, I struggle to slide out from under it. I have to crawl, and I feel my back shred against its teeth before I crumple on the wet ground, bleeding and exhausted.

The creature is dead and unmoving.

"Eat that, motherfucker," I rasp.

"Maeve! Please, Maeve!" I hear them yell, and I know I need to go back to the beach before they come after me. They have to focus on Logan. That thought gets me going, even as my body wants to give in to the agony coursing through me. Stumbling to my feet, I use their worried shouts as a beacon. My leg aches and wants to give out, my body deciding now would be a good time to pack it in. Adrenaline is the only thing that keeps me going until I stumble out onto the beach to find a panicking Aiy right in front of me.

"Maeve!" He yanks me into his arms. "What happened?"

I lean into him as Wilder and Way look at me. "It's dead," I say. "I killed it." Pulling away from Aiy, I sit in the sand next to Logan. "How is he?"

"He's going to be okay. They are almost there." I glance at Wilder as he sets off a flare. "You're fucking crazy, Carter."

"Don't forget it." I smile as I pant and lie back in the sand, exhausted and bloody.

Finally, I hear the sound of the rescue helicopter over the lap of the ocean waves. "I guess the calvary is here," I joke, and a trembling hand grips mine. I glance over to see Logan looking at me, holding my hand. Someone else takes my other one, and I turn to find Wilder there.

"We'll be okay." He nods. "Just hold on. Everyone, just hold on."

When the helicopter is above us, I struggle to my feet, and we help

Logan and Rick in first. Wilder shoves me in next, and once I'm in a seat, I watch as they work on Logan, quiet and numb.

"Maeve, are you okay?" Ajax yells over the helicopter engine as he leans in. "Maeve!"

"I'm fine, I'm fine," I say as they get the rest of the guys into the helicopter, and then we are on the move. Wilder crowds his brothers as Way holds Aiy and drags me under his other arm. I watch them from the shelter of his embrace.

"We are okay. We made it," he whispers. "We are going to be okay."

Everything catches up to me before I know it.

My last vision is of Logan bleeding all over the helicopter's floor as Wilder cries his name, and the monitor he's connected to alerts, his heart giving out.

# FORTY-FIVE
## MAEVE

**D**éjà vu, that's what I feel when I open my eyes to a familiar ceiling. Beeping sounds near me, and dim lights surround me. My heart thuds, and I jerk upright, scanning the room. I find my dad sleeping at my side. "Dad?"

He sits up, blinking. "Maeve," he whispers as he pulls me into a hug. I fall into his embrace, but I continue to search my room.

"Dad, where are they? What happened?"

Pulling back, he cradles my face in his palms, searching my gaze before he deflates. "I thought I'd lost you again, Maeve. Don't you ever do that again. I was so scared."

"I'm sorry. I really am. Please, Dad, where are they?" I'm panicking.

The last thing I remember was Logan's heart stopping.

"I know you aren't going to calm down until you see them, so give me one second," he whispers. He presses a buzzer, and within minutes, I'm being wheeled down the corridor. It must be nighttime because there aren't many staff members or visitors and it's quiet.

I lean forward like that will help me go faster. A couple of rooms down, they open a door and roll me inside, and I get my first glimpse of the guys. I feel like I can finally breathe again.

261

Logan is in a hospital bed like I was. His eyes are closed, and machines are hooked up to him, but he looks clean and less pale. Rick is in a bed next to him, his head turned away. Wilder is bandaged to hell but asleep in a large chair between them, while Way and Aiyaret are cuddled together on a sofa in the back of the room.

My dad lowers his voice so he doesn't wake them. "They kept swapping who stayed with you and their friends until I kicked them out. Their fussing was annoying me or they would have been by your side."

"Logan? Rick?" I whisper.

"They are going to be okay. Rick had some damage to his shoulder, but with physical therapy, it will be back to normal. He had a cut on his head, too, but the doctors weren't overly worried. They are all dehydrated and need rest," my dad explains.

"Logan?" I ask, and he winces.

"His condition is more serious. The lower half of his leg is gone. Luckily, he got here quickly, so infection hasn't set in. They did operate. Hopefully he won't need anything, but he has a long road ahead of him, kid. He'll need lots of rest and physical therapy. Ajax mentioned getting him the best treatment and prosthetic." The rest of his words fade off as I double over, tears filling my eyes.

Everything he worked for, all his dreams, was taken in an instant.

I know he's lucky to be alive, but his independence and mobility meant everything to him, and now it's just gone, and it's my fault.

He was protecting me.

"Kid, don't cry. They are all okay. They are alive thanks to you," my dad murmurs, but that just makes me cry harder. "Let me wake them," my dad offers, and I shake my head.

"No, let them sleep. I can't face them anyway." He frowns, and I wipe my eyes. "Take me back."

"Maeve."

"Take me back," I demand.

Frowning, he helps wheel me out, and we are down the corridor when I hear footsteps.

"Carter!" We stop, and I freeze in my chair. "That's it? You come in while we're asleep and then just leave? Nothing else?" Wilder hurries around, stopping before me. "You aren't even going to stay?"

I look away. "I was just checking on you."

"Bullshit. You can lie to yourself, but not me," he snaps, searching my eyes with desperation.

"I'm not lying," I retort, wishing more than anything I wasn't in this fucking chair so I could run away.

"Son, maybe this should wait," my dad cautions, but Wilder steps forward.

"No offense, Mr. Carter, but she's lying." He looks at me, his eyes hard. "You're being a coward, and Maeve Carter is not a fucking coward."

"It's my fault!" I yell, and he blinks. "It's my fault Logan is in there. He lost his leg, Wilder. All his dreams, his future, are gone because of me."

"That's what you think?" He purses his lips. "My brother's future is not gone, even without his leg, and no offense, Maeve, but not everything is about you, so you get your ass in that room and sit at his side, even if you feel guilty. He did everything to protect you. It's the least you can do."

"Son, stop," my dad interjects. "Everyone is worried and stressed right now. Let's give Maeve a minute, okay?"

Wilder looks from my dad to me, his eyebrow arched. "If you roll away, you've made your choice. We both know you aren't a coward who runs away because you feel guilty. Those men need you, and you promised to be there. Don't make yourself a liar." He steps back, letting me choose, and I hesitate.

"It's your choice, kid. Want me to slug him?" my dad teases, and I wipe my eyes, knowing my dad would, but Wilder is wrong.

I am a coward. I can't face them, not right now.

"Maeve," Aiyaret says softly as he appears at my side, and if it had been any of the others, I would have left, but it's Aiy. "Logan is awake. He heard your voice, and he's asking for you."

My dad waits, letting me choose, so I take a deep breath and nod. "Take me to see him."

My dad smiles as I turn around, and Wilder and Aiyaret follow me. Way is awake now, and so is Rick. I check them over before realizing I'm stalling. When my eyes land on Logan in the bed, I want to sob. He looks so weak, pale, and . . . small.

Logan always appears large with his personality and noisiness, but right now, he looks broken, and my heart breaks.

"There she is. How do you look hot even in a medical gown?" he teases, and my dad coughs. "Oops, sorry, future father-in-law. I couldn't help myself. Your daughter is just so beautiful."

My dad laughs and squeezes my shoulder. "I'll be outside, okay? Shout if you need me."

I nod and watch him leave before Wilder moves me closer and steps back. I linger at Logan's bedside, where he sits up slightly. "Don't look at me like that," he whispers.

"Like what?" I murmur.

"Like you're waiting for me to break down. I've had enough from these guys."

"We are just worried," I reply, placing my hand on the bed before I hesitate. He doesn't, reaching for it and taking it as he smiles softly. "Logan, I'm sorry."

"For what?" he asks, forcing a bright smile, but it's tight. He's holding on by a thread. I hate that he feels like he has to be strong right now.

"Your leg." He jerks, and I hold his hand tighter. "I'm sorry. I know you were protecting me. I'm so fucking sorry."

"It's not your fault." He pulls me closer. "Look at me, Maeve. It isn't your fault. I made a decision in that moment, and I don't regret it. I'd do it all over again. Yes, it sucks that I lost my leg, but we're alive, and that's all that matters."

When I'm quiet, he carries on, his voice too high and fast.

"I'm a fighter, Maeve, always have been. This will be no different. I know it won't be easy, but I never did take the easy route anyway. Don't blame yourself, okay? I don't."

"You don't need to be okay and strong for me," I tell him.

He goes to make a joke, and I squeeze his hand. "Logan, you don't have to be okay right now. You don't need to make jokes or make us comfortable. You are allowed to be sad, angry, or whatever you want to be. You don't need to pretend—not for them and not for me."

He holds my gaze, and I see his fragile walls crumble as he tries to hold himself together. It's a feeling I know far too well.

"Can you hold me?" he whispers, and I'm up in a minute. Ignoring Wilder's objections, I climb into the bed, careful of his leg and side, and tug him into my arms.

I don't say anything. There's nothing I can say that will make this situation better. Yes, Ajax will help, and he'll get the best treatment. He'll walk and have a new leg, but it doesn't change what he has lost.

His tears are silent at first, but as I hold him, he sobs louder and starts to shake.

The others are quiet as I hold Logan, and despite his assurance, my guilt will never go away.

"We are right here," I murmur, blinking back my own tears. "We are all right here, and we aren't going anywhere. We'll be with you every step of the way."

"But I can't do this job anymore. I'll be left behind," he sobs.

"Never," I vow. "We will never leave you, I promise you. We are in this together. You can't get rid of us, so don't even think about it. For now, you need to focus on resting, okay? Try to sleep. We are right here."

He cries for a little while longer until he finally falls to sleep, and I meet Wilder's heartbroken eyes. I know we have a long road ahead of us, but what I said is true.

I'm not going anywhere.

I must fall asleep at some point because I wake up to a soft voice. I feign sleep when I realize it's my dad.

"I know how you feel. When I found out about my illness, I thought it was a death sentence. The worst part was knowing I would never be out there at her side again. Son, whatever happens, you will never lose your family, but this is not the end. It's just another battle, another path. You're strong—you have to be for my daughter to care for you so much. If you are even half the man she thinks you are, then you're going to be okay. There are plenty of athletes and competitors out there with missing limbs. This isn't the end, not like it is for me. You just have to want it badly enough." He's quiet for a moment. "I can't be out there with her anymore, and it kills me, but you can be. She needs you. I knew it the moment she woke up and risked her life to come back for you. You're her team now, the family she needs, so be strong and tackle this like everything else. You're going to be okay, but when things get hard, you have a family to fall back on."

"I'm scared," Logan admits softly. "I'm scared I'll never get to see the world again, and that I won't be able to keep up anymore."

"Of course you are, that's normal, but you can't let fear stop you. You didn't when you saved my daughter, and you won't now, and you will always have a home with me, understood? Anyone who is willing to risk their life for Maeve is my family. Whatever happens, you aren't alone."

"Aren't you afraid?" Logan asks.

"I used to be, but want to know what truly terrifies me? It's leaving my daughter alone in the world, but she won't be anymore, and I owe all of you for that. I don't know what happened on that island, and I don't need to unless you want to tell me, but all I know is she risked her life to save you, and that tells me everything. She's the most loyal person in this world, and she chose you. Whatever happens now, I know she'll be okay. It's a relief," he replies.

"But there are five of us." Logan tenses, no doubt trying to convey his meaning. My dad must catch on.

"Meh, my daughter has never been one to do anything the same way as others. I don't care as long as she is happy and safe. Do you understand?"

"I do," Logan answers. "Thank you. I'm not usually this . . . troubled. I just—"

"It's to be expected. I can't begin to imagine what you are feeling, but if you let her, she'll be right there with you through it all. Now, get some rest. I'll watch over you, okay?"

I feel Logan slide down, and it doesn't take long before he's asleep. "I know you're awake, kid." I wince, and he chuckles softly. "You never could pull this trick on me, even when you were young. Sleep, tomorrow is a new day." He pats my head, and I nod, moving closer to Logan.

The next journey will be just as hard as the one we took to get here.

## FORTY-SIX
## RICK

We've been in the hospital for a few days, and it's driving us all crazy. Wilder and I have been given the all clear. I'll need physical therapy, but they want me to start in our home city when Logan is stable enough to move. Luckily, the first operation was a success. He might need another in the future, but they are hopeful he won't. The doctors said his mindset has a lot to do with it. His recovery hinges on it, so we need to keep his strength up and ensure his happiness.

Ajax checks on us daily and tells us not to worry about anything else. Since Maeve keeps sleeping in our room as well, he wrangles it so we can all share one. It's a squeeze, but none of us care. When Logan wakes up panicking, she's there, holding his hand, and we give them the privacy they need since he only seems comfortable letting her see that, not us. It hurts, but I know he's worried about upsetting us.

Maeve's dad is here every day, looking after us and making sure we rest and eat. He's a great man, and we get along well. He tells us his stories about his expeditions, and I love it.

None of us have spoken about what will happen when we go back. I know I don't want to be apart from Maeve. We wouldn't have survived that island without her, but it's more than that. It's the bond we created while we were there, driven by trauma, fear, and something deeper. I know none of us want to say goodbye, but I also know it's probably out of our hands. Ajax has contracts and plans, and we need to figure out a way around those, but for now, we are all focused on resting and relaxing. Soon enough, our need to move and do more will emerge, but we are all riding the wave of post-survival glow and making the most of it.

Way folds his cards on the table with a groan since this is the second hand he's lost in a row. Logan is sleeping, and when Way glances over, I follow his gaze. Logan's hand is in Maeve's, who's curled up at his side. He never wants her far from him, and I understand, but the strangest part is she doesn't seem inclined to leave him either.

"She's going to injure herself sleeping like that every night," Way grumbles as he climbs to his feet and stretches out.

"You try telling her what to do." I grin as I pick up another card and inspect my hand.

"Not a chance. She scares me." He grins as he walks over to them. Way pulls the blanket from the bed and drapes it around her shoulders, tucking it in carefully before lingering. I think he assumes no one is watching as he leans down and kisses her forehead, but when I glance back, I see all my brothers are staring too.

Aiyaret and Way are dating, but Aiy smiles as he watches them, seemingly happy, then focuses back on his cards. He's been bolder since we got off the island, more open to speaking and asking for what he wants. He still has nightmares, but he's changing, and we all know it's thanks to Maeve and Way.

How could we deny him anything that makes him happy?

"You know this isn't normal, right?" Wilder comments, his voice low as Way rejoins us, holding a water bottle in his hand. "When we get back to reality, she might walk away from us. Whatever this . . . thing is between us, it's not something the world would ever tolerate. She already fights so much more than us since she's a woman in our field and has to prove herself, so this might be too much."

"I think that's up to her," I say as I process his words. "No one tells

Maeve Carter what to do, and when she's made up her mind, she's sure. Besides, she never gave a damn what the world thought before."

"And you?" my brother asks. "What if it means losing our fans and our job?"

He's anxious, so I pat his shoulder. "Brother, stop worrying so much about the future, especially one that might never happen. You like Maeve, yes?"

His lips purse, but he nods his head.

"Then that's all that matters. Our relationships are between us, no one else. Besides, none of us have ever been normal, so why should our dating lives be standard? If anyone could keep up with us, it's her."

"What if this all goes wrong?" Wilder sighs, and I see the fear in his eyes. He's always trying to protect us from things that might hurt us.

"You can't protect our hearts, Wilder," Way says as if he were thinking the same thing. "Any relationship can fail, not just this one, but that doesn't mean we shouldn't give it a try. I say let Maeve lead, and we'll follow."

"It's her choice," Aiy agrees as he looks at Wilder. "We shouldn't take it from her or talk for her. Personally, I don't care if it seems odd to anyone else. She makes us happy, so why is that a problem?"

"You know, almost being eaten by a croc really enlightened you," I tease, and Aiy gives me a narrow-eyed look. "Just saying."

"And it didn't stop that mouth," he retorts, making my eyes widen as we all burst out laughing before becoming silent when there's a groan from the sleeping beauties.

We play a few hands before Wilder finally speaks up. "I'm just . . . worried—not just for us, but for her." His eyes go to Maeve. "She's been through enough. I don't want to be another reason she's hurting."

"So then don't be." I shrug. "It's that simple."

## WILDER

Everyone is asleep when I wake up to grab a drink, but Maeve's bed is empty. Frowning, I search the dark room in case I missed her. Sometimes she's in the bed with Logan, but he's spread out, snoring. Way and Aiyaret are curled up together on another bed, and Rick is hanging from a sofa, but she's nowhere in sight.

Slipping from the room, I stride down the silent corridor. Everyone else is gone at this hour, with only a skeleton staff. The room next to ours is technically Maeve's, but she hasn't spent a night there since Logan woke up. I check there first, though. Sliding open the door, I scan the semi-dark room. The soft neon lights inlaid around the bottom of the walls just give off enough illumination for me to see shapes, and there is a lump in the bed.

Closing the door silently, I tread closer, in case it's Maeve's dad or Ajax, but the person looks too small to be either. The blanket is up over the person's head, like a cocoon, and it seems to be shaking.

I pause beside them, listening hard, and I hear soft sniffles, like they are trying to hold back their tears.

Gripping the blanket, I rip it back, and she gasps as she turns over, her eyes bloodshot and puffy. Maeve stares up at me in horror. "Get out!" She grabs the blanket and tries to cover herself, but I hold it until we are playing tug-of-war. Smirking, I watch her struggle, and she swears and lets it go, rolling over and giving me her back. "I'm not in the mood, Wilder," she warns, her voice quiet, and it chases the last of my amusement away.

I sit on the edge of the bed, grab her shoulder, and try to turn her to face me, but she resists, so I stop. "I'm sorry. I was worried."

She stiffens under my touch and then slowly turns to look at me, her eyes brimming with tears that fall silently down her cheeks. Her chin wobbles as she tries to stop.

Fuck, that look . . . It burns me to my core.

I slide my hand down and grip hers. "Talk to me, Carter. What's going on? Did something happen?" I ask, my voice softer than it's ever been.

For a moment, I don't know if she'll answer.

"Talk to me, Carter. I'll fix it."

"You can't. I don't even know," she answers around her sniffles. "It's like everything has caught up to me, and I needed to get out of that room. I couldn't stop—" Shaking her head, she covers her face.

My brow furrows. This isn't like Maeve, but she's been through a lot, so it makes sense that all of her strength would eventually crumble. With a gentle grip, I tug her hands from her face and wrap my fingers around her wrists when she tries to escape me again.

"Carter, stop." She keeps struggling, and we fall back, her eyes wide as we both freeze. Her hands are still in mine, and I'm pinning her down. Every inch of me is touching her. I sit up, not wanting to put pressure on her bad leg, and she stares up at me, looking so lost and confused.

"Come here, baby." Gathering her into my arms, I lean back on the bed. She remains stiff at first before relaxing. Her hands fist my shirt before she buries her face in the fabric and cries for everything that happened, everything she endured and saw.

"That first night I cried so hard I threw up," I murmur. "Everyone else was asleep, but I was so scared for Logan and what it meant. I couldn't let anyone else see."

Her head lifts, and she meets my eyes. "Wilder crying? I don't believe it."

"I'll take a picture next time," I tease. "All I'm saying, baby, is that this is normal. You were running on adrenaline on that island, we all were, and we endured things we could never even begin to explain to other people. Thinking we were going to die nearly every moment of every day takes its toll, so if you need to cry, then cry. I won't tell anyone."

"Gee, thanks," she grumbles and smiles. I wipe her face before she lowers her head.

"Don't worry. Tomorrow, I'll go back to fighting you," I tease, and she smiles through her tears.

"Okay, tomorrow," she murmurs as she lies back down.

Resting my head on top of hers, I hold her tighter, my heartbeat easing in my chest. I'm always so worried about what tomorrow will bring and how I can keep my family safe, but in this moment, with her in my arms, I feel like I can breathe for the first time ever.

I don't know how long we lie like this before her breathing evens out, and when I glance down, I realize she is asleep. Pushing her hair back, I kiss her head just like Way did. "I wish we could stay like this forever, Carter," I whisper. "I don't want to go back. I don't want to face what that means, especially the possibility of losing you. It's selfish, but I don't want to let you go. You make me feel alive, Carter, and I don't think I can go back to a life before you." It's a stolen confession, words I'll never tell her. Carter isn't one to be tied down, but it's the truth.

I wish we could stay like this forever, but tomorrow always comes.

Sighing, I pull her closer and close my eyes. I don't know how long I sleep for, but when I wake up, we are still wrapped around each other. I'm facing away from the door, and her back is against my chest as she lies on her good leg. She burrowed into my arm that's under her head, but something woke me up.

A noise.

I strain my ears, and it comes again. It's from her.

She's moaning.

The sound is soft and breathy, and I look down, finally realizing where my other hand is. It's in her loose hospital pants, cupping her bare pussy and playing with it. She's wet and warm and grinding into me, and I was fucking feeling her up.

Bad fucking hand! I stiffen, knowing I'm taking advantage of her, though I don't know if it counts since I was asleep too, but obviously I'm a perv while I'm sleeping.

"Don't stop," she whispers, and I realize she's awake. Her head turns, and she boldly meets my eyes. "I think we both need something to cling to, some semblance of sanity . . . something good, so don't fucking stop, Wilder."

"Carter . . ." I swallow, fighting a losing battle to stop my hand from feeling her soft, warm heat again.

"You've never treated me like glass, so don't start now." Reaching up, she grips the back of my head and drags me down until my lips are close to hers. "Fuck me like you've always wanted, Wilder. Fuck me like you hate me."

Glancing from her eyes to her mouth, I groan and give in, pressing my lips to hers as I stroke her cunt. She rolls onto her back, giving me better access, her thighs falling open.

She's so fucking hot and wet, I need to taste her more than I need my next breath.

Sliding my hand from her pants, I get to my knees, grip the waistband of her pants, and slowly tug them down and off before throwing them behind me.

Lifting her bad leg, I press a soft kiss on the scars there, and she watches me, her throat bobbing. I lower it and lift her other leg, kissing down and back up until I'm right where I belong—kneeling between Carter's perfect thighs.

Her eyes find mine as she widens her legs, her chest heaving for me, and for a moment, I just stare, obsessed with how incredible she looks, until her eyes narrow.

"Wilder," she snaps. "If you don't fucking touch me—"

I drag my tongue up her pussy, silencing her as she groans. Her head falls back, and she clutches my hair. "Always so argumentative, Carter. Don't you know you catch more flies with honey?"

"Or you just burn the fucking place down instead," she retorts.

Chuckling, I hold her tighter, loving how she fights me even when my mouth is on her dripping cunt. She never backs down, and it drives me crazy. I lap at her pussy, tasting her cream on my tongue, sweet and utterly perfect. Her hand tightens in my hair, dragging me closer as she rocks into my mouth, chasing what she wants.

I'll give her anything she desires as long as she keeps making those noises for me. She's fighting to hold back her quiet moans but can't seem to. My fingers dig into her good thigh as I lift her to get a better angle, then I thrust my tongue inside her wet heat, fucking her with it. Her thigh trembles in my grip, and she presses against my mouth, her channel clenching on my tongue. I circle her clit, driving her mad, until she's panting and fighting to get off.

Her eyes are filled with fire as she glares at me. "Make me come," she orders.

"Ask nicely," I tease as I lick my lips, tasting her before I blow on her hot cunt, watching as she shudders.

"Wilder," she warns.

"Carter," I purr. My dick throbs in my pants as I grind against the bed, needing to be buried inside her while she glares at me like that.

Her eyes narrow further, and she goes to push me away, but I pin her leg and bite down on her good thigh until she hisses. "Don't you dare try to take this pretty pussy away from me. I haven't had my fill yet," I growl as I lap at her teasingly, winding her up further as I slide my other fingers over her wetness and shove two inside her.

She arches up off the bed, moaning loudly before she cuts it off. Panting, she writhes on the sheet, the bed frame creaking as she rides my fingers, and I can't do anything but give her what she wants. I need to see her come, even if she won't ask nicely.

I can stand losing if it's to her.

Sealing my lips around her clit, I suck and nip it as I add a third finger, crooking them inside her and stroking her walls until her legs start to shake. Her muffled cries grow louder, and then she comes all over me, her cunt fluttering around my fingers. The feeling is so fucking perfect, I memorize it as I lick her through it. She yanks on my head when she slumps, pulling me away, but I want to taste every drop of her cream, so I slide my fingers free and suck on them as she watches me with half-lidded eyes.

"You look good fucked, Carter," I tell her as I slide up her body and press my cock against her pussy, letting her feel how hard I am. "Are you going to be nice so I can give us what we both want?"

"Not a fucking chance," she counters as she tugs on my shirt. "Get naked."

Chuckling, I sit up and remove my shirt, then I shove my pants down. It's a struggle to get them off, and she smirks until my cock springs free, and then her smile drops. She eyes my length with awe and trepidation. I'm big, but it's the piercing that catches her eye.

Fisting my length, I stroke myself as she watches. "It's going to feel so good inside you, Carter."

"It fucking better," she retorts, meeting my eyes. "Shit, I don't have a condom."

Fuck.

I look from her to my dick, ready to stop if she tells me to, even though it's the last thing I want. Slumping back, she laughs before shaking her head. "Ah, fuck it. Just pull out." She slides her hand down my body until she covers my fist on my cock and tightens her grip to the point of pain. "Don't you dare get me pregnant, Wilder, or I'll fucking kill you."

"I'd probably enjoy it," I quip before I press my lips to hers, kissing her hard. I thrust into her grip, but we both want more. Knocking her hand aside, I lift her thigh, which she wraps around me, urging me on as I slide my length across her wet cunt. She rolls her hips, demanding more as she sucks on my tongue.

Lining up with her entrance, I bite her lower lip as I push in. She cries out, and I sweep my tongue over her lips, rolling my hips. I pull out then push back in, forcing her to take more of me until I'm buried deep inside her.

She feels so fucking good raw, so hot and tight, her body gripping my cock like she never wants me to pull out of her, and honestly, I don't want to either.

Her body is paradise.

She lifts her hips and pulls her mouth away from mine. "Stop being nice, Wilder. Show me what you can do. Let me feel your piercing. You promised."

Kneeling, I lift her ass into the air. "So I did. Hold on, Carter."

I slam into her, and her eyes close as she gasps, grabbing the bedding as I pull out and slam back in, watching her breasts jiggle from the force. The sight burns into my brain, pushing me past the limits of my control, but I know she can take it as I pummel into her body. She pulls me down, her lips finding mine again as her fingernails dig into my shoulders and back. I keep up my relentless force, pleasure spiraling through me with each perfect thrust into her incredible body, her little sounds of pleasure only urging me on.

The bed squeaks with the force of my movements, the flash of pain from her nails making me grunt. "Don't fucking stop!" she orders.

"Not a chance," I snarl, fighting her tightening cunt. My hand slaps the wall above the bed for leverage as I drive into her. "Jesus, who knew this is where we would be?"

"Don't lie, Wilder, you've wanted this since the moment you met me," she teases, but her words end in a moan as I twist my hips and press my piercing against her inner wall.

"Too fucking right. I wanted to bend your annoying ass over and fuck it raw until you shut your smart mouth."

She narrows her eyes and jerks up, but the force knocks us sideways, and we tip from the stupid hospital bed. I turn and wrap my arms around her, absorbing the impact against the floor, but it doesn't stop either of us. We twist and roll until I pin her down and drive into her harder. She cries out, meeting my thrusts with her hips. Her pussy tightens, and I know she's close.

Leaning down, I press my mouth to her ear. "Admit you've always wanted me and I'll let you come."

Her tongue darts out, wetting her lips that curve in a knowing smirk. Her back arches, and her cunt clenches around me, driving me crazy. "I've wanted you since the first moment I met you," she whispers.

It rips me apart because she's right. I wanted her all along, and now she's mine.

Pressing my hand into the floor beside her, I move faster and harder until her eyes roll back in her head and her cunt clenches around me as her orgasm tears through her. Her choked cry fills the air and sends me over the edge. I remember to pull out at the last second and come across her stomach instead.

My orgasm is so intense, I feel drained, like I've always needed this . . . needed her.

"Fuck," I rasp as her eyes open and lock on me above her. "We are doing that again, Carter."

"Don't get cocky, Wilder," she scoffs then groans as I kiss her.

Smirking, I pull away, and she sighs but lies back, and we both look at the bed.

"Oops," she remarks.

Our laughter mixes until there's a knock on the door. "You guys done?" We blink at Rick's voice. "Um, you pressed the emergency buzzer during your . . . carnal activities. I assured them you are okay, but I'd maybe go tell them yourselves before they burst in here."

Maeve groans, pressing her head to my shoulder, and a smile spreads across my lips.

"Guys?" Rick calls. "Guys? Seriously."

## FORTY-SEVEN
## MAEVE

"Can you pass me a towel?" I yell through the door. I forgot to bring one in here. I'm supposed to be careful when I'm in the shower, but I needed one so badly, I rushed to get under the hot spray. "Hello?" I call again, peeking through the cracked door.

Aiyaret appears. "Maeve, are you okay?"

"Where is everyone?" I frown. They were here when I came in.

"Logan had some tests, so the others went with them. I came back to check on you."

"Oh, uh, can you pass me a towel? I forgot one," I admit.

Chuckling, he disappears then passes one through the door.

"Thanks." I shut the door and dry off before struggling into an oversized shirt and pajama pants. When I open the door again, I find Aiy waiting for me. "What kind of test?" I ask as I turn to the mirror. My leg aches from standing for so long, and I rub it as I wipe the mirror and grimace at my hair.

Fucking Wilder last night didn't help—well, it helped my mental health and needs, but it made my already dirty hair worse. I don't regret it though. I worried I would this morning, but I felt good about it, like it had been a long time coming, and Wilder didn't seem to feel anything but happiness about it as well. Rick has been shooting me knowing looks all morning, but no one else has said anything, so either they don't know or don't care.

"Just routine stuff. What's wrong?" he asks, leaning against the doorframe as I sigh at the state of my hair.

"I couldn't wash my hair," I reply. "My shoulder . . ." Fingering the greasy locks, I debate shaving my head to make life easier.

"Let me?" he requests so softly, I almost don't hear it.

"You don't have to do that," I murmur, eyes widening.

"I want to." He smiles sweetly then hurries away. When he returns, he holds another towel. Aiyaret notices my hand on my leg, and he disappears again before coming back with a chair. Placing it before the sink, he pats it. "Sit."

Grinning, I sit down, and he drapes the towel around my neck, protecting my clothes. I relax back as he turns on the water and lays my dirty hair in the sink. After grabbing what he needs, he carefully wets it then lathers shampoo in his hands. I watch him as he does. He's leaning into me and doesn't seem to notice. He went from someone who recoiled at my touch to this man. It's a complete one-eighty, and I'm so proud of him. Moreover, I like that he is comfortable with my touch.

One of his hands covers my eyebrows, protecting the rest of my face, while the other rinses the shampoo.

My eyes shut as he massages the conditioner in, working out the tangles. I should be embarrassed by the state of my hair, but he doesn't seem to mind, so neither do I.

When he's done, he wraps my hair in a towel and helps me sit up. "Thank you." I smile tenderly.

"Not done yet."

Turning the chair, he grabs the hair dryer and works on it with a brush, and when he's done, he grabs a hair tie, braids it, and grins at me in the mirror. "Ta-da, how does that feel?"

"So much better!" I reply, smiling up at him. "How did you learn to do that?"

His face closes down for a moment. "My mom." He busies himself by cleaning up as I watch him. I don't press. If he doesn't want to share, then he won't, and I won't pry. I've learned enough to hate the bitch, but he surprises me when he speaks again. "She used to get really drunk, and when she did, she couldn't look after herself. I learned to do it because I would get hit. I used to hate touching her even like that, but with you, it was kind of relaxing. I like taking care of you."

"I like you taking care of me," I reply. "I never had a mom to do this for me, and my dad wasn't really the type," I explain with a smile. "Thank you, Aiy, for taking care of me and for trusting me enough to tell me."

Stopping behind my chair, he looks down at me as I lean my head back and smile up at him, covering his hands with mine.

He stares at me for a moment, and I worry I said the wrong thing until he blurts, "Can I kiss you?"

"Yes," I whisper, the response automatic. I slept with Wilder, but maybe I shouldn't blur things, considering Aiy is dating Way. When he looks at me with so much hope, though, I realize I want him to kiss me.

Leaning down, he kisses me gently, almost hesitantly. I let him lead, remaining still. His lips move shyly against mine before he grips my chin, tilting my head and kissing me harder. This time, I kiss him back, and when he doesn't pull away, I give as good as I get. Our tongues dance even in this awkward position until a noise has us breaking apart.

"Fuck, sorry!" Rick covers his face as we jump. Whirling, Rick tries to race from the bathroom, but he runs into the partially open door and bounces off it, hitting the floor. He raises his arm, giving us a thumbs-up. "I'm okay. Ignore me. Please continue."

"Why is it always me?" Rick grumbles, shooting Aiy and me a look. "I think we need a sock on the door policy."

"Jealous?" Aiyaret asks, and we gawk at him, but he continues eating without a care, wearing a proud smile on his lips. Male satisfaction, I realize.

"Yes," Logan says, and I spin to find him awake. He fell asleep as soon as he got back from his tests. Hurrying over, I sink into the chair at his bedside, which has quickly become mine. "Kiss me too, Carter." He smiles loopily.

"I see the new pain meds are working," I tease as I take his hand and kiss the back of it. "How are you feeling?"

I've asked a million times, but I'm worried. He hasn't broken down since the other night. I know he's trying to be strong for us, but I hope he's not forcing himself to be okay.

"I'm fine," he answers like always. "Stop worrying. Besides, I can get a kickass prosthetic. It's just another adventure." When I stare at him in disbelief, he sighs. "Yes, I was upset, Carter, and I think I'll always wonder what could have been, but what's the point in moping around? I'm still me. It won't be easy, but I'm determined to live the best life I can, and that means not sitting around feeling sorry for myself, so if you guys could stop looking at me like you're waiting for me to break down at any moment, then maybe I could stop acting like it."

"You got it, brother," Wilder murmurs.

"We were supposed to be worried?" Rick teases, but the tightness around his eyes gives him away. "I was just imagining all the robot jokes I could make."

Way smacks him without even looking, making us chuckle as I lean into Logan's bed. "Deal, but if you ever do feel like breaking down, we are right here."

"Fine, I'm upset, show me your boobs." His grin is sloppy again, and I can't help but laugh.

"I want to be on whatever you're on." I wink.

"You do. It's good. I feel floaty." Logan sighs, snuggling deeper into the bed. "What games are we playing tonight? Strip poker? Strip Monopoly?"

"Why do they all involve stripping?" Wilder mutters. "You perv."

"Hey, a crocodile ate my leg, so I deserve to see some skin, don't I?"

"He isn't wrong. Show the man some boobs!" Way comments as he shoves another piece of broccoli in his mouth.

"Fine!" Rick yells dramatically and rips his shirt up, pushing his pecs together and shaking his chest. "Boobs."

"I meant Carter's," Logan grouses. "Nobody wants to see those."

"I do," I comment as I give Rick a thumbs-up as he shakes his rack.

"Mine are better," Wilder remarks impassively. We gape at him, and then his shirt is suddenly up around his neck and he's flexing his pecs.

"Yours? Check these out." Still chewing, Way pulls his shirt up and flexes his chest as he wiggles his eyebrows.

"Well, if you can't beat them . . ." Aiyaret sighs and stands, shyly lifting his shirt and exposing one of his nipples, smiling brightly.

"There are so many nipples out, yet none are the ones I want to see," Logan whines.

"What the hell is happening in here?" We turn to find Ajax and my dad at the door, looking horrified, and I burst into laughter so hard, I almost piss my pants.

The others went in search of snacks and new games to play, so for once, the room is quiet. Logan is asleep, or so I thought, but his eyes open, locking on me. "You don't have to watch me all the time, you know."

"You love it," I tease, and his smile is slow and sure. The drugs have worn off, and there's a tightness around his eyes that betrays his pain, but I know he isn't due for another dose yet. He also admitted he didn't want to take them often and become dependent.

"Makes up for all the time I used to stare at you," he murmurs, and I must look confused because he turns his head to face me, his fingers playing with mine. "You had to know I watched you."

"Why?" I ask.

"Don't be dumb, Carter, it doesn't suit you. I wanted you—always did. You were just so . . . beautiful. Even when you were covered in mud and climbing mountains and being crazy, I couldn't look away. I used to sneak off and watch your videos so the others didn't know, but then I caught Wilder doing the same thing." The wicked smile he gives me as he betrays his brother makes me laugh. "I never thought I'd have the opportunity to get close to you, never mind have a . . . relationship like this."

"And what relationship is that?" I tease.

"Whatever one I can have with you. I'm not stupid. I know you want the others too." His smile is small as he holds my hand, his eyes filled with pain for a moment, so even though I'm uncomfortable, I press to distract him.

"And that doesn't bother you?" I ask as his thumb rubs back and forth across my knuckles.

"No," he replies. "I share everything with my family, so why not you? Besides, even if I get a little bit of your attention, I'm fine with that." He sounds so truthful, so honest, that it hurts, making me feel like shit.

I slept with his brother yesterday, then I kissed his friend, yet he stares at me like I'm the best thing to ever happen to him, and I don't want that look to change.

The truth is, I want Logan too, and I always have.

He's always been attractive, but seeing him on that island and working with him to survive showed me another side of him, and any man willing to get his leg bitten off to save me? Yeah, they are worth sticking around for.

I can't bring his leg back or make what will come next easier for him, but for one minute, I can give Logan what he wants—me.

Releasing his hand, I remove my stolen hoodie, which I'm pretty sure is Way's, so I'm in nothing but an oversized shirt and loose pajama pants.

"Maeve," he murmurs, "what are you doing?"

I grin. "You wanted boobs, didn't you?"

He's uncharacteristically serious as he watches me.

My smile fades, a nervous sort of energy filling me as I slowly remove my shirt, and then I'm naked from the waist up. His eyes resist lowering at first, searching mine before they drop to my mouth and then to my chest. I drink in his expression as he looks at me—the slow blink, his teeth sinking into his lower lip.

"You're so beautiful," he whispers. "Want to fool around?" he jokes, but it falls flat as his hand balls into a fist on the bed. "I can't even move to get you." He looks away, shame etched on his features.

I stand and step closer to the bed, tilting his chin back so I can look into his eyes. "I still want you as much as I did before, leg or no leg. Besides, I can move for you." Taking his hand, I press it to the base of my throat, and his fingers reflexively circle it, making my chest flush as desire hums through my veins. He slides his hand down my chest, between my breasts, and over my abs before gliding back up.

"You're so beautiful, Maeve Carter, more beautiful than any monument or world wonder I have ever seen. We've been to every unexplored corner of the world, searching for something beautiful, but nothing rivals you."

Holy fuck. My mouth drops open as he meets my eyes and his fingers circle my nipple, deft and sure, before he tugs it into a tight peak. Desire shoots from my nipple to my clit, throbbing in time with my heartbeat as he slides his hand over to my other breast, giving that nipple the same treatment.

"Even in comfy clothes, you are the most exquisite thing I've ever laid eyes on. Adventurers spend our lives chasing highs, but none have ever compared to touching you. You are my greatest thrill." Looking up at me through his lashes, he gives me a soft smile that makes my heart clench. "You are my greatest adventure, Maeve Carter."

"Logan." His name is more of a breath than anything. For once, I am speechless. I knew Logan wanted to fuck me, but the way he's speaking is like a confession of love, and it leaves me weak and desperate. I want to be the woman I see in his eyes.

I have never felt more beautiful and desired than in this moment, and despite only wanting to offer him a distraction, this has turned into much more, and I couldn't back out now even if I wanted to.

Sliding up onto the bed, I straddle his waist then grab both of his hands, dragging them up my stomach until they cup my breasts.

"Christ, M," he whispers, and the shortening of my name does something to me, like this is something private just between us. "Don't do this to me. I can't move enough to get what I want."

"Then let me help you," I murmur as I lower my breasts to his mouth.

Our eyes meet as he sucks a nipple. My hands fist the hospital bedding above his head as I rock on his lap. He grips my hips, urging me to move faster, but I keep my pace slow. There's no rush, after all.

I gasp as his teeth dig into the flesh of my breast, and when he releases me, his cocky grin is back, one that is all Logan as he soothes his tongue over the bite while his hand slips into my pants. In one smooth move, he buries his fingers inside me. My head falls back as pleasure courses through me, and his mouth explores my nipple again, sucking and biting until I'm struggling to hold back cries of pleasure as I ride his fingers.

"Look at you," he whispers. "Fuck, M, you're so perfect. If I could, I'd be on my knees with my mouth on your pussy. I'd spend forever there." His fingers speed up as he presses the heel of his hand to my clit. "You're so goddamn wet for me, darling."

"I want you." It's important he knows, especially now.

His gaze bores into me, burning with desire as he strokes my channel until I sway into him and shatter. He catches me as I tumble forward, kissing my cheek as he gently caresses my pussy.

"You did so well, M."

Shaking off my haze of pleasure, I remove his hand from my pants and suck his fingers clean before trailing my fingers down his torso, aiming for his dick. The desire in his eyes spills over, leaving me breathless.

He lifts up and then hisses, dropping back. The desire in his eyes dims a little at the reminder of his leg, and I don't want that. I want him to forget for a while, so place my hands on his chest.

"Let me," I murmur.

Sliding down his body, careful of his injuries, I push the bedding down until his bandaged leg is exposed. When I glance up, his cheeks are red, and he looks like he's ready to push me away. I keep my eyes on him as I press a kiss over it, letting him know it doesn't bother me. If anything, it just makes me want him more. "Let me take the pain away," I murmur as I settle between his parted legs, slide his gown up, and get my first look at his cock.

Need pounds through me, as I know he would feel so fucking good inside me. He's not as long as Wilder, but he's thick, and I shudder as I lick my lips.

Meeting his eyes, I let him see how badly I want him so he never doubts it again, and when he gulps, I press a kiss to the leaking tip of his cock. He groans, so I take it slowly, knowing I need to be careful. I sweep my tongue down his length and back up, tasting him as he jerks in my grip. My hand slides down to the base of his thick cock, and I'm unable to even close my fingers around him.

"M," he begs.

"I've got you," I promise as I lick my way up and suck his wide tip until he lifts his hips. He seems to forget his pain for a moment, or maybe he chooses to ignore it. I'm not sure, but I keep my eyes on him just in case as I open my mouth and swallow him back as far as I can. My jaw aches from his girth, but in a good way that has me sucking him harder as I wiggle on the bed.

I've always loved giving head, loved watching their reaction, and Logan doesn't let me down. His head drops back on the bed before he lifts it again like he can't bear to look away. Veins bulge on his neck as his jaw pops, his eyes dark with desire as he rocks into my mouth, taking over.

I let him take back every inch of control, knowing he needs it, and honestly, I enjoy the messy, sloppy head as I feel him losing control.

"Best pain relief ever." His chest heaves as he stares at me with shocked eyes. "But if you don't stop, I'm going to come."

Popping my mouth from his cock, I grin. "That was my plan."

"Not in your mouth," he implores, shaking his head. "Not this time. Please, I need you. I need to know I can . . . that I'm still me."

The desperation in his voice is my undoing. Despite the fact that I want to feel him spill down my throat, I kiss his leaking tip and slide up, resting my hands on his shoulders, and then I position myself carefully so my pussy is pressed against his cock. "Then let me show you."

I reach between us and lower onto his length. He's so wide it burns, but I keep going until I'm fully seated on his dick, and we are both groaning. His hands grip my hips with more strength than I thought he had, and he lifts and drops me onto him.

"Fuck, move, M, please," he growls, sweeping his eyes all over my body like he doesn't know where to look. "I've wanted you for too fucking long to be sweet and loving this time. I need to fuck you."

"I've got you." I cover his hands on my hips, and he jerks inside me as I take over, speeding up. I carefully ride him as he watches me with half-lidded eyes, his teeth trapping his lower lip. He looks so fucking sexy, I clench around him, my clit throbbing with need.

I'm careful as I rock, not wanting to make anything worse, but he tries to speed up, to move, and I slow him down. I kiss him as we come together, and despite his words, he's good at being soft and gentle. I feel his desire in every single touch. Each kiss is determined and hard, leaving me breathless. I did this for him and because I wanted it, but as we come together, I realize I needed this too. I needed to feel him alive inside me.

Fucking Wilder was a release, but claiming Logan is a celebration of life.

My forehead presses to his as pleasure spirals through me, growing stronger by the second. "M," he whispers. "Please, God, you drive me crazy. You always have. Please, I don't deserve it, don't deserve you, but let me have you. Let me be yours."

"You are," I murmur as I grab his hand and press it to my chest, over my heart. "You are right here, and you're never getting out now. You're mine."

His fingers curl in as he pulses inside me, and I know he's close. His other hand reaches down and rubs my clit, and it sends me over the edge. Pleasure explodes through me, leaving me crying out as the force of my orgasm shakes my entire body.

"M, fuck, lift up. I can't hold back." He helps me up then pulls out just as he comes, splashing his hot release across my stomach and breasts as he grunts loudly. His eyes are screwed shut, his lips are parted in pleasure, and I drink in his reaction as I shiver in his embrace.

I slump into him before remembering his leg, then I carefully climb off him. My leg almost gives way, but I make my way to the bathroom, and once I'm cleaned up, I help him before crawling back into bed and into his open arms.

"Thank you, M," he whispers as he kisses my head, "for still wanting me."

"I've never wanted you more," I murmur as I kiss his chest. "Get some sleep."

Snuggling into his side, I hide my satisfied smile, but when I look up, he's smiling too. His pain is forgotten, and his worries are gone. His hold tightens on me, and I never want to leave his embrace. I want to stay here forever.

# FORTY-EIGHT
## WAY

We are all giving Logan and Maeve time alone. It was obvious he needed it tonight. Our brother is hurting, and she's his balm. Wilder and Rick fell asleep over an hour ago in Maeve's old hospital bed, but I stare up at the ceiling from the floor next to the couch where Aiy sleeps. My mind won't calm down.

One glimpse of my boyfriend's chest and I'm like a horny teenager.

I've seen Aiyaret's skin before, but it's different now. He's mine. He was oblivious of his effect on me, and I have no plans to push him or take this further until he's ready. He might never be, and that's fine with me.

I rise and head to the bathroom to take care of my rock-hard cock in hopes I can sleep. Sliding the door shut softly, I stare into the mirror. I look haggard with desire. My eyes are bright, my face is flushed, and my cock is tenting my pajama pants. I lean one hand on the counter and shove the other under my waistband, circling my length. My eyes shut as I remember the flash of his skin and the way his lips felt on mine. My imagination goes wild as I visualize my lips gliding down his body as I strip off his clothes.

"Way?" The innocent, soft question has my gaze jerking up and clashing with Aiyaret's in the mirror as he lingers in the doorway. I was so lost in my fantasy, I didn't even hear him open it.

My hand stills on my cock, even as it jerks in my grip. I trace my eyes over his face and lower.

"I, um . . . You weren't there." His cheeks blush as he realizes what I'm doing. "Is this because of Maeve?"

Choking on a laugh, I slide my hand along my length as I watch him, wondering what he sounds like when he comes. Would he blush like that for me? Would he fight? Cry?

"No," I murmur. "It's because of you," I tell him truthfully, knowing he needs to hear it. "You stripped in front of me earlier. You're my boyfriend, Aiyaret."

"But you've seen me before." He shuffles forward, glancing back into the room to check on the others.

"It's different now," I say, tightening my grip on my tip as I try my best to hold back. I dig my fingers into the counter to stop myself from reaching for him and sating my lust.

"Oh." It's all he says, but his eyes are locked on my hand in my pants, desire in his gaze as he shifts from foot to foot. I try to breathe through need so strong, it physically hurts.

"Aiyaret," I warn, my cock jerking in my fist as his eyes clash with mine. He looks so fucking soft and innocent, it drives me crazy. "Go back to sleep."

He stares at me for a heartbeat.

Then two.

"What if I don't want to?" His soft words have me grunting as I thrust into my fist, wishing it were his touch. He's right there, the thing I want most, but I won't be like everyone else in his life.

His hand lingers on the door, and I see him hesitate.

"If you shut that door, I'm not holding back," I warn. It's a threat, a promise, so he'll turn away and I won't feel like a total tyrant.

Licking his lips, he stares at me for a moment before he steps fully into the room and shuts the door behind him. "I didn't ask you to," he says, and it's all the permission I need.

I slam him back against the door as my lips crash onto his. I try to slow down, to be gentle, but I need him too much. My fingers circle his throat while my other slides down to his waist and under his shirt, caressing his chest. He gasps, opening his mouth and letting my tongue in.

"Way," he whispers as I kiss down his cheek to his neck. I bite down until he cries out, covering his mouth with my other hand as I meet his wide eyes. "Shh, baby, or they'll think I'm hurting you." He nods, and I kiss my bite spot as I grip his pecs and squeeze before sliding my hand lower, across his incredible abs to the waistband of his pants.

"Can I?" I ask. If he says no, I'll stop, but fuck if I don't want to touch him more than I want to breathe.

His nod is jerky, and I slip my hand into his pants and fist his dick, feeling him for the first time. I've accidently seen him before, but he feels so good, so long, thick, warm, and hard. His back slaps into the wall as he whines behind my palm.

"That's it, baby. I've got you," I murmur as I slide him through my grip, but I need to see him. Clutching his shirt with my other hand, I drag it up and off before kissing him again. When he gasps, I kiss down his neck, biting and sucking as he thrusts into my fist.

"Way—" He stumbles over my name, and when I glance up, his eyes are wide and confused but needy.

"Shh, I've got you. I'll make you feel good, I promise," I murmur as I kiss down his abs. They clench as I lick them until his hips move again. Smirking, I let go just enough to tug his pants down, and he kicks them off so he's naked. I just kneel and stare.

"Way?" he whispers self-consciously.

"You're perfect, baby," I whisper, and I roll my eyes up so he can see it in my gaze. "I never thought I'd ever be so lucky to call you mine, never mind have you. Just give me a moment so I can prove it's real."

His smile is shy, but he reaches for me, stroking my cheek. "It's real. Please. I need you."

"Not as much as I need you," I tell him as I wrap my hand around his length, watching his precum bead on his tip. I'm not sure how far he wants to take this, but I'll keep going and checking in. I just want him to feel comfortable and experience nothing but pleasure, so despite how badly I'm shaking with desire, I go slowly. Leaning in, I lick away the taste of him and watch his reaction. He gasps as I suck on his tip before swallowing him inch by inch. My other hand strokes his thigh before sliding up and cupping his balls, rolling them in my fingers as he jerks and fucks my mouth with unsure movements, but as I urge him on with my eyes, he gets more confident. A blush spreads down his cheeks and neck to his chest until he's heaving above me, shoving deeper into my mouth.

"Way," he begs, his eyes wild. "I want us . . . I want you to fuck me."

Jesus. Popping my mouth from his cock, I rest my head against his stomach and breathe, trying to control myself. "Are you sure?" I ask as I look up at him. He nods, but I narrow my eyes. "Words, baby."

"Yes, I'm sure. I want you to fuck me."

I surge to my feet, and he jerks back but lets me kiss him until he relaxes into me, stroking my skin. Each brush of his hesitant hand drives me wild until I thrust against his stomach, needing more.

I pull far enough away to look around. I don't want this to hurt, but I'm not exactly prepared. Groaning, I spit on my palm and circle his cock, wishing I had more. I'll just have to be careful. I wet his cock as much as I can before sliding my hands down his thighs and behind, then I lift him up.

His legs wrap around me, and I turn and press his back to the wall to stifle the noise of the door. I massage his plump ass. "Are you sure?" I ask. I'll stop right now if he isn't.

"Yes, please," he whispers. "I'm ready."

I search his gaze, but all I see is desire.

Nodding, I lean in and kiss him. "If it hurts or you want to stop at any point, tell me. I won't be mad. I want you to enjoy this."

"I will." He slaps my shoulders. "Please."

Grinning, I widen his legs and grab my length, rolling it across him until he moves his hips, his lips seeking mine. I kiss him as I press against his rear entrance and slowly push past the ring of muscles, and then I pull out and rock deeper, sliding in slowly, inch by inch. He whimpers into my mouth, digging his nails into my shoulders, but he doesn't stop me. He kisses me harder, so I keep going until I'm buried all the way inside him. Breaking the kiss, I press my forehead to his, letting him adjust to my size. "That's it, baby, just relax. You're doing so well. It will feel amazing when I start to move. Trust me."

"I do," he whispers, and he pushes down experimentally. I let him until he looks at me for help. The slight pain and shyness in his eyes are gone, replaced by a feral need that matches my own. Kissing him, I pull out and slowly push back in, working him up as I slide my hand between our bodies and circle his length, letting him fuck my hand as I take his ass.

He's so fucking tight around me and so goddamn perfect that I have to hold back my pleasure, but soon, he's demanding more, and I can't restrain myself any longer.

"Faster," he begs, his dark eyes pinning me in place. "Harder, Way, fuck, please."

I can't deny him anything.

I slam into him, and he cries out loudly.

Covering his mouth with my hand, I drive into his perfect ass, pounding into the wall with our rapid movements.

"Eyes on me," I order as he goes to shut them. I need him to see I'm the one who is touching him. I need him to associate pleasure with me rather than everything that happened before.

His eyes open and lock on me as I claim him. Our lips come together, silencing our noises of pleasure, our bodies slapping loudly. Pleasure spirals through me, burning like acid down my spine as my balls draw up, but I hold it back. I need to feel him come first, need him to enjoy this more than anything else.

We find a perfect rhythm, both of us desperate as we touch each other all over, unable to get enough. His head falls back, his eyes wild. "Way, I can't."

"Shh, baby, let go. I've got you," I tell him as I feel his cock swelling and jerking in my hand. "Let go, baby. I'm right here. I'll always catch you."

It seems to be what he needs to hear because his eyes shut, and he jerks in my grip. I feel his cum spray across us as our bodies move together. His cry of pleasure is muffled as he bites his lip, and I tilt him to hit that spot that drags out his release and makes his cry louder.

I can't take it anymore.

My release erupts from me, filling his perfect ass as I bury my head in his throat. I jerk and force my cock deeper, until I know he'll never get me out of him.

His fingers stroke my back as he shudders in my arms, kissing every inch of skin he can. Lifting my head, I press my lips to his. "You did so well, baby."

He seems to brighten, smiling so vividly it steals what is left of my heart and soul.

My legs want to buckle, so I sit my ass on the counter before I fall and drop both of us. "Are you okay?" I ask worriedly. I was hard and unrelenting, and it's his first time with me.

"Better than okay," he assures me as he lifts his head, showing me his smile. "Thank you."

"For what?" I ask.

"For not touching me like I'm broken or holding back just because of my past . . . . For still wanting me," he whispers.

"Always," I vow. "Your past changes nothing. I've wanted you for years, and I just want to make you happy. I want to give you everything you need and desire."

His smile is so bright it must hurt, and he buries his face in my neck.

"Hiding?" I tease.

"I'm shy," he murmurs, and my grin widens.

"After what we just did? Babe, how are you shy?" I tease, and he smacks me. "Okay, okay, come on, let's clean up and then get some sleep."

Turning the shower on, I wait for the water to warm up, and then I carry him in, making sure he's steady on his feet before I start washing his body. He's blushing hard and tries to protest, but I clean every inch of him, including his beautiful ass, and when we're done, I dry him off and help him dress again. We sneak back into the room hand in hand, only this time, he pulls me down onto the sofa with him and sprawls across my chest. Wrapping my arms around him, I kiss his head and sigh.

"I love you, Way," he whispers in the dark. "I never meant to fall in love with you, but I did. Every time you held my hand through a nightmare, every time you woke me, protected me, and treated me like a normal human being . . . You stole a piece of me, and I don't want it back." I meet his gaze. "But I want that piece of you too. Even if I share it with Maeve, I want it."

"It's yours," I tell him. "It has been for years. Nothing will change that. I love you, Aiyaret. I'm sorry it took me so long to realize it."

Kissing me softly, he leans down with a happy hum. "It's okay, just don't waste any more time."

Smiling, I close my eyes. "I won't. That's a promise."

## FORTY-NINE
# RICK

Time in the hospital is moving weirdly. I know Ajax and our company are protecting us, giving us time to rest before we return. I also know we'll have to move eventually, but for now, this is our own little paradise. It can be stifling, however, and my wanderer's soul yearns for fresh air and the outdoors, so the next night, when everyone is doing their own thing, I head out in search of the quietness of nature.

I sneak up to the roof, not wanting to go too far in case something happens. The door doesn't alarm, which is lucky. A few nights ago, I heard the nurses admitting that the doctors sneak up here for a break and a smoke since there are no cameras, which is why I hoped I could too.

There's no staff up here at the moment, and I'm grateful as I walk to the ledge and lie down, dangling a leg off the rooftop. One of my arms hangs, my fingers playing with the air as I stare up at the night sky. My lungs slowly expand with fresh, warm air.

I lie like this for a while, letting it heal me. I'm comfortable in cities and around people, but my heart always belongs to the wilderness.

"Rick?" Turning my head, I lock eyes with the person my heart also belongs to, someone equally as wild as the world I love—Maeve Carter.

"Are you stalking me, pretty girl?" I tease.

"I heard the nurses talking about the cutie sneaking up here." She smiles as she heads over, and I sit up, crossing my legs as she sits beside me. She winces when her bad leg causes her pain, so I grab it and lay it over my lap. "What are you doing here?"

"I just needed some fresh air," I reply. "Too long inside and I start to go a little crazy."

"Only a little?" She bumps into me with a grin as she leans back on her hands, dropping her head back so she gazes at the sky, but I'm looking at her. "It's beautiful here."

"It is," I murmur, but she's the view I'm talking about.

Her head lifts as if she heard something in my voice, and she meets my gaze. "Flirt," she retorts.

"It isn't flirting if it's true." I shrug. "How long before you get the itch?" I know she understands what I mean. We all have the urge to get back out there and explore. It's why we do what we do.

"Usually a few weeks, maybe a little longer this time since I'm healing. I want to spend some time with my dad at home and feel safe for a little while. What about you?"

"Already got it," I respond, "but we need some peace and time at home. I can wait."

"You're restless," she murmurs, and I nod, looking back at the stars.

"I've always been this way, unable to stay in one place for too long. There's just so much out there to see and do, so much I want to achieve and experience, that it feels like a waste to sit around."

"And this, right here, right now, is it a waste of your time?" she asks carefully.

Dropping my chin to my chest, I meet her gaze. "Any time with you is not a waste," I answer truthfully.

Her lips purse as she hides a smile. "You're good at saying what people want to hear. I bet the girls love it."

"There are no girls." I shrug. "There were some in the past, but never anything serious. I don't stick around long enough for relationships, nor did I ever want one with people who couldn't understand why I want to be out there rather than settling down. Pretty words only last so long. They all say they are okay with it."

"But they aren't," she says. "They start getting angry and impatient. It becomes a fight, and then they leave, unable to handle the lifestyle. It doesn't matter how much you warn them or give them outs; they all say they can handle it. They can't. How could they understand why I'd rather be standing on a random beach across the world or scaling a dangerous mountain? I can count the number of relationships I tried before I realized it wasn't worth the heartache—mine or theirs."

She understands—of course she does. She's just like us—a soul filled with the need for more. Partners don't usually understand that. They think it means they lack something and they aren't enough for us, but the truth is, it isn't them—it's us.

"We are never going to be this world's norm," I murmur, "and that's okay. We just have to find people who are the same . . . the ones not afraid to take risks."

"Are you afraid to take what you want?" she asks, and something in her voice indicates she means more than this life I lead.

"You tell me," I counter.

"Well, you haven't taken me," she responds, refusing to back down. "You want me, yet here we are, so I think you're afraid."

"Of you? No. Of taking you and being so close to heaven then losing it? Yes," I reply, but I reach for her anyway. I slide her onto my lap until she's pressed against my chest, her legs on either side of me. The warm air of this foreign land wraps around us, and I know this will be my favorite memory I've ever made on any of these trips. "You scare me, Maeve Carter, in the way scaling mountains does. You're just as unpredictable, wild, and beautiful."

"Your brother—"

Covering her mouth, I lean in. "This isn't about my brothers. This is about us. I don't care what goes on between you. I never have. You make them happy, so why would that bother me? All I care about is that you want me as much as I want you. If you don't, then tell me now and let me go because I couldn't stand falling deeper in love with you if you don't feel the same way."

"And what if I feel the same? What if I'm greedy and want you as well?" she asks, searching my gaze.

"Then take me." I swoop in, my lips above hers, and let her make the decision.

Her eyes peer into mine until suddenly, with an audible groan, she closes the remaining distance. I let go, handing everything I am over to her. Our kiss turns feral as she grips my hair, and I tug her closer so she's pressed against me. My head tilts back since hers is above me, and I deepen the kiss, tasting every inch of her mouth as her hands find my shirt then slip under it. She strokes my muscles until they clench for her. Careful of her leg, I lift her and open my eyes to see where I'm going as I turn us and lay her across the ledge, coming down above her.

Her eyes open as she turns to see the drop-off, but when she looks back at me, she's grinning. "Ever had a danger fuck?"

I blink in confusion, my brain not working well enough to form words, and she laughs. "Rick, the big, bad flirt, has never had a danger fuck? Well, let me be your first." Her smile only grows as she slides her hand down my chest to cup my hard dick. "Check my pocket for condoms. I figured I couldn't be too careful around all of you. Put one on and fuck me right here where we could fall at any minute. It will make it even better, and it will fill that itch for now."

Lowering my head, I nip her pouty bottom lip. "And what about my itch for you?"

"Sorry, you're stuck there," she whispers as I kiss down her throat and across her shirt before pushing it up to expose her abs. I lick them as my hand slides into her pocket. As I extract the condoms, I want to ask where and how she got them, but I decide I really don't care. I pocket one and toss the rest down next to us as I grab her pants and yank them off, draping them next to us. She's naked underneath, and I blink at the sight.

"It's annoying putting underwear on when people keep taking it off." She laughs, and I can't help but smile. I know she's had the others, and it doesn't bother me. She'll be more willing to stay then, and I'm not above fighting dirty to get what I want, which is having Maeve Carter by my side forever.

Kissing up her legs, I force them open and throw them over my shoulders as I get my first look at her pussy. It's pink and glistening for me, and I swear my dick practically bursts as I drag my tongue across her wet folds, tasting her. Her sweetness fills my mouth, and I'll never taste anything more glorious.

Her moan fills the night air, and I slide my hands up to her breasts, tweaking and rolling her nipples. I tease her swollen clit with little, sure licks until she grinds into my mouth, making a gasping, moaning noise that has me leaking in my pants. She drives me crazy, all perfect, tan skin, hard-earned muscles, and a face to rival the greatest of paintings. She's all I need, all I've wanted since the first time I saw her, and now I'm here with her cream smeared across my mouth. I suck on her clit until she arches off the ledge of the roof, rolling her hips to get closer. I feel her lock up and watch as she comes apart for me. Her cries of pleasure are swallowed by the night as she finds her release, but I don't relent. I slide my hands down and slip two fingers inside her, wanting to feel her inner muscles massage me as she rides out her orgasm. I lick her through it, winding her back up until she can't catch her breath.

"Rick, Rick," she rasps. "Fuck, wait—"

I don't, and I don't bother speaking. My words wouldn't make sense right now anyway. I'm continually making a fool of myself around her, but I don't care when she grinds down into my mouth, begging for more despite her words.

"Merrick!" Hearing my full name on her lips drives me crazy. I grab her hips and yank her under me, devouring her pretty cunt as I spear a third finger into her and rub her wall until she's riding me again. One orgasm flows into the next as she screams. Her thighs clamp around my head tightly as I feel her come.

"Merrick, Merrick," she chants, trying to push me away, but I'm not done yet. I drag my tongue down as I pull my fingers free so I can catch every drop, and only then do I lift my head.

Her eyes are wild as she watches me, then she tackles me back. I hit the concrete roof hard, but I don't care as she tears at my clothes, quickly stripping them off me. Grabbing a condom, she rips it open with her mouth. Fuck, that does something to me, almost as much as when she deftly puts it on, rises above me, and sinks down on my length. My hips lift involuntarily, a groan leaving my choked throat as I look at her above me.

The stars shine brightly in the sky, fighting to shine brighter than she does, but they lose.

She's all I see as her palms press against my chest and she starts to move. The crooked smirk she aims at me has my balls drawing up as she rides me fast and hard, taking what she wants.

"You still with me, Merrick?" she teases.

"Look at you," I rasp. "Maeve, you can't be real."

She rolls her hips before sliding down my cock, bending over me until she can bite my lip. "I'm real, and I'm right here. What are you going to do about it, Merrick?" I don't know how she figured out what hearing my name on her lips does to me, but it's what shatters this speechless awe I've fallen into.

Snarling, I chase her lips, but she laughs and leans back, grinding on me.

"I thought you wanted a danger fuck," I growl and stand. She gasps as I hold her, then I drop her onto the ledge, following her down so her back and head hang in the air while her thighs wrap around me.

"Fuck yes!" she cries loudly, her arms floating in the air. She trusts me to hold her as I take her cunt, faster and harder. "Merrick, please."

I give her what she wants, giving her freedom as I take her. Her smile is wide before it morphs into a moan of pleasure as I slide my hand between us and flick her clit.

Her eyes close, her back arches, and the sight wrecks me. I'm nothing but a wild animal rutting into her, and her noises of pleasure only grow, encouraging me as she meets me halfway. Sitting up, she drapes herself over me and meets my thrusts.

Our heavy breathing echoes through the night, just us and the stars, and when she leans in and whispers my name, I can't hold back.

My release slams through me, and I rub her clit until she follows me with a soft cry, her body stiffening as I thrust as deeply as I can, holding her there against me as I ride out the pleasure. My lips press to hers in a breathless kiss as she whimpers, her hips jerking. Pleasure locks us together until it finally releases us, and we slump, sweaty and satisfied.

Blinking my eyes open, I pinch her chin, tilt her head up, and kiss her as her eyelids flutter open. "I'm in love with you, Maeve Carter. I have been for a long fucking time. My heart belongs to you, and so does my family. Do with them what you will, just don't leave."

Licking her swollen lips, she wraps her arms around my shoulders and kisses me softly. Unlike our feral fuck, it's slow and loving. "I love you too, Merrick," she murmurs, and the words shock my fragile heart. I feel too full, too happy. It can't be real. "And I'm not going anywhere."

I can't articulate how I feel, so instead, I show her by kissing her. I pour everything I feel into the kiss, and when we break apart, we hold each other. The cool night air dries the sweat on our skin. We should probably move, but neither of us want to, and for that, I'm happy. I'll take as much of her time and life as I can—until I hear voices.

She must hear them at the same time I do. We break apart and grab our clothes. Maeve heads to the exit, but I catch her hand as the voices draw closer, and we run to the side of it, shoving our clothes on. I press her against the wall hidden behind the door as a nurse and a doctor head to the edge of the roof and light up cigarettes.

She giggles, and I cover her mouth with my hand, but I'm smiling as well, and when I look into her eyes, I have to bite back my own laughter. She presses against my chest, and I lower my head automatically, our lips meeting in a smiling kiss.

# FIFTY
## MAEVE

The last two weeks have been so calm and peaceful, I should have known something was occurring. My dad had to fly back two days ago for his appointments, but I chose to stay with the guys, promising I would return home when they did, but as I stare at Ajax, I know my choice is being taken away from me. He pulled me from Logan's room not long ago, claiming he needed to speak to me.

"Don't do this," I beg as we sit in the hallway.

"Carter, I tried my best to delay it. The board has tied my hands. They need reports and answers and to go over the footage. You also need to be checked out over there. It won't be forever, just for now," he explains. "They'll be coming home soon as well—"

"But you want me to fly back now and leave them?"

"Please, I've tried everything to put this off, but I'm at a loss. Wilder can't leave his brother, so that leaves you. The public wants answers, as does the board. I don't know what else to do," Ajax admits, stress lining his features.

I'm surprised my reprieve lasted this long, but maybe Ajax has been running interference on our behalf.

"They will be left here?" I ask, my eyes dropping to the floor as my heart aches with the idea of spending even a minute away from them. We've been inseparable, and my life has begun to revolve around them.

Maybe that isn't a good thing, since it will change when we go back. I should get used to this now before it's too late and I'm in too deep.

My mood spirals, and I clench the armrests of the chair I'm on.

"I'm leaving a team behind, so they won't be alone, and when they can fly, we'll get them straight home. We don't want to risk further injury. They also won't need to report as quickly since we will have your account," Ajax rationalizes. "But I'm on your side, so if you say no, I will find a way around it. I had to ask, especially since your dad has returned. I figured you would want to go back too."

Usually I would, but they are here, and that makes me hesitate.

"Maeve?" Ajax prompts.

"If I want to stay?" I see the stress triple on his face and he sighs. "I don't really have a choice, do I?" Ajax's expression tells me I don't. "Fine, I'll leave with you. When?"

"You're leaving?" My head jerks up, and I see Aiyaret in the doorway of Logan's room, looking betrayed.

"Who's leaving?" Way asks as he appears behind him and sees me. "Maeve? Maeve's leaving? What do you mean?"

Sighing, I rub my face and stand, dragging ass as I trudge into their room to see the others, not wanting to discuss this in public.

"What's going on?" Wilder asks, glancing between Ajax and me.

"The board is demanding one of you return to report what happened and do some interviews. Logan can't fly, so I can't ask you. I asked Maeve," Ajax replies as he hesitates in the door, sensing he wouldn't be welcome right now. It's become public knowledge we are not to be separated, even for treatment.

Wilder's eyes land on me, anger and hurt in his gaze as he silently pleads with me to deny Ajax. "You're leaving with him?"

It's almost an accusation, and the atmosphere in the room intensifies. I feel their eyes on me, and I'm filled with guilt, but my thoughts circle back to earlier.

Maybe having some time to myself to think about my future would be good.

"I have no choice. You all need rest, and Logan needs you here, so if I can take this off your plate, then I will," I answer.

"Tell the board to go fuck themselves!" Wilder roars. "We just went through hell and barely survived. They can wait."

"Wilder," I caution, and he calms at my voice. "I can do this. It will be okay."

"M," Logan protests, but he says nothing else.

"Don't go," Aiyaret murmurs, and Way wraps his arm protectively around his shoulders. I hate it.

I smile softly, but it feels wobbly. How did they come to mean so much to me in such a short amount of time? They need me right now, and I can't be here. "It isn't forever, just for now," I tell them, repeating Ajax's earlier words, but it doesn't make me feel better, and from their expressions, it clearly doesn't pacify them either.

"We'll come back too," Wilder states.

"Logan can't fly yet." Ajax sighs. "I thought about that too. I'll take care of her, and it won't be long, just a few weeks apart. You guys can manage that. Hell, you never even used to want to be around each other."

"It's different now," Wilder grumbles.

"He's right. We've spent longer apart," I reason. "I'll go back and sort everything out so you guys can rest. We'll see each other again when you're home."

Looking at their anguished expressions, I feel my heart sink. I don't want to go either, but if I can take care of this for them, then I will. They don't need any more stress than they already have.

Logan is quiet and withdrawn, and I worry. Walking over to his side, I take his hand and say, "Tell me you need me to stay and I will. Fuck the board, and fuck Ajax—no offense, Ajax. Tell me and I will."

"How long until I can fly?" Logan asks, looking at my hand on his.

"A few weeks at most," Ajax murmurs.

"I suppose I can bear that," Logan concedes as he squeezes my hand. "Go, you need to. We'll be okay, trust us."

"Logan!" Rick protests.

"She has no choice. If she doesn't, the board could punish her. I'm not wrong, am I?" Logan looks at Ajax, who shakes his head. "She's already in trouble for using funds to come back and help us. We'll follow her as soon as we can."

We are both trying to protect each other. He wants to make sure I don't lose my job, and I don't want him to have to think about work while he heals.

I kiss him, uncaring that Ajax is watching. "I'll see you back home, okay? Call me day and night, whatever you need."

"You bet," he replies as I step back and look at the others.

"That goes for all of you. Don't go back to radio silence," I warn.

Arms wrap around me, and I realize it's Wilder, his mouth brushing my ear. "Let us know when you get back. If the board gives you shit, then kick their asses. Wait for us, okay? We'll be back soon."

Nodding, I sink into his embrace, and the others join us, holding me until Ajax clears his throat. "The plane will be here soon," he says.

Pulling away, I look over them and step back. "I'll see you at home," I tell them as I hesitate, my heart torn. "Bye."

Turning away before I cry or do something stupid, I stride swiftly past Ajax and into the corridor, their chorus of goodbyes chasing me.

Why does this feel so final?

Why does it shred me to pieces?

I haven't seen the guys in three weeks. I heard they are back in the US now, but I feel weird just appearing at their door. What if things have changed? It was easy to go along with this when we were together constantly, but after spending time apart, I started to question everything.

I'm scared, which isn't something I'm used to.

It took a week of meetings and interviews before Ajax let me go home, and I went to my dad's to spend time with him. I've texted the guys a few times, but I never know what to say anymore, and they were so busy preparing to come back that we didn't have a lot of time to call despite our parting promises. Instead, I throw myself into looking after my dad and rehab for my leg. I can walk a lot better now. I think I will always have twinges of pain, but I'm not going to let it stop me.

Reaching over, I push a mug closer to my dad's shaking hand. "Drink. Green tea is good for you," I admonish. It's the same fight we have every day.

"No offense, Maeve, but you're annoying me. Go on, get out of here," my dad snaps, and I jerk my head up from fussing over the tea.

"Gee, thanks, Dad," I mutter, feeling hurt.

"You've been flitting around me with nerves for weeks. It's time for you to get back out there. What did I always teach you?" he asks.

"Face your fears," I grumble when he stares at me with a hard look only a parent can manage. "It isn't that simple."

"Like hell it isn't," he retorts. "No daughter of mine will mope around like this. Don't use me as an excuse, Maeve. I don't want you here." I flinch, and he softens. "I love you, and I'd love to have you here forever, but this isn't where your heart belongs. I don't want to be your crutch. I'd never forgive myself. What are you so afraid of?"

That's the question, isn't it? I was so certain in the hospital and on that island, but everything is different now. I don't know if it was the board's analysis and questions or facing reality in the interviews, but it feels . . . strange, like it's wrong to want to be with them. Maybe things should go back to the way they were before.

Maybe they don't need me like I need them. It could have just been the desire to survive driving us.

"Have you spoken to them?" he asks when I don't respond, smiling gently. "Kid, I saw you with them in the hospital. You care for them, so why are you pushing them away?"

Again, I have no answer, just worries and regrets.

The doorbell rings, and I stand, happy to escape my dad's prying and knowing eyes. "I'll get it. It's your prescription." Shuffling down the corridor, I open the door and freeze.

Five familiar faces stare back at me. "Surprise." Rick grins.

I gape like I'm seeing ghosts, and Wilder smirks. "Since you didn't come to us, we came to you."

"Are you going to let us in?" Way mutters. "These bags are heavy."

Aiy waves at me happily, and Logan grins at me from his wheelchair, and yet I just stare.

"Who is it? Oh, hey, guys! Glad you made it. Did you find us easily from the address I gave you?" my dad calls, and I whirl around, shocked as I peer at my grinning father.

"Easy-peasy. We can find mountaintops, so your house was simple," Wilder teases.

"I'll let Miranda know we have guests. You're staying for the night, right?" my dad asks as I continue to stare at him in shock, my eyes bugging from my head.

"Absolutely." Rick pushes past me. "Nice to see you again, Mr. Carter. You can show me that boat you were talking about—"

"I—we—what?" I turn around to look at them as Way grunts, walking by with five backpacks weighing him down. Aiy follows, leaning in to kiss my cheek as I stand like a statue. Wilder wheels Logan in and stops in front of me.

"Didn't think we'd let you escape that easily, did you? We made a promise." Wilder winks, and then they are gone, their voices filling my dad's house as I stand in the entryway, wondering what the fuck just happened.

They make themselves at home, which shouldn't surprise me. What does, however, is how welcoming my dad is. He gets them settled and even lets them help cook with him and step-monster. I watch the entire time, gripping a beer I was given, silent and unsure.

They update us on what's been transpiring as we eat outside by the fire as night falls. Logan is going through therapy, which I knew. He's been vlogging his story to inspire others, and I watch religiously. He's doing well, and I have no doubt he'll be back out there before long, but until then, his team is waiting. They never ask me anything, but their eyes are always on me, and it makes me feel insecure—something I don't like. I feel awkward around them.

"You'll soon be as fast as I am in this wheelchair," my dad jokes with Logan after step-monster heads to bed.

"We should race tomorrow," Logan replies, making my dad chuckle before he catches my eye. I look away, and he sighs.

He gave them this address and brought them here, but why?

For me, I realize. He noticed his daughter was hurting and lost, and he gave her what she needed, even knowing it means I will leave him again.

"How long are you back for?" my dad asks.

"Until Logan is ready. We plan to do some activities close to home. Ajax is happy for us to do that . . . for us to be close to what we want," Way answers, and his gaze lands on me. I see a new determination there that makes me quickly avert my eyes.

It's like they've all come to break me down.

"Good, that's good." Everyone becomes silent, just the crackle of the fire providing background noise as I peel the label of my warm beer, wondering what to say.

Are they mad?

I didn't meet them like I promised.

Are they done?

Have they realized what I have?

Questions that keep me up at night crowd my head, and I don't know what to say, so I remain silent, just as I have online other than the interviews the board wanted. I know my fans are curious and worried, but I couldn't bring myself to pretend I'm okay right now. For once in my life, I wanted time away from cameras to figure out what I want, and Ajax gave me that.

"Well, that's me calling it a night," my dad says. "These old bones aren't what they used to be. Don't cause trouble for the neighbors, and don't burn my house down," he teases. "Night, kid." Leaning close to me, he lowers his voice. "Be kind, and stop being afraid." He wheels back inside, leaving me with the guys and the questions I see on their faces.

"I spoke to Ajax, you know?" Wilder starts, and I wince. "He told us that you took the blame for everything."

Shrugging, I focus on the flames, knowing if I meet their gazes, I'll melt into them.

"Despite everything that happened, we found what we were employed to find," Wilder carries on. "We corrected him since you seemed to let him believe we found it. You got there first, Maeve, so it's yours, as is the payday. He's going to donate half to your dad's charity and name it in his honor."

My head lifts, and I meet his eyes across the fire. "It was your find," he states as I stare. "Now, let's talk about you avoiding us."

"I wasn't," I protest. "I was taking care of my father—"

"You were hiding from us," he interjects. "Why? We were fine when you left."

"We missed you," Aiyaret admits, and fuck if that doesn't make me soften toward them, because the truth is, I missed them too.

I never needed anyone before, but now, it's like I don't know how to be me without them.

"Talk to us, what's going on? Did we do something?" Logan pleads.

I look around at their hopeful faces and then back at the fire.

"You didn't do anything," I murmur.

"Talk to us, Carter," Wilder demands, and his bossy tone grabs my attention, but there's an edge of desperation in his voice, which is new, and I fall into that, the truth pushing out.

"You know what? That island was a special kind of hell. We almost died every way imaginable, and we had to fight just to survive every minute of the day, but I kind of miss it as well. We were together, we were a team, and we had each other's backs. I miss hearing your voices around the fire. I miss you." A tear finally falls, and I see their faces crumple. "I know I can do this alone, but I realized I don't want to." Wiping my tears away, I meet their gazes. "But everything has changed. In some ways, it was easy on that island and in the hospital to be what we wanted, but here, it feels like it was a dream. We aren't a team. We can't be what we want. It isn't what the world wants."

"Bullshit." I startle at the venom in Aiyaret's voice. "We can be whatever we want. We are right here, Maeve. We were waiting for you. Nothing has changed for us." He glances around. "We spoke about it. It's what we want—you, us, this team. We haven't changed. Have you?"

I stare at him, and he waits.

"Do you still want us?" he prompts when I don't respond.

"Yes," I whisper.

"Then why does anything else matter? You're overthinking it, babe," Rick teases.

"I never thought I'd see the day when Maeve Carter backed away because she was scared, so don't start now," Wilder remarks. "Just so you know, we already applied for you to be a member of our team if you want it. We did it first thing when we returned. The world doesn't have to know more than that. It's your decision, Carter. Are you with us, or are you running away?"

"What if it doesn't work?" I ask.

"What if an avalanche comes? What if our boat sinks? What if our plane crashes? What if a crocodile stalks us?" Logan challenges. "Nothing is guaranteed, Carter. We live our lives day by day. It's who we are. Don't change now. I love you. My brothers love you. We want you to be one of us. Will you?"

As I look around at them, I know there is only one answer I can give. "Yes."

Their whoops fill the air before they quiet down, remembering my dad's warning, which makes me smile even as tears fill my eyes. I was so lonely, so lost without them. I never even knew I was before them, but everyone changed on that island, including me and my future. Previously, I would have done anything to prove myself solo without them, but now, all I want is to explore the world with them and make memories.

I don't want to be alone anymore.

I realized I didn't need to go alone just to prove I can, just to prove I'm strong, brave, or independent. I can still be all of those things with them.

I look around at them with wet eyes. "Are you sure this is what you want?"

"Yes," they agree, and I look at Wilder.

He toasts me with his beer. "I guess I can deal with losing to you for the rest of my life."

I smirk. "Looks like you have no choice."

It's like nothing and everything has changed between us, and I know I'd follow them anywhere. I'm one of them now, or maybe they are part of me.

Either way, we are stuck together.

# FIFTY-ONE
## AIYARET

The tension is broken, and Maeve's smile is wide as she looks at us around the fire. We contacted her dad as soon as we got back, and he told us to give her time, but as the days went by, we grew impatient, and he finally gave us their address, admitting he was worried about her. It seems she was struggling, but now that I know why, I sigh in relief.

She was worried about us.

That's adorable.

She's relaxed now, and Logan starts telling her stories about his physical therapy, making her laugh. The others join in, but I just observe her. I never thought I could love a woman, never mind have a future with one, and despite being in love with Way, I'm not complete without Maeve, and our time apart showed me that.

We need her.

I need her.

Way's hand loosens in mine, and I glance at him. "Go." He jerks his head. "Maeve, can you grab us more drinks? Aiy will help you." He pushes me up, and I frown, not comprehending what he wants. The others urge me on, and I still don't understand, but I nod as she stands.

"Sure, the beer fridge is in the boathouse. Follow me." She slips her hand through my arm, a habit I've missed as we walk across the grass toward the red boathouse. Pulling the door open, she flips the light on.

There's a small fishing boat anchored between the pylons, some tools on the back left wall, and fridges and freezers along the opposite wall. She hums as she steps away from me, heading to a fridge, and the reason Way pushed me to go with her finally clicks.

He's giving me a chance. He knows how much I've missed her, and he loves me so much he's provided me with a chance to fix that. Grabbing her arm, I swallow hard as I call her name. "Maeve?"

She turns to me, tilting her head. "Yeah?" She looks confused and so fucking beautiful, I can't hold back.

I steal a kiss, and she jerks, gasping as I pull away.

"Sorry, but I missed you," I tell her as I stare into her eyes. "Actually, I'm not sorry." Swooping in, I press my lips to hers.

I grip her hips and back her up into the closest wall, but tools rattle and fall. I raise my arm to protect her head, and she giggles as she pulls away, the sound making me smile as I sweep my thumb over her lips.

"Did you miss me?" I whisper.

"Yes," she replies. "Every day."

"Can you show me?" Her eyes widen at my request. "I'm tired of letting fear control me. I don't know if I can, but I want to try. I love you, Maeve, and that isn't going to change. We are starting over. I want this. I want you."

"Aiyaret, are you sure?" She looks around nervously.

"I know this isn't the most romantic spot. Sorry, we can wait. I just —" My cheeks heat with embarrassment.

Her lips find mine again before she takes my hand. "Follow me."

I'd follow her anywhere.

Any of us would.

She steps down on the wooden plank and then onto the boat, holding my hand as I clamber over less gracefully than her, but she just smiles, tugs off a tarp, and throws it aside to reveal a nest of blankets and pillows. There are journals and maps spread around.

"My escape. It's my boat." She turns to me before sinking to her knees. "How do you want me?"

My cock jerks at her words, and wicked thoughts fill my head. For the first time ever, nothing else exists—just us, just her and me.

"Aiy?" When I continue to stare at her, she smiles and toys with her shirt. "Do you want me naked?"

I nod jerkily, and she slowly tugs her shirt up and off, exposing her beautiful tan skin. Her abs tighten with the movement, her nipples pebbling in the cool air as she kneels in front of me, her breasts high and tight. My mouth waters at the sight before she rises, unbuckles her cargos, and slides them off. Now, she's in nothing but a tiny pair of low-rise underwear, which she quickly removes. "I won't ask about your past, but please tell me how to do this. I want you to think of me, nothing else, so please tell me how."

It didn't even cross my mind, but my heart melts at her concern, and I lower to my knees, cupping her jaw as I gaze into her eyes. "I don't think it will matter when I'm with you." I hope, at least, that it won't. "But this time, maybe if I'm in control—"

She covers my hand. "Whatever you need. I'm yours, Aiy, and if we can't this time, then it doesn't matter. We have all the time in the world. We can take it slow."

"I don't want to go slow," I blurt out. Way and I have spoken at length about this. Unleashing my lust with him was an eye-opener. I like to be controlled when I'm with him, and although I enjoy making love, I love hard, rough sex, and when I imagine Maeve and me together, that's what I want. I want to hear her scream for me. I want to lose myself in her and let go.

I want to control every inch of her pleasure. I want to be its master.

There are probably reasons linked to my past, but I don't care. Way encouraged me to explore that side of myself, and maybe he was right, so I allow myself to be honest and say it out loud.

"Then tell me what you want, Aiy." Her voice is quiet and thick with need as she watches me from her blankets.

"I want you. I want to take you in every single way I've only dreamed about. I want . . . I want all of you to be mine. I want to . . ."

"Control me?" she finishes, as if sensing what I need.

I swallow, my jaw clenching in embarrassment, but she trails her finger across it, a smile curling her lips. "Who said you couldn't?" Leaning in, she hovers over my lips. "Take what you want, Aiy. I guarantee I want it too."

I freeze, her words hanging in the air until she leans back. "Well?" Her hands rest on top of her thighs. The only sign she feels as antsy as I do is the slight tremble in her voice and the rapid rise of her chest.

Wetting my lips, I debate if I can follow through, but I want this. I don't know if I'll be able to perform, since she would be the first woman I have ever been with voluntarily, but all the times before, I was never in charge, and it was taken. This time, I want it.

I want her, and maybe with Maeve, I can find that part of me again—the part they stole and ruined.

She's healed so many other parts of me I had given up on, so why not this one?

With shaking hands, I reach behind me and remove my shirt, dropping it to the blanket. She inhales, watching me for a moment to make sure I'm okay before her eyes dip to my chest and rove over my skin.

I know what I look like. I've been called pretty since I was a kid, told I was attractive. It was a curse then, but as she looks into my eyes with awe and lust, it feels like a blessing to earn her desire.

Standing, more confident now, I unbuckle my belt and remove it. The sound is loud as I drop it on the blankets and then tug my zipper down. Her breathing picks up and she glances from my eyes to my hands, and something comes over me—a feeling of control from knowing I'm doing this to her.

The shake in my hands lessens, and I slide my pants and boxers down, stepping out of them. My hard cock points toward her, knowing what it wants.

Her inhale is loud, and when I meet her eyes again, they burn with desire. "You're stunning, Aiyaret," she whispers. It's not a disgusted sneer or command. It's an awe-filled compliment meant to make me feel good, and it does.

"I know." It's not pride, just the truth, but my cheeks heat.

I've taken back my body with Way, but with Maeve, I want to regain my soul.

I need her just like she needs me. Dropping to my knees, I crawl toward her and push her back so she tumbles into the blankets and I'm above her.

I'm still shy, but the more she looks at me like that, the quicker my hesitancy seems to disappear, until we have our own little nest. Everything else strips away, leaving nothing but two beings who want to crawl inside each other.

She waits, her chest rubbing against mine, and I pin her until I can't take it anymore. I want to touch her, but I need to focus on that, so an idea comes to mind.

Grabbing my discarded belt, I wrap it around her wrists, careful it isn't too tight, and then I lift her hands and hook them above her. "Is your shoulder okay like that?" I ask carefully, knowing she's still undergoing therapy for it.

"Fine." She wiggles her hips impatiently. "Aiyaret."

"Hmm?" I lean down, press my nose to her neck, and inhale deeply. She smells of smoke from the fire, and under that is her scent. "You smell good."

She shivers as I run my nose across her collarbone and down between her breasts before I slide my lips over her nipple in a teasing, open-mouthed kiss. She whines, lifting her chest, but I only suck her nipple into my mouth when I want to, and when she moans, I pull back and turn my attention to the other one. I kiss and lick around her nipple until she's panting, her hands twisting above her. I watch her reactions, obsessed with them, but she still doesn't stop me.

Maeve is always in control, even now, so she could quickly flip the script, but she doesn't, and I fall even more in love with her as she lets me have this.

Biting her nipple, I listen to her hiss as she writhes below me, but then I soothe it as she lifts her chest for more. Grinning, I lick up her neck to her chin, placing a kiss there before I meet her bright eyes for a moment.

When I lick her lips, I taste beer, and I love it. "Does your pussy taste as sweet?" She startles at my words, and I hum. "I guess I'll find out. Way and I have a bet."

Sliding down her body, I part her thighs and look at her.

"What kind of bet?" she asks, her voice hoarse.

Settling between her thighs, I grin up at her. "The kind we'll both win," I answer before I seal my mouth on her pussy, tasting as much of her as I can.

I was right. She's sweet—sweeter than her pretty mouth. She drips on my tongue, and I groan, licking every inch of her as her hips wiggle. Maeve lets me play, lets me torture her until she's shaking, and then all it takes is for me to bite her swollen clit, and she arches with a scream, her release tightening her muscles. I sit back and watch her, my cock leaking at the sight.

"I want to feel you do that when I'm inside you," I murmur. I used to hate it and want it. It meant it was over and I was free, but now I want to experience it so many times so I can memorize every facet of her release.

Slumping into the blankets, she pants and slowly opens her eyes. "Then do it," she says, her voice thick.

Climbing to my knees, I reach into my wallet and pull out a condom—a habit for her and Way. I open the packet, toss it aside, and roll the condom down my length, stroking my cock as she watches. I know it will feel better once I'm inside her, so I toss her legs over my shoulders. Her ass presses against me as I notch my tip at her entrance, her eyes wide as she grips the belt to hold on.

"Aiyaret!" she cries out as I thrust into her, burying my length deep within her core. She said I could take her however I wanted, and watching her eyes roll back as I claim her pussy unlocks the wildness inside me. The sense of control goes to my head, and I can't stop myself.

I lift her higher, the new angle causing her to cry out and place her hands on her stomach as if she wants to reach for me. The sight of her bound wrists has me jerking inside her wetness. She's tight, so fucking hot, and gripping my cock like a vise as I pull out and slam back into her, rocking her entire body.

"Fuck, fuck, Aiy, please," she begs. "Give me more. I can handle it."

My lips twist in a smirk, and I yank the belt off her hands, grab her waist, and flip her. She yelps as she hits the blanket, but I haul her ass up and slam into her cunt, cutting off her noises.

"Yes, fuck, like that!" she implores, her head hanging down.

Her hands press against the blanket for leverage as she pants, pushing her ass backward to take me deeper as I drape myself over her back, sucking and nipping her neck. Her pussy clenches around me so tightly, it almost makes my eyes cross.

Her hips dent from my cruel fingertips, but I can't stop. Seeing her like this is driving me crazy. There's just us and pleasure forcing us to move harder and faster.

Her touch is a comfort rather than a poison, and her words are a balm to my jagged heart.

I need more of it. I need everything.

Cupping her chin, I pull her head back until her neck is strained in a long line. She raises her hands and hangs on as I hammer into her.

"Aiy!" I have no doubt the others can hear us, but the thought only makes me move faster, wringing more noises from her.

The boat rocks on the lapping water, even though it's anchored on either side, and as I stare down at her, I can't help but fall in love all over again. The moonlight shines into the boathouse, the echoes of our family's laughter reaching us from the fire, but this moment is all for us.

"Maeve," I growl into her ear as she gasps. "You're the first woman I chose."

She melts into my hold as her eyes meet mine. "And I'll be your last."

That makes me snarl, but she's right. I take her harder, until we can't speak, can't breathe. My free hand slides down her chest, playing with her jiggling breasts and then petting her cunt. I feel it stretch around me before I rub her clit, and she screams so loudly I know they definitely heard it, since their laughter cuts off. A satisfied smile spreads across my lips as she clenches down on my cock so tight and hard, I can't move, and she drags me with her.

My bellow of ecstasy fills the boathouse as I freeze, buried deep inside her as pleasure washes through me. Before, I used to fight the ecstasy that comes with release, I used to hate it, but not anymore. Now, I just let it sweep me away.

When I come back to, we are cuddled together, my cock slipping from her body, and she holds me tighter as I rest my head on her chest. I listen as her heartbeat slows and her erratic breathing evens out.

"That was amazing," I murmur.

She laughs softly, shaking against me. "Better than amazing," she replies.

We lapse into silence, listening to the soft purl of the water and the creak of the wood around us.

She strokes my head, our legs and arms tangled. "I guess we should get back to the others," I murmur, but I make no move to stand.

"Not yet." She sighs, holding me. "They can wait. They won't mind. They'll just be happy we're happy."

"They knew what we were up to anyway." She shakes with laughter, and I smile and hold her tighter as it fades, then I look up at her. "I'm never letting you go, Maeve. I mean it."

"Good, I don't want you to." Leaning down, she kisses me softly. "We are family, and nothing will change that."

"Family never meant anything good until those guys and now you," I admit. "I like family now. I can't wait to spend the rest of our lives together."

All my other worries have disappeared. Wilder won't leave, and neither will Rick or Logan. They have her to link us together forever, and Way is with her and me. She gave me my family back and took away all my fears.

She helped me reclaim my body and stole my heart in the process.

How could I fear forever when it's with her?

# FIFTY-TWO
## MAEVE

The guys are still asleep. Although I only got a few hours, it was the most restful slumber I've had since I last saw them. I feel different, reenergized and hopeful, but as I watch my father read his newspaper with shaking hands, I worry this will hurt him.

"I like them, you know," he comments as he drops his newspaper. "I can practically hear your thoughts from here. They are good guys. I might have also threatened them on the phone to make sure they are serious." My eyes widen. "Whatever you choose for your life, Maeve, I will be happy as long as you are."

"They want me on their team," I blurt nervously.

"And is that what you want?" he asks, no judgment, just curiosity.

I nod, biting my lip. "But we were a team—"

"Maeve." He chuckles as he leans in. "I can never join you again. We know that, and I've long since accepted it. You have to stop holding onto what was, kid. It's time to find a new partner or team. I'll always be your family, but I don't want you out there alone, so walk this path with them, and I'll be right here whenever you get back."

I hold his hand. "I'm sorry, Dad." Tears fill my eyes as I stare at my father. He's changed so much in such a short time, and I know he hates this as much as I do.

327

"Me too, kid. I'm sorry I can't be there with you, but knowing you aren't alone will make sleeping a little easier. When I found out you weren't alone on that island, I could breathe. I've met them, Maeve. They would do anything to keep you safe. There is clearly a bond between you, isn't there?"

"I enjoy working with them," I hedge.

"Then do it. Life is too short for regrets, kid. Trust me on that. It's time for you to find your own adventure. All I've ever wanted is for you to be safe and happy and lead the life you want. Raising you without a mother, I did my best to ensure money and your gender wouldn't hold you back, and I'm proud of the woman you have become. You don't need to prove yourself to anyone anymore, kid, so enjoy it. Find your place and your family. If it's them, then that's okay with me. Besides, I kind of like all the noise in this place. It reminds me of our trips when we would stay at hostels and meet all those people along the way. That's the key to exploring—not just experiencing the world and other countries, but the friendships and memories you make along the way. Go make your own."

"I feel like I'm betraying you," I murmur, my chin quivering. "I guess I always thought it was you and me until the end."

"Me too, kid, but life changes pretty quickly. I'm happy. I know you don't think I am, but I like this life, I really do, so be happy, Maeve—if not for you, then for me. Wherever life takes you, know I love you, and you will always have a home to come back to, but you were made to explore, kid, so make me proud and maybe send a postcard or two." I laugh, and he wheels closer until I can lean my head on his shoulder. When he speaks again, his voice is low and soft. "I love you, kid, never doubt that." We stay like that for a while before I pull away, and he brushes my hair from my face. "Besides, they are kind of cute."

"Dad," I protest, which makes us both laugh just as a sleepy looking Way stumbles into the kitchen. He freezes when he sees us and starts to back up.

"Don't worry, we're done. Come eat. Are the others up?" my dad asks.

"Just waking up," he replies as he ruffles his hair. "Please tell me there's lots of coffee."

My dad chuckles. "Over there."

"Maeve, do you want one?" Way asks around a yawn.

"Maeve?" my dad mocks, and I shoot him a glare.

"Sure, thanks," I answer, and when Way comes over, he hands me a mug and kisses my cheek before sinking into the chair next to mine.

The others file in soon after. Luckily, my dad's house is modified for a wheelchair, so it's easier for Logan to move around, though I know he's practicing on crutches as well. By the time they all arrive, the table is full of food, and they dive in like starving animals. As I watch them, I realize they fit in my life with ease, like they belonged in the first place.

I observe as my dad talks to them, regaling them with his own travel stories and becoming a dad to them as well. I know he wishes he could be with us, and I think that will always sting us both, but as I watch him, I realize he's not lying.

He's happy here, so maybe it's time I found my happiness too . . . or maybe I already have.

# FIFTY-THREE
## WAY

*One month later . . .*

While Logan learns to use his new prosthetic and vlogs his journey with us, we have taken small jobs closer to home —some base jumping and plane walks, those kinds of things—as well as charity events which are good for the company. Today is no exception as we make our way into a party dressed to the nines. We have to shake hands with the rich and philanthropic sponsors of Venture and play nice. Usually, I wouldn't even bother to turn up, but after one look at Maeve in a dress, you bet your ass I got mine in a tux and followed her.

It's black and clings to her incredible body. There's a strap over her left shoulder, while her right one is bare, showcasing her amazing scars. The fabric dips under her breasts and flares out a little at her knees, gathering at the side to show her leg. I know she is self-conscious about the scars on her thigh, but she's getting better about it, and I'm so proud of her for showing them off tonight. She is the most beautiful person in the entire party, and she seems oblivious to the effect she has on us all. We've had a month of learning our way around this new relationship together. Rather than having separate houses, Ajax found us one that was big enough for all of us, and that's where we live now with Maeve. We claimed it was for ease since we are a team, but it just makes life easier since we are dating as well.

Dating.

She officially agreed to date all of us. We haven't made it public knowledge, and we might never do that, since the world might not accept it, but it's enough that we and the people we care about know.

There have been some fights and jealousy, but we are navigating our way through it, although there is never a dull moment with her around. I know she, like us, is itching to get back out there, but for now, we settle for this, and when the first song of the night kicks up, I steal her hand before any of the other hungry beasts she's dating can and pull her onto the dance floor, leaving Wilder and the others to schmooze and make nice.

I swing her around, and her eyes widen. "I didn't expect you to know how to dance."

"My mom used to teach me," I tell her, pulling her close, my hand on her waist as I lean down. "You look incredible tonight."

"I know." She chuckles. "Your hands are wandering."

"Can you blame me?" I murmur, glancing at Aiyaret to check on him, but he's laughing with Logan and Rick. He looks so fucking handsome in his suit that I nearly didn't let him out of the house. When he catches my eye, he winks at us and turns away. We are learning how it works as we date each other, but there don't seem to be any issues between us. Maeve cares for both of us, and we care for her.

"I don't know. You're usually so restrained." That's the truth. Maeve and I have kissed and fooled around, but I've never had her in my bed. I was worried about rushing it with her and how Aiy would feel, but he doesn't seem to care. If anything, he's pushing me to take that step. He says our relationship is different from the one I have with her, that they are separate things and my heart is big enough for both of us.

I don't make any stipulations on their relationship. If anything, they are closer than any of us. They sleep in the same bed most nights, and it got so bad, I just started sleeping with them so I could be close to them.

Some nights, it's a puppy pile as the others join them, and other nights, it's just us. Maybe it should be weird, but it works.

"Not tonight. Tonight, you're mine," I tell her, and I mean it. Her shudder makes me grin, and I slip my hand lower still, feeling every soft inch of her against me.

"Promises, promises." She steps back as the song ends. "We'll see." Wilder is there before I can respond, and he sweeps her up in a dance as I walk back to our table.

Aiyaret's hand covers mine as I sit, and I share his drink as I watch them. "She looks amazing." He sighs. "So do you. I'm one lucky man."

"No, I am," I reply as I kiss his cheek. "Are you sure you're okay with her and me dating?"

"Way, how many times have we discussed this?" He sighs, sounding annoyed.

"Too many," I answer. "I just never want to do anything to hurt you."

"And you won't. I love Maeve, and I love you, so why wouldn't I want the two people I love most to be together? Stop fighting what you want just for me. She wants you." I follow his gaze to see her watching me, and I see the hungry look in her eyes. "Though, she might eat you alive."

"Shut up," I mutter, but I lean into him. "It changes nothing between us."

"No, it doesn't," he murmurs. "Just like my relationship with her doesn't, but if you don't hurry, you might lose your spot in her heart and bed."

Those words haunt me all night as I'm paraded around and forced to interact. My eyes find her constantly, and by the time we are back home, I'm almost crazed by them. Aiy chuckles like he knows and wraps his arm around Logan's waist to assist him since he's tired. "Let's go get a drink." The others follow him to the kitchen. Maeve begins to walk in their direction as well, when I take two steps and block her path.

"Did you forget?" I ask. "You're mine tonight." Before she can speak or give me sass, I bend over, scoop her over my shoulder, and turn. I march upstairs to my room, where I kick the door shut and toss her on my bed. She watches me with wide eyes before she lurches off it and tackles me.

Catching her midair, I slam her against my door as her lips find mine, her hands tugging at my jacket and shirt until she's touching skin.

I shove it off for her so she can explore, sliding her hands across my muscles before she trails her lips down my chest and bites my pec.

"Maeve," I hiss.

Her eyes meet mine, dark and lustful, as she sinks her teeth in deeper. My hips flex as pain mixes with the pleasure, and then she pulls back, licking the mark she left behind. I hoist her up, knocking her hands away. She can play later. Maeve grips my arms, digging into the muscles there she loves.

She adores that I'm able to throw her around—I know that from experience—and that look in her eyes when I do it always makes me grin.

"The dress and heels will stay on," I warn her as I pull the black material up and slide my hand inside her panties. Groaning, she digs one of the heels into my ass, the pain making me groan and kiss her. I spin us and throw us down across the bed, my fingers finding her clit and rubbing it as I suck on her tongue.

After months of teasing, flirting, petting, and touching, neither of us can stand it anymore. I should be soft and gentle, since it's our first time together, but I can't, and she can't seem to either.

She turns her head as she pants, and I lick down her neck, sucking the juncture of it until she writhes, pressing against my hand and body for more.

Gripping her chin, I guide her head toward me and suck on her lips until she whines. "I've wanted to fuck you for so long, Maeve." I have, but I was worried about Aiyaret. I wanted our relationship to be solid. We talked about it at length, and she understood, but all that waiting has driven me insane with need for her.

"Then what the hell are you waiting for?" she snaps, smacking my hand aside and rolling us so she straddles me. Maeve shoves the top of her dress down, causing it to gather around her waist, her curls tumbling over her shoulder. "You've been winding me up all night. I don't need your fingers or your mouth. I want your dick."

Lifting my hips, I dislodge her, and when she rolls, I pin her down again, my lips finding her nipple and sucking as her legs wrap around me.

"Stop being a brat," I growl, biting her nipple until she cries out.

"No," she retorts, unfastening my pants before she grips my cock. My head hangs as pleasure washes through me from her expert touch. I thrust into her grip, trying to stop myself, but she feels so fucking good.

"You like that, big guy? You'll like my pussy more, so stop fucking around." She lets go and slaps my side.

"I'm big, Maeve. You know that—"

"And I can take you, so shut the fuck up," she snaps, "or I'll find one of the others." She goes to move past me, so I slam her down, circling her throat with my fingers and squeezing until her eyes bug from her head.

"Not tonight you won't," I promise darkly. "You'll be here until morning, and even then, I won't have had my fill." Yanking the dress up higher, I rip her thong and toss it aside before I shove my pants down. "Such a fucking brat."

"You love it," she teases with a grin, but it falls away when she feels me at her entrance. We've all been tested and talked about safety—not a very sexy conversation, but necessary—so I know tonight, I can take her raw. She even asked me to.

Tightening my hand on her neck, I force her to look at me as I push into her, slow and steady even as she wiggles, wanting it faster. Every time she does, I stop until she relents. "Good girl," I praise, and then I slam all the way inside her, letting her feel every long, hard inch of me.

Her cry of pleasure is like music to my ears, so I pull out and slam back in until she makes it again. Her fingers dig into my shoulders before they slide down to my ass and grip it as I flex, fucking her as her chest arches.

"Fuck, you should see yourself," I praise in a rush. "So goddamn beautiful. Wait." Standing, I lift her, and she gasps, clinging to me as I carry her to the huge mirror in the corner of my room. I bought it for vlogging and Aiy, but as I lower and spin her, it does the trick. Her hands press to the glass as I kick her legs open and press inside her.

She looks so fucking small in front of me, even though she isn't. I just dwarf her. Her sleek, tan skin glows in the low lighting of my room, and her breasts move with the force of my thrusts, her perfect pink nipples ripe for sucking.

She's sin incarnate right now and all mine.

"We look good together," she rasps as she pushes back, using the mirror for leverage. "You should put a mirror above your bed so you can watch me ride you."

"Jesus." My cock throbs at her thought, and that's what I'll be doing tomorrow, but right now, I focus on her. My mouth brushes her ear as I bottom out inside her, giving her every inch before tilting her forward to drag it over her G-spot. "If you're a good girl, I'll let you come until you can't see anymore."

"Me? Good? Never." She leans back into me, squeezing her cunt around my length until I yank on her hips and drive into her. "But if you're bad, I'll let you fuck me until you can't walk."

Maeve fucking Carter is the only person to ever meet my challenges with one of her own, and I can't wait to find out which one of us is wrong.

My palm presses against the mirror above hers as the slap of our bodies joining fills my bedroom. My chest heaves with my breath, every muscle locking up as I hold back my release. She's just so fucking sexy, so hot and wet, dripping down my cock, but I won't come until she does.

We have all night to enjoy each other. All of our lives, actually.

"Call me that again," she mutters, her eyes shutting as I nip her ear.

"Call you wh—" My lips tilt in a smile. "My good girl?"

I feel her clench around me and chuckle. "So, you misbehave, but you like to be called my good girl." I bite her earlobe until she hisses and opens her eyes. I meet her gaze in the mirror. "Good to know. Now come for me, my good girl. I want to feel you drench my cock with it. I want them all to hear."

My hand slides around her neck, lifting her again, while my other one grips her hip. She gasps as I drive into her until she falls over the edge, writhing on my cock, but I still fuck her, moving harder, faster, until one release flows into the next. She claws at my hand and arm, the slight pain making me roar as I slam into her, my release exploding from my cock.

Falling forward into the mirror, I keep her pinned in place as we pant. I leave my dick deep inside her, keeping my cum where I want it. When I eat her later, I want to taste us mixed together.

Her eyes open as she relaxes into my hold, and I tilt her head up, kissing her as I recover. "Good boy," she teases, and my softening cock quickly hardens again, making her laugh.

"Oh, that's it, Maeve. You're in for it now," I warn.

"Oh, I'm so scared," she teases. "How ever will I survive multiple orgasms? Oh, wait . . ."

"Such a fucking brat," I grumble as I smile, meeting her eyes in the mirror again as I hear the others downstairs, talking and laughing. She must hear them, too, because her smile matches mine.

Our family is in our home, and none of us have ever been happier.

Who knew this is where we would end up? Not me, but I have everything I could ever dream of and more, and I'll spend the rest of my years exploring this happiness with them.

Lifting her, I stumble to the bed and lower us down. "Now, time for round two," I say as she groans, but she screams not long after, just like I wanted and promised.

# EPILOGUE

*A year later . . .*

The sun is so bright, it almost blinds me, and the air is lighter up here. My heart beats steadily, even as excitement nearly makes me bounce on the spot. This is our first real exploration since the island. Logan was cleared to go, and although we had to alter some things, we happily did so. He's thriving with his prosthetic, and I think he's won more hearts than ever with his positive attitude, showing people there are no limitations other than what you place on yourself.

The last year has been one of pure happiness. We've created a bond so strong and tight, it's unbreakable.

I love each and every one of them.

They still get on my nerves every now and again, and they are still Adreno boys, but now I'm an Adreno girl, and I couldn't be happier. Seeing the world with them and pushing limits is so much better together. We are still scarred from what we survived, but we use it as a lesson, refusing to let it stop us.

Turning the camera, I film the sky around us before panning up to see the brightly colored hot-air balloon above us then turning it to face us, knowing the guys are crowded together behind me. Hands slip around me and faces press to mine as I smile into the camera. "Are you ready, guys?"

"Ready!" they yell in unison before their voices come again. "Love you, Dad!" It's a habit they've picked up from me. Every trip, every video, they tell my father they love him. They make him a part of our expeditions, and I know he's touched by that as much as I am.

"I love you, Dad!" I shout into the camera after them. "I'll see you soon. Well, not too soon." I hit end, drag my mask down, and backflip over the edge of the hot-air balloon, falling into the sky alongside my team, my family . . . my explorers.

**THE END**

# ABOUT K.A. KNIGHT

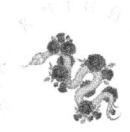

K.A Knight is a New York Times Bestselling Author trying to get all of the stories and characters out of her head, writing the monsters that you love to hate. She loves reading and devours every book she can get her hands on, and she also has a worrying caffeine addiction.

She leads her double life in a sleepy English town, where she spends her days writing like a crazy person.

Read more at K.A Knight's website or join her Facebook Reader Group. Sign up for exclusive content and my newsletter here http://eepurl.com/drLLoj

# OTHER BOOKS BY K.A. KNIGHT

## CONTEMPORARY

### LEGENDS AND LOVE *CONTEMPORARY*

Revolt *RH*

Rebel *RH*

Riot *MF*

Resist *MM*

### PRETTY LIARS *CONTEMPORARY RH*

Unstoppable

Unbreakable

### PINE VALLEY COLLEGE *CONTEMPORARY*

Racing Hearts *MM*

Crashing Hearts *MM*

Bleeding Hearts *FF*

### DEN OF VIPERS UNIVERSE STANDALONES

Scarlett Limerence *CONTEMPORARY*

Nadia's Salvation *CONTEMPORARY*

Alena's Revenge *CONTEMPORARY*

Den of Vipers *CONTEMPORARY RH*

Gangsters and Guns (Co-Write with Loxley Savage) *CONTEMPORARY RH*

### FORBIDDEN READS *(STANDALONES)*

Daddy's Angel *CONTEMPORARY*

Stepbrothers' Darling *CONTEMPORARY RH*

## STANDALONES

The Standby *CONTEMPORARY*

Diver's Heart *CONTEMPORARY RH*

# DYSTOPIAN

## THEIR CHAMPION SERIES *Dystopian RH*

The Wasteland

The Summit

The Cities

The Nations

Their Champion Coloring Book

Their Champion - the omnibus

The Forgotten

The Lost

The Damned

Their Champion Companion - the omnibus

# PARANORMAL

## THE LOST COVEN SERIES *PNR RH*

Aurora's Coven

Aurora's Betrayal

Book 3 - *coming soon..*

## HER MONSTERS SERIES *PNR RH*

Rage

Hate

Book 3 - *coming soon..*

## COURTS AND KINGS *PNR*

Court of Nightmares *RH*

Court of Death *MF*

Court of Beasts *RH*

Court of Heathens *RH*

Court of Evil *RH*

## THE FALLEN GODS SERIES *PNR*

Pretty Painful

Pretty Bloody

Pretty Stormy

Pretty Wild

Pretty Hot

Pretty Faces

Pretty Spelled

Fallen Gods - the omnibus 1

Fallen Gods - the omnibus 2

## FORGOTTEN CITY *PNR*

Monstrous Lies

Monstrous Truths

Monstrous Ends

# SCIENCE FICTION

## DAWNBREAKER SERIES *SCI FI RH*

Voyage to Ayama

Dreaming of Ayama

**STANDALONES**

Crown of Stars *SCI FI RH*

## SHARED WORLD PROJECTS

Blade of Iris - Mafia Wars *CONTEMPORARY RH*

## CO-WRITES

**CO-AUTHOR PROJECTS - *Erin O'Kane***

HER FREAKS SERIES *PNR Dystopian RH*

Circus Save Me

Taming The Ringmaster

Walking the Tightrope

Her Freaks Series - the omnibus

THE WILD BOYS SERIES *CONTEMPORARY RH*

The Wild Interview

The Wild Tour

The Wild Finale

The Wild Boys - the omnibus

STANDALONES

Kingdom of Crowns and Daggers *Dark Fantasy RH*

The Hero Complex *PNR RH*

Dark Temptations *Collection of Short Stories, ft. One Night Only & Circus Saves Christmas*

## CO-AUTHOR PROJECTS - *Ivy Fox*

### Deadly Love Series *CONTEMPORARY*

Deadly Affair

Deadly Match

Deadly Encounter

## CO-AUTHOR PROJECTS - *Kendra Moreno*

STANDALONES

Stolen Trophy *CONTEMPORARY RH*

Fractured Shadows *PNR RH*

Shadowed Heart

Burn Me *PNR*

Cirque Obscurum *PNR RH*

## CO-AUTHOR PROJECTS - *Loxley Savage*

THE FORSAKEN SERIES *SCI FI RH*

Capturing Carmen

Stealing Shiloh

Harboring Harlow

STANDALONES

Gangsters and Guns *CONTEMPORARY*, IN DEN OF VIPERS' UNIVERSE

## OTHER CO-WRITES

Shipwreck Souls *(with Kendra Moreno & Poppy Woods)*

The Horror Emporium *(with Kendra Moreno & Poppy Woods)*

## AUDIOBOOKS

The Wasteland

The Summit

The Cities

The Nations

Rage

Hate

Den of Vipers *(From Podium Audio)*

Gangsters and Guns *(From Podium Audio)*

Daddy's Angel *(From Podium Audio)*

Stepbrothers' Darling *(From Podium Audio)*

Blade of Iris *(From Podium Audio)*

Deadly Affair *(From Podium Audio)*

Deadly Match *(From Podium Audio)*

Deadly Encounter *(From Podium Audio)*

Stolen Trophy *(From Podium Audio)*

Crown of Stars *(From Podium Audio)*

Monstrous Lies *(From Podium Audio)*

Monstrous Truth *(From Podium Audio)*

Monstrous Ends *(From Podium Audio)*

Court of Nightmares *(From Podium Audio)*

Court of Death *(From Podium Audio)*

Court of Beasts *(From Podium Audio)*

Unstoppable *(From Podium Audio)*

Unbreakable *(From Podium Audio)*

Fractured Shadows *(From Podium Audio)*

Shadowed Heart *(From Podium Audio)*

Revolt *(From Podium Audio)*

Rebel *(From Podium Audio)*

Riot *(From Podium Audio)* Coming soon…

Cirque Obscurum *(From Podium Audio)* Coming soon…

Kingdom of Crowns and Daggers *(From Podium Audio)*

Diver's Heart *(From Podium Audio)*

Racing Hearts *(From Podium Audio)*